THE WORDS

ASHLEY JADE

THE WORDS

ASHLEY JADE

"Every saint has a past, and every sinner has a future."
— **Oscar Wilde**

DEDICATION

In loving memory of my Dad,
I love you more.

The Words

Photographer: Michelle Lancaster

Cover Design: Lori Jackson at Lori Jackson Design

Editors:

Kristy Stalter

Ellie McLove

Rosa Sharon

Proofreader: Jo Annette

SPOTIFY PLAYLIST

For your enjoyment, here is a Spotify playlist.

https://open.spotify.com/playlist/0JOpbihYgKnj06TtxP6hk0

Happy Reading,
A Jade

PROLOGUE
PHOENIX

Four years earlier…

"**C**ome here, you little shit."

I haven't been a *little shit* since the seventh grade. Not that he would know.

Brushing him off, I walk the five steps down the tiny, narrow hallway leading to my bedroom.

I'm twisting the doorknob when a glass bottle hits my back.

It's empty. *Always fucking empty.*

Because Vance Walker would never waste a drop of booze.

Seeing red, I turn around and grab him by his dirty shirt. "You're drunk."

"And you're worthless." He swings his fist, but his coordination is fucked, so he misses and stumbles back. "Bastard."

The goddamn irony. "Only because you made me one."

My mind flashes back to a time when my life wasn't a train wreck. Before the alcohol and drugs. Before this piece of shit trailer in this shithole town. Before the affair. Before the abuse.

Before she left us.

I should hate her for it...but I can't.

She saw the opportunity for freedom—a chance at a life where cracked ribs, broken noses, and bruises weren't an everyday occurrence—and she took it.

Even though it meant leaving her seven-year-old son behind to fend for himself.

I look into his hazy, glazed-over blue eyes—eyes I inherited from him—wondering how he let himself slip so far down the rabbit hole.

Once upon a time, my father was a legend. Or at least on the verge of becoming one.

People said he was the next Jimi Hendrix. Hell, some even claimed he was better.

He also had a gorgeous wife who loved him and a son who looked at him like he was a hero.

Once upon a time—he had it all.

And then he lost it.

I refuse to make the same mistake.

CHAPTER 1
LENNON

I'm downing my second bowl of *Captain Crunch* when my father strides into the kitchen, patting his pockets.

"Have you seen my keys?"

I point to the island where they're in clear view. "Over there."

"Ah." Walking to the marble island, he grabs them. "Thanks, monkey face."

You'd think someone with his talent would have come up with a better nickname for his daughter, but alas, I'm stuck with it.

According to him, when I was born, I looked just like a monkey— big ears and all.

Instantly, there's a sharp tug on my heart and I put down my spoon.

Unfortunately, it was the only positive memory associated with my birth for him, given my mom—his soul mate—died minutes later.

"Do you know where my—"

"Over there," I tell him, pointing to the notebook he placed on the counter next to the fridge.

Relief washes over his face. "Thanks. I have a meeting with Black Lung today."

That gets my attention. "Black Lung?" I stifle the laugh working its way up my throat, because my dad definitely doesn't fit Black Lung's fan base. "Aren't you a little...you know."

He adjusts the thick-framed glasses slipping down his nose. "A little what?"

I'm not Willy Wonka, so I don't sugarcoat shit. "You're pushing fifty, Dad."

The confused expression on his face makes it clear he doesn't get it. "So?"

"Have you ever been to a Black Lung show? Most of their fans are *my* age."

Although I don't know why because they aren't very good. Even if my dad manages to work his magic and write them some hit songs, it won't fix their biggest problems.

The band's lack of harmony.

And the lead singer's lack of...well, *everything.*

He shrugs, not looking the least bit concerned. "Their manager sought me out. Not the other way around."

No surprise there. Age aside, my dad is still the greatest song-writer since his personal favorite, John Lennon. Who—*surprise*—he named me after.

"Besides," he continues, popping his collar. "I'm still hip."

It's on the tip of my tongue to point out that only old people use terms like *hip,* but I've insulted him enough for one day.

"Knock 'em dead, Pops."

He winks. "If I do that, they won't cut me a check." His eyes drift to the clock above my head. "Shoot. I'm late, monkey face. Gotta go." Bending down, he kisses my cheek. "Have a good day at school."

I stifle a groan because it's impossible for me to have a good day at Hillcrest High. The place has been my personal version of hell since the moment I walked through the doors.

"Try not to join any mosh pits. You don't want to *break* a hip."

"Very funny." He ambles to the front door but pauses before opening it. "Dammit. Where'd I put my keys?"

I pick up my spoon. "In your pocket."

I tug on the bottom of my blouse as I walk toward the brick building flooding with students. I really wish I'd purchased the top in a bigger size so it would stop riding up. Lord knows the last thing anyone wants to see is my stomach peeking out. Drawing a breath, I try to suck it in, but it's no use. I could inhale until my lungs explode, but my belly will still extend beyond the waistband of my size eighteen jeans.

Jealousy blooms in my chest as I look around the parking lot, taking in every pretty girl with a toned, flat abdomen.

The small town of Hillcrest might only have a population of four thousand and one, but there must be something in the water here because almost everyone is good-looking.

And that included my mom.

According to both pictures and my dad, she was gorgeous, tall, and thin with the voice of an angel. However, I didn't inherit any of those qualities from her. Well, other than my love of singing in the shower when my dad isn't home.

No, I'm the spitting image of my dad. Short, brunette, brown eyes, bad eyesight, ordinary looks…and stuck somewhere between chubby and obese.

"Take a picture, fat ass. It will last longer."

Sabrina Simmons. My archenemy and the bane of my existence. The girl is such a bitch she makes Regina George look like Mary Poppins.

Beautiful, popular, and the captain of the dance team—everyone at Hillcrest is obsessed with her.

However, she hates me.

Which, of course, makes everyone else follow suit.

I quickly realize there are two choices. One—I could ignore her, which will only make it worse. Or, two—I could give her a taste of her own medicine…which will also make it worse.

Basically, there are no good options here, so I go with the one that won't make me late for class. I stride past her.

"Either your clothes shrunk or you're getting fatter," she calls out behind me.

"Come on, we all know it's the second one," Draven Turner, football team captain and Sabrina's sometimes boyfriend, adds. "The bitch is so fat when she steps on the scale it says, *to be continued.*"

Their little group erupts in laughter and I want nothing more than for the ground to open up and swallow me whole.

Whoever said ignoring a bully was the best course of action was either a fucking idiot or someone who never experienced true torment.

The fact we're graduating in a month and they're still making fun of me is honestly absurd.

Absurd *and* scary. I used to tell myself all this fat-shaming bullshit would end after high school, but now I'm beginning to think that asshole kids grow up to become even bigger asshole adults and society is doomed.

One thing's for sure, though. I'm sick and tired of being their punching bag.

I spin around. Draven's arm is slung around Sabrina's slim shoulders, making it clear they're back together again.

I might not be able to attack their looks, but I can still hit them where it hurts.

"Wow." My smile is every bit as fake as Sabrina's extensions as I recall the latest drama circulating around Hillcrest. "I thought after you caught Sabrina screwing Phoenix in the parking lot during prom, you'd be done with her for good." I hike my purse up on my shoulder. "But look at you two...back together *again*. I guess true love really does exist."

The group goes silent, but it's clear by the anger illuminating Draven's face and the daggers Sabrina's glaring at me that my work here is done.

I've barely turned around when the happy couple starts yelling at each other.

Truth be told, it's not like I can blame Sabrina for hooking up with Phoenix Walker.

He's as gorgeous as he is mystifying.

He doesn't hang with the popular crowd, but he's definitely not in Loserville, either. He doesn't talk much, but when he does, you can't help but listen because there's something about his deep, raspy voice—about *him*—that puts you under a spell.

The second he walks into a room, he sucks all the oxygen out of it and commands your attention.

God must be a comedian listening in on my thoughts because goose bumps break out along my flesh and my temperature rises.

Don't look.

But I can't help myself. I'm a masochist.

My mouth goes dry, and the earth tilts on its axis when I turn and piercing blue eyes hold me hostage.

I bet even in the dark, he could look right through me.

Dressed in black from head to toe, he leans against his beat-up Toyota Camry, looking like he doesn't have a care in the world. His dark-blond hair is long enough to fall into his eyes when he moves, making him appear even more enigmatic. A cigarette hangs from his full lips...affirming he doesn't give a fuck about school policy or the possibility of getting into trouble.

We've never spoken, but I've watched him over the years.

I know he lives in the Bayview Estates trailer park.

I know there's only one person at school that he considers a friend—Reese Storm.

I've seen the way he sizes people up when they approach... silently determining if they're worth his time.

The cruel mask he wears when everyone is looking.

The torment in his eyes when they're not.

We've never uttered a single word to one another...

But sometimes I feel like nobody knows him better than I do.

CHAPTER 2
LENNON

"I need to see you after class, Lennon."

Twenty pairs of curious eyes look my way. My stomach twists because those are words you never want to hear from a teacher. Especially one month before graduation.

I scan my brain as Mrs. Herman turns back to the board and continues her lesson about Renaissance literature versus that of the Middle Ages. I've been an A student since the first grade. Heck, I would have been valedictorian if David Paul hadn't scored a one hundred on our last math test, beating me by two points. *The bastard.*

I'm not sure what's going on, but it has me on edge. So much so I barely concentrate during the remainder of class.

After everyone's cleared the room, I approach her desk. "Is everything okay?"

She purses her lips, studying me intently before she smiles. "I just wanted to personally tell you how proud I am of you for getting into Dartmouth. You've always been a hard worker and I'm so happy you're coming out of your shell and thriving."

I've never been good at receiving compliments, and right now is no exception. "Oh…um. Thanks."

To be honest, even though I had applied to a few Ivy League schools, my plan was to attend the local community college.

The thought of my dad being alone at home while I'm hours away doesn't sit well with me. However, he assured me he would be fine, and as much as he would miss me, he'd be upset if I missed the opportunity of a lifetime just because I was scared to flee the nest.

He insisted it was time to spread my wings, but not to worry, because he'd always be there whenever I needed him.

As anxious as the thought of leaving makes me, deep down, I know he's right. There's more to the world than Hillcrest and I can't wait to start exploring it.

I feel compelled to say something in return before I take off, so I utter, "You're a great teacher."

At that, she frowns. "I'm not so sure about that anymore."

Well, this is awkward.

Arranging her pens in a straight line on her desk, she sighs. "There's a student who's been giving me a great deal of difficulty. I believe he's motivated to do well, but no matter how many times I stay after school to give him extra help, I just can't seem to get through to him. I've suggested that he would benefit from hiring a tutor so he can pass the upcoming final, but he can't afford one." Her brows knit together. "As of now, it's highly unlikely he'll graduate."

I'm not sure why she's telling *me* this, but my heart goes out to whoever it is.

Unless it's Draven. That shithead can kick rocks.

"That really stink—"

"I've seen you help other students, Lennon. You're patient and kind…even when they don't deserve it, and you have a way of turning on the light bulb for them. I know I have no right to ask you to take on something like this—especially for free—but I really feel for the kid. His home life—" As if sensing she's said too much, she clamps her mouth shut. "Him not graduating will do him far more harm than good. However, in order to avoid that, he *needs* to pass the final in addition to completing an extracurricular project to further boost his English grade."

Oh, boy. This is a lot to think about. It's not that I don't want to help, but it sounds stressful. Not to mention… time-consuming.

Not that I have a social life or anything.

"Is it just English that he needs to pass, or are there more subjects he's struggling with?"

"I've spoken to his other teachers and while his grades aren't great, he'll squeak by in those classes. It appears English is his weakest subject."

Given English is my best, it seems I might be able to do some good.

Part of me wants to decline and not get involved, but I know if I don't at least try to help, it will gnaw at me.

"I have some time after school and on the weekends." I swipe my books off my desk. "I can't promise my tutoring will make him pass, but I'm willing to give it a shot."

She lights up. "That's wonderful. Thank you so much, Lennon." She looks around her empty classroom. "There's a faculty meeting after school today, but I can leave my classroom unlocked for you to use so you two can get acquainted and set up a schedule."

"Sounds good. Thanks." I'm heading toward the door when it occurs to me that I don't even know who it is I'll be tutoring. "Who's the student?"

She looks up from the pile of papers on her desk. "I'm not sure if you know him since you two aren't in the same class, but it's Phoenix Walker."

It feels like someone pulled the rug out from underneath my feet. "Oh."

She blinks. "Is that a problem?"

Not unless she considers my stomach bottoming out, my sudden case of sweaty palms, or the inability to draw air into my lungs a problem.

"Nope. Everything's fine."

Just fine.

Maybe I should tell Mrs. Herman I came down with mono.

Or malaria.

I could say there's an emergency at home.

Or that my goldfish died.

I tug on the hem of my shirt as I walk down the empty hallway, silently cursing myself for ever agreeing to this in the first place.

Stupid, stupid, stupid.

I was hoping my nerves would have subsided throughout the day, but they've only gotten worse.

And now here I am…ready to tango in the lion's den.

Not that Phoenix is a lion.

He's more like a lone wolf.

Especially with those icy-blue eyes and his *don't fuck with me or I'll tear out your jugular with my teeth* demeanor.

I'm relieved when I find the classroom empty. Arriving first gives me the upper hand…and some extra time to chill the fuck out.

Placing my book bag on the long table in the back, I plop down in a seat.

Five minutes soon turns into ten, and there's still no sign of him.

Relieved, I pack up my stuff while humming one of my favorite songs, "Cryin," by Aerosmith.

Music has always been my first love. Whenever I'm stressed or sad or nervous…it's there with open arms. Wrapping me up like a warm blanket on a cold day.

It's not long before my humming turns to full-on singing. I'm belting out the line about love being sweet misery when I see a tall form enter the classroom in my peripheral.

Oh, God.

I freeze. The only sound I can hear now is my pulse thrumming in my ears.

Don't look.

I kind of have to though, given he's here to see me.

When I finally muster the courage to angle my head, I find him propped against the doorway with his hands in the pocket of his jeans and a sly smirk on his face.

Awesome.

"Don't stop on my account."

His voice is crushed velvet wrapped in silk and gravel.

Luckily, mine comes out sounding way more in control than I feel. "You're late."

He strides inside like he owns the place. "Had to take care of something."

I have to stop myself from asking what that was because it's none of my business.

He stands, hovering over me like an impending storm cloud as I take a few books and folders out of my bag. "Mrs. Herman said you're having some trouble in English class."

I feel like a moron because, *duh*, that's why he's here, but I have no idea how to get the ball rolling because he's not exactly Mr. Talkative.

After what feels like an eternity, he joins me at the table, but still remains silent.

I decide to try a different tactic. "What days and times are you available? I'm usually free after school and on weekends."

I mentally smack myself because I just made myself sound like a loser.

He leans back in the chair with his legs spread and a pissed-off expression on his gorgeous face. As if it's *my* fault he's here.

Opening a folder, I take out the essay we're supposed to read and analyze, and a list of questions about it. "Okay. We can set up our schedule later." I slide the paper across the table. "I'll give you a few minutes to read this and then we can—"

Do nothing…because he's walking out of the classroom.

I sit there stunned for a few moments because *the audacity*. Here I am trying to help him so he can graduate and he just up and leaves without so much as a thank you or a fuck you.

Irritation simmers in the pit of my stomach, and I storm out after him.

I'm tired of people mistaking my kindness for weakness. Tired of assholes thinking they can just walk all over me because I don't look like an Instagram model or wear a size two.

Tired of accepting shitty behavior that I don't deserve.

Phoenix is gone by the time I reach the end of the empty hallway. I debate running out to the parking lot, but why bother? If he doesn't want my help—and he's made it crystal clear he doesn't—I'm not going to waste my time.

Gritting my teeth, I make my way back to the classroom so I can collect my things and go home. I'm approaching the door when the melodic sound of the piano fills my ears. The notes are familiar, but it still takes my brain a second to realize it's a stripped-down version of the song I was singing earlier.

And then I hear it.

My heart stops cold before awakening with a great big thump that sends everything inside me spiraling.

There are good voices.

And then there are once-in-a-lifetime voices.

The hypnotizing kind that holds you hostage and demands every ounce of your attention…every piece of your soul.

The kind that makes you follow the sound like a moth to a flame.

A craving you can't ignore.

My skin prickles as I enter the band room where I find Phoenix sitting at the piano with his eyes closed and his head tilted toward the ceiling as he sings.

Although singing seems like the wrong word for what this is.

It's like he's siphoning every note into his bloodstream so he can spin it into something even more beautiful with his vocal cords.

I feel like I'm watching a spiritual experience…a *metamorphosis* taking place.

His low, raspy voice envelops me like a thick fog. I couldn't take my eyes off him, even if I wanted to. He's utterly mesmerizing.

Like he was born for this.

The song ends and I'm not sure he's even aware I'm standing there.

Not until he snarls, "I don't want your help."

I should be insulted with his rejection and the harsh edge to his words. Instead, I blurt out, "You come alive when you sing."

I don't get a response, but it doesn't matter. I take a step in his direction. "Your voice…watching you do *that*…" Inching closer, I inhale a deep breath. "You have a gift, Phoenix."

I don't even realize I'm next to him until I hear the legs of the piano bench scrape against the wood floor and he stands, towering over me.

He's like the sun. The energy radiating off him pulls you in and you can't help but get closer. Aching to feel the heat on your skin. To make contact with something so powerful. So beautiful.

Even if it burns you.

"I don't want your help," he says again.

His low, raspy voice is a turbulent current of water, pulling me under. However, it's the haunting, desperate look in his eyes that's my undoing.

"But I need it."

CHAPTER 3
PHOENIX

I f someone told me Lennon Michael would be the key to my freedom, I would have asked them to pass me the good shit they were smoking.

Despite attending the same school for the past four years, I've never talked to the girl. Hell, I don't think anyone talks to the girl.

They're too fucking busy talking *about* her.

I'm not blind, Lennon isn't skinny by any means. Ergo her appearance doesn't warrant any interest or attention from guys. The chicks at this school, though. They're like flies on shit. Especially Sabrina.

That girl practically makes it her life's mission to bully Lennon.

Probably because she's jealous.

While Sabrina's hot as hell on the outside, she's weak as fuck on the inside. It's painfully obvious she's desperate for people's approval.

Lennon's not like that, though. While the girl doesn't hesitate to help out others—even my ass on account of her offering to tutor me—she's not a pushover.

I've never seen her so much as shed a tear from Sabrina's—or anyone else's insults. She takes everything in stride, like she genuinely doesn't give a fuck what they think.

That alone is appealing.

So is her voice.

While not conventionally perfect—the hoarse, sultry tone is a slow tug on my cock. There are these tiny cracks in it that make you think her voice is going to give out, and she's about to dive off a motherfucking cliff...but it never happens.

Her voice is as resilient as she is.

I could listen to her sing all fucking day.

Not today, though. I need to get my ass to Storm's house so we can practice.

Our *band* consists of just the two of us. Me—a singer who can play the keyboard. And Storm—a drummer with skills that make him sound like the love child of John Bonham, Neil Peart, and Tommy Lee.

The latter is because he has a unique style that's all him. It's like every time he beats down on those things, he's pounding out his demons.

It's a common denominator that makes him not only my band-mate, but my best friend.

Every time I close my eyes and sing...all the bad shit just fades into the background.

When I'm lost in the music, I'm no longer Phoenix Walker. Stupid kid from a trailer park who got the shit beat out of him daily by his drunk dad and was left behind by his mother.

I'm Phoenix Walker.

The guy who's gonna command the stage, steal every ounce of your attention, *and* make you drop to your knees so you can suck my motherfucking dick while I do it.

Storm and I have a plan. The second we graduate high school, we're heading to Los Angeles so we can be discovered. If it doesn't work out for us there, we'll try New York.

Despite my shitty grades, I'm not a total dumbass. I'm well aware that more aspiring musicians fail than ever make it big. And while Storm and I are fully prepared to live off ramen and cohabitate with roaches for the next five years, we're gonna need some income while we do it.

Hence, I'll need to get a job while I'm chasing my dreams. No potential employer likes a high school dropout though, so in order to secure a semi-decent one, I'll have to get my diploma.

Which is why I find myself in the unfortunate position of needing Lennon Michael.

I have to get the fuck out of this town—the fuck away from my father—before I end up just like him.

You're only young once, so it's now or fucking never.

I know I'll never forgive myself if I don't at least try. Even if I fail, it's better than not trying at all.

"I'm willing to help you," Lennon says, tearing me from my thoughts. "Let's go back to the classroom and get started."

I'd rather shove nails into my scrotum.

"Can't." I pull my car keys out of my pocket. "I have plans."

I go to brush past her, but she steps in front of me and places her palm to my chest.

Her mouth drops open, like she's equally insulted and shaken by my departure. "Are you serious? In case you didn't hear me, I'm offering to help tutor you so you can *graduate*. We don't have a lot of time. The sooner we get started, the better."

I'm well aware the clock is running out. However, music takes precedence over anything and everything.

Always will.

I peer at the hand that's still on my chest. "Move."

Cheeks pink, she removes it and takes a few steps back. "If you're not going to take this seriously, I'm out."

Christ. Leave it up to *this* girl to bust my fucking balls.

"I'm free tomorrow night after nine. I'll pick you up."

At that, she lifts a brow. "Pick me up? What? How—"

"In my car," I interject. "Unless you wanna walk to the other side of town." I drop my gaze, giving her body a slow, threatening perusal from head to toe. "In the dark…all by yourself."

I'm willing to bet my left nut that Little Miss Innocent has never crossed the tracks and played with the big, bad wolves.

She's too busy living the life of luxury on the nice side of Hillcrest in an even nicer house.

"Well, no, but—"

"Didn't think so."

Pushing past her, I shoulder-check her in the process. "See you tomorrow."

"You don't even know where I live," she calls out behind me.

She's wrong. I know exactly where she lives.

The big house on top of the hill on Baldwin Avenue.

Lennon isn't the only one who's been watching a person they've never spoken to over the years.

Only unlike her motives, mine are strictly business.

Her father is Don Michael. A man who's written a couple of hit songs for a lot of great musicians.

And while I'm too proud to ask him to put a word in with his connections, I have every intention of hiring the man once I make it big.

But in order to do that, I need to graduate.

And find a way for Lennon to tutor me without discovering one of my biggest secrets.

"Where the fuck have you been?" Storm bitches as I enter his garage.

Ever since his parents abandoned him, he's lived with his grand-mother in a tiny house not too far from the trailer park.

Fortunately, the tiny house has a decent-sized garage. One his grandma let us convert into a place we could practice.

Even better? She doesn't give a shit about all the noise we make. She's almost fully deaf, so she just takes out her hearing aids when-ever we're jamming out.

I'm appreciative of that *and* the futon Storm lets me sleep on whenever things reach unbearable levels at home.

I don't say shit as I walk over to the mic stand.

But Storm doesn't drop it. "Fucking hell. How many goddamn times do I have to tell you to quit fucking bitches before practice?"

Too many times to count. However, that wasn't the reason I was late today.

Sabrina sucked my dick *before* I met Lennon.

I turn to look at him. "I was at school…meeting my new tutor."

His eyebrows rise. "New tutor? For what?"

Here goes nothing.

"Mrs. Herman's gonna fail me if I don't do some extracurricular bullshit and pass the final."

Five. Four. Three. Two…

"Are you fucking kidding me?"

One.

He throws his drumsticks on the floor like a toddler having a temper tantrum. "You told me you had that shit handled."

I do.

"I'll pass the fucking shit, man. Don't worry." That reminds me. "Can I bring her here after practice tomorrow night? Fuck knows I won't be able to study with…you know."

My drunk asshole father around.

Picking up his sticks and placing them on top of the drum, he nods. "Yeah." His eyes narrow. "Swear to God, Phoenix, you better not let your dick get in the way." He takes a cigarette out of the pack and lights it. "I don't give a shit how hot she is. Do *not* fuck this girl until you graduate."

"It's Lennon Michael."

Instantly, whatever concern he had fades, and he laughs. "Never mind then."

Exactly. There's no way I'd ever fuck that girl.

Not only is she not my type, I now know she's going to be a pain in the balls to deal with.

I turn back to the mic. "Let's go, asshole."

CHAPTER 4
LENNON

I'm parking my bicycle in the garage when I hear it.

Meow.

"I don't have any food for you, Mittens."

Not that she needs it. My neighbor's cat is *very* pleasantly plump. Mrs. Palma and her husband feed her plenty…along with the rest of the neighborhood, since the Persian feline scours the block, working her charm on all of us.

Not taking no for an answer, she swats the air with her paw and gives me a little purr.

I fold like a cheap lawn chair. Walking over to the bag of cat food I keep around for her, I pull a couple of pebbles out and place them on the floor.

The moment she devours them, I scoop her up. "Now that you got what you came here for, it's time for you to go home."

She meows as I start the walk to Mrs. Palma's, still begging for food.

I hear you, sister.

Music might be my first love, but food is my best friend…always there to give me comfort.

Mrs. Palma stops her gardening when she sees me…and her cat.

"I'm so sorry." Standing, she removes her gloves and takes

Mittens from me. "I've put her on another diet, but she isn't too happy about it and keeps trying to escape."

Smiling, I give Mitten's head a little scratch. "No need to apologize. I love when Mittens comes over to say hello."

Her lips twist as she studies me. "Who's the boy?"

I'm not sure how this woman knows these things, but I swear she must be part psychic.

And ever since I was eleven and came running over here crying because I had gotten my first period and didn't know what to do... she's also been a sort of mother figure to me.

"No one." I wave a hand. "It's nothing. Not a big deal."

Except it is. Because Phoenix Walker is picking me up tomorrow night.

Despite looking unconvinced, she lets it slide. "If you say so." She scratches Mittens behind the ears. "I have to go inside and start dinner, but I'll be around later if you want to have some girl talk."

Usually, I'd take her up on that, but she's just going to tell me for the millionth time that I'm beautiful and that my size doesn't define me.

She'll tell me that guys like Phoenix Walker would be crazy not to date me.

While I always appreciate her kind words...I know they're not true.

Guys like Phoenix won't ever be into girls like me. It's just a fact of life.

One I've learned to accept.

Giving her a small wave, I trek back to my house. My dad still isn't home, so I raid the cupboards and grab a bag of chips and a candy bar. After stopping to take a soda out of the fridge, I head into my bedroom.

Music posters of my favorite bands line the walls, along with physical records of my favorite songs that I keep framed.

Dropping the bag of chips, candy, and soda onto my bed, I close my eyes...

Then I take off my clothes.

Walking over to the large full-size mirror on the opposite end of my bedroom, I inspect every inch of myself.

"Take a picture, fat ass. It will last longer."

"Either your clothes shrunk or you're getting fatter."

"The bitch is so fat when she steps on the scale it says, to be continued."

Today's insults reverberate throughout my mind in a loop, forcing me to face the cold, hard truth.

And then I take out the marker.

"Where are you going?" my dad asks when I pass the living room on my way to the front door.

Phoenix didn't say a word to me in school today, but I assume we're still on since he didn't tell me otherwise.

I glance at the clock on the wall above my father's head. It's 8:58. Which means he'll be here in two minutes.

I think.

Although I have no idea how he knows where I live.

"I'm tutoring a friend."

Friend sounds way better than *hot guy from school I'm obsessed with.*

My dad pivots on the couch, now looking at the same clock I am. "But it's nine. On a school night."

"Technically, it's eight fifty-nine. And last I checked, I turned eighteen last month," I remind him, much to his chagrin.

"Last I checked, you still live under my roof," he reminds *me.*

Not wanting to lose this battle, I pull an Uno reverse. "Are you saying you want me to move out because—"

"No, Lennon. Don't be ridiculous." He pushes his glasses up his nose. "What time will you be home?"

I have no idea. "Two—" I start to say, but then he scowls.

"Try again."

"One thirty?"

Another scowl.

"Midnight," he says. "Not a minute later."

That's so not fair. "Dad, that's only *three* hours."

I have no idea how long Phoenix will need me. Plus, I don't want to come across like a loser with a curfew.

At least I can feign tiredness at one a.m. since we have school tomorrow.

"Come on. Let me stay out until one—"

"What could you possibly need to do in four hours that you can't get done in three?" Horror crosses over his face. "This isn't a *boy* you're tutoring, is it?"

He spits the word *boy* out like he tastes something rancid.

"Uh—" I start to answer, but the sound of someone honking their horn cuts me off.

My dad practically leaps off the couch and walks over to the window. He pulls back the curtain, and sure enough, Phoenix's Toyota is parked at the very end of our driveway.

Thankfully, it's too dark, and he's too far away to make out his face.

Not that it matters.

"Only an obnoxious teenage punk honks their horn like that." My dad looks at me. "An obnoxious teenage *boy* punk."

Good Lord.

"It's not like that," I sputter, my brain scrambling. "He's... Phoenix is gay."

My dad blinks. "Oh."

I take the opportunity to sprint toward the front door. "Love you. Buh-bye. See you at one."

"Twelve thirty," he yells as I'm closing the front door behind me. "Not a moment later."

Ugh. It's not much, but at least it's better than what Cinderella got.

I can't wait until I stop chickening out about taking my driver's test. Although I'm sure the newfound freedom will only make my dad even more nuts.

I open the passenger side door of Phoenix's car and get in.

"Down with the Sickness" by Disturbed blasts through my ears and I can't help but grin before mouthing the words.

People my age tend to listen to the latest pop or hip-hop crap on the radio. Not rock or alternative rock music...which is my personal favorite.

I wish an amazing rock band would come along and save my peers from all the bullshit they're filling their ears with.

Every generation before me was lucky enough to get more than one.

God knows it's time for us.

The fact Phoenix knows what good music is only makes him that much more irresistible.

I can feel him studying me as he backs out of the driveway.

"*You* like this song?" he questions, or at least I think he does because the volume is turned up so loud.

"Rock music is my favorite," I shout over the music. "And Disturbed is *awesome*. Although, technically speaking, they lean more toward the heavy metal spectrum of rock."

Regardless, they're a timeless classic. Practically a prerequisite for those claiming to be a true fan of rock music.

I watch the tendons in his hand and wrist flex as he clutches the steering wheel and speeds out of my neighborhood, breaking a handful of traffic laws.

When the song ends, Phoenix presses the pause button on the stereo. "What time is your curfew?"

"What makes you think I have a curfew?"

And how the hell does he know?

His lips curve into a smirk. "You seem like the type."

I want to ask what *that's* supposed to mean, but then he tosses me his phone, which is feeding music through the stereo.

"Come on, Groupie. Play me something good."

The insulting name has me narrowing my eyes. "Fuck you. I'm not a groupie."

I'm a fan. Big freaking difference.

Annoyed, I scroll through the playlist on his phone. We have similar tastes. He even listens to a few of the same bands that aren't super well known. He gets props for that.

However, I'm still irritated by his groupie remark, so I choose a song to reflect that.

I give him a smirk of my own as "I Hate Everything About You," by Three Days Grace comes through the speakers.

His lips twitch before curling into a sexy smile that makes my heart stop.

I'm thankful we spend the rest of the ride listening to music.

I'm confused when he pulls to a stop on the street in front of a small house. "Where are we?"

I figured he was going to take me to his place so we could study.

"Relax," he says as he gets out of the car. "It's not a crack house."

I don't know how to take that remark. Is he assuring me…or making fun of me?

I seriously hope it's not the latter because I'm not like that at all.

I climb out after him. "Excuse me for wanting to know where a guy I've barely even spoken to is taking m—"

I stop talking when he advances on me…slowly backing me up until my spine meets the window of his car.

"What's the matter?" A menacing glint darkens his eyes as he sweeps his gaze up and down my body in a way that makes me feel naked and exposed. "Scared I'm gonna have my wicked way with you? Do all the dirty little things you think about when you're alone in your bed at night…touching yourself?"

God, I wish.

A buzz goes through me when he leans in, his lips ghosting over my ear. "Or is that what you're *hoping* will happen tonight?"

My mouth goes dry. I try to form words, but none come out.

"You can feign innocence all you want, but I know you like to stalk me, Groupie." He edges away. "But I'm gonna need you to keep your little crush in check so I can graduate. Think you can manage that? Or do I need to ask Mrs. Herman to find someone else?"

It feels like he just poured a tub of ice water over my head.

"I don't..." I fight the wave of embarrassment coursing through me. "You know what? Screw you. I didn't ask to tutor you. Therefore, I don't need to spend *my* free time doing it."

I'm about to walk away and pull up the Uber app so I can get home, but his hand wraps around my wrist.

"Look at me, Lennon."

The commanding tone combined with his touch makes me fold.

The second our eyes lock, he says, "I just want to make sure we each know where the other stands, so shit doesn't get complicated."

"Why would shit get complicated?"

The only way it could is if Phoenix returned my little *crush* as he called it. And we both know that will never happen.

I've accepted it.

But for some odd reason, it seems like *he* hasn't gotten the memo.

"It won't." He shifts his weight onto one leg, and once again, I'm aware of just how tall he is. Easily over six feet. "Not on my end anyway."

"Not on my end either."

"Good." He lets go of my wrist. "Glad we got that cleared up."

He gestures for me to follow him. I assume we're going inside the house, but he opens the garage door.

I take in the microphone and stand, keyboard, amp, and drum set as I enter.

"Are you in a band?"

I mean, if he isn't, he definitely *should* be. Despite being an asshole, he has the voice of a god.

He walks over to the futon on the opposite side of the garage. "Yeah. It's just me and Storm who's the drummer, but we make it work. This is his house, by the way."

That's...surprising. "Oh. Are you sure—"

"It's fine. He said we could chill here."

I don't know much about Storm. Other than he's pretty scary looking, and Phoenix's friend...but it was cool of him to offer up his place.

It's even cooler that they're in a band together.

I'm about to suggest they hold auditions to find a guitarist, but then Phoenix sits on the futon. "Let's get this shit over with."

Opening my bag, I take out the same essay from yesterday so he can read it and answer a list of questions about it after.

Our English teacher isn't a heartless bitch who's looking to fail him. She just wants to make sure he's able to do the bare minimum in order to graduate.

Once he answers this set of questions, and a different set from another essay—in addition to writing a short essay of his own—his extracurricular *project* will be done.

Then we can focus on studying for the final.

"I'll give you a few minutes to read this."

He snatches it out of my hand.

His brows knit and I watch the way his lips move as he reads.

"Can you stop staring at me?" he snaps a minute later.

Geez.

Getting off the futon, I make a beeline for the instruments.

They aren't expensive. In fact, everything looks second—maybe even thirdhand—but they do keep them in good condition.

I'm so absorbed in imagining what it would be like to watch him perform, I don't realize how much time has passed until I glance at my phone. It's almost ten-thirty.

I walk back over to him. "Sorry. I kind of zoned out."

Phoenix doesn't look up. "I need more time."

While I admire him wanting to do everything on his own, the reason I'm here is to tutor him and make sure he's on the right path.

"It's okay. I'll look over your answers and give you feedback. This way, I can see what you're struggling with and come up with a game plan to get you back on track."

His jaw tics. "I haven't finished reading this shit yet."

I don't know whether to laugh because he's pulling my leg...or be concerned because he's been reading for over an hour now.

It's a five-page essay. Not a book.

"Um—"

"I need more time," he grits through his teeth.

Holding my hands up, I back away. "No problem."

I wander back over to the instruments, only now I'm solely focused on watching him as he reads.

I have no doubt he's concentrating, it's obvious by the way his face scrunches as he looks over the paper.

However, I also notice that he *never* moves on from the first page.

An awful feeling comes over me, but I shake it out of my head because that would be ridiculous.

Of course, Phoenix can read. He's a freaking senior. Surely *someone* would have caught on to him being illiterate by now.

And yet...he's still scanning the very same page. Looking like he's trying his absolute hardest to make sense of it.

I glance at my phone. It's after eleven now.

Nerves bunch in my stomach as I approach him again.

I'd never in a million years make fun of someone with a learning disability. However, I need to know what I'm dealing with so I can help him.

If I even *can* still help him at this point.

Sitting beside him on the futon, I gently touch his knee. "Phoenix?"

His deep voice is laced with hostility. "What?"

I hold his gaze. "I need you to understand that I will never, *ever* judge you." I pry the essay from him. "But you've been reading for a very long time now."

I expect him to give me an explanation, but that's not what happens.

"Fine. Let's do the questions."

Looking down at the paper, I read the first one. "What exploration was the sixteenth century great for?"

This one is a multiple-choice question, so it should be relatively easy.

Phoenix gets it wrong, though. He tells me the answer is A when it's actually B.

Keeping my expression neutral, I ask him another question, followed by another.

He answers each one incorrectly.

"Phoenix," I whisper, trying to be as compassionate as I can. "You didn't get any of the questions right. But it's okay—"

Words jam in my throat when he snatches the paper from me and rips it in half. "Fuck you." He stands. "I don't need this shit. I'll get someone else to tutor me."

I'm not the problem here. The problem is him.

Or rather, his refusal to confide in me about what's going on.

"You can get another tutor if you want, but I don't think it will matter. Heck, I haven't even had a chance to actually tutor you yet since you still haven't read it."

"I *did* read it," he booms.

"Then what exploration was the sixteenth century great for?"

He doesn't answer…because he can't.

Picking up the two halves of the paper he tore, I hold them up next to each other. "The answer is in the second sentence. Read it to me."

I can see him struggling as he tries to, and it breaks my heart.

"It's okay," I assure him. "I'm not going to make fun of you, I promise. I just want to help."

He averts his gaze. "I'm not a fucking idiot."

"I know you're not." I draw in a breath. "An idiot can't sing or play piano the way you do. An idiot can't drive. An idiot doesn't have great taste in music like you do…so no, you're not an idiot. But I do think you're having difficulty when it comes to reading. Can you try to explain what happens so I can better understand?"

He's silent for so long I fear I'm wasting my time…but then he finally speaks.

"The words…the letters. They get all jumbled up. I can't keep them straight."

I think about this for a moment. "You mean like dyslexia?"

He shrugs. "Don't know what the name for it is. Just know that's what happens."

Wanting to investigate further, I read the first two sentences aloud and ask him the same question I did before.

Phoenix gets it right.

Making sure it's not a fluke, I read the entire essay. Then I ask him all the corresponding questions. He gets all but two right *and* he's able to provide decent answers to the ones that aren't multiple choice.

It's clear he definitely comprehends this stuff…as long as it's not in written form.

How the hell did no one notice this before?

"Okay. So, I can't officially diagnose you with dyslexia or anything, but I'm pretty sure that's what you have." I expel a sigh. "I don't understand how none of your teachers caught on to this."

Not even Mrs. Herman.

He looks sheepish. "They wouldn't."

"Why?"

He scrubs a hand down his face. "Because whenever we have to read a book for class, I make sure to get the audio version. I also have an app that scans and reads things aloud to me. Storm reads shit to me too whenever I ask."

Okay, that makes sense…and it doesn't.

"The tests aren't given in audio form. How do you pass those?"

"Most of the time I don't, which is why I'm failing. But every once in a while…" His Adam's apple bobs. "I manage."

"What do you mean?"

"When a test is multiple choice, I'll peek over at someone else's scantron and scope out the pattern." He shrugs. "If I know there won't be a scantron, I'll find a girl who's already taken the test and ask her for the answers."

I balk at him. "And these girls just do it?"

I want to mentally smack myself because, *of course,* they do.

He's Phoenix Walker.

He simply just has to exist, and girls line up to throw themselves at him.

Me included.

I have no intention of helping him cheat, though. I would, however, like to help him pass legitimately so he can graduate.

Problem is, I have no idea how to do that.

Phoenix glances at his watch. "What time do you have to be home?"

"Twelve thirty, why?"

"It's twelve forty."

"Shit."

He takes his keys out of his pocket and opens the garage door. "Come on. I'll take you home."

We ride in complete silence the entire way.

It's only when he pulls up in front of my house and cuts the engine that I speak. "If I can figure out a way to help—genuinely help you—would you let me?"

His eyes dart over every inch of my face, like I'm a puzzle he can't seem to figure out before he nods.

"Pick me up tomorrow," I tell him as I get out of the car. "Same time."

My dad is still wide awake when I walk into the house. No doubt waiting up for me.

"Were you stuck in another galaxy that has no concept of time? Or is the clock on the phone that's always attached to your hand broken? I said twelve—"

"What do you know about dyslexia?"

I tend to tell my dad almost everything because *he* tends to give the best advice.

Unfortunately, this isn't his area of expertise because he says, "Not a whole lot. Why?"

"I'm pretty sure the guy I'm tutoring has it. And I have no idea how to help him now."

But I want to.

He thinks about this for several moments before speaking. "As much as you'd like to help him, monkey face, I'm not sure you can. Teachers are the ones qualified to deal with learning disabilities. Not you."

"Teachers let him slip through the cracks."

Not that I can really blame them for it. Phoenix specifically does things to hide it.

I follow him into the kitchen, where he pours us both a glass of milk and takes out a package of cookies. "How bad is it?"

"Bad enough he couldn't even get through the first page of an essay I had him read. He says all the words jumble up and he can't keep them straight."

No wonder he looked like he was concentrating so hard. It must be torture.

Bringing a cookie to his mouth, my dad cringes. "That sounds pretty bad. I think this is out of your hands."

I refuse to believe that.

"The thing is...he answered most of the questions correctly when I read the essay to him. He said he has an app on his phone that reads things aloud so he can do homework. He also gets audio versions of the books we need to read in class." I dunk my cookie in the glass of milk. "He's motivated..." Just like Mrs. Herman said. "It's just his brain that isn't cooperating."

Through no fault of his own.

He chews another cookie. "I get that—"

"I'm not giving up on him." Feeling a sense of gusto, I head out of the kitchen. "I know there's gotta be something I can do to help him."

There *has* to be.

I stop and look at my dad before I exit. "Sorry I was late."

He closes the package of cookies. "I'll let it slide, given the circumstances."

I chew the corner of my lip as I ponder the best way to say this.

"I'm eighteen, Dad. I'm also going to keep tutoring Phoenix at night. You're gonna need to loosen the reins."

"Why does this tutoring have to be so late? Can't you two meet up during normal hours?"

Nighttime *is* normal. My dad is just a fossil.

I scan my brain, trying to come up with a reason he'll not only accept but respect.

"He works after school and doesn't get off until after nine."

I mean, it's *kind* of true since he's in a band. I assume he practices a lot.

Despite it being clear that my dad still doesn't like this arrangement, he caves. "Fine. But don't walk in this house after one a.m."

"One fifteen," I counter.

"We'll see," he says, which is good enough for me.

"Love you, Dad."

Picking up the carton of milk, he places it in the cupboard. "Love you, too."

"Uh, Dad?"

"Yeah, monkey face?"

"Last I checked, milk goes in the fridge."

Laughing, he opens the cabinet door. "Whoops. I was so distracted by this curfew talk; I must have mixed it up with the cookies."

I hightail it out of the kitchen so he doesn't change his mind about my new curfew.

After changing into pajamas, I take out my laptop and sit on my bed.

Then I spend the rest of the night and early morning researching everything I can about dyslexia.

CHAPTER 5
LENNON

Phoenix found me after school yesterday and told me he couldn't study that night. I was about to lay into him for avoiding his issues, but he said he had something important he needed to take care of.

Then he asked for my number.

I didn't think he'd use it, but tonight at approximately eight fifty, my cell vibrates with an incoming text from an unknown number.

Unknown: You free tonight, Groupie?

His nickname makes me grind my molars as I save his contact info.

Lennon: That depends.
Phoenix: On?
Lennon: Are you going to take this seriously and let me help you?

I watch the dots appear and disappear before another text comes through.

Phoenix: Look out your bedroom window.

Confused, I peel back the curtain and peer down.

I bite back a smile when I see his car parked under a large tree that's a little down the street from my house.

Lennon: You could have parked in the driveway, you know.
Phoenix: Get your ass down here.

After changing into jeans and a T-shirt, I stuff the ruler I picked up for him yesterday into my purse and grab the folder with the essays and questions.

I also take my laptop with me.

"Bye," I call out as I pass my dad in the living room.

"One o'clock," he calls back. "I love you."

After walking down the steep hill that is my driveway, I meet Phoenix at his car.

This time, "Zombie" by The Cranberries blasts through the speakers.

"Good song," I yell as I slide into the passenger seat and put my seat belt on.

He gives me that infamous smirk.

I wait for the song to end before I press the pause button on the stereo.

"You answered my texts right away. How did you read them so fast?"

The tendons in his forearm flex as he speeds down the road.

I never thought veins and tendons were hot before, but I stand corrected.

"I use text-to-speech to listen to my messages. It helps a lot." A wry smile stretches his lips. "Unless I'm texting Storm and he's having a bitch fit while I'm out in public. Then I get a bunch of dirty looks."

I laugh, until another thought occurs to me.

The research I did said there were different types of dyslexia and not everyone has issues writing. I'm wondering if he does.

"Do you have difficulty when it comes to writing?"

He makes a face. "That's not a strong point of mine either, so I use speech-to-text, too. For assignments, I type shit on the laptop Storm's grandmother got me last year. I still struggle, but it's a fuckton easier than writing by hand."

"Storm's grandmother got you a laptop?" I ask as I process all this.

"Yup." He draws in a breath. "The woman is a sweetheart with a heart of gold. I didn't want to accept it because I know money's tight and she couldn't afford it, but she *made* me. She said I wasn't allowed to come over and practice until I took it. When I protested again, she swatted me out the front door with her broom. Then she locked it." He laughs to himself. "I still mow her lawn every Sunday as a thank you."

My heart warms because it seems there's some good in Phoenix after all.

Although it's sad that Storm's grandmother appears to be the only adult in his life who seems to care enough to help him.

I wonder what the deal is with his parents.

I can feel his brooding stare boring holes into me right before he grits out, "Any other questions, Groupie?"

Since he's offering.

"Actually, yes." I shift in my seat to look at him. "How did you know where I live?"

Because I *never* told him.

Ignoring my question, he pulls to a stop in front of Storm's house. "I didn't mean to blow you off yesterday. Storm and I had a meeting with the manager of Voodoo. After some convincing, he scheduled us to play there a month from today. They can only squeeze us on stage for three songs, but it's something."

It's *everything*.

Excitement races through me as I get out of the car. "Holy shit. That's awesome."

Granted, Voodoo is a hole-in-the-wall bar-slash-venue, but amazing undiscovered artists play there a lot.

A few have even gone from undiscovered to discovered shortly after their gigs there.

Since I just turned eighteen last month, I've only been to Voodoo once, but I plan on going back soon.

The genuine smile on Phoenix's face tells me he's equally excited about his upcoming show.

"Do you mind if I come?" I ask as he opens the garage door.

Ever since his little *comment* about knowing I stalk him; I've made a conscious effort to pretend like he doesn't exist when we're at school.

I hate that he thinks I'm some pathetic—well, *groupie*—who watches his every move.

Although, there is some truth to it, I suppose.

"The more tickets we sell, the better, so yeah. Come if you want."

While he doesn't sound elated about me being there, he doesn't sound irritated about it either.

I'll take it as a win.

He walks over to the futon and sits. "Let's get this shit over with."

I take a seat next to him. "First, we need to talk about your options."

I truly feel like Phoenix would benefit from telling our teachers about his dyslexia.

His brow lifts. "What options?"

"Option one is—you talk to Mrs. Herman and tell her the truth. She's very understanding, and she wants to see you succeed, so I'm positive she'd help you." I hold his gaze. "You have a learning disability, Phoenix. It's not your fault, and it's *nothing* to be ashamed of. The school can help. Granted, it would mean you'd have to stay back another year, but once the school knows, you can take special classes and have an IEP—"

"Staying back another year isn't a fucking option for me, Lennon." His nostrils flare with frustration, but there's also a hint of fear in his tone. "I need out of here *now*."

He says it like he's not only determined, but *desperate* to leave.

"Okay. That leaves us with option two."

"Which is?"

"We try like hell to get you to pass the final."

He hangs his head. "I appreciate it, but I can pass the final on my own—"

"Flirting with some girl so she gives you all the answers isn't passing the final on your own. It's *cheating*." I reach for my folder. "Anyway, I did some research. And while I don't think it's going to magically fix your dyslexia, I got you something that might help make things a little easier."

He looks taken aback. "You got me something?"

After taking the essay out of the folder, I pull the ruler from my purse. "This is a reading ruler." I place it over the paper. "You said the letters become jumbled, which makes sense because dyslexia can give you visual difficulties while reading. Basically, this thing is a colored transparent ruler that individually highlights the sentence you want to read. I'm hoping it can help you focus better on one word and one sentence at a time."

This way, it won't be so overwhelming.

"But if it doesn't, that's okay. There's different stuff we can try. This one just happens to be the simplest."

I have no idea what to make of the look on his face. "Fine."

Not wanting him to feel like I'm breathing down his neck, I get off the futon. "I'll be over there if you need me."

I wander over to the instruments. Even though they're second-hand, they still cost money.

So does Phoenix's car and phone.

I wonder what he does to earn it.

I turn around and look at him. He still appears to be struggling, but not as much. The ruler is halfway down the first page already... which is further than he got the other day.

A half hour later, he's made it to the end of the second page.

"This isn't working. It's taking me so long that by the time I figure out what a sentence says, I'm forgetting everything else I read."

I knew the ruler wouldn't be a miracle worker, but I was hoping he would find it beneficial.

Sad thing is, I know if I went over there and read it to him, he'd be able to answer most of the questions correctly.

I can tell he's frustrated, though, so I decide to change tactics.

"Put the essay down." I walk back over to him. "We're gonna focus on something else for a bit."

I reach for my laptop and plop down next to him. "Part of your extracurricular project is writing your own essay. Let's work on that."

Sinking against the futon, he makes a gruff sound in his throat. "I think I'm tapped out."

I can tell. Perhaps a brief change of subject is in order.

"What do you do for money?"

"Is that your way of saying you want me to pay you?"

"No. I'm just curious how you afford instruments and stuff."

"I landscape over the summer. I also do some construction at my dad's job sometimes."

So, his dad *is* in the picture.

"Are you guys close?" I shift to face him. "What about your mom?"

Visibly annoyed with my line of questioning, he grunts. "Let's start that essay."

I boot up my laptop and open a new Word doc. "The topic is— what drives the human spirit. I figure it might be easier if you talk and I transcribe."

This way, he can completely focus on what he wants to say without having to worry about typing it.

He exhales slowly. "I don't think I can answer that because it's different for everyone," he starts as my fingers tap the keys.

"It depends on their intellect, emotions, fears, the shit they've been through...what they truly want and need. I only know what drives mine." His eyes squeeze shut. "For me...it's music. Creating."

He's so candid right now. So *raw*. I feel like I'm getting a glimpse at the real him under the mask.

I have to remind myself to keep typing as he continues.

"When I get lost in music, nothing else matters…because all the bad shit has been stripped away, and I become a brand-new canvas. One that turns me into whatever the notes, chords, and lyrics need me to be. It's like a spell has been cast, and I'm no longer human. I'm no longer matter taking up space…I'm sheer energy. A vessel for magic I can't even begin to explain. All I know is those sparks of magic…it's the best feeling in the world. It's what I live and breathe for. It's what drives *me.*"

His eyes open and lock with mine. "Whenever I'm singing or playing, I'm the most authentic version of myself. It's the only time I don't want to be anyone else."

My heart squeezes as I finish typing up his words. "That was…wow."

I don't think Mrs. Herman will have a problem with this one bit.

Far from it. *She'll want to get close to the sun.*

After clicking save on the document, I email it to him so he can turn it in. The clock on the right-hand corner of my laptop reads twelve-fifteen. Which means we still have some time before I have to go.

"My curfew is one now." Not wanting to come off desperate, I quickly add. "But if you're tired, you can drop me off early."

With a humorless laugh, he takes a pack of cigarettes out of his pocket and lights one. "Must be nice having parents who give a shit." Before I can ask what he means, he grits out, "Living in that nice, big house with plenty of food and whatever else you fucking want."

The smoke from the lit cigarette hanging out of his mouth wafts through the air, and his upper lip curls in contempt. "Bet they always say how proud they are of their sweet, innocent little girl."

I'm not sure where all this is coming from, but his cruel words feel like a punch to the rib cage.

"It's parent. Not parents." Confusion spreads across his face as I stand up. "And I have no idea if my mom would be proud of me because she died a few minutes after I was born." I gather my things.

"She's never been anything more than a ghost whose death broke my dad's heart." *A missing piece I can never get back.* "But by all means, keep telling me how great my life is."

"Lennon."

Ignoring him, I march toward the garage door.

I know he doesn't live in a nice house and his family struggles financially, but that doesn't give him a right to make assumptions about me and my life.

Especially when he has something I'll *never* have.

Something I'd kill for.

I feel a sharp tug on my wrist before he spins me around.

"I was a dick." His ragged breath fans my face. "I'm sorry, okay?"

His earnest expression tells me he means it.

But what he said still hurt.

"It's fine." I fetch my phone out of my pocket with my free hand. "I'm gonna get an Uber."

Instead of backing off, the grip on my wrist tightens. "No. I can drive you." He visibly swallows and his voice lowers…like whatever he's going to say next physically pains him. "I don't have a mom either."

This is news to me.

Then again, it turns out…I don't really know Phoenix after all.

"Your mom died, too?"

"Worse," he bites out. "She *left*."

Oh, God. That's horrible. My mom didn't desert me on purpose…the choice was completely out of her hands.

Being intentionally abandoned by your parent must hurt like hell.

"How old were you?"

"Seven."

Dealing with that at any age is awful…but he was so young when it happened.

We're both quiet for what feels like an eternity before I break the silence.

"I'm sorry."

He lets go of my wrist. "Wasn't your fault." He digs in his pocket for his keys. "I'll take you home."

I don't want him to after that, but something tells me he needs space.

"Okay."

Just like the first night, we drive home in silence.

CHAPTER 6
PHOENIX

"**Y**eah, just like that," Sabrina cries out.

Usually, it's a turn-on when chicks are vocal, but since I'm fucking her in the band room, there's a chance someone might hear us.

"That's it, baby." She tries to kiss me, but I turn away. Just like I always do. "You're gonna make me come, Phoenix."

I don't give a shit. I just want her to shut the fuck up while she does.

That doesn't happen, though. Tossing her head back, she proceeds to scream my name—like she wants anyone who might be walking by to know *exactly* who she's screwing.

Christ. Her orgasm is just as phony as she is.

Thankfully, whether she gets off or not has no bearing on me busting a nut.

Shortly after I do, I put some distance between us and discard the condom.

"That was so good, baby," Sabrina purrs as she fixes her sequin dance uniform. "No one fucks me like you do."

Including her boyfriend…given she's always chasing *my* cock behind his back.

Not that I give a fuck. That's Draven's shit to deal with.

I'm just here because I like sticking my dick in something wet and pretty.

Although the appeal is starting to wear off, because Sabrina's annoying the living shit out of me.

Not only does she keep trying to kiss me during…she keeps trying to talk to me *after*. Fuck that shit.

She has a boyfriend, and it sure as fuck ain't me. This thing between us is nothing more than a transaction. She likes getting fucked by me…and I like to fuck.

Simple as that.

Only it isn't anymore, because she's trying to make shit more than it is.

"Lillian's having a huge party after graduation," she says as I tuck my dick inside my jeans. "Promise me you'll come."

I tug up my zipper. "No."

Fuck that. The second they hand me a diploma, I have no intention of seeing any of these assholes again. Aside from Storm.

And maybe Lennon.

For some fucking reason, the girl is starting to grow on me.

Like a fungus.

Nevertheless, I'm not opposed to the idea of keeping in touch with her from time to time after we graduate.

If I even graduate, that is.

"Come on, Phoenix." She walks her red talons up my torso. "*Everyone* is going to be there. Even that lard ass Lennon."

That's…fucking weird.

Lennon's always been an outcast, and as far as I know, she's never gone to a party.

Hell, she didn't even attend prom.

"Why was Lennon invited?"

Because I don't think she'd go unless she specifically was.

Sinking her teeth into her bottom lip, Sabrina smiles coyly. "You'll find out if you come."

I don't like the sound of that, but I can't drill Sabrina about it because I hear footsteps approaching.

"What are you doing here, fat ass?" Sabrina snaps before I can even turn my head.

When I do, an unexpected twist goes through my gut.

School ended a half-hour ago. I figured Lennon would be long gone by now.

Evidently, I was wrong.

Those baby-brown eyes widen with shock before she speaks. Or rather, *tries* to.

"I...um..."

It's not like Lennon to trip over her words...no matter how mean Sabrina is.

Her nemesis takes the opportunity to close in on her like a goddamn vulture. "What's the matter, fatty? Cat got your tongue?" She laughs. "Oh, that's right, it can't. Because your mouth is always stuffed with food."

Jesus. What a cunt.

I'm sure Lennon has a mirror, therefore she's well aware that she's heavy.

I don't get Sabrina—or the rest of the school's obsession—with constantly ripping into her about it.

Funny thing is, her losing weight would be a threat to Sabrina. Not only because it would take away her ammunition, but Lennon isn't ugly.

Hell, I'd even call her cute in the right light.

So cute, I have no doubt that if she dropped a few pounds, Sabrina would shit a goddamn brick because all the guys would be chasing *her* instead.

I throw Lennon a bone. "She's tutoring me."

Sabrina directs her irritation my way. "Tutoring you for what? We graduate in two and a half weeks."

A trail of tension rides down my neck. I don't owe her a damn thing. Least of all, an explanation for why someone's helping me out.

"None of your fucking business."

That makes her mouth clamp shut. With a huff, she grabs her purse off the piano.

"Whatever." Blowing me a kiss, she pushes her way past Lennon, intentionally bumping into her. "Text me later."

I won't.

Lennon still isn't making eye contact with me.

It shouldn't bother me...but it does.

"Sabrina's a bitch."

Her head snaps up and there's no mistaking the anger flashing in her eyes.

"Then why do you fuck her?"

I didn't owe Sabrina an explanation, and I sure as fuck don't owe her one either.

Only unlike Sabrina, I need Lennon.

My progress is slow and most nights, I want to bash my head through a wall and give up.

But there's something about knowing that I might not have to cheat my way out of the hole I dug myself into that gives me a sense of pride.

I want to *earn* it.

But in order for that to happen, I have to keep my tutor around.

So, I lie.

"I didn't fuck her."

Lennon's stare drops to the floor—briefly lingering on the used condom I dropped in my haste to get away—before trailing up to my face.

She no longer looks angry...her expression is pure hurt.

And then she walks away.

Fuck.

I chase after her, my long strides quickly eating the distance between us.

"I don't appreciate being lied to," she snaps when I grab her arm.

"Me either."

She whips around to face me. "When have I *ever* lied to you?"

"When you told me you could keep your little crush under

control and shit wouldn't get complicated," I point out. "Acting jealous and hurt because I fucked another girl is a complication."

One I don't need.

Her mouth drops open. "You're unbelievable, you know that?"

So I've been told.

I tighten my hold when she tries to walk away again. A little too hard, though, because she winces. "You're hurting me."

I promptly let go. "Tell me I'm wrong."

But we both know I'm not.

She gives her head a shake. "Fine. Jealous—no. Hurt—*yes*." She looks me over, like I'm nothing but a piece of trash littering the street. "Only because I was dumb enough to think we might actually be friends."

"We are friends."

Maybe not in the conventional sense. But shit, I spend more time with her than I do with Storm lately.

"No, we're not." Sadness twists her features. "Because friends don't fuck people who bully their friends."

With those parting words, she walks away.

And I let her…

Because she's right.

CHAPTER 7
LENNON

I'm tossing and turning in my bed when I hear something hit my window.

At first, I think it's just a reckless chipmunk, but then it happens again.

I look over at the clock on the nightstand. It's just after two a.m.

When something hits my window a third time...I get out of bed so I can check it out.

I nearly fall over when I see Phoenix swinging like a monkey from the large oak tree directly across from my bedroom...while the rain beats down on him.

I swiftly open my window. "What the hell are you doing?"

"You weren't answering my texts."

Damn right I wasn't. I have nothing to say after catching him with Sabrina.

I heard they had sex in the parking lot after prom...but I didn't think they were an actual *thing*.

Rumor has it Phoenix is a one-time-only screw.

Clearly, Sabrina's the exception to that.

"That's because I don't want to talk to you."

I go to slam the window, but he grunts, "Christ, Groupie. My arm strength is good, but not good enough to hang here all fucking night. For fuck's sake, just hear me out."

I cross my arms. "You have five seconds."

"You were right earlier. We are friends—" he starts to say, but I cut him off.

"No, we're not. I don't want to be friends with someone who's balls deep inside *her* on a daily basis."

His lips quirk. "Check out the mouth on Little Miss Innocent."

I'm about to shut the window for a second time, but then he says, "I know you're angry, but it's not serious. Sabrina's just something I stick my dick in—"

"I don't need details."

"Fuck." The muscles in his arms strain as he speaks. "What I'm trying to say is...you're more important. I won't fuck her again, okay?"

I should tell him to go fuck *himself*, but he is hanging from a tree outside my bedroom. In the rain.

All so he can try and make things right between us.

"Promise?"

Eyes locked with mine, he nods. "Yeah."

And then he falls.

Fortunately, the wet grass below breaks the brunt of it.

My phone lights up with a text as soon as he makes it to his car.

Phoenix: We cool?

Lennon: We're cool.

Phoenix: I'll pick you up tomorrow night.

I try to quell the rush of exhilaration those words fill me with but fail miserably.

Because Phoenix wasn't the only one who lied before.

I was angry...

But I was also jealous.

Even though I have no right to be.

Because I'm not the kind of girl who gets the guy.

The final is three days before graduation, which means we have less than two weeks to get Phoenix ready for it.

He's been working really hard, so I'm trying to make tonight fun. Which is why I asked Storm to join us for our study session.

Even though dyslexia is the main problem we're facing, Phoenix still has to know the material because there will be more than essays on the final. Therefore, I declared tonight flashcard night.

Storm picks up a card from the stack and reads it. "In the following sentence, which word is an adverb? The events in the movie are mostly true."

Phoenix thinks about this for several moments before he answers.

"Mostly is the adverb."

Despite sounding unsure, he's correct.

"Yep," Storm tells him.

With a cocky grin, Phoenix looks at me. "Make sure it's pepperoni, Groupie."

I told him if he got more questions right than wrong by the time we reached the halfway mark, I'd order a pizza.

As if on cue, Storm's grandmother opens the door, carrying two large pizzas and some paper plates.

The three of us quickly rush over to help her.

"Goodness gracious, settle down." Breezing past us, she walks over to the futon and sets the boxes on one of the crates we set up as a makeshift table. "Y'all act like I'm *old* or something."

The three of us exchange a glance, but wisely stay silent.

"I hope you took some for yourself," I tell her when she starts to leave.

She waves a hand. "Thank you, dear, but cheese gives me the Hershey squirts."

"Jesus Christ, Grams," Storm mutters under his breath as Phoenix laughs.

For a moment I don't think she heard her grandson because

Phoenix told me she's hard of hearing, but she must have those aids turned up to max because she wags a finger at him. "Oh, hush, Reese. It's a normal bodily function."

I mean, the woman isn't *wrong*.

"Anyway," she continues. "I'm going to bed, but enjoy your pizza and study hard for that big test." Her eyes land on Phoenix. "I like her. You better keep this one around or I'll kick your handsome little ass."

Storm snorts and I stand there utterly confused because his poor, sweet grandmother must be deaf *and* blind if she thinks Phoenix would ever be into me.

"I gotta take a leak," Storm announces shortly after she leaves.

I can feel Phoenix eyeing me as he digs into his pizza. "How'd the pizza get here so quick?"

"I ordered it before we started." I shuffle the small pile of flash-cards he didn't get right and add them to the stack we still have left. "I knew you had it in the bag."

His expression is inscrutable before changing to one of curiosity. "Why aren't you eating?"

Because fat girls don't eat in front of hot guys they have crushes on.

It's sort of an unwritten rule.

It's almost as if not drawing attention to my fatal flaw will somehow make him forget about it.

My cheeks heat with embarrassment, so I look anywhere but at him. "I ate dinner right before you picked me up."

He opens his mouth to say something, but thankfully Storm comes back.

I shuffle the stack of flashcards again. "Okay, you two eat and I'll ask the questions this time." I shoot them a hopeful look. "Maybe after we're done, I can hear you two play?"

Storm speaks through a mouthful of pizza. "That depends. You like rock music?"

I start to answer, but Phoenix beats me to it. "She fucking loves it. Not only does Lennon know all the lyrics to every song I play in the car, her taste in music is *almost* as good as mine." Those full lips curl into a smirk. "It's why I call her groupie."

I flip him the bird. "I can't be your groupie if I've never heard you play, now can I?"

I want to smack myself as I replay those words back, but it's too late. They're already out there.

His smirk deepens. "I guess we'll have to change that then, huh?"

My insides swoop and I'm positive I'm blushing.

Storm claps his hands. "That's what I'm talking about. Let's get this studying bullshit over with so we can jam." He looks at Phoenix. "I'm with Grams. Keep her around."

I'm speechless as Phoenix belts the final verse of "Man in the Box" by Alice In Chains.

He sings it with such raw passion it steals my breath.

It took me mere seconds to ascertain that he was a phenomenal singer and great piano player...

It took even less for me to discover that he's also one hell of a performer.

From the moment he grabbed that mic and opened his mouth, he reached inside my chest and seized my soul.

Phoenix was right...what happens to him is pure magic.

Only, *he's* the magician.

And one day, the entire world will be under his spell.

I *feel* it.

I also have to give credit to Storm because he sure knows how to play drums. Despite looking like he's losing his fucking mind when he pounds on them, he never misses a beat.

I'm so enamored I don't even realize they've been playing for so long. Not until Phoenix ends the song and looks at Storm. "I gotta take her home."

Dammit. I *hate* having a curfew.

I get off the futon. "You guys...that was..." I clutch my heart, trying to come up with the right words for what I just experienced but there are none. "Insane in the very best way and nothing I say can do it justice."

I have to stop myself from asking for their autographs.

Storm grins. "Glad you enjoyed it. We'll give you a concert whenever you want."

"Remember you said that, because I'm definitely going to take you up on it."

He places his drumsticks down. "I'm gonna head inside. Thanks for the pizza."

"No problem. And hey, maybe next time you guys can play some of your own songs."

God knows they surpassed the originals, but every song they did tonight was a cover.

I'd love to hear some original stuff.

Phoenix and Storm exchange a glance before Storm says, "We'd love to...but we don't have any."

Phoenix grips the back of his neck. "*Yet*. We're working on it."

I'm sure they'll come up with some amazing ones soon enough. And if not...maybe I could ask my dad to sit down with them.

"Well, I can't wait to listen to them whenever you do."

Storm and Phoenix exchange a quick goodbye before we head out.

"You're going to blow everyone away at Voodoo," I tell him after we get inside the car.

"I hope so." He starts the engine. "Rumor has it there's going to be a record executive in the crowd the night we play."

Oh, shit. "Really?"

He nods. "Yeah. But it's just a rumor, so who knows."

"Well, if there's any truth to it, don't worry. They're gonna go crazy when they hear you. Trust me."

A dimple peeks out of his right cheek. "You're really good at that."

I'm not sure what he means. "Good at what?"

"Hyping me up." His expression turns serious. "Believing in me."

"How could I *not* believe in you?" My heart begins to race. "There's no one in the world like Phoenix Walker. You're special."

"You really think so, huh?"

I smile. "I *know* so."

And soon enough the world will, too.

CHAPTER 8
LENNON

A surge of excitement runs through me as we enter the garage. The gift I ordered Phoenix a couple of days ago finally came in and I can't wait to give it to him.

I'm hoping it not only works but puts him in a good enough mood that he'll be on board with an idea I've been ruminating on for a bit.

"I got you something," I tell him as we sit on the futon.

Since we'll be working on reading passages and answering questions tonight, it's the perfect opportunity for him to test it out.

His eyebrows shoot up. "Again?"

"Yup. Only this time, I *know* it's gonna work." I root around my purse for the pen and pull it out. "This is a reading pen. Basically, you scan a line of text and it reads it aloud for you." I open my folder and take out a piece of paper containing one of the passages. "Here. Try."

He examines the pen. "It looks expensive."

It was. But only because I wanted to get him a really good one.

It was totally worth digging into my car fund, though, because I know this will be a game changer.

Especially if he agrees to let me talk to Mrs. Herman.

Shaking his head, he places the pen down. "I appreciate it, but I can't accept this."

Is he crazy? "Of course you can. I know the ruler didn't help that much, but this will. I did a lot of research and this one is supposed to be the best—"

"It's too much money."

I don't understand why he keeps focusing on the price tag. "So what? I don't want you to pay me back, I just want you to use it."

A sound of irritation escapes him, and he stands. "I'm *not* a charity case, Lennon."

I honestly don't get why he's making such a big deal about this.

"I never said you were."

"Pizza is one thing. Lavish gifts are another."

I can't help but laugh because he's being ridiculous. "It's just a damn pen, Phoenix. I'd hardly call it *lavish*."

My comment only makes him angrier. "Maybe not to you, *princess*. But not everyone has a rich daddy who shells out money whenever they want."

Ouch. I'm the farthest thing from a princess.

I also didn't ask my dad for a penny. I bought it with money I saved up over the years from babysitting and tutoring.

And while my dad makes a very good living and I've been fortunate to never have to go without, I'd hardly call him *rich*.

Songwriters aren't millionaires like people seem to think. Even after they write a hit song.

"My dad didn't pay for this." Tears prickle my throat, but I force myself to swallow them. "I did." To my absolute horror, my voice cracks and my vision blurs. "I just wanted to help you."

Humiliated at the thought of him seeing me cry, I turn around.

"Shit." I hear his sharp exhale of breath before his fingers skim my shoulder. "I'm sorry. It's just…you do so much for me as it is. Way more than I deserve."

That's not true. He has more raw talent in his pinkie finger than most musicians out there today have *combined*.

But even if he didn't, he still deserves my friendship and support.

I just wish he knew how much faith I have in him.

"You're going to change the world one day, Phoenix. And when that happens, I'm going to cheer you on from the sidelines with the biggest smile on my face."

I knew from the first second I laid eyes on him that he was special.

So does everyone else.

The fingers brushing my shoulder glide up the side of my neck. I feel the contact *everywhere*.

His voice is such a low rasp I almost don't hear him. "Lennon."

I close my eyes as heat floods my body, settling between my thighs. For the briefest of moments, I give myself permission to pretend I'm not the fat girl...but the kind of girl Phoenix Walker is attracted to.

All too soon, his touch is gone, though...and I'm faced with reality again.

"Thank you for the pen."

After taking a cleansing breath, I turn and sit back down on the futon. "You're welcome."

He places the pen over the paper, smiling a little when it reads a sentence aloud. "This thing is pretty sweet. Too bad I won't be able to use it for the final."

Here goes nothing.

"About that." I tuck a strand of hair behind my ear. "I've been thinking..."

"The suspense is killing me," he jokes after another minute goes by.

"I want to tell Mrs. Herman the truth."

He shuts it down instantly. "No."

"Come on, Phoenix." He's failed to comprehend what this could mean for him. "I know once I explain the issue, she'll have no problem accommodating you. And then you'll be able to pass the final...all on your own."

"I don't need everyone knowing I can't read," he grinds out.

"I'll ask if you can take the final after school. In private. No one will know."

"I don't think it's a good idea." Trepidation contorts his features. "What if she says no? Or worse—what if she insists on holding me back another year so they can stick me in a special class. I can't take that chance, Lennon. I *have* to get the fuck out of here."

I know.

I place my hand on top of his. "Do you trust me?"

His throat works on a swallow and it feels like a century goes by before he answers. "Yes."

"Good. Because I've got you."

"Is everything okay, Lennon?" Mrs. Herman asks when I hang back after class.

"Actually, I was hoping you had a second."

Placing her red marker down, she smiles. "For you, I have several."

I return her smile. "I want to talk about Phoenix."

Her forehead creases. "Oh, no. Is it not working out? I know he can be difficult—"

"No. Phoenix is great. He's been working really hard."

She nods. "That he is. The essay he turned in was excellent. I never even knew he was a musician."

"He's an amazing musician." I wipe my damp palms on my jeans. "However, there's an issue. It's not his fault, but it's definitely the reason behind his poor grades."

Her expression pinches. "Are you referring to his homelife because I've tried setting up a meeting with his fath—"

"No. I'm talking about his dyslexia."

She's visibly confused by this. "I'm sorry, but you must be mistaken. Phoenix doesn't have dyslexia."

"Yes, he does." I lick my dry lips. "It's why he's been struggling so much. He said the words get all jumbled. The first night we studied, he couldn't even read the first page of an essay."

Her mouth opens and closes in shock before she speaks. "He never...how come I didn't know about this? I would have made sure to get him help—"

"Phoenix didn't want anyone to know. He's...embarrassed."

She rubs her forehead. "He's turned in assignments before that were rather good. I don't understand how that happened." Her eyes narrow. "Unless he's not the one who did the work."

"No," I say quickly. "He gets audio versions of the books we read in class from the library. He also uses an app on his phone that reads aloud to him so he can do the homework. As far as tests...he tries his best to guess the answers."

"I can't believe I didn't know this. Whenever I asked him to stay after so I could help, he looked like he was concentrating, yet he never seemed to know the answers. I thought he just wasn't processing it. Not that he had trouble reading." She steeples her fingers. "I'll set up a meeting with the principal. If we hold him back another year, I can ensure he gets the help—"

"I know a much better way you can help him."

Her nose scrunches. "What do you mean?"

I can't expect her to tailor the final for him or anything.

I just want her to give him a fighting chance.

"I got him a reading pen. Basically, it scans a sentence and reads it aloud. I'm hoping you'll let him use it for the final...and let him take it after school so no one else knows about it."

Her eyes widen. "Oh...that is." She shakes her head. "I mean, if he had an IEP, I'd have no problem accommodating his needs but—"

I pull out the big guns. "You once told me that Phoenix not graduating would do him more harm than good...and you were right. I know this is a lot to ask, and it means you'll have to stay after, which will require even more of your time, but I know in my gut he'll pass. *Please*, don't let something that's not his fault hold him back."

I can see her mulling this over before she speaks. "All right. I'll allow it. But the reading pen *only*. No phones, no tablets...no other devices. And he is not to leave this classroom once he starts the final. Are we clear?"

"Absolutely."

I breathe a sigh of relief as I scramble toward the door.

"Lennon?" she calls out before I leave.

"Yes?" I ask, hoping she won't change her mind.

"I'm glad I paired you two up. It seems you've done a lot of good for him. I hope he knows how fortunate he is."

My chest contracts. Because I feel like *I'm* the lucky one.

I didn't see Phoenix in the hallways after I spoke to Mrs. Herman, so I decide to wait by his car after school. This way I can tell him the good news in person.

Wanting to pass the time until he arrives, I pull my journal and a pen out of my bag.

Most of the lyrics I scribble down in here aren't very good and I'd *never* share them with anyone.

Especially my dad because they're nowhere near as great as his are.

I'd be afraid of getting his hopes up about his daughter sharing his gift…only to end up disappointing him once he heard them.

Not that he'd *ever* tell me that.

All that aside…writing songs is cathartic.

A way for me to purge some of the pain away.

Channel my emotions and feelings into something that heals me.

It's like my own secret form of therapy.

I'm so into the one I'm working on, I don't realize Phoenix has walked out of the building until he's halfway to his car.

However, he's not alone.

Sasha Williams is beside him. And just like her friend Sabrina— she's beautiful and thin.

Unlike me, she looks like she belongs with him.

Someone he wouldn't mind being seen with in public...and touching in private.

Feeling stupid, I head over to the bike rack so I can pedal my ass home and sulk over a tub of ice cream, but Phoenix spots me.

"Lennon." His strides pick up until he's in front of me. "Everything okay?"

"Yeah."

Sasha sidles up beside him then, and it's clear my presence annoys her because she looks like she smelled something rotten.

I put in the combination for my bike lock. "I have some good news...but I can tell you another time."

"Change of plans," he says. "I'm busy tonight."

Of course, he'd ditch me for Sasha.

"Okay—" I start to say, but then I realize he's not talking to me.

He's talking to *her*.

The look on Sasha's face makes it clear she's equally shocked by this. "Wait...are you for real?"

He doesn't even look at her when he speaks. "Yes."

Outrage spreads over her pretty features. "This is...you're an asshole." Tossing her auburn hair over her shoulder, she murmurs, "Have fun hanging out with butterball."

"Points for creativity on that one," I say to her retreating back. "Most people just call me fat ass."

"Most people are dicks," Phoenix mutters under his breath. "Anyway, fuck that bitch. What's up?"

"I spoke to Mrs. Herman." I can't contain my smile. "She not only agreed to let you take the final while using the pen...she agreed to let you take it after class."

His jaw drops. "What? Are you serious?"

I nod so hard I get dizzy.

And that dizziness only grows when Phoenix wraps his arms around me.

Oh. My. God.

Phoenix Walker is *hugging* me.

I swear my feet almost lift off the ground as I fill my nostrils with the earthy scent of him before he breaks contact.

"Thank you. So fucking much." He gestures to my bike. "Let's stick that thing in my trunk."

"I don't think it will fit." I shake my head, feeling all sorts of perplexed. "And *why*?"

He looks at me like I sprouted another head. "So we can grab some food and head over to Storm's. Unless you'd rather leave it here...just don't blame me if it gets stolen."

Grabbing the handlebars, I walk my bike to his car. "You sure you want to start studying this early?"

It's still daylight out.

"Fuck no." Opening the back door of his Toyota, he takes out a few bungee cords. "I've been doing enough of that lately. I want to hang out."

Yup. This day just keeps getting weirder and weirder.

In the absolute best way.

"Oh."

Taking my bike from me, he places it in his trunk and secures it with the bungees. "What? You got something better to do?"

"No." I hike my purse up my shoulder. "I'm totally down to hang out."

I have to bite the inside of my cheek to keep from smiling as I get into his car.

We really are friends.

CHAPTER 9
LENNON

"How come you're not eating your burger?" Phoenix questions around a mouthful of the one he's currently stuffing his face with.

Because it's the equivalent of taking a giant dump in front of you.

We stopped at a fast-food place on the way to Storm's and despite me telling him I didn't want anything, he ordered me a burger with the works anyway.

He said it was the least he could do for getting Mrs. Herman to agree to let him use the pen.

"I'm not really hungry," I lie.

I'm so famished my stomach is legitimately growling for once. I talked to Mrs. Herman during my lunch period and by the time I finally made it to the cafeteria, the bell rang.

"We've been in school all day." A drop of ketchup drips down his chiseled jaw and holy hell, I've never had the urge to lick something so bad in my life. "There's no way you're not hungry."

"I'm really not," I fib again, only this time my stomach betrays me because it growls...loudly.

Giving me a look that says—*I told you so*, Phoenix picks up the burger on the makeshift crate table in front of us. "Eat the fucking burger, Lennon."

I take it, but have second thoughts as I unwrap it because this is a big deal.

Everyone knows food is what makes you fat, so it goes without saying that when a heavy person eats in front of those who aren't, they're being judged.

As if we're expected to eat salads and veggies only.

Because we no longer deserve to indulge and enjoy food since we abused it and let ourselves go.

Thoroughly annoyed, Phoenix places his half-eaten burger down.

"You're not skinny."

I. Want. To. Die.

"But you're human," he continues, much to my embarrassment. "And humans need to eat when they're hungry. So, either pick up that burger, or I'm taking you home. Because at least I know you won't starve yourself there."

I'm torn between wanting to run right out that door and wanting to call him an asshole for being so blunt.

However, there's something to be said about him seeing me for exactly who I am...and not judging me for it.

I take a small bite. "Happy?"

He picks up his burger. "Almost. Eat some more."

I'm desperate to change the subject, so I scan my brain for another topic as I take another bite. I almost choke when I realize. Phoenix never mentioned it, but it's kind of important.

"What's your band name?"

His lips twitch as he finishes his food. "Sharp Objects."

"That's..." *Oddly perfect.* "How did you come up with that?"

Blue eyes pierce mine. "Storm and I...we have a tendency to hurt people...cut them with our words and actions. So, it fits." He wipes his hands with a napkin. "That and a sharp note is one you can't help but pay attention to."

"Because it's a higher pitch," I whisper. "Special."

Just like he is.

"Exactly." His gaze drops to the now half-eaten burger I placed down while he was talking. "You gonna finish that?"

Normally I would not only finish it, I'd chase it with two more.

Even though I'm five foot two and two hundred and thirty pounds…I can't seem to find the off switch when it comes to food.

I eat so much because I'm trying to fill a void.

Because it gives me a false sense of happiness…even though it always turns to shame afterward.

But that's not the case right now. Even though mentally, I'm *dying* to finish the rest. Physically, I'm satisfied.

"No. I'm actually full."

I start to wrap the remaining burger back up, but Phoenix takes it. "In that case, more for me."

Rolling my eyes, I laugh. I thought my appetite was insatiable, but it has nothing on his.

Only *he* has the advantage of having a fast metabolism because he's long and lean.

Flawless.

I feel him studying me intently as he polishes off the rest of my food. "What's the deal with that notebook you were writing in before?"

I shift uncomfortably. I feel like I could tell Phoenix anything at this point, but what's in there is private.

Plus, the latest song I'm writing is about *him*.

"It's nothing. I just doodle stuff down sometimes."

That only seems to interest him more. "What kind of stuff?"

My palms begin sweating, so I wipe them on my jeans. "Nothing. It's not a big deal."

I wish he'd take the hint and drop it.

But he doesn't.

"If it's no big deal, then tell me."

Jesus. He's like a dog trying to dig up a bone buried six feet underground.

"Would you stop?" I lash out with way more hostility than necessary. "It's none of your damn business."

Visibly insulted, he runs a hand through his hair. "Fuck me for asking."

It's obvious I offended him, and I feel terrible. He was only trying to ask me about something he saw, and not only did I not answer him, I bit his head off.

I'm about to apologize, but then it dawns on me that there's also something I've been dying to know about him. Perhaps we could trade secrets.

"I'll tell you what's in my notebook if you tell me how you knew where I lived."

Grabbing a pack of cigarettes off the crate, he brings one to his mouth. It's on the tip of my tongue to tell him smoking is a surefire way to ruin his amazing voice, but then he says, "I did some land-scaping work for your neighbor, Mrs. Palma, last summer and I saw you outside."

"Oh."

I'm happy he finally told me, but he's definitely getting the juicier secret out of this deal.

Here goes nothing. "I kind of…sort of…write songs."

His expression remains neutral as he lights his cigarette. "You mean like lyrics? Or music?"

"Both."

He rubs his jaw, dissecting me. "I want to hear them."

I'd rather swallow nails than sing one of my songs to him, but I'm willing to compromise.

I fish my notebook out of my purse. No way in hell would I ever show him *all* my songs, but there is one that's my favorite.

Although it is incredibly personal…and kind of strange.

"Here." I flip to the page it's on. "You can read this one."

I want to kick myself the moment the words leave my mouth.

I'm about to suggest he use the pen I got him, but he takes the notebook from me and closes it.

"I have trouble reading, remember? That includes reading music."

How is that even possible? "But you play piano."

I took piano lessons for three years and learning to read music was not only necessary, it was a basic requirement.

He points to his ears. "Because I have these."

Holy shit. I know musicians who can solely play by ear exist, but it's usually ones who have been doing it for decades.

Then again, I once heard that some people with learning disabilities are incredibly gifted in other areas.

It's clear that's the case with Phoenix.

Every cell he's made up of lives, breathes, and creates music.

It's why he was put on this earth.

"Anyway," he continues, as if what he said was no big deal. "I want the full experience." He juts his chin at the instruments set up across the room. "I don't know what you'll need, but help yourself to whatever you want."

I shake my head because that's completely out of the question. "Absolutely *not*—"

"Come on, Groupie." He stubs his cigarette out in a nearby ashtray. "You can't tell me you write songs and not play any for me. That's like telling a kid you have candy, but you won't share any with them."

He has a point, but still. I don't want to share something so personal.

I don't want him to laugh at me.

"No."

Phoenix isn't giving up, though. "I played for you."

It's true. He did. And he was phenomenal.

However, my voice isn't raspy while simultaneously being smooth and velvety like *his*.

Mine is scratchy and hoarse. Like my alter ego is a seventy-year-old smoker named Bertha who has a perpetual sore throat.

"Both my voice and song are weird," I warn him.

"I like weird." Those ice-blue orbs sharpen on me, sucking all the oxygen out of the room. "And I love your voice."

I'm rendered speechless, any argument I had vanishing into thin air.

Because Phoenix Walker is looking at me like *I'm* the talented one in this room.

My legs feel like Jell-O when I stand.

Let's hope I don't disappoint him.

CHAPTER 10
PHOENIX

There's nervous…and then there's petrified.

Lennon is unquestionably the latter right now.

I've never seen this girl so much as break a sweat, so watching her get worked up is strange as hell.

Christ. She looks like she's going to puke any second.

I'm about to ask if she wants a bucket as she walks behind the keyboard. "I don't play as well as you do."

I don't give a shit how well she can play. I just want to hear her sing again.

Given I'm over a foot taller than her, the mic is positioned above her head. "Lower the mic."

The look she gives me makes it clear she doesn't want to.

Tough shit. I want to hear every sound that comes out of her mouth.

"Promise you won't laugh," she says as she adjusts it. "Actually, promise you won't say *anything*."

I'm a dick, but not when it comes to music. I know firsthand that it takes a lot of balls to bare your soul in front of others.

"I won't laugh."

Not unless she's about to start playing clown music.

Her gaze rests on the keyboard as her fingers begin to move, filling the garage with a dark melodic sound that has a bite of edge to it.

I shift to the edge of the couch, because already she's got my full attention.

And then she starts to sing.

I'm tough as a nail
Sharp as a blade
But I'm still lying here...
In the mess you made.

Jagged and broken
Dull and washed out.
Everywhere I turn...
I breathe you in and bleed you out.

Because I'm supposed to be the cutter...
But you're the one who cut me.

Fuck the memories I'll never have.
Fuck the pain of your knife.
Fuck these feelings you left me with...
Fuck this thing they call life.

I don't move a muscle as the song comes to an end. I *can't*.

Because Lennon Michael just made me hard without even touching me.

Her low, sultry voice wrapped around my dick and tugged.

And don't even get me started on the lyrics. They're painful and real...

They're the purest form of art.

That combined with the slow edgy melody that built up into a hypnotic crescendo with every verse until it reached inside your chest and pulled out your beating heart…

Fuck. The girl has a gift.

Averting her gaze, she ambles back over to the futon.

Like she didn't just do something that left me breathless and wanting more.

"Lennon."

I know she didn't want me to say anything, but I *have* to.

If only so she'll transfer even half the belief she has in me onto herself.

I turn to face her. "That was…"

Words don't do it justice.

"I'm…you…"

Shit. *I'm* the one tripping over my words now.

I clear my throat. "You wrote that? By yourself?"

I won't judge her if she had help from her dad. It makes what I just witnessed no less incredible.

"Yeah." Her face pinches. "Why?"

My knee bumps hers as I move closer. "It was per—"

"What up, fucker?" Storm interjects.

His gaze lands on Lennon as he walks into the garage. "Hey, Groupie."

My eyes snap to his as irritation snakes up my spine.

I have the sudden urge to walk over there and launch my fist into my best friend's face.

Lennon's *my* friend. Not his.

Unbothered by him calling her my nickname, Lennon smiles. "Hey."

Lighting up a joint, Storm regards me again. "We have to practice."

Lennon's face lights up. "Can I stay and watch?"

"Yeah," I say at the same time Storm does.

Standing, she tugs her bottom lip between her teeth. "Um…sorry, but can I use your bathroom first?"

Storm gestures to the door he just came through. "Second door on the right. Grams is cooking dinner though, which means she won't let you pass by until you try some of her sauce. Consider yourself warned."

After Lennon leaves, his gaze ping-pongs between me and the door. "What's the deal with you two?"

I want to tell him to put down the joint because it's killing his brain cells.

"She's tutoring me," I remind him.

He takes a long pull off his joint before clipping it. "Didn't look like she was tutoring you when I walked in." His expression turns curious. "And last I checked, you don't bring chicks to practice."

Because it's too much of a fucking distraction. The only time I did bring a girl to one, I ended up cutting it short so we could go fuck in my car.

I don't have that problem with Lennon.

But unlike those girls who can't even name their top five favorite rock bands—or tell me the difference between alternative rock and heavy metal—Lennon can name fifty off the top of her head *and* cite their B-side songs.

She also seems to genuinely enjoy listening to us play, which is an added bonus.

"I—"

"Bro, it's fine." He walks over to his drum set. "I'm cool with it."

I don't give a shit that he's cool with it. I don't need his approval.

Besides, there's nothing going on between us.

"There's nothing to be cool with," I tell him as I walk over to the mic stand and adjust it. "Lennon's chill, but it's not like that. We're friends."

"If you say so," Storm mutters behind me.

Tilting my head, I glare at him. "Are you really that stupid, asshole? She's not my fucking type."

"All right, man. Goddamn. Let's fucking play."

CHAPTER 11
LENNON

"Everything will be great," I tell him as we walk down the hall to Mrs. Herman's room.

Phoenix doesn't seem convinced.

I know he's nervous, because what happens on that final determines his fate.

But I *know* he's going to pass.

"I'll buy you dinner after so we can celebrate," I prattle on, hoping to ease some of his anxiety.

It doesn't work. By the time we reach the classroom, he looks like he's two seconds away from saying *fuck this* and bolting.

Grabbing him by the shoulders, I peer up at him. "You got this, you hear me? You're gonna make this final your bitch because you're Phoenix motherfucking Walker."

I'm grateful the hallway is empty because I shouted that last part.

Not that I regret it because it manages to get a little smile out of him.

Mrs. Herman pops her head outside the door. "Everything okay out here?"

"Yes," I answer.

She looks between us. "I'll give you two another minute to say your goodbyes. Then I'll need you to come inside so you can begin."

With that, she disappears.

Phoenix's voice is so low I almost don't hear him. "What if I fail?"

"You *won't*." Closing the distance between us, I give him a quick hug. "I believe in you." I walk backward. "Now get in there and kick that final's ass. I'll be waiting for you in the band room."

I say a silent prayer that everything works out in his favor as he walks inside.

"Lennon's chill, but it's not like that. We're friends."

The tail end of the conversation I overheard the other day echoes through my head as I enter the band room.

Maybe it should have hurt because I have feelings for him, but he said we were friends. And I've always known that's the most a girl like me could ever hope for when it comes to Phoenix.

I take a seat at the piano bench.

"Are you really that stupid, asshole? She's not my fucking type."

That's the part that hurt.

Even though he didn't insult me, hearing him say those words still felt like a punch to the heart.

Because it's the truth.

I've been playing so long my fingers are starting to cramp up.

I look up at the clock on the wall. He's been in there for over two hours now.

A horrendous thought slams into me.

What if he left already? *Because he failed.*

No. There's no way he did. I refuse to even entertain the notion.

I'm on the last verse of the song I've been working on when the door swings open.

I'm on my feet so fast the bench almost tips over.

I don't know what to make of his expression, or the fact he's just standing there…not saying a word.

But then he gives me the biggest, most beautiful smile I've ever seen in my life.

"I got an eighty-one."

A rush of exhilaration surges through me, and I race over. I'm so happy I feel like I could burst wide open with the force of it.

I throw my arms around him. "I *knew* you were gonna pass." I grab his face. "I didn't doubt it for a second. You're—"

Soft lips crash against mine.

I'm torn between wanting to pinch myself because there's no way this is real life, and not wanting to move or breathe ever again… because this is a dream I *never* want to wake up from.

He makes a noise deep in his throat and my back slams against a wall. That's when I realize this isn't a hallucination, after all.

Phoenix Walker is *kissing* me.

My mouth opens and his tongue ardently slides in, tasting mine.

I'm so close to the sun I go up in flames.

I was thirteen when I had my first—and until this moment, last— kiss with a guy named Kelly, who was visiting his grandparents for the summer. It was awkward, sloppy…and not even close to how I always envisioned the magical moment would be.

But *this* kiss? It's everything I've ever wanted and then some.

He's kissing me like he's parched and I'm the only drop of water for miles. I arch against him as his tongue thrusts deeper and his hand cups the side of my neck, keeping me there…as though he's afraid I might escape.

But the building could explode—hell, the earth could explode— and I still wouldn't put an end to this kiss.

However, *he* does.

His eyes are wide as he backs away from me slowly…like we're in an apocalypse and he just discovered I'm a zombie.

I can't differentiate if the expression on his face is because of shock or horror.

Perhaps my kissing skills are worse than I thought, and I messed something up?

I'm not sure what went wrong. The only thing I *am* sure of right now is that he regrets it.

"Phoenix—"

As if the sound of my voice was some kind of alarm warning him of imminent danger, he turns and bolts out the door.

While I'm left standing there, wondering what the hell just happened…

And what I did wrong.

Later that night—after debating for hours—I finally give in and text him.

Lennon: I'm proud of you.

Yes, we kissed. But it doesn't have to ruin our friendship.

He can chalk it up to a mistake he made due to his excitement over passing the final…and I can chalk it up to the best moment of my life.

Then we can go back to normal.

Only we can't…

Because he never responds.

CHAPTER 12
LENNON

I t's been three days since Phoenix kissed me and took off. I knew he needed some space, but I figured he'd get over it the next day and we'd be cool again.

That didn't happen, though. Not only did he avoid me like the plague in school *and* after, he still didn't return my text.

I don't want to come off clingy, but I really miss my friend.

Which is why I end up sending him another text.

Lennon: Congrats.

We'll be graduating in less than an hour, so I'm *sure* he's going to put an end to this silent treatment and tell me the same.

No such luck. Just like my last one, I get no response.

"Lennon, we're gonna be late," my dad hollers from downstairs.

Glancing in the mirror, I finish bobby-pinning the stupid blue cap to my head. "I'll be right there."

I check my phone one last time before chucking it into my purse. He can't avoid me forever. Not only will I see him at graduation, he'll be at the party tonight.

I look over at the outfit hanging on the door of my closet. Usually,

I wear T-shirts and jeans, but I decided to step out of my comfort zone and purchase a new dress for tonight. It's short, A-line, and black. I love it because the bottom flares out, giving my figure a flattering shape. Plus, the dark color is slimming.

I ended up confiding in Mrs. Palma about Phoenix because I really needed to vent. After telling me boys were stupid and that he'd come to his senses, she offered to help me do my hair and makeup for the party.

I'm under no illusion that wearing a dress and makeup will make Phoenix fall at my feet, but if he doesn't pull his head out of his ass, then tonight's the last night we'll ever see each other.

Therefore, I might as well look my best.

"Lennon," my dad yells again. "Let's go."

I went temporarily blind from the flash of my dad's camera thanks to him snapping no less than a thousand pictures of me walking across the stage.

Fortunately, my vision is back to normal by the time it's Phoenix's turn. Somehow, he even manages to make the ugly cap and gown look sexy. My fellow classmates and I erupt in loud cheers as he accepts his diploma. When I glance back at the audience, I see Storm's grandmother standing and yelling her heart out while she takes a few photos.

As far as I can tell, she's the only *parent* here for him.

Shortly after he walks off, the announcer tells us to move our tassels to the other side and declares us official high school graduates.

I'm thrilled when we get to toss the caps in the air because those damn pins were starting to give me a headache.

It feels like an eternity by the time everyone exits the oversized tent the ceremony took place under.

I spot my dad instantly once I make it out...because he's holding the biggest bouquet of flowers I've ever seen in my life.

Running over, he hugs me so tight it hurts. "I'm so proud of you, monkey face!"

I laugh into his shirt because he's making a bigger deal out of this than necessary. "Thanks."

After he finally lets me go, he hands me the gigantic bouquet. It's so big, I need two hands to hold it. "I told the florist to give me the prettiest flowers in the store because my baby girl deserves nothing less."

She most certainly did. Not only is there one heck of a *variety*, every single flower is so vivid and beautiful.

"They're gorgeous, Dad."

Out of the corner of my eye, I spot Storm, his grandma, and Phoenix talking. I really want to walk over there, but despite only being a mere ten feet away, he isn't looking my way.

"Dartmouth, here you come," my dad says, drawing my attention back to him.

Sheer pride illuminates his face as he smiles from ear to ear, but nerves coil in my belly at the thought of moving away from the only parent I have left. "I could always stay here."

"Absolutely not. It's okay to be scared, but it's not okay to let that fear hold you back from experiencing life." Leaning forward, he kisses my forehead. "Besides, you'll be home every holiday and summer."

Deep down, I know he's right. It's time for me to grow up.

Get out of this tiny fishbowl that is Hillcrest and jump into the ocean.

He puts his arm around my shoulders. "Come on, let's go to lunch."

I bat my eyelashes. "Can we go to that seafood place I like?"

It's super expensive, but they have the *best* lobster.

"We can go wherever you want."

We're about to leave, but I halt my steps and hand him my bouquet. "Can you hold these for a second?"

In a desperate attempt to salvage our friendship once again, I pull my phone out of my purse and shoot him one last text.

Lennon: I knew you could do it.

My heart clenches when I see Phoenix glance at his phone... before shoving it back into his pocket.

CHAPTER 13
PHOENIX

I mutter a curse when I make the mistake of rolling over in bed. Even though the sharp, stabbing pain spreading throughout my side has now reduced to a dull ache, putting pressure on it wasn't a good idea.

I'm just glad there wasn't more damage. *Drunk motherfucker.*

Practice with Storm ran until three a.m., and I had to get up early for the graduation ceremony today, so I was tired as hell.

The moment I came home, I went straight to my room and passed the fuck out.

Only to be woken up hours later by a bat striking my hip.

The asshole only got one swing in before I wrangled it from him and punched him in the face so hard I knocked him out.

After that, I dragged his unconscious ass out into the hallway.

It's almost midnight now, and the bastard is *still* passed out cold.

Grabbing my phone, I scroll through my texts, stopping on the one I got from Lennon earlier.

I should reply, but I don't know what to say.

Because I royally fucked up.

I told her not to make shit complicated, and then I did by *kissing* her.

Goddammit. That was so fucking stupid.

Not only are we friends, I'm about to split.

Our gig at Voodoo is in four days, and a week after that Storm and I are leaving for Los Angeles.

I can't fucking wait to get out of here.

My phone vibrates and Storm's name flashes across the screen. Fucker probably needs a ride home because he got plastered at the graduation party.

Clicking the green button, I bring it to my ear. "You need me to swing by and get you?"

"Nah, man. Some shit just went down."

I'm expecting him to tell me that the cops were called, and half our graduating class was arrested.

"You need me to bail you out?"

If that's the case, it's gonna put a dent in our LA fund.

"Not tonight." He blows out a breath. "Anyway, I was outside in the hot tub getting a hand job from Sasha. I was about to suggest that we go inside and screw, but then I heard a ton of commotion."

"Let me guess, a fight broke out."

I'm gearing up to tell him not to be too disappointed about the interruption because Sasha's a lousy lay, but then he says, "Nah. It was your girl."

My girl? "Can you be more specific?"

"*Lennon,* motherfucker."

My mind spins back to what Sabrina said after I fucked her in the band room.

I bolt up in bed. "What the fuck happened?"

I'd been so busy practicing for our upcoming gig *and* ignoring her, I forgot to warn her not to go to the party.

"Sabrina and a bunch of other assholes threw pig slop on her. Then they circled around the poor girl and oinked while someone kept yelling, '*Sooey.*' It was fucking brutal."

Jesus fucking Christ.

"Anyway," he adds. "I have her in my truck. What do you want me to do with her?"

He says it like she's a goddamn appliance he's delivering. Then again, that's Storm. The only emotion the fucker is able to register is anger.

I swipe my keys off my dresser. "I'm on my way."

"I'll keep her until you get here. Although I should warn you, the girl still hasn't said anything. I think she's in shock or something."

The towel I swiped from the bathroom on my way out isn't gonna cut it.

Lennon's covered head to toe in pig slop. It's so bad it's caked onto her clothes, eyelashes, and hair.

She keeps her gaze cast down as I help her out of Storm's truck.

She definitely needs a shower, but I can't take her back to my place.

Not with *him* there.

I don't think bringing her home is a good idea, either. Lennon's dad actually gives a shit about his daughter, so I wouldn't put it past him to not only flip out, but march over here and yell at everyone... which will only make things worse for her.

I look at Storm. "Can I—"

"You don't even need to ask." He gestures to the house where the party sounds like it's still in full swing. "I'm gonna head back in there and get my dick sucked. See you in the morning."

With those parting words, he bounces, and I lead Lennon to my car.

She doesn't say shit to me on the drive to Storm's.

Lennon protests as I usher her through the front door. "Can you take me home—"

"My word," Grams exclaims when she sees us, nearly dropping her cup of tea. "What happened?"

"Some bitches attacked Lennon at a graduation party."

As a Southern Christian woman who attends church for *fun*, she usually scolds me whenever I curse, but she's too focused on Lennon.

After handing me her tea, she grabs Lennon's hand and escorts her to the bathroom. "You go and shower, sweet pea. I'll wash your clothes."

Lennon isn't having it, though. "Thank you, but I don't want to impose. I'll just call an Uber and—"

"Nonsense," Grams says, and I can't help but laugh because there's no arguing with the woman. "Go on in and get cleaned up." She opens the bathroom door. "Towels are in the cabinet over there."

Realizing she's not going to win this battle, Lennon concedes. "Thank you. I really appreciate it."

Grams frowns after the door closes. "What a cruel thing to do." Shuffling toward the kitchen, she lets out a long sigh. "May they rot in hell. Every last one of them."

Amen to that.

It dawns on me that Lennon's going to need something to wear while her clothes are being washed, so I head into Storm's room. I make a beeline for the duffel bag I keep here for when shit gets bad at home and I need to crash for a few days.

As I'm rummaging through it, I come across a faded black Papa Roach T-shirt Grams got me for my birthday a few years ago.

I have a feeling Lennon will prefer this over one of Gram's hideous nightgowns.

The shower is running by the time I reach the bathroom, so I open the door. "I brought you—"

"Jesus. Don't you knock?" Lennon screeches, quickly reaching for a towel.

I catch the briefest glimpse of a purple bra and flashes of ink before she clutches the towel to her body.

I'll be damned. Little Miss Innocent and I have something else in common.

"You have tattoos?"

Lennon shoots me a look like she wants to rip my head off. "Get out of here!"

For fuck's sake. She's not the first naked chick I've encountered. It's practically a daily occurrence.

"Relax, it's nothing I haven't seen before."

Not that I even saw much of anything in the first place.

I place the T-shirt on the sink. "I brought you something to wear."

A half-hour later, the interior door opens, and Lennon enters the garage. Her dark shoulder-length hair that's usually tied up is now loose and wet, and she keeps tugging down the T-shirt even though it grazes her knees. That, along with her expression, makes it clear she's uncomfortable.

However, she's no longer covered in pig slop, so she should take it as a win.

"Hey."

"Can you take me home?"

I *could*, but I don't want to. I figured we could hang out for a bit.

"Why don't you stay a little while?"

Lennon's not into it though, because she's quick to shut that idea down. "No. I just want to go home."

Growing annoyed, I cross my arms. "Wait for your clothes to dry."

"I'll come back and get them tomorrow."

Dammit. I was hoping we could squash the bullshit between us and go back to the way shit was.

"Hang out with me."

She laughs, but there's not an ounce of humor. "Why would I want to hang out with you?"

Christ. This morning she was texting me and now she's acting like she can't put enough distance between us.

"Because we're friends?"

"We're not friends." Those baby browns turn glassy. "Friends don't ghost friends."

She's right, but before I can say that, she marches past me, heading for the exterior door.

I chase after her. I get that she's pissed, but leaving in the middle of the night wearing nothing but a T-shirt isn't fucking smart.

"Lennon."

I reach for her wrist, but she whips around and pushes me. "Leave me *alone*."

"I know you're upset—"

"I'm not upset. I'm *mortified*." Her lower lip trembles and her voice cracks. "They fucking poured pig slop on me."

I'm about to remind her that she'll never have to deal with them again, but then Lennon does something I've never seen her do before...

She cries.

CHAPTER 14
LENNON

As if being covered in pig slop wasn't enough of a reason to be humiliated, I now have another one.

I'm a fountain of tears and jittery breaths that I can't seem to stop. I want to run right out that door and never come back, but Phoenix wraps his arms around me.

The urge to push him away again is strong, but it's overshadowed by my need for comfort.

And because he smells good. *Damn him.*

His voice is a low rumble in my ear as he tightens his hold. "They're fucking bitches."

That only makes me sob harder. I spent all afternoon getting ready, hoping to not only see him, but enjoy a night with my peers before we all went our separate ways.

A night where I wasn't the fat girl being bullied...because for once, I fit in.

But I don't fit in. *I never will.*

"I just wanted to get drunk and have fun," I croak against his chest, my tears saturating the thin material of his dark-gray T-shirt.

"I have a bottle of Jack in my car." When I peer up, his mouth curls into a smirk. "Let's party."

I didn't think it was possible to laugh and cry at the same time, but I was wrong. "Very funny."

"I'm serious." Breaking the hug, he walks backward. "We just graduated motherfucking high school, and I want to kick back and celebrate with one of my favorite people." He waggles his eyebrows. "I'll be right back."

I should turn him down since he's ignored me for the last three days… but he didn't have to show up at the party and get me.

It would also be nice to pick up the pieces of what's undoubtedly been the worst night of my life.

Hanging out with my friend seems like a good way to do that.

Plus—much to my father's reluctance when we discussed it—I no longer have a curfew since I'm not only eighteen, but a high school graduate.

Phoenix walks back inside holding a bottle of Jack Daniels in one hand and two red Solo cups in the other.

Gesturing for me to follow, he walks over to the futon.

I plop down next to him as he places the bottle and cups on the crate in front of us.

"So, is the plan to just sit here and get wasted all night?" I ask as he fills both Solos to the halfway mark.

"Yeah." After giving one to me, he lightly taps his cup against mine. "Pretty much."

Granted, I've never gotten drunk before, but that doesn't seem very exciting.

"That's not really fun."

Phoenix snorts. "Wait till the alcohol hits you."

Fair enough. Although, it might be more entertaining if we found a way to make it more interesting while that happens.

"We should play a game."

His forehead creases. "What kind of game?"

"A drinking game." *Obviously.* "How about Never Have I Ever?" I haven't personally played it, but it's a fairly easy concept. "Basically, we each take turns saying something we've never done before, but if the other person *has* done it…they have to take a drink."

"That sounds stupid," Phoenix mutters. "But, fine. I'm down. You start."

He won't think it's so stupid when I win and he's hammered.

I go with the obvious one. "Never have I ever sang on stage."

That surprises him. "Really?"

"Yup."

My own peers have always ostracized me, so the thought of ever singing on stage in front of a bunch of people I've never met before scares the shit out of me.

Although I'd be lying if I said I didn't secretly wish to know what it feels like to have everyone look at you like you actually matter.

Like you're special.

Bringing the cup to his mouth, Phoenix takes a sip. His lips twitch with amusement before he speaks.

"Never have I ever had a curfew."

Damn him.

I take a big gulp, which wasn't the brightest idea, because I start coughing as the amber liquid goes down my throat. *Geez.*

Phoenix laughs at my inexperience. "What's the matter, Groupie? Can't handle your liquor?"

Flipping him off, I pay him back with a zinger of my own. "Never have I ever cheated on a test."

"Cute." Eyes narrowing, he takes another swig. "Never have I ever had pig slop thrown on me at a party."

Ouch. Raising the cup to my lips, I hold up the pointer finger of my free hand. "Too soon."

My second gulp is still harsh, but it goes down much easier.

Since he's pulling out the big guns, I will too.

I hold his gaze. "Never have I ever fucked a *skank* in the band room."

"Someone's claws are out tonight," he mutters before taking a sip.

Warmth rushes through my veins and my head feels lighter. "You started it, pal."

Reaching for his pack of cigarettes, he brings one to his mouth and lights it. "Never have I ever spent a ton of money on a fucking pen."

He has me there. I happily take another swig. My body feeling nice and cozy. "Wow, this stuff is strong."

His gorgeous face pinches with concern. "You should probably slow down."

Screw that. I want to have fun.

"Hell no," I tell him. "I don't have a curfew tonight."

Celebrating that small victory, I take another sip.

My mind whirls as I try to think of something else I haven't done that Phoenix has. I snicker when it comes to me. Lord knows his dick makes its way around.

"Never have I ever had an orgy."

Phoenix takes another drag of his cigarette, making no move for his cup.

I wave him on. "Come on, buddy. Drink up."

"I've never had an orgy." A glimmer of humor lights his face. "Threesomes? Yes. Orgies? Too much fucking work."

Can't argue with *that* logic.

I take another mouthful. "Amen, brother."

A soft touch to my arm makes me shiver. "Maybe we should stop."

"Thanks for the advice, *dad*." I fill my now empty cup back up. "But I'm not a quitter."

He makes a sound of irritation deep in his throat. "Fine. Never have I ever given a blow job."

The arrogant look in his eyes tells me he thinks he's won this round.

However, I'd rather end up shit-faced drunk and barfing my brains out than give him confirmation that I'm a loser who can't manage to get a guy to let me suck him off.

Keeping my expression neutral, I take a sip.

He stubs his cigarette out in a nearby ashtray. "You're *not* supposed to drink when you haven't done something, remember?"

"I know the rules," I deadpan.

The triumphant expression on his face vanishes, and he falls silent.

Wanting to keep the game going, I scan my brain for another thing I haven't done that he has. "Never have I ever been arrested."

Once again, Phoenix doesn't drink.

"Why aren't you drinking?"

He gives me a cocky wink that makes my heart kick up. "Because I don't get caught."

Studying me like I'm a specimen under a microscope, his face goes slack, and he runs a finger over his sharp jaw, like he's debating his next words.

"Never have I ever fucked a dude."

In for a penny, in for a pound. Just like before, I don't want to verify that I'm a nerd who can't get laid.

So, I drink.

"Who did you fuck?"

There's a slight edge to his tone and I'm not sure why.

Playing coy, I return his wink. "We'd have to play Truth or Dare for that."

"Truth or Dare it is then."

Ah, crap. "Okay." I swallow. "Truth or—"

"You went first last time," he interjects as he lights up another cigarette. "Truth or dare, Groupie?"

It's apparent he hasn't quite caught on that there's an easy way out of this for me. "Dare."

Boom. *Safe.*

The smoke from the lit cigarette hanging out of his mouth wafts through the air. "Let me see your tattoos."

What. The. Fuck.

I'd rather sing him every song in my notebook while standing in front of our entire graduating class than let him see *that*.

How the hell am I going to get out of this?

Thinking quick, I realize honesty is the best policy. *Sort of.*

"I don't have any."

It's evident he doesn't like that answer, but there's nothing he can do about it. He can't see my tattoos because there are none. *Tough cookies.*

And now it's my turn. "Truth or dare?"

There's no hesitation on his part. "Truth."

I could go easy on him, but I'm hoping if I can make him even half as uncomfortable as he made me with his last request, he'll agree to stop playing this game.

"Why did you kiss me?"

His nostrils flare on an indrawn breath, and for a moment I don't think he's going to answer…

But then he does.

"Because I wanted to."

Little tingles shoot up my spine and I press my legs together.

Phoenix *wanted* to kiss me.

Thank God I'm buzzed because I have no idea how to fully process the magnitude of that.

He tosses his cigarette into his cup and it hisses. "Truth or dare?"

I don't want him to ask me what's on my body, so I say, "Dare."

It feels like he's spearing my soul with a dull knife when he utters his next statement. "Show me the ink on your upper thigh."

My lips part on a shaky inhale. Clearly, I'm the one who's slow on the uptake because he just one-upped me. *Big time.*

I can't do this. I *can't.*

But I have to. Because something tells me he won't let me squeak out of this.

I hate to say it, but the fact Phoenix has difficulty reading is a major bonus for me right now.

My legs feel like rubber as I stand. "Okay."

I go to move the T-shirt up, but Phoenix beats me to it. The second he touches me, I grow light-headed.

Frustration creeps over his features as he tries to decipher the three words on my upper thighs.

I'm about to tell him his time is up, but then he shifts off the couch and moves closer, inspecting the ink.

He brushes over one of the words. The contrast of his calloused finger and gentle touch sends heat between my legs.

"Fat."

My heart thuds against my ribs.

Brows furrowing, he reads another. "Pig." Anger colors his tone as he utters the last one visible to him. "Fat ass."

Bringing his thumb to his mouth, he wets it...then rubs it over one of the words, trying to erase it.

But he can't. Not that easily anyway. "It's permanent marker."

"Why..." The line between his brows grows deeper and his voice drops to a faint rasp. "Why do you do this to yourself?"

Because it's what I am.

What everyone sees me as.

Blinking back tears, I move his hand away. "You can't ask a question unless I pick truth. Plus, it's my turn." I sit back down on the couch. "Truth or dare?"

A muscle in his jaw bunches. "Dare."

My chest feels like it's been cracked open, exposing my darkest secrets. I've never felt more vulnerable in my whole entire life.

I think it's only fair that he lets me see *his* secret.

"Show me where you live."

He looks at me like I'm certifiable. "No—"

"I just showed you something no one else knows about. Something incredibly personal and private." *Something that almost broke me.* "The least you can do is show me the trailer you live in."

Even though it's clear he doesn't want to, he caves. "Fine." He digs his keys out of his pocket. "Let's go."

Dirt and gravel crunch under the tires of Phoenix's Toyota as he drives through Bayview.

After making a quick right, we pass a line of run-down trailers, each one shoddier than the last.

My stomach bottoms out when he pulls to a stop in front of the worst one at the very end.

The small trailer is so rusty and dingy I can't even make out what the color of it once was. There's a small staircase at the entrance, but it—along with the roof—are so dilapidated it borders on unsafe.

This place is so awful it makes Eminem's trailer in *8 Mile* look like a luxury home.

I don't mean that in a judgmental way…I'm just sad.

No one deserves to live like this.

"We're not going inside," Phoenix grits out.

"We don't have to."

Jaw working, he glares at the trailer, then at me. "Get your fill yet, princess?"

His comment stings like a slap. "I didn't ask you to take me here to be mean and make you feel like shit. I asked because I wanted to know more about you." I scowl at him. "Same reason *you* asked to see what I write on my body."

He has no argument for that because he goes silent.

Hoping to change the subject, I shift in my seat to face him. "It's your turn."

His low voice fills the space between us. "Truth or dare?"

I don't want him to ask me *why* I write the things I do on myself —because then he'll know it's all a ruse and I'm not even half as strong as I pretend to be—so once again, I make the same decision as before.

"Dare."

Tilting his head, he holds my gaze. Those icy-blue eyes pierce through me like a burning arrow. "I dare you to give me a blow job."

Wait…*what*?

I search his face for signs he's joking, but there are none.

My mind spins and it has nothing to do with the alcohol I consumed. Despite me telling him otherwise, I've never done it before.

I also don't want my first sexual experience to take place because of a dare. I might not have the greatest self-esteem, but I deserve more than that.

"I...uh..."

Phoenix starts laughing like I just said something hilarious. "You should see your face right now. I'm just fucking with you." He starts the engine. "Let's grab some food and head back to Storm's."

I have an out. I should take it.

A weird twinge of disappointment hits me square in the chest. If this was any other guy, I'd be relieved...but it's not.

It's Phoenix.

And dare or no dare...this might be my only chance to be *that* girl.

The one who gets the guy.

Even though it's just for tonight.

I place my hand on top of his when he shifts into reverse. "I can't do it while you're driving."

I mean, I *could,* but that's not very safe.

He cuts a look my way. "Very funny, Groupie."

Liquid courage makes me bolder than I ever thought I could be. "Unlike you, I'm not joking."

Shifting the car back into park now, he studies my face.

All I can hear is the rapid thud of my heart, for one...

Two.

Three.

Four.

Five seconds...

And then he moves his seat back.

"If you want it..." He looks at me through lowered lids. "Then take it."

Nerves flutter like a swarm of unruly bees in my belly because I feel like I've just bitten off way more than I can chew. Which is saying something considering my bingeing habits.

I've watched porn—and practiced with a cucumber once due to sheer curiosity—so I'm familiar with the basic concept of what I'll need to do.

However, I have no idea how to *start*. Something Phoenix is now catching on to.

The corner of his mouth quirks up slightly, almost like he can sense my anxiety and finds it comical. "Nervous?"

Petrified. But I force myself to push that down because I will not let my fear get in the way of something I've been fantasizing about for years.

"No."

I can feel him sizing me up before he rasps, "Then come here."

My pulse thrums in my ears as I inch as close as I can without sitting on his lap. I want to kiss him, but the last time that happened he freaked out, so maybe it's best we avoid doing that again.

I pluck his shirt. "Take this off." When he raises a brow in question, I deliver the very same words he said when he wanted me to sing my song for him. "I want the full experience."

Reaching behind him, he grabs hold of his shirt and tugs it over his head in one swift motion.

My eyes immediately go to the large black music clef directly over his heart. A set of five horizontal lines—otherwise known as the staff—are next to it. However, there are no notes. It's completely blank.

"Why don't you have any notes?"

"I'm waiting until I write the song that will change my life."

That's a good reason.

I feel his heart rate pick up as I gently trace the tattoo with my finger. "How long have you had this?"

"Two years."

"It's beautiful." My eyes drop down, taking in his lean, toned stomach. *He's* beautiful. "Do you have any others?"

"Why don't you find out for yourself?"

Guess that's my cue.

Another wave of nervousness comes over me as my fingers find the button on his jeans. The denim is stretched tight over his prominent erection, and the sound of me forcing his zipper down is so loud it's almost deafening.

Whatever apprehension I had disappears as I come to the stark realization that Phoenix Walker is hard…

For *me*.

Lifting his hips, he tugs down his jeans a little, causing his cock to spring out.

That…can't be real.

I mean, obviously it is, but…holy hell. It's *huge*.

And I don't mean huge in a porn-star dick kind of way. I mean huge in a it's legitimately alarming and science should probably study him kind of way.

"Jesus." Swear it grows bigger the longer I stare at it. "What the fuck do you feed that thing?"

A choked laugh escapes him before his expression evens out and he presses his thumb to my bottom lip. "Your mouth in a minute."

Right.

I wrap my hand around his thick girth. Despite being hard as a rock, he feels like heated satin as I slowly stroke him from root to tip.

Phoenix sucks in a sharp breath when I repeat the movement and I can't help but glance up. His lips are parted, and his eyes are hooded as his chest rises and falls with ragged inhales. Ribbons of heat unfurl low in my belly as I circle the pad of my thumb over his wide, shiny head, spreading the pearlescent drop of liquid around it.

His throat flexes on a hard swallow. "Lennon."

There's a hint of desperation in his tone and that only spurs me on as I begin jerking him.

Shifting, I lower myself until my head hovers above his lap. "There's no way I can deep throat you."

Figure we might as well get *that* out of the way now. And if by some crazy chance there is a woman out there capable of sucking this thing down to the hilt? Science should probably study her too because she must be part snake in order to unhinge her jaw.

His voice is a deep rumble. "I don't care, just put your mouth on it."

Brushing my lips against his tip, I give it a little kiss, tasting the salty liquid before pulling back. "You need to show me exactly what you like so I can keep doing it."

Because I want to make this good for him.

Wrapping my hair around one hand and fisting his dick with the other, he guides me back to his cock. "Open."

When I do, he pushes his swollen head into my mouth. "Lick."

I flick my tongue against the small slit and he groans. "More."

Running the flat of my tongue all over his crown, I lick him like he's the best thing I've ever tasted and I don't want to waste a single drop.

"Fuck." His grip on my hair tightens. "Now, suck it."

His dirty commands drive me crazy and I take him deeper, eliciting another groan from him.

Replacing his hand with mine, I eagerly pump and suck him in tandem, paying special attention to the noises he makes.

When I find a rhythm he particularly likes, he grunts and bucks his hips into my face. "Fuck yeah. Suck me just like that."

Knowing he's losing control because *I'm* bringing him pleasure is almost enough to make me orgasm.

My jaw aches as I continue sucking him with quick, deep pulls, but I power through, wanting to bring him to the finish line.

His whole body shudders. "Fuck. I'm gonna—" He pushes down on my head so hard I gag. "Don't move."

The tone of his voice is downright lethal.

I'm bracing myself to swallow his cum...but that doesn't happen.

Instead, he goes still.

I'm about to ask if I'm doing something wrong, but then I hear it.

Some guy is shouting—or rather *slurring*—things at Phoenix.

"Get back in here, you piece of shit. I'm gonna kick your ass again."

What the hell?

Feeling helpless, I swivel my gaze around, but a deep dark bruise spanning across the sharp V-cut of his lower abdomen catches my attention.

As far as I know, Phoenix doesn't play any sports, so I wonder where that came from. God knows it has to hurt.

The slurring gets closer, along with the sounds of unsteady footsteps.

"You stupid shit stain," the man yells. "Your whore mother should have done the world a favor and aborted you. You're not my son, you're a good-for-nothing leech and one day I'm gonna fucking kill you."

Holy crap. Anger races through my veins as I release him from my mouth. The awful things that crazy man is yelling are positively vile.

You're not my son. Disgust rolls through me as I realize the belligerent asshole is most likely Phoenix's dad.

I'm about to give the bastard a piece of my mind, but Phoenix reverses, peeling out of the trailer park so fast I get whiplash.

I sit up in the passenger seat. "Was that your father?"

Jaw clenching, he tugs his pants up, but otherwise remains silent.

It's enough confirmation for me.

"Where are we going?" I ask when he speeds past Storm's house.

Only then does he speak. "I'm taking you home."

I don't want to go home, but what happened has obviously put a damper on what was turning out to be the best night of my life.

But way more important than that, I don't want him going back to that trailer. Ever.

His piece of shit father threatened to *kill* him. That's not only scary...it's straight-up abuse.

While my dad won't like the thought of a guy crashing on our couch, I know once I explain what happened, he'll give in and let him stay for however long he needs.

Instead of pulling up my driveway, Phoenix parks under the large oak tree a few feet down the street.

"I'm gonna ask my dad if you can stay. He won't like it, but—"

"I'm not staying at your house," he interjects. "Storm lets me crash at his whenever I want."

I was already eternally grateful to Storm for breaking through the pig-slop crowd and ushering me out of the party, but now I have another reason because he gives Phoenix a safe haven.

"Okay." I squeeze my eyes shut as a swell of pain flows through me. "Does what happened tonight happen often?"

Once again, he doesn't answer. I'm now realizing that his silence following difficult questions *are* the answers.

When I open my eyes, I notice that he never put a shirt back on and his pants are still hanging open.

Reaching over, I ever so gently sweep my fingertips over the bruise. "Did he give you this?"

Nothing.

The need to soothe him in some small way comes over me, so I lean over and softly brush my lips against the bruise over and over, wishing my touch alone could make all his pain disappear.

Phoenix releases a jagged breath, and I notice his cock is rising.

His voice is a rough scrape. "Lennon."

I can't tell if it's a warning or a request, but I go with the second option and wrap my hand around him.

A low groan pushes past his lips when I tongue and suck his plump head.

However, when I stretch my mouth over his length, he halts me.

My cheeks heat with embarrassment because of course he doesn't want a blow job right now, he's going through something traumatic.

I start to move away, but he grabs my hand and places it back on his dick, guiding it up and down.

A startled gasp flies out of me when his free hand tightens around my throat. His hold isn't strong enough to suffocate me, but enough that it makes breathing a little more difficult.

Inclining his head, he inhales me.

"Jerk it faster," he rasps, running his lips along the side of my throat. Both his words and the vibration have my nipples hardening.

Closing my eyes, I speed up my movements.

His deep, melodic voice rolls over me, holding me hostage. "You're so sweet and innocent." I'm about to remind him that what I'm doing right now is neither sweet nor innocent, but his teeth graze my neck. "The thought of corrupting the shit out of you turns me on so fucking much."

That makes two of us.

He draws my skin into his mouth with enough suction I know he's going to leave a mark.

I not only welcome the pain, I crave more of it. "Harder."

His teeth clamp down, nipping and biting until I whimper and shudder.

A low groan tears out of him and he fists the base of his dick while I'm on the upstroke. "I'm gonna come." Taking over, he gives himself a hard and fast tug. "You want some of this?"

I want whatever he's willing to give me.

Dipping my head, I close my mouth over his tip and slide down as far as I can. A moment later, a coarse, ragged sound cuts through the air and a spurt of hot liquid hits the back of my throat. I suck him down, not wanting to waste a single drop.

He slumps against the driver's seat. "Fuck."

I'll say. Phoenix might have been the one who came, but I feel like *I'm* the one who derived all the pleasure from it.

Until a depressing thought hits me.

What happens after tonight? Is he going to act like I don't exist? End our friendship for good?

"Are you gonna ignore me again?"

"No." Cocking his head to look at me, he lights a cigarette. "But I don't do girlfriends, Lennon." A regretful note enters his voice. "And even if I wanted to pursue this thing with you, I can't because Storm and I are leaving for LA in eleven days. We're hoping to make some connections and catch a break there." He expels a sigh. "I probably should have told you that before…you know. I'm sorry."

I get it. Though I can't help but wonder now.

"If you weren't leaving…would you?"

"Would I what?"

"Pursue this thing with me?" When I see uneasiness spread over his face, I quickly add, "Just so we're clear, I'm *not* asking you to stay." I'd never want him to stop chasing his dreams because of me.

"I'm leaving for Dartmouth at the end of the summer, so I'm not looking for a relationship, either." I lift a shoulder. "I just want to know."

If a girl like me could get the guy.

He takes so long to answer I'm about to tell him to forget it…but then I hear it.

"Maybe," he whispers.

My heart squeezes painfully. *Talk about bittersweet.*

But it doesn't have to be. We can't be in a relationship, but it doesn't mean we can't keep in contact and be friends.

I could visit him in LA during breaks from school and I'm sure he and Storm will be back to visit his grandmother from time to time.

Plus, he's not gone yet. Granted, we don't have much, but we have a little time. Which is better than no time.

"We still have eleven days."

"Yeah." He tosses his cigarette out the window. "But three of those will be spent practicing for Voodoo."

True.

"If you and Storm are okay with it, I'd like to come to practice."

"It's cool with me. Although you'll probably get bored after a while."

That's not possible. "I'm never bored when I'm hearing you sing and watching you perform." I look out the window just as a light turns on in my house. I have no doubt my dad is waiting up for me. "I should probably head in."

Something tells me he'll have *lots* of questions regarding my current wardrobe.

I'm about to grab my things and leave, but then it dawns on me. "How come you always park here and never in my driveway?"

"Because you have security cameras." He smirks. "None of them point over here, though."

Huh. *The more you know.*

I grab my purse off the floor. "I'll see you tomorrow."

On impulse, I lean in…then freeze.

How does this work? We're friends, but what we just did was a little more than friendly.

Do I hug him? Shake his hand? Or just say to hell with it and kiss him?

As if reading my mind, Phoenix says, "I never kiss my hookups." It's on the tip of my tongue to remind him that we've already kissed, but then he adds, "It complicates shit. Makes them think it's more than what it is."

Can't really argue with that.

"No kissing. Got it."

I reach for the door handle at the same time he reaches over and cups my jaw.

My breath stills as he comes closer.

There's no tongue when he kisses me, just a soft press of his lips against mine before he pulls away. "I'll text you tomorrow."

"Okay."

I bite my cheek to keep from smiling as I run across the street and sprint up the driveway.

I was hoping my dad went back to bed, but he's sitting on the couch when I walk in. Drinking a cup of coffee.

In other words, intentionally waiting up for me.

"Seriously, Dad?" I roll my eyes. "I'm not a baby."

"You're *my* baby," he argues. "And one day when you have children of your own, you'll understand the fear that comes with your teenager attending a party where something bad might happen—" His eyes widen as he looks me up and down. "What happened to your clothes?"

Thinking fast, I utter, "We had a massive water balloon fight at the party." I shrug. "My dress got drenched, so the girl hosting it gave me a T-shirt to wear and offered to wash it for me."

A dark brow lifts. "She couldn't have given you some pants, too?"

"She's…a lot smaller than I am."

He seems to buy this because he stands. "If water balloon fights were the worst of it, I should probably count my blessings." He smacks a kiss on my cheek. "It's almost three. I'm going to sleep."

I'm about to follow him, but my phone vibrates with an incoming text.

Phoenix: It's tomorrow.

Grinning, I type out a reply.

Lennon: Thanks for not ignoring me this time, pal.

I watch dots appear and disappear across my screen as I walk up the stairs and into my bedroom.

Phoenix: Thanks for the blow job, buddy.
Lennon: What can I say? I'm a great friend.
Phoenix: That you are. I'm gonna have to tell Storm to step up his game before you take his spot.

Crawling into bed, I type a reply text.

Lennon: Do you want Storm to suck your dick, too? No judgment here if you do. I can give him some tips.
Phoenix: Hard pass. Storm's not my type.

A flicker of pain shoots through my chest.

Lennon: I'm not either.
Phoenix: That's true. You're nothing like the other girls I hang out with.

The flicker of pain turns into a full-blown ache, but then a follow-up text comes through.

Phoenix: You're better.

I fall asleep with the biggest smile on my face.

CHAPTER 15
LENNON

A majority of the last forty-eight hours have been spent holed up in Storm's garage, listening to them rehearse.

Unfortunately, there's a bit of a rift going on because Phoenix and Storm keep arguing about what song they should open with.

Phoenix wants to start off with "Enter Sandman" by Metallica, and Storm wants to open with "My Generation" by The Who because it's big on drums.

Tension is mounting by the minute and I'm a little scared it might come to blows soon.

Even Grams gave up and went back inside after listening to their bickering. But not before the poor woman ripped out her hearing aids.

Storm launches his drumsticks across the room with a force that makes me happy I ducked in time. "We only get *three* songs, asshole. All I'm asking is for one of them to be heavy on drums."

Nostrils flaring, Phoenix grips the mic so hard his knuckles turn white. "Are you deaf, motherfucker? 'Enter Sandman' *has* good drums."

He looks at me. "Help me talk some sense into this idiot, Lennon."

Oh, boy. "The song *does* have good drums—"

Storm's bitter snort cuts me off. "Of course your little girlfriend is going to take your side."

Whoa. That's not fair. He didn't even give me a chance to finish my sentence.

"She's not my girlfriend, dipshit," Phoenix grits through his teeth.

"What the fuck ever—"

Bringing my fingers to my mouth, I let out a loud whistle because this is getting out of hand.

They play at Voodoo tomorrow night, so this is not the time to fall apart. If they don't get their shit together and settle on an opening song soon, they're screwed.

"Enough," I scream over the loud rumble of thunder.

There's a bad storm going on outside, but it pales in comparison to the one happening in here.

"If you two would just stop arguing and put your stubbornness aside, you could figure this out and continue rehearsing."

Phoenix looks at Storm. "Lennon's a huge rock fan, and she thinks we should start with the Metallica song—"

"No," I cut in. "I don't."

Phoenix whips around to face me again. "I thought you just agreed?"

"I agreed it has good drums, but not that you should *start* with it."

Storm smiles smugly. "The Who it is then."

"I don't think that's the right choice either."

I personally love the song, but it doesn't scream *stop what you're doing and listen*. And while Phoenix can sing the pants off of anything, that one doesn't really show off his insane vocal range.

"There's a happy medium," I say. "You just have to figure it out and be open to suggestions."

"Fine," Storm huffs. "What do you suggest then, Groupie?"

"Don't call her Groupie, fucker," Phoenix mutters low and deadly under his breath.

Yeah. I'll come back to *that* later.

"Do you like the Metallica song?"

"Obviously," Phoenix says, but I hold up a hand.

"I was talking to Storm."

Storm looks at me like I've sprouted another head. "Of course. It's fucking *Metallica*."

Now we're getting somewhere. "In that case, would you be open to moving Sandman to number two and scraping 'Welcome to the Machine' by Pink Floyd since it doesn't have any drums?"

"Whoa," Phoenix chimes in. "That's a great song."

"I know," I grit through my teeth. "But this is about *compromise*."

And I'm willing to bet Storm's plight is less about the opening song choice and more about the second song not having *any* drums.

Phoenix didn't mean to, but he inadvertently excluded his best friend and band member from an *entire* freaking song by doing that. No wonder his passive-aggressive response to that was "My Generation."

"I'm fine with it," Storm says at last. "But then we don't have an opening *or* closing song."

He's right. I scan my brain, recalling everything I've heard them play before.

I snap my fingers when it comes to me. "What about closing out with 'Man in the Box'? You guys *murder* that one, and the drums are definitely a big part of the song."

Phoenix and Storm exchange a glance that quickly turns into a mutual nod.

"That works for me," Storm agrees.

"Me too." Phoenix rubs his chin, studying me intently. "Any suggestions for what we should open with?"

Pacing, I try to think of a song that will showcase both Phoenix's incredible voice and Storm's awesome drum skills at the same time, as well as individually.

I wince when it hits me because it's a little trite, but they could totally make it work.

"'Voodoo'," I exclaim.

"Yes, Lennon," Phoenix says condescendingly. "That's where we're playing—"

"I meant the song by Godsmack."

They exchange a perturbed glance.

"Yeah, no," Phoenix grunts. "That's hokey as fuck."

"It will only come off hokey if you're not good enough to make whoever thinks that eat crow…but you guys *are*."

Granted, the original band isn't exactly known for their incredible vocals, but that song is amazing.

"Come on," I continue. "Not only does it start off a cappella, you have a lower register that will kick the fucking shit out of it."

Walking across the room, Storm picks up his drumsticks. "Your girl's not wrong."

I give Storm a smile. "And right after Phoenix's a cappella, there's a dark and hypnotic drum segment that *you'll* make your bitch before you both merge and slaughter it together."

It's the best of both worlds.

"Just try it," I urge when Phoenix starts to protest again.

"Fine."

Storm gets back behind his drum set and a moment later, Phoenix's deep, dark voice surrounds me like a fog before the drums kick in.

I've always loved this song, but what's happening now is absolutely captivating. People are going to lose their shit. If there were actually seats at Voodoo…they wouldn't be dry after this performance.

Midway through, Phoenix looks back at Storm, who gives him a nod. All the anger from before vanishes and their amazing chemistry is back.

I have to stop myself from jumping up and down like a fangirl when they finish. "I vote hell yes."

Not that I get a vote in this, but dammit. They should do *this* song.

Phoenix looks at Storm. "What say you?"

Storm rubs his chin. "I'm with her. We're already doing cover songs, so fuckers are gonna think we're unoriginal anyway. Might as well go up there and make them eat shit like Lennon said."

"Exactly."

"All right," Phoenix agrees. "Voodoo it is." He juts his chin at Storm. "Let's go again."

I take a seat on the futon as they rehearse it a few more times, each rendition sounding better and better. However, halfway through practice number five, the power flickers on and off due to the storm.

They manage to make it through to the end, but when it happens during their next run-through, Storm throws his drumsticks on the ground. "Fuck this. I'm taking a break."

I assume he's going to grab something to drink or smoke, but he takes out his phone and starts texting someone.

Then he pulls out his keys and walks toward the door.

Phoenix must be wondering the same thing I am because he grunts, "Where are you going?"

Pausing midstep to text again, Storm says, "Sasha's." He shrugs. "We won't be able to practice until this shit dies down. Might as well do something fun."

It's clear by *fun* he means hooking up with Sasha.

I can't help but wonder if Storm knows about her trying to get with his friend first.

Phoenix snorts. "Won't be having all that much fun, bro. I told you she—" Glancing my way, he stops talking. "Text me when you're done."

"She what?" I urge, more out of curiosity than anything.

Storm waggles his eyebrows at Phoenix. "I'll be having more fun than you."

Then he ducks out.

Crossing my arms, I look at Phoenix. "Why do I feel like the butt of a joke I'm not in on?"

He reaches for his bottle of water. "It's nothing."

I don't buy that for a second. "If it's nothing, then why won't you tell me?"

He stops gulping his water. "You really want to know?"

I nod.

"I gave Storm a heads-up that Sasha was a lousy screw, but I guess he wants to find out for himself. Either that or he's into chicks who lay there like a corpse."

Safe to say I'm seriously regretting inquiring about it now.

"Oh."

He finishes the rest of his water. "You asked."

He's right. I did. And now I know better.

We're not a couple, but it doesn't mean I want to hear about his hookups.

I'd also be lying if I wasn't questioning whether him warning Storm about Sasha had more to do with him feeling resentful over his friend sleeping with a girl he once did.

"Kind of sounds like you might be bitter that he's hanging out with her."

He laughs, but there's not an ounce of humor. "Trust me, I'm not."

"You sure about that?" I press, fully aware I'm provoking him.

His shoulders tense as he stares down at me. "I'm not the jealous type, Groupie." The punishing look in his eyes cuts me to the bone. "That would require me actually giving a fuck about a chick and I never do."

It would hurt less if he punched me. "Got it."

For a brief second, remorse flashes in his eyes, but then it's gone, and he changes the subject. "Thanks for your help tonight." Lifting his T-shirt, he wipes the sweat off his face. "I probably would have decked him if you didn't intervene when you did."

My eyes fall to the bruise on his hip. It's no longer dark blue, but colorful…like a vibrant sunset.

Only unlike a sunset, it's not beautiful. It's ugly and cruel.

Because someone hurt him.

"Have you been back there since?"

Once again, he freezes me out. "I'm gonna grab a bite to eat. Want anything?"

Disappointment punches through my chest. Every time I try to get under the surface, he puts the lock back on and throws away the key.

I wish he'd open up to me. Because *all* I want to do is help him.

"Yeah. I want you to stop shutting me out whenever I ask about your dad. I know what you're going through is hard, but—"

A sound of repugnance cuts me off. "You don't know shit."

"What the hell is that supposed to mean?"

The lights flicker as he takes a step in my direction. "You sit there in your ivory tower, loved and cared for by your daddy."

My heart pounds painfully as he continues.

"You don't have to lock your door to avoid getting hit by the bat your drunk father is wielding because he wants to kill you in your sleep. You don't have to live in a shithole where every day is a constant reminder that one wrong move means you'll end up just like him. You don't have to wonder where your mom is and hope like hell she's doing okay, even though she didn't give a fuck about you because she left *you* behind."

His declaration rips through my chest. "Ph—"

"You don't know what it's like to be hungry. And I don't mean a few stomach growls." His upper lip curls. "I mean the kind of hungry that *hurts* and makes you pray to a god you're not so sure exists anymore that you find a way to get something to eat before your body gives out."

A tear rolls down my cheek but that only makes him angrier. "You don't know shit, Lennon." Advancing, he corners me into a wall. "Because *you've* never had to want for shit. You have things people like me would die for."

Inclining his head, his lips ghost over my ear. The threatening tone of his voice sends a shiver through my body. "Don't you dare cry for me." I wince when he grips my chin between his fingers, forcing me to look up at him. "I don't want your bullshit martyr tears. And I sure as fuck don't want your pity."

The despair brewing in my gut turns to anger.

I want to help him, but that doesn't mean I'll be his punching bag.

"Fuck you. Just because you have a shitty life doesn't mean it's okay to push away the people who care about you and treat them like trash. Neither of us had a choice in the hand life dealt us. I *hate* that yours is so awful, and if there was a way I could swap with you, I would. However, I also know you're not the first person who's had to crawl their way out of the gutter and you won't be the last."

I wipe my tears with the back of my hand. "And for your information, I don't pity you, because horrible father aside, you have *everything* I want."

Pure envy burns through my veins as I unleash every bit of pain I keep inside onto him. "You don't have to fear entering a room or meeting someone new because people don't make fun of you. They fucking worship the ground you walk on."

Losing what's left of my composure, I punch my chest. "You'd die for the things I have? Well, I'd *kill* to know what it's like to be you. To be so fucking talented and mesmerizing people can't take their eyes off you. I'd *kill* to experience even just a tiny fraction of that magic you talked about in your essay." A lump rises in my throat and my voice cracks. "But I never will."

Because I'm not special.

I go to shove him away so I can leave, but he catches my wrist.

"What are you doing?" I seethe as he drags me over to the keyboard.

"You want to know what it's like, don't you?" He lowers the mic stand. "Fucking sing."

If I thought he was unhinged before, it pales in comparison to right now. "Are you crazy? No—"

He grips my face. "Stop being a fucking coward and *sing*."

I should run right out that door...but I can't.

The allure of the sun is too strong. Like a tsunami pulling me under.

I stare down at the keyboard. "I don't know what to sing."

He stands behind me. "Anything."

I go with the one I sang for him last time.

The lights flicker and the power goes in and out as I press down on the ivory keys, causing me to mess up the first few notes.

Phoenix's lips brush the shell of my ear. "Close your eyes. And no matter what happens, don't you fucking stop. Got it?"

Nodding, I squeeze my eyes shut and begin. My pulse drums in my ears so hard it nearly overpowers my voice.

Gentle fingertips run down my arms, leaving goose bumps in their wake.

I stumble over the lyrics when his lips graze my neck and I feel his cock harden. "Don't stop."

My head feels hot and heavy as his warm breath gusts over my skin and he runs his hands down the sides of my waist.

The realization that he's touching my body and what he's feeling makes me tense up. "Pho—"

A sharp bite has me gasping. "You're not the one in control." His tongue darts out, soothing the sting. "Keep singing."

God help me because I do.

I sing my heart out as I transform into someone else. Someone who's confident and skilled.

Special.

With a low grunt, Phoenix grinds his massive erection into my ass, like he can't help himself.

Another rush of adrenaline spirals through me, but it's quickly followed by a trail of nerves when he palms my breast.

Sadly, I didn't get the consolation prize that tends to come with being a big girl. While I have slightly more than a handful, they're not huge. I'm afraid Phoenix will be disappointed.

His voice is a rough scrape against my shoulder blade as he pinches my nipple through my bra. "Get out of your head."

It's a struggle to swallow past the panic, but I know if I don't, it will ruin this moment and I won't get another one.

Stuffing down my anxiety, I force myself to go to that place again. The place where I no longer have control of my mind or body, because I'm a vessel for something far more powerful.

Heat blooms over my chest and face when his hand disappears under my T-shirt. When he reaches my bra, he tugs it down and plumps my bare breast in his big hand.

The note I was singing comes out breathless, but I keep going.

So does Phoenix.

A shiver courses through me when his free hand finds the waist-band of my jeans. I start to protest as he flicks open the button, because there's no way he can touch me *there* without feeling my lower stomach.

"Phoenix—"

A startled, strangled sound leaves me when he shoves his hand inside my underwear and cups me.

It happened so fast I barely had time to think about it, let alone put up much of a fight.

Since he's not running away screaming, I continue singing.

His finger slides over my slick flesh, teasing me.

My vibrato turns into a moan when the pad of his finger finds my clit and he makes a wet little circle around it. *Taunting.*

I've played with myself lots of times, but nothing compares to this. It's like he's making my body his instrument, producing whatever sensations and sounds he wants from me.

In the span of minutes, I've gone from sheer panic to wanting to beg him to take me right here, right now.

A whimper fills the room when his long finger plunges inside me.

I become so dizzy *my* fingers fumble over the keys like intoxicated frat boys.

His dark voice is an electrifying live wire. "Don't stop."

I want to tell *him* that when he drags his finger out and pushes it back in, causing a bolt of pleasure to shoot between my legs.

He adds another finger, stretching me so much it aches.

Then he starts pumping them.

My breath comes out in choppy, desperate pants when his thumb rubs my clit in a measured rhythm while he drives his fingers inside me frantically.

The contrast is too much for me to take. I grip the edges of the keyboard, unable to keep playing.

I moan into the mic, the lyrics I was supposed to be singing trapped in my throat because *all* I can focus on is this euphoric feeling taking over.

I feel like a spell has been cast, and I'm desperate for it to reach the peak and never end at the same time.

The lights flicker and my moans fade in and out of the mic with the sporadic power.

"Phoenix."

I arch against him. All my senses are lost and quickly being replaced by the potent ones he's giving me.

He speeds up his movements and I squeeze my eyes shut as pleasure overcomes me.

"Oh god."

I'm no longer matter taking up space. I am energy.

I am his.

A loud boom of thunder vibrates the house before the electricity shuts off completely.

I sag forward, but Phoenix grips my waist with his free hand, tugging me back against him.

His voice is jagged gravel abrading my insides. *"That's* what it feels like."

Those long fingers seesaw inside me one last time, gathering the remnants of my orgasm before his hand slips out of my pants.

My blood quickens when he paints my lips with my wetness. "Open."

When I do, he shoves his fingers inside, making me taste myself.

I can't see him because my eyes haven't adjusted to the darkness surrounding us yet, but I *feel* him because he spins me around.

"Give me some of that."

Grabbing my jaw, he kisses me, thrusting his tongue in and out of my mouth with greedy, fervid strokes.

My head spins as he takes hold of my hips and leads me across the room.

We end up near the futon, but when I go to sit, he halts me. "Wait."

In the shadows, I see him bend over and hear a faint click.

His lips capture mine and my pulse skyrockets as we tumble onto the futon turned bed.

Our choppy breathing, along with the soft bite he gives my neck, makes the already muggy summer air even hotter.

He maneuvers my still open jeans past my hips. "I want to hear you sing my name when I make you come again."

Holy hell. The thought of him giving me another orgasm practically makes it happen.

He tugs my underwear and jeans down my legs and I eagerly kick off my shoes to help him remove them.

I'm happy we're in a blackout because it means he won't see my body.

Then again, it might come back on. Which is why when he goes to remove my shirt, I divert his attention by pulling down his zipper.

I'm wrenching his pants off so I can take him into my mouth when he halts me. "Let me grab a condom."

My lungs seize with the realization. *He wants to have sex.*

And why wouldn't he? As far as he knows, I'm not a virgin so this shouldn't be a huge deal.

I debate spilling the truth, but this is Phoenix Walker. The guy I've secretly stalked and wanted for years.

Losing my virginity to him is the stuff all my dreams are made of.

I'm afraid if I tell him, not only will it ruin the moment…he'll see what a loser I am and put a stop to any future hookups.

He might even ignore me again.

The sound of foil tearing assaults my ears. "Spread those legs for me."

Giving myself a mental pep talk to not be a corpse like Sasha, I part my thighs.

Looming above me, he settles between them.

The tip of his cock nudges my entrance and I hold my breath, awaiting the invasion…but it doesn't come.

"You've done this before, right?"

Panic rises within me. Did I do something wrong?

Or can he just sense my anxiety?

"Yeah," I lie, willing my body to relax and my mind to pretend like I've had sex lots of times.

He moves his hips…and that's when I remember how *large* he is.

He has to work just to fit the head of his cock inside me. "You're so fucking tight."

"You're so fucking *big*," I counter, and he laughs under his breath.

However, the laughter turns into a grunt when he pushes in a little more.

I bite my lip as he stretches me. He's barely even halfway in and already it's painful.

Bracing myself, I whisper, "You can just…start."

I've always been a rip the Band-Aid off type of girl, and the quicker he pops my cherry, the quicker we can get to the good stuff.

I immediately regret telling him that, though when he pulls back and drives forward with so much force, white spots form in front of my eyes.

A severe burning, stinging pain envelops me and I dig my nails into his back so hard I'm positive I draw blood.

"Fuck," he groans, his hips snapping against mine.

Jesus. This hurts like a bitch.

I accidentally cry out.

His movements come to an abrupt halt. "You okay?"

"Yeah. It feels good," I assure him as the legs wrapped around him begin trembling from the pain.

"Christ." He makes a low noise in the back of his throat and thrusts again. "Your pussy's so goddamn ti—"

Two things happen at that moment.

One. The lights turn on.

And two…Storm walks through the door.

"Shit. My bad."

The door quickly shuts behind him.

Being covered in pig slop was the most humiliating moment of my life, but this *definitely* comes in second.

The interruption and the electricity coming back on is a mood killer because Phoenix tenses before he grunts, "Get dressed."

Then he rolls off me, not even bothering to look my way as he puts his clothes on.

It hurts worse than losing my virginity.

I can only assume that seeing me half-naked in the light ruined the moment.

Ashamed, I collect my clothes. It's a struggle to put my under-wear and jeans back on in a way that doesn't expose too much skin since I've already turned him off enough.

I'm tying my shoelaces when I notice Phoenix glaring at me. He looks downright *pissed*.

"Did I do something wrong?"

If he doesn't want to fuck a fat chick, he should just man the hell up and say it instead of putting me through these mental gymnastics.

I might not be his *type*, but I'm still a human being.

I deserve more than his bullshit mood swings and being made to feel bad about myself. I didn't put a damn gun to his head and make him stick his cock inside me. He did that all on his own.

Jaw ticcing, his eyes lock on something behind me.

When I turn around, the color drains from my face and my knees grow weak.

There, in the middle of the bed—staining the light-blue sheet—is a pool of blood.

I knew there was a chance there might be some, but I didn't think it would be *this* bad. I've heard some girls don't even bleed at all.

Evidently, I was not one of the lucky ones.

It looks like my freaking vagina was massacred by Phoenix's giant dick.

Fuck.

I'm debating whether it would be better to say I got my period or fess up about me being a virgin when he storms out of the garage.

I'm starting to think God truly is a comedian because this tops the pig slop and Storm walking in on us *combined*.

Since I can't remove the stain, I quickly roll up the sheet. I'm grateful the mattress underneath is black.

As I pass the garbage cans on the way out to his car, I stop and toss it in one.

Phoenix doesn't say a word as I climb into the passenger seat, or during the drive home.

Neither do I.

By the time he pulls up my driveway, I can't take it anymore. "So that's it? You're never gonna talk to me again?"

His expression is like a stone.

Tears sting my eyes. I can only bend so much before I finally break.

I go to leave, but his hand closes around my forearm. "Why did you lie to me?"

His tone makes it clear he's equally disgusted and angry.

My heart twists painfully in my chest. The only way to fix this… is to give him total honesty.

"Because of the way you're acting right now," I whisper, releasing myself from his hold so I can curl my arms around myself. "It's bad enough I don't look like the other girls you mess around with. I didn't want you to also think I was a loser who couldn't get laid." My throat swells tight. "I know I should have told you before we…but I…" I glance out the window as another tear rolls down my cheek. "I didn't want to give you any more reasons not to be with me."

"So you tricked me."

My head whips around at his accusation. "Oh, please. It was hardly a trick. I'm sure you've fucked *lots* of virgins."

Only unlike me, they got the *full experience*.

"You're wrong," he snarls. "I haven't fucked *any*."

I blink in surprise. "What?"

"Virgins complicate shit." An ugly snort leaves him. "Girls get clingy enough after sex, and the last thing I want is to escalate that bullshit by popping someone's cherry."

Emotion punches through my chest and the need to protect myself runs rampant throughout me. "Guess it's a good thing we were interrupted then, huh?"

I reach for the door handle, but his hand latches on to my knee. "I'm not looking to hurt you."

"Funny. Because you just did."

"Goddammit," he snaps when I snatch my purse off the car floor. "This conversation isn't over."

I don't know whether to laugh or cry. "It's over for me."

For once, *he* can see how it feels to be ignored.

I go to exit the car for a final time, but Phoenix grabs my face. "This is *not* fucking over."

And then his mouth is on mine, kissing me so hard my mind whirls and I forget we're fighting.

"You're complicating shit," I breathe against his lips before his tongue plunges inside.

"No." His hand tangles in my hair as he pulls back slightly, looking down at me through lowered lids. "I'm pursuing this."

My heart takes flight, but my brain doesn't want to hop on board just yet. I have so many questions. Like—how are we going to make this work when both of us are leaving? And does this make me his official girlfriend now, or is he only *pursuing* for the next week?

All my worries jump to the back burner when Phoenix palms my breast. "You drive me fucking crazy."

Not nearly as crazy as he drives me.

"I'm sorry I lied." I never looked at it from his point of view and now that I am…I see I was in the wrong. "I kept telling myself you'd never be attracted to a girl like me and I let my insecurities take over."

But if I don't get a handle on them soon, it will ruin everything between us.

I close my eyes as his mouth moves to my neck and he places my hand over his erection. "Does this help clear things up?"

My heart takes off in a gallop and warmth pools between my legs.

"Do you have another condom?"

The need to finish what we started is greater than my need for air.

"In my pocket," he rasps, nipping my collarbone.

Reaching inside his pocket, I pull out the foil packet as his fingers toy with the button on my jeans.

A hard knock on the window, followed by an angry throat clearing, makes us both jolt.

"What the fuck—" Phoenix growls at the same time I screech, "Oh my god."

My dad's glare bounces between us...and if looks could kill, we'd *both* be in caskets right now.

"Shit," Phoenix mutters under his breath as we break apart.

I silently tell God to knock it off and stop upping the humiliation ante as I exit the car.

"Inside, Lennon," he seethes. "Right now."

I love my dad, but he needs to stop treating me like a baby. I know witnessing his daughter getting hot and heavy with a guy upset him, but I'm a grown-up now.

I cross my arms. "No."

That's when Phoenix steps out of the car.

My jaw drops because I expected him to drive off. I wouldn't even blame him for it.

"Who the hell are you?" my dad barks, even though his intimidation tactics are almost comical since he's a good five inches shorter than Phoenix. "And what were you doing with your paws all over my daughter?"

Given the latter is pretty obvious, I answer his first question.

"His name is Phoenix."

Confusion spreads across his face. "I thought you said he was gay?"

Beside me, Phoenix coughs. "What?"

Crap. I completely forgot I told him that.

I wince. "Um...he's not anymore?"

"Clearly." My dad narrows his eyes. "When did you two start having sex?"

Less than forty-five minutes ago.

A furious blush creeps along my neck and cheeks. "That's none of your business."

"The hell it isn't," he argues. "You're my—"

"Eighteen-year-old *adult* daughter," I interject. "Who's going off to college at the end of the summer and will no longer be living under your roof."

My words hit him like a freight train, and he stumbles back.

Guilt prickles my chest because I didn't mean to hurt him. However, he can't tell me to spread my wings, only to clip them the second I test them out.

I'm about to tell him this, but all his attention is now directed at Phoenix.

"My daughter is not a piece of ass, young man."

Oh. My. God. He's *incorrigible.*

Phoenix looks him right in the eyes. "I know."

If someone would have told me one month and three days ago that Phoenix Walker and my father would be having a conversation regarding us having sex, I would have asked them to walk a straight line.

Despite Phoenix keeping it respectful, my dad glowers. "No, you don't. If you did, you'd realize she deserves a lot more than two minutes in the back seat of your damn car."

Disappointment slashes his face before he turns on his heel and stomps back into the house.

Groaning, I rub my forehead. "I am so sorry."

"Don't be." Scrubbing a hand down his face, he blows out a

breath. "Can't fault the man for being mad at the guy who was seconds away from screwing his daughter in his driveway."

I glance at his car. "That's two for two tonight." Apparently, the universe wants me to remain half a virgin. "Unless you want to go back to Storm's...or park down the street?"

Taking a step toward me, his hand curls around my hip. "I've had blue balls *twice* in the last hour, so I'm probably gonna regret this, but I think we should let the dust settle and pick up where we left off tomorrow night."

I'd be lying if I said I wasn't disappointed. I want him *now*.

"Oh." I'll want him just as much tomorrow, though, so I guess I can deal. "Okay."

His brows furrow. "You're still coming to the show, right?"

I wouldn't miss it for the world. "Yeah. I bought a ticket."

He takes another step, pressing me against his car. "Fuck that. I'll leave your name at the door so you can meet me backstage."

My heart swells to twice its size because not only does that sound like something a guy would say to his *girlfriend*...it sounds like something a guy who's not ashamed to be seen with her would say.

"Are you sure?"

He tips my chin. "Positive."

I press up on my toes when he drops his mouth to mine. I'm slipping my tongue past his lips when he pulls back, breaking the kiss. "Go inside before I give your dad another reason to hate me."

"He has no reason to hate you. *He's* the one who was in the wrong."

"He cares about you," Phoenix counters, his gaze darting over every inch of my face. "You should probably talk to him."

Hell no. I'm not talking to him until he apologizes for acting like a lunatic.

"And say what? I'm sorry your overprotective, nosy self caught me almost having sex?"

"How about—sorry the asshole I'm with fucked up. Because even though the two-minute remark was wrong, he was right about the rest." He cups my face. "Your first time shouldn't have been on a futon in my best friend's garage."

My first time was everything I've always wanted, and it has nothing to do with the location. It's because it was with *him*.

"I don't regret it," I whisper.

"Good." He fists my shirt, pulling me closer. "Because next time? I'm gonna fuck you so good it *will* end with you coming all over my cock." My heart flutters when he catches my lower lip between his teeth. "So good it will be worth those forty-four-hour drives."

With that, he releases me and opens his car door.

He's reversing out of the driveway when I realize he was referring to the drive from Los Angeles to Dartmouth.

CHAPTER 16
LENNON

My dad refuses to look at me when I walk through the front door.

One of us has to break the ice, but it's clear he's still angry, so I brush past him and head up the stairs.

He can't stay mad at me forever.

Once I reach my room, I swipe my laptop off my desk and sit on my bed.

I've been putting off scheduling my road test because of my anxiety, but Phoenix just gave me a damn good reason to get over it.

Less than five minutes later, my test is officially scheduled for the day after he leaves.

This way I can make those forty-four-hour drives, too.

I'm in the middle of texting Phoenix the good news when there's a knock on my door.

"Come in."

My dad's expression is still sour as he enters my bedroom, but at least he's willing to talk this out now.

"I never meant to hurt you," I begin. "But I'm not a little girl anymore."

"I know." Looking defeated, he lets out a heavy sigh and takes a seat at the end of my bed. "Tell me about this Phoenix guy."

I grin, my heart skipping several beats. "Well, for starters, he told me I should come inside and talk to you."

He gives an approving nod. "Keep going."

My grin grows. "He's had a hard life, so he's a bit rough around the edges, but he has a good heart." I look down at the carpet. "Sabrina and a bunch of her friends threw pig slop on me at the graduation party—"

"What?" he booms. "Why didn't you tell me?"

"Because I was embarrassed, and I didn't want you going apeshit and calling everyone's parents." I tuck a loose strand of hair behind my ear. "Anyway, Phoenix was there for me. He not only picked me up from the party, he took me to Storm's house so I could shower." I gesture to his Papa Roach T-shirt near my pillow. "I didn't have anything to wear while my clothes were being washed, so he gave me that."

The groove in his forehead deepens as he takes all this in. "I'm glad he came to your aid, but I still wish you would have called me." He cocks his head to the side. "And who's Storm?"

At that, I laugh. "Storm is Phoenix's best friend...and bandmate."

Whatever progress we were making dies with those words. "He's in a band?"

Here we go. "Yes. And before you freak out, he's *incredible*. And I swear, I'm not just saying that because he's my...you know." My hand finds my heart that beats out of my chest every time I think or talk about him. "His voice...his talent. It's out of this world—"

A hostile snort cuts me off. "Wait until he breaks your heart."

"He's not going to break my heart," I defend, growing upset over his assumptions. Not only did he meet Phoenix for all of two seconds, it was while the circumstances weren't in his favor. It's not fair for my dad to judge him or our situation. "You don't even know him."

Standing, he dismisses both me and my statement. "Oh, but I do. I work with guys like him all the time, remember? They're all cocky, selfish assholes who only want one thing when it comes to girls." He crosses his arms. "I give him a week before he's replacing you with another girl and you're crying yourself to sleep...and that's being generous."

That's not true. Phoenix isn't looking to hurt me. He said so himself.

"Phoenix won't do that to me."

"For such a smart girl, you're acting real dumb when it comes to this boy."

"The boy has a name." My chest tightens with anger. "And for such a great father, you're acting like a real shitty one right now."

"No, I'm not," he argues. "I'm simply trying to protect the thing I love most in this world." He jabs his finger in the air. "I don't want you to learn this lesson the hard way."

"The only thing I'm learning is that *you* can't handle the fact that there's another guy in my life."

"Not for long," he scoffs.

Exasperated, I stomp my foot. "Dad—"

"How do you know he's not just using you so he can take advantage of my connections? Ever think of that?" He snorts. "Of course not. Because those damn stars in your eyes have rendered you blind."

Whatever hope I had of asking my dad to help Phoenix and Storm is dashed with those words.

Screw it. They don't need him.

"I know you think I'm just an old guy on a power trip right now, but I've been around the block a few times. I know guys like him. I know how they think. Hell, I *was* one."

Then he should know people are capable of changing for the better. Not that Phoenix even has to because he's surprised me at every turn.

Every time my insecurities convinced me he would go right... he'd do the opposite and go left.

Because he cares about me.

And I'm not going to let my dad fill my head with doubt because

I have spent my whole life believing I'm not the kind of girl who gets the guy.

But I *am*.

"I don't want to keep fighting with you about this," he says softly as he ambles to the door. "I just wish you'd listen to me."

I know my dad is only saying this stuff because he's worried and he loves me...but in my heart, I know he's wrong about Phoenix.

Because I love him.

CHAPTER 17
PHOENIX

Adrenaline courses through me as I roll my shoulders back and close my eyes, letting the energy hum and vibrate before it becomes a roar.

A lot of artists get nervous before they perform, but not me. I know once I'm on that stage…nothing else matters.

"When's your girlfriend coming?" Storm questions, spinning around on the only chair inside the dressing room.

Like me, he doesn't get nervous either.

I glance at my watch. We aren't on for another forty minutes, so Lennon still has plenty of time to get here.

"Don't know. I'll shoot her a text in a bit."

It's only then that I realize I didn't bother correcting him about the girlfriend comment, but before I can scrutinize it any further, Storm mutters a curse.

"What?"

If he's going to throw another one of his bitch fits, he can take his ass outside.

He stares down at his phone. "My buddy Mike just texted me and said he spotted Vic Doherty from Phantom Rock Records in the crowd."

I heard the rumor going around about a record executive showing up tonight, but not *the* record executive.

Dude is a motherfucking legend in the music world. Hell, the world in general. He's the name behind some of the greatest rock legends on the planet.

The adrenaline surging through me quickly turns to a nauseating mixture of anxiety and dread.

We're so fucked.

"What the fuck are we gonna do?" Storm grunts, echoing my thoughts. "We can't just go out there and play a bunch of covers. Without original music, there's no way in hell he'd even think twice about us."

He's right.

While I'm confident in both mine and Storm's capabilities, it won't be enough. He's not gonna be impressed by us performing another band's greatest hits...no matter how fucking good we are.

He wants originality. Something rare and unique.

Something special.

The dread and anxiety coiling in my gut kicks up a few notches.

Because I have exactly what he's looking for...

It's just gonna cost me the only person who's ever believed in me.

I hate the forked road I find myself standing in front of, but only one of those roads will lead me to my dreams.

An opportunity like this comes once in a lifetime...if you're lucky.

I have to take it.

Blowing out a breath, I turn to Storm. "I've been working on something."

Storm's eyes nearly pop out of their sockets. "Way to wait for the last fucking minute to tell me."

 "I'll give you the rundown, but we don't have time to rehearse, so you'll have to follow along while we're up there. Drums are heavy at the end."

Normally it wouldn't be an issue because we're always in sync, but this is completely new material.

Despite looking uneasy, he gives me a nod. "I can work with that."

With those words, I know there's no going back and our fate has been sealed.

I just hope like hell it will be worth it.

Taking out my phone, I use the voice-to-text option and hit send.

CHAPTER 18
LENNON

I finish putting on another layer of lip gloss and close my compact. Once again, I enlisted Mrs. Palma's help with my makeup and hair, and she did an amazing job.

Instead of nerdy Lennon, I'm now cute and—dare I say—*sexy* Lennon.

Only this time, while she worked her magic, I gushed about Phoenix and she squealed like *she* was the teenage girl dating the hottest guy in Hillcrest.

She also assured me that my dad would come around eventually. He just needs a little more time to deal with his baby girl growing up.

I smooth down my dress as I step out of the Uber. It's the same one I wore to the graduation party, but since Phoenix never saw it sans pig slop and it makes me feel confident, I figured it was a solid choice.

There's already a line out the door as I walk up to the venue. I had planned on getting here earlier, but Mrs. Palma decided at the last minute that my hair needed more oomph and whipped out her curling iron.

Fortunately, they don't go on until ten, which means I still have approximately seventeen minutes to get my booty inside.

Some people grumble behind me as I make my way to the front of the line.

Being the girlfriend of a lead singer definitely has its perks.

"Hey," I greet the grumpy-looking man standing at the entrance. "My name is Lennon Michael. Sharp Objects put me on their backstage list."

After briefly scanning the paper in his hand, he gives me a lanyard. "Here's your pass." He hikes a thumb behind him. "Down the hallway, third door on the left."

The place is buzzing when I open the door and I let myself revel in the fact that I get to go backstage as I cut across the main floor and turn down a long hallway.

I find Storm furiously banging on one of the doors. "What the fuck are you doing in there, asshole?"

Uh-oh. That can't be good.

"Everything okay?" I question as I sidle up beside him.

"No," he grunts. "Your man has been in there for the last fifteen minutes." He bangs on the wood. "And he won't open the fucking door."

Oh, shit. Maybe he's nervous.

Granted, Phoenix doesn't strike me as the type to get cold feet before a performance, but fear can strike at any time and happen to anyone.

Closing my eyes, I press my forehead against the mahogany panel, willing him to feel just how much faith I have in him. "You got this, Phoenix. You're gonna kill it tonight. I believe in—"

The door opens…only it isn't my boyfriend standing on the other side of it.

It's *Sabrina.*

"Sorry." Crinkling her nose, she gives me a smug smirk. "We were busy."

I stand there paralyzed…aside from my heart, that feels like it's cracking into a thousand tiny pieces.

Each and every one of those tiny pieces slices through me when I shoot my gaze past her and see Phoenix doing up his fly.

This can't be happening.

My heart, desperate to put itself back together again tries to come up with a feeble excuse in an attempt to reconcile how the guy I lost my virginity to less than twenty-four hours ago—the guy who said he wanted to *pursue* this and talked about forty-four-hour drives—is the same one I'm staring at.

Every part of my body is screaming at me to turn around and walk away. To preserve what little dignity I have left.

Fuck that.

This cut is too deep to pretend like it doesn't hurt like hell.

If he didn't want to be with me, he never should have led me to think otherwise.

Despite how much I wanted him, I was more than willing to be friends. Because I had long accepted that it was all we'd ever be.

Until *he* made me believe we could be more.

That a girl like me could get a guy like him.

Which can only mean one thing.

Our relationship—both the friendship and sexual parts—were nothing but a sick little game to him.

Rage mixed with agony is a violent tidal wave ripping through my body as I trek inside.

I could call him an asshole and tell him how much he hurt me.

I could ask him *why.*

But none of it matters…because it won't change what he did or take away this pain.

"I never want to see you again. *Ever.*"

For the very first time, I don't want to get closer to the sun.

I want out of his atmosphere. *For good.*

He takes a step forward—almost like he wanted to reach out and touch me—before he edges away and focuses his attention on something behind me. "I'll text you later, Sabrina."

Whatever self-control I had snaps and I kick him in the balls so hard he keels over and Storm mutters *ouch* under his breath.

That doesn't give me the vindication I was seeking, though, so I grab the large pitcher of soda resting on the table and pour it over his head. This way when he goes on stage, he'll feel foolish and humiliated…just like I do right now.

"I *hate* you."

With that, I walk out…and the first tear falls.

They don't stop falling as I march out of the venue, trudge down the street, and call my dad.

He answers on the first ring. "Hey—"

"Can you pick me up?" I croak through hysterical sobs that I can't seem to make stop.

"Of course. Where are you?"

"Voodoo. Well…down the street."

Because I want to be as far away from him as I can get.

"I'm leaving right now."

"Thanks." A sharp pain singes my chest. "You were right about Phoenix."

I'm grateful he doesn't rub it in or say I told you so.

"I'll be there soon, monkey face."

Another swell of agony pummels through me as the line disconnects. It's so sharp it nearly takes the strength from my knees.

When you fall off a building, all your bones break.

But when you fall in love? It's your heart that breaks.

CHAPTER 19
LENNON

"Thank you," I tell the drive-through attendant as she hands me my bag of food and a giant soda.

I can see the judgment in her eyes before I peel away.

It's been four months since the worst night of my life, and in that time, I got my driver's license, purchased a car, started college...and gained fifteen pounds.

Unwrapping my burger, I take a big bite. Sad thing is, I'm not even hungry.

I just want the endorphin kick.

Even though the shame will come soon after.

I'd love to be able to conquer my food addiction instead of letting it control me, but I don't think that will ever happen. Especially now that my void feels bigger than ever.

This school is large, but I have no friends. Sure, I have a roommate who's nice and all, but she has a boyfriend who also attends Dartmouth.

When she's not over at his dorm, he's at ours.

Something I only know because the scrunchie on the outside doorknob of our room gives me a heads-up not to interrupt them.

Reaching inside the bag, I grab the second burger as I pull up to a stop sign.

I need to quit doing this.

Taking a bite, I turn up the volume on my stereo. I don't usually listen to the radio—because hello *Spotify*—but this channel not only plays awesome rock music that I love, they do interviews with musicians every so often.

That's not the case today, though. The radio host's annoying voice spills through my speakers. "I was a goner the second I laid eyes on my wife. And now I want *you* to tell me if you've ever experienced love at first sight. The tenth caller will get a pair of tickets to the upcoming Christmas rock festival."

Blah, blah, blah.

I'm about to switch to Spotify, but the next words out of his mouth hold my attention. "In the meantime, I've got a little treat for you all. The brand-new, self-titled single that just came out yesterday but is already blowing up the charts by Sharp Objects."

My car nearly swerves off the road.

Holy shit.

"I gotta tell ya," the radio host continues. "I'm really digging this one."

I go to turn it off because even though I'm happy for Storm, I don't think I can handle listening to Phoenix's voice without crying.

Then…I hear it.

> *I'm tough as a nail*
> *Sharp as a blade*
> *But I'm still lying here...*
> *In the mess you made.*

Everything inside me freezes.

I don't even realize I've veered off the road and popped my tire on a curb I jumped until some woman runs over and asks if I'm okay.

I'm not okay. *Not even close.*

They say when you play with fire, you get burned.

But when you love it?

You get destroyed.

CHAPTER 20
PHOENIX

Four years later...

"**G**rammy!" a voice on the other side of the house shouts.

On cue, everyone takes a sip of whatever's in their hand.

Last night, myself and the three other members of Sharp Objects became official Grammy winners when we took home Album of the Year.

I'd be lying if I said I wasn't worried about walking away without one. Four years ago, when we struck gold and made it big, we were nominated for Best New Artist and our self-titled track "Sharp Objects" was nominated for Song of the Year. The disappointment from not winning either felt like a brick to the face.

But we finally did it. To celebrate, our manager Chandler and the rest of our team rented us a sweet house on the beach and invited all our favorite supporters—i.e., groupies and roadies—to join us.

We've been partying for the last twenty-four hours, and I have no desire to slow this train down. I'll be twenty-three this year and I already have a motherfucking *Grammy*. I'm the shit legends are made of.

I finish the rest of the Jack in my glass and head to the table so I can refill.

Storm, who's leisurely smoking a blunt, makes a face as I fill it up to the brim. "You should probably pump the brakes on that shit, man."

He's still my best friend, but fuck him and his buzzkill ass.

"We won a Grammy, bitch. I'm celebrating."

Josh, our bassist—and one of the craziest motherfuckers I've ever met—strides over to us.

Before Vic signed Storm and me to Phantom Rock Records, he had us meet with a bassist and a guitarist who happened to be foster brothers.

Like Storm and I, they were from the wrong side of the tracks and got dealt a shitty hand in life, but music was what got them through rough times. The second we started jamming, I got goose bumps and you could practically see dollar signs flashing in Vic's eyes. The stars aligned that day and it was without a doubt fate.

Josh and Memphis needed a lead singer and a drummer, and we needed a guitarist and a bassist…but what we got was a family.

"Fuck yeah, we're celebrating!" Josh yells before he grabs the bottle of Jack off the table and takes a big swig.

Visibly annoyed, Storm grunts something under his breath and Josh flips him the bird. "No one likes a party pooper."

Placing an arm around my shoulders, he points to two hot half-naked chicks across the room. "See those bitches over there?" I'm about to remind him I'm not blind, but then he says, "Those are blow jobs with our names on it." He waggles his brows. "And I got a bag of coke we're gonna snort off their giant titties."

Sign me the fuck up.

"What are we waiting for?"

He kisses my forehead. "And that's why you're my boy."

Since I am his boy, I do him a solid and scope out the surrounding area for his fiancée Skylar. Despite being together since they were kids and Skylar being a sweet little blonde dime piece, Josh cheats on her left and right. The rest of the guys and I have long since given up trying to tell him to knock it off because that fucker never listens.

And Skylar always ends up forgiving him.

But it looks like the tides are changing because I catch her huddled in the corner of the living room, having what looks like a very heated conversation with Memphis.

Josh is so high these days he doesn't realize his own brother and band member is in love with his girl.

Skylar is far more perceptive, though, because the second we start ushering the girls into the nearest bedroom, she closes in on her man like a vulture. "Josh!"

Despite being loaded, Josh picks up his pace, laughing as he pulls the girls into the bedroom and locks the door behind us.

"Take off your clothes," he tells the redhead as I escort the blonde over to the first of the two beds in the room.

"Your new piercing is so hot," blondie purrs. "I *love* kissing guys with lip rings."

She won't be kissing this one.

The chick goes to sit on the mattress, but I shake my head. "On your knees."

Giggling, she eagerly tugs down my zipper. A moment later, she's swallowing my cock. Or rather, trying to because she gags and says, "You're so big."

I press down on the back of her head. "Suck it anyway."

And she does.

That's the great thing about groupies. There's no bullshit or pretenses. They're just here to serve, fuck, and suck us like the gods we are.

It's fucking beautiful.

Until a loud knock on the door makes Josh spill the bag of coke he's pouring on the redhead's tits.

"Josh, I swear to God—"

"Relax, baby girl," he yells. "We're just talking." Sucking her nipple into his mouth, he murmurs, "These taste good...but they're about to taste even better."

That only makes the frantic pounding get louder.

Ignoring his fiancée's pleas for him to exit, both Josh and the redhead walk over to me. "Give daddy Phoenix a little sample."

The redhead enthusiastically holds up her big tit like a shelf and Josh takes out a new bag of coke and pours some on it.

I don't make it a habit to fuck with the hard stuff, but winning a Grammy calls for a little extra fun.

Lowering my head, I snort the line.

It takes me all of five seconds to realize something's different about it. "What kind of coke is this?"

Those blond eyebrows dance and he grins like the cat who ate the canary. "The heroin kind."

Motherfucker. He knows I don't fuck with that shit.

"What the fuck—" I start to grunt, but a rush of nausea knots my stomach.

And then I puke…

All over the chick giving me a blow job.

Jesus Christ.

Reaching over, Josh slaps my back. "Enjoy the ride, kid."

I want to yell at him, but the euphoric feeling pumping through my veins can only be compared to the kind I feel whenever I'm on stage.

Another surge of pure bliss hits me, and I feel like I'm in my own little world where nothing and no one can ruin this peaceful feeling.

Not even Skylar's loud sobbing on the other side of the door.

"Good, right?" Josh says as he undoes his zipper, and the girl in front of him falls to her knees.

I close my eyes, getting lost in the sensation as I turn Skylar's knocking into a melodic beat in my head.

"Goddammit," Josh roars. "Suck it harder."

"I'm trying," she whines.

"You're not trying if you're talking." A moment later, I hear a loud huff. "You're hot, but I can suck dick better than you. Get the fuck out, you worthless piece of shit."

"Be easy, asswipe," I bark.

For fuck's sake, the chick is in here to get him off.

A new set of sniffles assaults my ears because Josh has managed to make *two* girls cry now.

"It's not my fault," he argues. "This bitch can't get me hard."

It's not her fault, either.

I start to look down but think the better of it because although I give the girl blowing me an A for effort, the visual is something that will ruin my hard-on real fast. "Well, *I* don't have that problem, asshole. Shut the fuck up so I can finish."

He does me a solid and fifteen minutes later I'm busting a nut that leaves me satisfied.

"Thanks, sweetheart." I jut my chin in the direction of the adjoining bathroom. "Shower's in there."

My blonde and Josh's blubbering redhead make a beeline for it.

I'm whipping off my shirt because there's some puke on it…

when the door opens and an irate Skylar barrels in with a screw-driver in her hand.

Wonder where she got one of those?

Dropping the tool, she pounds her fists into his chest. "I fucking hate you."

"Relax," he soothes, trying to pull her into a hug. "Nothing happened." He looks at me. "Tell her, Phoenix."

I ain't saying *shit*. This is his tornado to deal with.

"You know how much I love you," he continues, but Skylar isn't having it because she shoves him.

He's so high he nearly falls and busts his ass.

"It's over."

He starts to chase after her, but she screams, "Do not fucking follow me. I'm *done*."

He rolls his eyes as she storms out of the room. "She knows damn well we're not over."

Despite being pretty convincing about it this time, he's probably right.

Skylar has a bleeding heart…one that continuously bleeds out because of him.

Unbothered by his relationship going up in flames, Josh looks at me and grins. "What do you say we go on a little adventure?"

"What kind of adventure?"

Because with Josh you never know.

"The kind that involves us getting the fuck out of here."

Yeah, he's high as a kite. Not only will our security team be looking for us after we leave, hiking on the beach in the middle of the night isn't my idea of a good time.

"I'm not in the mood to go walking—"

"Who said anything about walking?" He dangles a pair of keys in front of my face. "I stole the keys to Chandler's Stang earlier. Let's take it out for a spin."

He must sense I'm about to turn him down because he taunts, "Come on. Don't be a pussy."

Once this numbnut sets his sights on something, it's a wrap. The only thing you can do is supervise the fucker, so he doesn't cause too much destruction.

   Dodging people left and right, we make our way outside, heading for our manager's red mustang.

He tosses the keys to me. "I'll let you do the honors."

Opening the driver's side door, I climb inside. "We're only dipping out for a few minutes."

The moment I start the car "...Baby One More Time" by Britney Spears blasts through the speakers.

Josh and I exchange a glance...and then we burst into laughter.

"Holy fucking shit," Josh says between fits of chuckles.

"I know."

Our manager has been in the industry for fifteen years and is not only a hard-core rock enthusiast, but a hard-ass in general.

Then again, the dude wears cargo pants.

Taking the lit cigarette he passes me, I reverse out of the driveway. "I'm never gonna let him live this shit down."

Josh pulls something out of his pocket. "Fuck no. Next time he starts bitching at us, I'm gonna start singing *this*."

A snort leaves me as I head down the coast. The look on that dickhead's face will be priceless.

"We should make this our pregame song on tour," Josh continues.

We'll be starting our month-long South American tour in five weeks, followed by another month-long stint in Australia, and then our US tour this summer.

After that...we'll be headed to Europe for six weeks.

And then? I'm sleeping for the next fucking decade.

"Fuck no."

I go to shut the stereo off, but Josh stops me. "Nah. Leave it on." Bopping his head to the beat, he dumps some powder on the dashboard and snorts it.

"Seriously, dude?"

He just did a few bumps back in the room.

"Relax. I saved you some."

I'm about to tell him I'm good because I'm feeling *nice* right now, but my phone rings. When I take it out of my pocket, I see Storm's name flash across the screen.

I hit the speakerphone button. "Yo."

"Where the hell are you?"

That only makes Josh and I crack up.

Reaching over, I rub Josh's head. "Our crazy bassist stole the keys to Chandler's car, so we're taking it for a joyride."

He goes silent…and then.

"What the fuck, Phoenix? You're shit-faced—"

"I'm fine—" I start to say as the car swerves.

"Party foul," Josh calls out.

Fuck. I'm more messed up than I thought.

"Damn, bro. That shit got me fucked up."

"Pull over now," Storm barks. "And tell me where you are so I can come scoop you two assholes."

I pull to a stop on the side of the road as another wave buzzes through me. "Not far. Still driving down the coast."

"I'll be there soon."

I take one last drag of my cigarette and chuck it out the window. "Fuck."

"Man, forget Storm's bitch ass." Josh gestures for me to give him the keys. "I can drive us back."

The warm, euphoric feeling intensifies. "Yeah?"

"Look at me."

When I do, he points to his face. "It's all gravy, baby. I got this." He nudges me with his elbow. "Switch places with me."

"Aight."

Hopping out of the car, we exchange seats. I shoot Storm a text and tell him not to bother coming because we'll be back soon.

Pulling a U-turn, Josh presses repeat on the Britney Spears song and turns up the volume.

"You sure *you're* not into this shit?"

Bopping his head, he steps on the gas. "Nah, bro. I'm just trying to learn the lyrics so I can fuck with him." The car accelerates as he moves his shoulders up and down to the beat, causing the mustang to veer sharply to the left. "Hit me—"

And then everything goes black.

White-hot pain shoots through my head and liquid runs down my face. "What the *fuck*?"

A coppery tang fills my mouth, mingling with the taste of something dusty.

When I open my eyes, I'm surrounded by airbags, broken glass, and branches from the trees we must have hit.

"Whoops."

Ignoring the throbbing in my neck and rib cage, I look over at Josh. There's a lot of blood on his face, but at least we're both alive.

Josh's hysterical laughter fills whatever's still left of the car. "Chandler's gonna be so pissed."

Hell yeah, he is.

"I should probably wait a while to give him shit about listening to Britney, huh?"

The dust in my mouth irritates my lungs and I cough...which only makes the piercing pain in my head and rib cage worse. "Let's get out of here."

I look around the rubble for my cell so I can tell Storm what happened, but the car is so wrecked I can't find it.

"Do you have your phone?"

I turn to look at him when I don't get a response.

His eyes glaze over. "Skylar."

"Huh?"

"Sky—"

His eyes roll back.

A flood of panic surges through me.

"Josh?" Reaching over, I shake him. "Come on, bro. Wake up."

I get no response.

Using what's left of my strength, I shake him harder...but his body goes still.

No. This isn't fucking happening. He was fine a minute ago.

"Wake up!"

The intense pain in my head grows. It's followed by a rush of exhaustion I can't seem to fight against.

"Josh!"

Faintly, I register voices and a tugging sensation.

"Fuck!" someone who sounds a lot like Chandler screams. "Fuck!"

"Stay with me," someone else says, and I immediately recognize the voice as Storm's.

When I look up, he's hunched over me, looking more scared than I've ever seen him in my life.

"Josh." Bile burns my throat. "He's in bad shape."

"I know," he whispers, gripping my hand. "So are you, Phoenix. The ambulance is on the way, though. I just need you to hold on, okay?"

"The people in the other car are dead," Chandler shouts.

Other car?

I want to ask what he's talking about, but every drop of strength I have is being sucked out of me.

"Thirsty." I can't keep my eyes open any longer. "Tired."

So fucking tired.

"Stay with me," Storm screams, only his voice is fading in and out, like he's yelling into a broken mic. "You're not dying on me."

But as I drift off...it's no longer his voice I hear.

It's hers.

CHAPTER 21
LENNON

"**S**cotch on the rocks with a twist."

"Coming right up," I tell the guy in a business suit.

After filling the lowball halfway with some ice, I toss a lemon peel into the glass. Business suit guy eyes me up and down the whole time.

"The owner of this place is an idiot for sticking a beautiful girl like you behind this bar instead of up there."

Up there would be the stage where Angel is currently twirling around the pole.

I wasn't sure what I was going to do after Dartmouth, but tending bar at Obsidian—a gentleman's club—definitely wasn't on my radar.

However, sometimes life throws you major curveballs and the only thing you can do is keep pushing forward.

Sliding the man his drink, I study him. Dark hair, dark eyes, and judging by his appearance, he looks to be in his late forties. While he's not unattractive, there's nothing particularly distinctive or alluring about his features.

I give the guy a coy wink because *tips*. "I'm behind the bar because I want to be."

Bringing the glass to his lips, he takes a sip as his gaze drops down, taking in my black corset and dark jeans.

Four years ago, a guy like him—hell, any guy for that matter—wouldn't have spared a girl like me a second glance.

As devastating as hearing *my* song on the radio was that day, it also ignited a fire inside me.

While I couldn't change what that pilfering asshole did, I realized there *was* something I could change.

Myself.

All my life, I attempted to fill the large, gaping void inside me with food.

Problem was, it didn't work. Because no matter how great I felt when I was in the middle of a binge, I always felt like shit after.

Which in turn would only make the void grow bigger.

Deep down I was miserable...but only because I was continuously choosing to be.

Learning to build a better relationship with food was a lot of hard work and took some deep soul searching.

I didn't force myself to go on a crash diet, nor did I starve myself in order to be thin. I simply made some healthier choices and stopped eating once I became full. Well, that and I cut out soda because that crap isn't good for anyone. Especially the excessive amount I was drinking.

I'm still not what society would consider *skinny* given I'm a size ten on a good day and a twelve on a PMS day, but screw society. The only thing that matters is that I like what I see when I look in the mirror.

Because I didn't conquer my demons for some stupid guy or because I wanted acceptance.

I did it for *me*.

The guy's eyeballs finally travel back up to my face. Thanks to Mrs. Palma, I finally learned how to do my own makeup. I also grew my shoulder-length hair out and dyed it jet black, something I've always wanted to do but was too afraid to try.

"You in college?" the guy asks.

His question makes me inwardly flinch, so I distract myself by grabbing a rag and wiping down the bar.

Despite my first few months at Dartmouth being lonely, once I started working on myself and stopped letting fear hold me back, I flourished. I made friends, maintained good grades, enjoyed a few hookups and a couple of one-night stands.

I even had a boyfriend named Harry for six months during my second year.

Then everything changed.

"No," I tell the guy. "I'm not."

I'm thankful he doesn't pry and hands me a twenty instead. "Have a good night, beautiful."

"You too."

It's just after three by the time I walk in the door. As I toe my shoes off, I say a silent prayer before heading into the living room.

Mrs. Palma's sitting on the couch watching old sitcom reruns on the television, but she smiles when she sees me. "Tonight was a good night."

I breathe a sigh of relief. "Thank you."

I honestly don't know what I'd do without this woman. She's proof angels really do exist and some are right here on earth.

"Always." Standing, she gives my hand a small squeeze. "I put some leftovers in the fridge for you. Richard wasn't a fan of tonight's meatloaf, but your dad seemed to like it."

I follow close behind her as she walks to the front door. "I'm sure it's amazing. Thank you again, Mrs. Palma."

"How many times do I have to tell you to call me Sue?" She gives me a quick hug. "And you don't have to thank me, Lennon. I'm happy to help however I can. I'll see you tomorrow, sweetie."

After she leaves, I head up the stairs so I can check on my dad. He's sleeping soundly, for which I'm grateful.

Three weeks before the end of my second year at Dartmouth, I received a call from Mrs. Palma.

A few days before said phone call, she was awoken by a loud sound in the middle of the night. Given her husband Richard was in bed next to her and no one else lives in the house, she was understandably spooked.

However, when Richard grabbed his gun and went downstairs to investigate, it wasn't an intruder like they thought.

It was my father rummaging through their refrigerator…naked.

When Mr. Palma asked what he was doing, my father mumbled something about keeping the party going. Figuring he must have had too much to drink at a get-together he attended, he walked my dad back to his house and told him to sleep it off.

Though strange, both Mr. and Mrs. Palma decided it was best not to make a big deal out of it because they didn't want to embarrass him.

But he came back three nights later.

Only this time…he crawled into their bed.

Mr. Palma was ready to kick his ass, but my dad freaked out and asked Richard what he was doing in bed with *his* wife. Realizing something wasn't right, they brought him to the hospital and called me.

Although he was better by the time I got there, they ran a bunch of tests anyway.

I remember the exact moment they diagnosed him with early-onset dementia…

Because it was the moment my entire world stopped.

I left Dartmouth and started my summer break early so I could be with him. I figured with medication and rehabilitation, things would get better, and I'd be able to go back for my third year in the fall.

However, life had other plans because despite the treatment a dementia specialist prescribed…my dad declined much sooner than anyone anticipated and there was no way I could return to school.

Harry tried to be supportive, but ultimately, the distance and him not being able to handle all my focus being on the most important man in my life had him calling things off.

His doctor suggested I place my father in an assisted living facility and go back to college, but while that might be a good solution for others, I couldn't bear the thought of doing that.

He was so lost and confused already, it felt wrong to add to it by taking him out of the home he loved.

The only thing I could do was figure out how to make our new normal work.

My dad had done well financially, but being a freelancer meant he didn't have traditional benefits and required him to pay for most of his medical costs out of pocket, which put a huge dent in his savings. Given he had just turned fifty, there wasn't much in his retirement fund, but I used that to pay off the house.

I still had to cover daily living expenses and support us, though, so I briefly took a job as a bartender at a restaurant. Unfortunately, I was barely making enough to get by. Plus, most of my shifts were during the day, which is when my dad is the happiest and active.

Being a bartender at Obsidian kind of fell into my lap thanks to a coworker knowing a girl who stripped there.

I was hesitant at first, but it worked out for the best. Things are still tight, but I make better money than I did at the restaurant, and because I work nights, I'm able to spend my days with him.

"I love you," I whisper before heading back downstairs.

While the world is full of horrible illnesses, dementia is by far one of the worst.

The disease is a heartless, cruel trick because even though physically my dad still looks like my dad...he's a mere shell of the man he once was.

With every passing day, dementia steals another piece of him from me.

The first time he forgot who I was, I cried myself to sleep for a week straight.

But there are still times—albeit few and far between now—where I get flashes of the dad I remember.

I live and breathe for those moments.

After microwaving some of the meatloaf Mrs. Palma left in the fridge, I head into the living room.

Bringing the fork to my mouth, I plop down on the couch.

I'm about to change the channel because watching the news can be depressing, but the next words out of the reporter's mouth make me choke.

"There's been a fatal accident involving members of the popular Grammy award-winning band Sharp Objects."

I clutch my chest as he continues.

"According to authorities, it was a two-vehicle crash. Sadly, bassist Josh Roland was pronounced dead at the scene as well as the two occupants in the second vehicle. Lead singer Phoenix Walker has been taken to a local area hospital and is listed in serious condition. The details of the accident are still pending further investigation, but we'll continue to report as more information comes in."

Oh. My. God.

A range of conflicting emotions hit me all at once, but one stands out among the rest.

Relief.

Because as much as I hate him and want him to suffer… a *very* small part of me is relieved it wasn't Phoenix who died.

CHAPTER 22
PHOENIX

"I quit."

My head pounds like it's being struck by the world's biggest hammer. *Repeatedly.*

When I make the mistake of opening my eyes, I see my publicist Alexis standing over me...looking ticked off as hell.

"Great. Now shut the fuck up."

I'm drifting off to sleep again when she squawks, "I'm serious, Phoenix. I've tried to be sympathetic and cover your ass, but last night's shenanigans were the last straw. I'm done."

Last night?

That's when it dawns on me that I'm not lying in the bed inside my hotel room.

I'm in the hallway.

When I shoot my gaze past Alexis, I see Chandler, Storm, and Memphis glaring at me.

It's apparent whatever I did pissed them the fuck off, too.

"It wasn't that bad," I protest, even though I have no idea what happened.

I'm just trying to smooth things over so I can go back to sleep.

Narrowing his eyes, Storm opens the door to my suite.

All the furniture is tipped over, the television is smashed, and there's a shit ton of bottles and trash littering every square inch of the floor.

There's also an unidentifiable, thick red goo covering the walls and furniture.

It's a mess, but it can easily be taken care of.

I peer up at Alexis. "I'll write the hotel a check."

"Your room isn't the problem," she grits through her teeth. "The problem is what *else* you did."

I scan my brain, trying to recall the events of last night, but come up empty.

Sensing my confusion, she screeches, "Not only did you break a window in the hotel lobby...you had sex on top of the bar."

"Good for me."

Growing frustrated, she stomps her heel. "No, it's *not*. Not only did everyone at the bar take videos of you screwing your brains out on their phones, you were visibly drunk and high off your ass."

I'll have to take her word for it since I don't remember shit.

"Still not understanding what the issue is."

Our fans aren't gonna give a fuck that there's a sex tape of me circulating around the internet. If anything, it will probably increase revenue.

Hell, everyone should be *thanking* me.

Her red talon swipes the air. "In case you forgot, one of your band members died due to drugs three months ago."

How could I forget? I relive the accident every time I close my eyes.

I never should have let him drive.

"Needless to say, it's not a good look. Fans are growing concerned and unhappy with your intoxicated antics," she prattles on. "Which is exactly what you *don't* want days before your US tour starts."

The throbbing in my head increases as I stand. Yawning, I slip my dick out of my boxers and piss on the large plant in the hallway.

Fuck. That feels good.

"Are you kidding me right now?" Alexis wails before turning to Chandler. "That's it. I'm *done*."

"You said that already," I remind her.

"I know he messed up, but we can work something out," Chandler offers.

That only makes her quicken her steps.

"We're beyond that. You couldn't pay me enough to deal with his shit anymore," she yaps before entering the elevator.

Fuck knows we were already paying her plenty already.

With another yawn, I lay back down on the hallway floor.

"I hope you're happy," Chandler snaps.

Thrilled. Alexis might be the best in the business, but she's an uptight bitch.

Memphis scrubs a hand down his face. "Dammit, Phoenix. This is the last thing we need right now. Especially after the shitstorm you caused in Australia."

I'm not sure what he means because I had a great time there.

Aside from being detained.

Apparently, it's a crime to drink on the beach I wandered off to.

So is getting naked and jerking off.

Evidently, the families enjoying their afternoon by the ocean weren't too pleased with my one-man show. Neither were the police.

Chandler looks like he's going to have a hissy fit. "How the hell are we going to find another publicist before the tour starts?"

Storm, Memphis, and I exchange a glance before Storm speaks.

"Well, there is someone who's always wanted to be a publicist."

Skylar. She used to ask Josh all the time if the band would consider taking a chance and hiring her, but he was always quick to shut it down.

A pang of guilt shoots through me because forcing her to have to see the guy who didn't stop her fiancé from killing himself isn't the best idea.

Memphis is in agreement because he grunts, "Not fucking happening."

"It's not a *terrible* suggestion," Chandler says while rubbing his chin. "Think she'd be able to start today?"

"No," Memphis grumbles. "Because we're not hiring her."

"Why not?" Storm argues. "Not only does she know everything about us, it will ensure she's taken care of."

Which is exactly what Josh would want.

Bile rises up my throat as I look up at the ceiling. Skylar has every right to tell us to go fuck ourselves, but the least we can do is offer her the position first.

I can tell Memphis is having a change of heart as well, because he doesn't say shit.

"Let's put it to a vote," Storm declares.

Three hands shoot up.

It used to be four.

Although technically it's still four on stage, because with being forced to go on tour five weeks after Josh's death, we had no choice but to hire a traveling musician to fill in.

None of us like the asshole, though.

Because he's not Josh.

"Then it's settled," Chandler says. "I'll contact Sky—"

"I'll do it," Memphis bites out.

"Fine, but make it quick. We don't have much time." Attention back on me, Chandler pinches the bridge of his nose and sighs. "Now that the publicist crisis is handled, what are we going to do about the *other* issue?"

Placing a hand inside my boxers, I scratch my nuts. "What other issue?"

As if on cue, three women walk out of my suite. They're all wearing tiny dresses and holding a pair of heels in their hands.

"Bye, Phoenix," one of them purrs while blowing me a kiss.

"We had a great time," another one chirps before they step over me and head for the elevators.

Guess I can cross orgy off the bucket list.

That's when I notice one of the girls is still lingering.

Dammit. There's always a stage-five clinger.

"That," Chandler says while pointing to the girl with a sheepish expression on her face. "Is the issue."

"Can you be more specific?"

His face turns red with anger and Memphis snorts. "You have no clue who she is, do you?"

None.

"*She*," Chandler bellows. "Was supposed to be your sober companion."

Squinting, I look the girl up and down. Come to think of it, she does look familiar.

"Am I fired?" the girl whispers.

"Do bears shit in the goddamn woods?" Chandler shouts and the girl scurries to the elevators.

"Bye, Phoenix," she calls out. "Text me later."

I don't even know her name.

"Wasn't she the counselor who came highly recommended?" Storm questions.

Chandler nods before narrowing his eyes.

"We've gone through *ten* sober companions in the two months you've been on tour, and you've fucked all of them."

"That's not true," I defend. "I never fucked the dude."

I had my groupies do that for me.

This way, he'd get off my case and have some fun.

Worked like a charm, too. Turns out the guy was almost a bigger party animal than me.

"It doesn't matter," Chandler gripes. "What matters is that everyone I hire lets you get away with too much."

"Not my problem—"

"Yes, it is," Storm interjects. "Vic's pissed. You need to cut this shit out before he drops us."

Not a chance.

Because when I'm drunk and high, I can't feel shit.

Like guilt.

Josh might have been the one driving, but I'm equally responsible.

And everyone here knows it.

"You'll just have to keep looking and hire someone better," Memphis says, coming to my defense, even though he's the last person who should.

Because I killed his brother.

"I've been trying," Chandler claims. "But every guy wants to be his best friend, and every chick wants to fuck him." Walking over, he peers down at me. "Everyone out there loves this asshole. I need to find someone who hates him."

"Oh, there's someone who hates him all right," Storm mutters under his breath.

Closing my eyes, I nod off again.

Yeah, there is.

CHAPTER 23
LENNON

"How's my favorite bartender?"

I glance up at a familiar face. Brian might not be the biggest tipper, but he's a friendly regular.

"I'm doing good. How about yourself?" I set an empty glass on the bar. "Jack and Coke tonight?"

He grins. "You know me so well."

Sadly, he's not wrong. Most of my social interaction these days consists of talking to the patrons at Obsidian.

After filling the glass with ice, I reach for the soda gun. "How's that merger coming along?"

Brian starts to answer, but a man marches up to the bar and interrupts. "Are you Lennon?"

I'm seriously regretting not using an alias.

"That depends. Who's asking?"

"Me."

I pass Brian his drink. "Gee, that really clears things up."

Brian hikes a thumb at the intruder wearing cargo pants and a crisp white button-down. "Want me to take care of this guy?"

Cargo pants looks like he's trying not to laugh. "You needn't embarrass yourself. I'll have you sprawled out on the floor, begging for your mother." He turns his attention to me again. "I—"

"Better be ordering a drink if you intend to stay." I gesture to the sign behind me that clearly states it's a two-drink minimum. "Club rules."

Grumbling, he fishes his wallet out of his pocket. "Fine. I'll take two Manhattans."

Bit of an odd choice, but this guy seems a bit *odd* himself, so I guess it fits.

I give Brian a smile as I fix up the first Manhattan. "I'll be okay." I gesture to the stage where Fantasia is currently dancing. "Go enjoy the show, sweetie."

He places a five down on the bar. "I'll be back in a little while to check on you."

I give cargo pants his drink. "What can I do for you?"

"My name is Chandler Dicky. I'm—"

"Wow. What an unfortunate last name."

Now I'm just fucking with the guy. Although the surname *is* pretty funny.

His irritation grows. "I can see why you and Phoenix dated, you're both giant pains in the asses."

I nearly drop the glass in my hand. "I'm sorry…what?"

Who the hell is this guy? And why is he talking about Phoenix and I dating?

Ignoring me, he keeps talking. "I'm the manager of Sharp Objects."

For a moment, I get my hopes up that Phoenix did the right thing and came clean, but they come crashing down when I hear the next words out of *Dicky's* mouth.

"I'm here to offer you an opportunity to help Phoenix."

A maniacal laugh flies out of me.

And then I give him a look that makes it clear he can shove this *opportunity* up his ass.

"After what he did to me, he can fuck off for eternity."

So can this guy.

Seemingly pleased by this, he smiles. "And *that* is precisely why I'm here. Storm told me about your volatile relationship. Or should I say, the way it ended." He takes a sip of his drink. "You're the perfect one for the job."

He's lucky I'm not throwing the second Manhattan I'm making in his face.

"What the hell are you talking about? What job?"

"I'd like to hire you to look after Phoenix while he's on tour."

"There's a day care down the street," I inform him, because what the actual fuck?

He's not amused. "What I mean is, I'd like you to be his sober companion and make sure he doesn't get into trouble. Our tour starts in two days. I'll pay you one hundred thousand dollars for eight weeks, with a bonus at the end. Provided you make it to the end, that is." He takes another sip of his drink. "Something tells me you will."

I'm seriously regretting not asking Brian to handle this guy now.

"Hate to break it to you, but your crystal ball is broken because I'm not interested."

I recently overheard someone in town mention that Phoenix was spiraling out of control ever since the accident that killed his bandmate three months ago, but it's worse than I thought if this guy is willing to come here and offer me that much money to be his personal babysitter.

Not that it matters. I'm not budging.

He blinks in confusion, like he wasn't prepared for me to turn him down. "There must be some way I can change your mind."

I look him right in the eyes. "Trust me. There isn't."

"Lennon—"

"If you don't quit bothering me, I'll have security throw you out."

Because something tells me this guy won't take no for an answer.

Huffing, he takes a card out of his wallet, along with a fifty-dollar bill, and slides them across the bar. "Here's my card. Please, just think about it."

Not a chance in hell.

Spending my days and nights thinking about Phoenix Walker and worrying about his well-being is long over.

"How is he?" I ask Mrs. Palma as I walk inside the house.

She shuts off the television. "He was a little restless this evening, but we listened to The Beatles and it put him in a better mood."

I smile, because when in doubt, music always helps. Especially his all-time favorite band.

"Thank you."

"Stop thanking me, Lennon." Standing, she gathers her things. "I put some leftovers in the fridge for you. I made salmon, though, so I'm not sure how well it will heat up."

I follow behind her as she makes her way to the front door. "I'm sure it will be perfect."

"You're off tomorrow, right?"

"Yeah—"

The sound of the doorbell ringing cuts me off.

I'm not sure who's on the other side of it, but I'm about ready to wring their neck because it's three-thirty in the morning and my dad is sleeping.

Moving in front of Mrs. Palma, I answer it. "This better be—"

I stop talking when I see that Chandler guy from earlier. "How the hell did you get my address?"

Immediately, Mrs. Palma takes a protective stance. "If you don't leave this instant, I will get my husband."

Bracing an arm on the side of the house, Chandler sighs. "One hundred and fifty thousand dollars."

"No."

Then I slam the door in his face.

"Who was that?" Mrs. Palma questions.

"That was the manager of Sharp Objects."

And a persistent asshole.

Her eyebrows shoot up to the ceiling. "You're kidding. What in the world did he want?" Her mouth drops open. "Did Phoenix tell the truth?"

I ended up confiding in her about everything shortly after I found out he stole my song and took credit for it.

Unfortunately, she was just as sad and perplexed as I was.

She suggested telling my dad, but he would have wanted to take Phoenix to court.

I didn't have a leg to stand on, though—because, unlike my dad —I didn't copyright my music.

I was just a dumb teenager sharing something personal with a guy she thought she could trust.

A guy who pretended to be interested in me so he could plagiarize my art.

And not only did no one else witness me singing him my song. No one else ever heard my song period. *Just him.*

In the end, my dad would have spent a lot of money on a case we never would have won.

"No." I rub my forehead, trying to thwart off the headache I can feel coming on. "His manager wants to hire me to be his sober companion on his upcoming tour for eight weeks."

Her mouth opens and closes like a fish before she speaks. "What? That's..."

"Weird as hell, right?"

She nods. "Very."

"Safe to say there's no way I'm doing it."

"Right." She makes a face. "Although..."

"Although what?" I ask when her voice trails off.

She waves a hand. "Nothing. Forget it."

If only it were that easy.

Because God knows I've been doing everything in my power to forget that asshole and what he did to me.

CHAPTER 24
LENNON

"**W**hat are you making for dinner, Mom?"

Keeping my face neutral, I answer my dad's question. "I was thinking chicken and veggies, but if you don't want that, I can order out for pizza."

He smiles. "Pizza sounds good."

"Pizza it is then."

Sometimes it's a struggle not to correct him, but I have to keep reminding myself that this is *his* reality, and just because it doesn't match mine doesn't make what he's experiencing any less valid.

Which means today...I'm my late grandmother. The other day I was a former teacher. And a couple of weeks ago, I was Joan Jett.

Although I didn't mind that one so much.

The most important thing is that he's in good spirits.

Even though I'm silently hoping he'll remember I'm his daughter again soon. *Just for a little while.*

But even if he doesn't...I'll still find him wherever he is.

Because no matter who I am to him, he will always be *my* dad and the person I love most in this world.

"I'm tired," he says. "I think I'm gonna take a nap before Kate gets home."

Kate was my mom. I remember he once told me they briefly

moved in with my grandmother shortly after they were married so they could save up for a down payment on this house, so that must be where his memories are taking him today.

"Okay. I'll wake you up when the pizza gets here." Leaning over, I kiss his cheek, feeling grateful he thinks I'm his mother right now because it's safe to do so. "I love you."

So much.

"I love you, too." I start to leave, but he reaches for my hand. "I hope one day when I have kids, I'll be a great parent like you."

My heart cracks and a wave of sorrow drives over the jagged pieces like a steamroller. "You're gonna be the best dad."

He ponders this for a short moment before speaking. "You think so?"

I squeeze his hand. "I *know* so."

I wait until I'm out of the room before I give in to my emotions and let the first tear escape.

Like most kids, I used to take my dad for granted. I thought he was too overprotective at times and didn't know best, despite him always thinking he did when it came to me.

But God knows I'd give *anything* to hear him nag or give me advice again.

To hear him tell me he's proud of the person I am, even though I'm not perfect and I don't always make the right decisions.

That I'm doing a decent job of navigating this fucked-up thing called life without his guidance.

That it will get better.

That one day it won't hurt so damn much.

After I've collected myself, I walk back downstairs. I find Mrs. Palma in the kitchen, washing the dishes.

"You don't have to do that," I tell her.

Lord knows the woman does way too much as it is.

She waves a hand. "It was only a few. Plus, I was bored and needed something to do." Turning off the faucet, she looks at me. "How is he?"

"He's good. Me, on the other hand? Not so much." Frowning, I take a seat at the table. "Today, I was my grandmother, and he said he hoped he'd make a great parent just like her."

"Oh, sweetie." She gives my shoulder a squeeze before sitting in the seat across from me. "Take solace in the fact that it means he wanted you and being your father was important to him long before you were here."

Somehow this woman always knows what to say to make me feel better.

"Yeah—" A knock on the front door cuts me off.

"Expecting any visitors?"

Getting up from the table, I shake my head. "Nope."

I mutter a curse the moment I open the door.

Because Chandler Dicky is standing on the other side of it. *Again.*

"Two hundred thousand."

I go to slam it in his face, but he wedges his foot between it and the frame.

"Our first show is tomorrow night in California," he says in a big rush. "We'll be going on the road right away, so you'll need to make a decision soon."

For fuck's sake. Is he deaf?

"My decision is *no.*"

This time when I slam the door, I lock it afterward.

"The manager came back again?" Mrs. Palma exclaims when I return to the kitchen.

"Yup. The asshole doesn't understand the meaning of no." I grab a water bottle out of the fridge for myself and her. "Luckily the tour starts tomorrow so he'll be out of my hair for good."

That same weird look from last night is back on her face as she takes the bottle from me. "Oh."

This woman is the closest thing I have to a mother figure *and* best friend, so I know when something's not sitting right with her.

"What's wrong?"

"Nothing." Averting her gaze, she takes a small sip of water. "But just out of curiosity, how much money would you have made if Phoenix didn't steal your song and you had been paid for it?"

I think about this for a long moment because there are a lot of variables to consider.

While my dad has written songs that have been featured on albums, he's best known for writing two hit songs during his career. I remember he once said he made around three hundred and seventy-five thousand in royalties the initial year his first hit song came out…after taxes.

However, he *also* told me the first year is when you make most of your money…because the older a song is, the more it loses value over time. Also, if the song is cowritten with anyone, even just a line or two—like his second hit was—you have to split all the royalties with them.

However, *my* song was solely written by me, and Sharp Objects not only blew up, it was also nominated for a freaking Grammy.

A sharp sting of pain strikes through my heart, because I know my dad would have been proud of me for accomplishing something so prestigious.

And equally devastated because I was dumb enough to let Phoenix use me.

Just like my dad told me he would.

"Off the top of my head, I'd say half a million in royalties for the first year alone. Bare minimum."

But there's no way to know for sure. Hell, I'm probably underestimating.

She blows out a breath. "Wow."

"I know." I raise a brow. "Why do you ask?"

She places her water bottle on the table. "This guy seems like he's willing to give you whatever you want in order to do this."

"And?"

"I know the thought of involving yourself with Phoenix again is not only scary, it's downright senseless."

She's got that right. "Agreed."

"For the girl who had a huge crush on some punk kid in a band and thought he was a rock star," she continues. "But you're not that girl anymore, Lennon. You're an independent, strong, confident, self-assured young woman. And as crazy as it sounds, I think doing this would not only be a way for you to conquer your demons with the guy who screwed you over...it's also a way to get some of the money you so justly deserve."

As much as I want to protest—because the thought of being anywhere near Phoenix makes me homicidal—my brain can't seem to formulate a proper argument.

Except one.

"I get what you're saying, but even if I wanted to, I can't. There's no way I'm leaving my father for eight weeks to run off on some rock tour."

He needs me.

"I can take care of him," she proposes. "He's been in good spirits lately and it's not like we won't keep in touch every day. You can talk to him on the phone and we can do video—"

"No. Not only is that way too much to ask of you, it wouldn't be right of me to accept. I'm his daughter. It's my responsibility to make sure he's taken care of."

Just like he's always taken care of me.

Her expression becomes serious, a sure sign she's not ready to give up just yet.

"You're only twenty-two years old, Lennon. These are supposed to be the best years of your life. The years where you're supposed to have fun, make mistakes, go a little wild, and learn and grow along the way." Her gaze cuts to mine. "Your father wouldn't want you to waste them trapped here taking care of him where the only reprieve you get is working behind a bar at a strip club just so you can make ends meet."

I open my mouth to protest, but she's not done yet. "I know what I'm about to say will hurt, but most days he doesn't even know who you are, so he'd be peacefully oblivious to your temporary absence."

As awful as hearing that is...it's the sad truth. I'd be missing him far more than he'd miss me.

However, I'm terrified of not being here for those moments when he does remember me.

I don't want him to think I abandoned him.

"But—"

"All a good parent ever wants for their child is for them to figure out what makes them happy. Music is that thing for you, Lennon."

Looking ready to throw down the gauntlet, she stabs the table with her finger. "Despite Phoenix being there, it's still a great opportunity to be around what you love. Not to mention, doing this means you won't have to struggle financially anymore. Being able to provide for yourself is something your father would also want."

My chest caves in because she's making it harder and harder to say no with every point she makes. "Mrs. Pa—"

"For heaven's sake, it's eight weeks, not eight years, Lennon. You will be back. In the meantime, I will take care of everything while you're gone. Physically he's fine, so you have nothing to worry about. Plus, Richard and I enjoy his company so it's really no bother."

It's not that I don't trust Mrs. Palma to take care of him, I know she will. It's the thought of leaving that makes me feel guilty. Along with inconveniencing her.

"I appreciate it, but I can't ask you to do this."

"You're not asking. I'm offering." Her expression softens. "Richard and I weren't lucky enough to have children, and I know I'm not your mother, but I care for you as if you were my own. So, please, let me do this."

My throat prickles. She brought out the big guns.

"I'll think about it," I settle on, because I need to take some time so I can weigh the pros and cons.

That said…there's an important motive Mrs. Palma failed to mention.

One that's urging me to turn my maybe into a yes.

Revenge.

CHAPTER 25
LENNON

My gaze ping-pongs between my empty suitcase and my phone, unable to bring myself to make a decision.

As luck would have it, my dad remembered me earlier…and Mrs. Palma spilled the beans.

Not about Phoenix stealing my song, but that I've been given an opportunity to join a band on tour and make some money.

He seemed happy for me.

It should probably make it easier, but it doesn't.

I'm going to miss him so much.

But eight weeks' worth of my time means I'll no longer be so strapped for cash. I'll also be able to quit my job, spend more time with him, *and* relieve Mrs. Palma from the hassle of watching him four nights a week.

I hate to admit it, but temporarily being in Phoenix's orbit again will solve some major problems.

I just hope it won't cause a whole set of new ones.

As if on cue, Mrs. Palma walks into the room. "You still haven't packed?"

"I still haven't called."

For all I know, Chandler might have found someone else after he left my house yesterday.

She pinches the bridge of her nose. "Lennon, honey."

"I know."

My wishy-washiness is not only annoying her, it's annoying me.

It's time to put my big girl panties on and do this.

Make Phoenix pay for what he did and get the money I deserve in the process.

Picking up my phone, I punch in the number on the card Chandler gave me and hit the speakerphone button.

He picks up on the second ring.

"What?" he barks.

Yup. Working for him is going to be *fun*.

"It's Lennon."

"Go on," he drones. "I haven't got all day."

Mrs. Palma and I exchange a glance because *rude*.

"I'm in. Under one condition."

"Which is?"

Here goes nothing. "I want five hundred thousand."

"You must be on drugs, too," he exclaims before expelling a sigh. "Three hundred thousand. That's my *final* offer. Take it or leave it."

My gut tells me he's probably right. That's an insane amount of money.

Money I deserve.

"Three hundred and fifty thousand."

"Christ almighty. Fine. I'll make it work. But you have to get here *tonight*. The concert starts at eight."

Before I can say another word, he hangs up the phone.

"That went better than expected."

Mrs. Palmer looks at her watch and blanches. "Except for the time difference." She winces. "You need to be in California by eight…which means you should have left two hours ago."

Shit.

"Don't panic," she says, despite looking like she is. "I'll go on the computer and book you a plane ticket. While I do that, you throw some things in a suitcase. Richard gets off work in five minutes so he can drive you to the airport. You'll be late, but I'm sure he'll understand."

I want to throw my arms around her, but she waves me on. "Go pack."

"You're late," Chandler snaps when I meet him outside the airport.

Is he for real right now?

"I'm not sure if you're aware," I tell him as I walk over to the black SUV he's leaning against. "But there's this crazy thing called living in a different time zone."

Dicky grumbles something under his breath as we climb into the back seat.

I take a moment to study him. He has beady dark eyes and styled dark hair that's graying at the temples and sideburns. I'm guessing he's in his early forties. Although he wears a perpetual scowl on his face, so it might just be premature wrinkles.

Once again, he's wearing cargo pants and another button-down, only this time, the sleeves are rolled up and I see a tattoo on his fore-arm. Upon closer inspection, I realize it's a lyric to the song, "Boule-vard of Broken Dreams" by Green Day.

Okay, so despite his geeky appearance, he's definitely a fan of rock.

"Good song."

"I know," he says snidely as the driver hits the gas.

Since he isn't one for conversation, I look out the window, however he snaps his fingers, drawing my attention back to him.

I'm about to tell him finger snapping isn't necessary, but he shoves a stack of papers at me.

"What's all this?"

He points to the first paper. "That one is an NDA. Which is an agreeme—"

"I know what an NDA is," I interject.

I just don't like that I'm being made to sign one.

Kind of messes up my goal of getting vengeance and all.

Although, I'm sure I'll figure out a way around it.

"Bravo. You're smarter than the last three girls before you," he murmurs while handing me a pen.

After reading it over and deciding there are no red flags, I sign it and hand it back to him.

He points to the next paper in the stack. "Given the money you requested was substantial, I needed to speak to the record company. They're willing to pay half your salary, provided you abide by their contract in addition to mine."

A weird twist of nerves churns in my stomach. I'm not sure why I expected this to be a little more *laid back*, but all these contracts and rules make it evident that's not the case.

"Okay."

I scan the document from Phantom Records but freeze when I get to the part that states I'll only get paid *after* I complete the full eight weeks.

"I don't get paid until after the tour's over?"

He nods. "That's right. We've wasted enough money paying people who can't fulfill the job requirements over the past two months. We need to ensure you'll stay until completion."

"My dad is sick," I whisper, but he holds up a hand.

"I'm not your therapist, so save your sob story for someone who cares." He shifts in his seat. "You're going to receive six figures at the end of this, remember? So, I suggest you decide right here and now whether you intend to take this job seriously. If not, I'll have the driver turn around so you can go back home. However, let it be known that I will *not* extend this offer again."

I give him a sugary sweet smile. "I read you loud and clear, *Dicky*."

He narrows his eyes. "Glad to hear it. If you're worried about funds, you needn't be. You'll receive three square meals a day and your room and board will be provided for."

But that doesn't help me pay bills back home. Shame snakes up my spine when I realize I'll have to ask Mrs. Palma for yet *another* favor.

One that will require me to stay on this damn tour no matter what, so I can pay her back in full.

Grimacing, I scribble my name on the bottom of the company's contract and give it to him.

Dicky's contract is not only the last...it's the longest. Go figure.

"Before you sign this one, we should go over the rules so there's no confusion and you understand exactly what's expected of you." His gaze turns hard. "Because if you break any of them? I'll drop your ass off at whatever city we happen to be driving through. Understand?"

I hate both his tone and his threats, but I bite my tongue since this is important.

"Got it." I motion for him to keep going. "What are the rules?"

"Of course, we'd like Phoenix to be sober and all that jazz. But more imperative than that...we'd like him to be in control."

"Control...meaning?"

"Nothing that hits the online gossip sites, tabloids, or social media." He makes a face. "Such as the recent video in which he had sex on top of a bar at a hotel while blitzed out of his mind."

Lovely.

"Simply put," he continues. "Your job is to keep him out of the news, out of trouble, and off hard drugs. I want him performing at his maximum capacity during every single show. Are we clear?"

"Yes." Although I need him to clarify something. "Phoenix never had an issue with drugs when I knew him. How long has this been going on?"

Chandler's *professional* demeanor morphs into something a lot more human. "While Phoenix never missed a party and dabbled from time to time, it's never been this bad. Ever since we lost Josh...he's been stuck in a downward spiral." He rubs his chin. "Hopefully, things improve soon, or we'll have another dead band member on our hands. Only someone with *his* talent can't be replaced, so we'll be screwed."

"Right."

He's not worried about Phoenix because he gives a shit, but because his death would impact his bottom line.

Not that it concerns me. I don't care.

He clears his throat. "Anyway, tonight he's in a suite, but going forward, you'll have adjoining rooms. You'll also have the key to his room in case he locks you out."

"We have to sleep in the same room tonight?" I bite out.

"Yes. I wasn't aware you were joining us until last minute, remember?" He takes a breath. "Anyhoo, there are six bunks on the tour bus and one very small bedroom in the back that's *mine*."

At least it's a whole lot better than sleeping in the same room. "Okay."

"You'll be expected to accompany him everywhere," he carries on. "Even the bathroom if need be."

Hard pass.

"I'm not following him into the bathroom."

Those beady eyes become tiny slits. "Then you run the risk of being fired in the event he does drugs, goes apeshit, and ends up on the news again."

Dammit. "I'll pat him down beforehand."

"It's your money at stake."

The driver slows to a stop in front of a hotel.

I'm about to gather my purse and luggage, but he stops me. "Not so fast. We haven't gone over the most important rule."

What's more important than keeping him out of trouble?

"Which is?"

"There is to be absolutely no sexual relations between you two. We hired *you* specifically, so we don't have to worry about that." He crosses his arms. "Screw anyone else you want, but under no circumstances are you to ever screw him. Understood?"

Oh, I'll be screwing him all right. Just not the way Chandler thinks.

"Trust me. There's no way I'd ever have sex with him."

"His suite is at the end," Chandler says as he leads me down a long hallway.

Not that I need directions. The sounds of people partying are unmistakable.

When we reach the double doors, he hands me a key.

"Good luck."

That's all I get before he turns and walks away.

Thanks, Dicky.

Squaring my shoulders, I force myself to take a deep breath as I grab my suitcase with one hand and swipe the key card with my other.

The muffled noises I heard in the hallway are now so loud I wince as I cart my luggage inside.

"All right, everyone ou— "

Words die in my throat...because there *he* is.

My mouth falls open as I peer up at him—and then down at the not one, but *two*, half-dressed women giving him a blow job in the middle of the room—while others carry on partying around them. Like this is completely normal behavior.

I'm too shocked to speak as I gape at him.

Despite my animosity—and disgust—Phoenix is still utterly gorgeous and mesmerizing.

Even more so given he looks slightly older now. *Edgier.*

Yet, those once intense blue eyes of his are dull.

Like the life's been sucked right out of him...but not by the two blondes on their knees.

My stare lands on the new scar spanning from his chest to his navel.

Ripping my gaze away, I take a quick inventory of my surroundings. There are at least twenty people in the room, not counting the little threesome going on. When I look to my right, I see a man and two girls snorting blow off a coffee table. When I look to my left, I see another man snorting something off a naked girl's ass as a line forms behind him…awaiting their turn.

In addition to drugs, there are liquor bottles everywhere.

I knew it would be bad, but not *this* bad.

I'm looking for the source of the music so I can shut it off and kick everyone out, but that deep, raspy—and very *slurred*—voice rolls over me like a boulder.

"Why don't you come over here and join us, baby?"

Sheer revulsion and rage light me up. Of all the things he should have said to me after what he did, *that's* what he chooses to start with?

My hand squeezes the handle of my luggage so hard I'm surprised it doesn't snap off.

The fucker is lucky it doesn't, though, because I'd beat him over the head with it.

"Excuse me?"

Phoenix sways like a tree in a hurricane, his head lolling from side to side as he fights to keep his eyes open.

It quickly dawns on me that he's so bombed he has no fucking idea who I am.

Hell, I don't even think he's fully cognizant of the blow job he's currently receiving…let alone enjoying it.

Jesus. This isn't the Phoenix I know.

Correction—the Phoenix I *thought* I knew, because it turns out I didn't back then, either.

I'd almost pity this pathetic, intoxicated mess of a guy if I didn't loathe the asshole so much.

His head flops to the side and the glint from the lip ring he now has catches my eye. "Don't be shy, beautiful. We're all friends here."

We most certainly aren't friends. *We never were.*

The two girls on the floor maneuver a bit, making room for me.

Fuck *that*. I'd rather eat my own intestines.

Gritting my teeth, I march out the door. I spot Chandler waiting by the elevators at the other end of the hall, so I accelerate my steps.

"Wait!" I call out just as the doors open.

He looks up at the ceiling before walking toward me. "You can't quit. Not only have you already signed the contract, it's only been two minutes."

"I'm not quitting." No matter how much I want to. "But there are some things I'm going to need as soon as possible."

Otherwise, I'm never going to get Phoenix or the situation in his room under control. *Not without killing him first.*

Chandler blinks. "What kinds of things?"

I start ticking stuff off with my fingers. "Handcuffs, a gallon of water, some smelling salts, and aspirin."

As much as I'd like the jerk to be in pain, he has a show tomorrow and it's now *my* responsibility to make sure he performs at peak capacity. Which means no hangover headaches for him.

I'm fully prepared for Dicky to argue, but to my surprise, he agrees. "Okay. I'll get you what you need."

I'm expecting him to head back to the elevators, but he strolls down the hallway, stopping at a room near Phoenix's.

"I need your handcuffs," he demands when the door opens. "And the keys."

I have no clue who's on the other side—or *why* they have a set of handcuffs on them—but three minutes later, he's tossing them to me before strolling along to the elevators.

"The rest will take a bit longer," he calls out. "But I'll leave everything outside your room."

Of all the things I asked for, I figured the cuffs would be the hardest for him to procure, not the easiest. "Thanks."

Jumping into action, I return to the suite. After shutting the music off, I bring my fingers to my lips, letting out a loud whistle. "Party's over."

As expected, there are dirty looks and protests all around.

"No, it's not," Phoenix slurs loudly and everyone cheers.

Goddammit.

Thinking quick, I give him a flirty smile and twirl the handcuffs around my finger. "I was kind of hoping we could have a party of our own."

Dopey eyes widen ever so slightly before he yells. "Party's over. Everyone out." He glances down. "Including you two."

Whines and objections fill the room as people stagger to the door.

"Buzzkill," someone sneers as they pass me.

One of the blow-job twins tries to kiss Phoenix goodbye, but he turns his head. "Get out."

"Bitch," one of them mutters under her breath as she gets dressed.

"Guess he's a chubby chaser," the more offended of the two spits as she stomps toward the door.

Years ago, those insults would have gotten under my skin, but I know she's only saying that because deep down she's miserable and feeling rejected.

I also know it's not true.

She's just a bitter bitch who's trying to pick out something she thinks I must be insecure about because I'm not a size two like she is.

Screw her. I have half a mind to mention that Phoenix has kissed me lots of times before the door closes behind her, but the asshole in question starts swaying again.

"You're hot," he mumbles as I grab his bicep.

When he stops tottering, I pick a pair of boxers up off the floor.

Sadly, that dick of his is still massive. Too bad the specimen is attached to a giant douchebag.

"Lift your leg," I instruct.

"I don't fuck without a condom," he babbles, despite me placing clothes *on* him.

At least he still remembers that small precaution. Needless to say, it won't be necessary.

"There's one by the bed." I tug on his arm. "Let's go."

"Have I fucked you before?" he questions as I haul his stupid, staggering ass to the other room. "You seem familiar."

Not familiar enough apparently.

I push him onto the mattress. "You only half fucked me."

With his cock. Because God knows he fully fucked me overall. *Bastard*.

That dopey expression is back again. "What?"

"Nothing."

He seizes the cuffs from me. "Get on the bed."

A laugh flies out of my mouth as I snatch them back. "I'm not the one getting restrained. You are."

My laughter dies when I realize the only way to secure him without having him suspect something is amiss is to straddle him first.

Fuck my life. *Hard*.

"Oh, you're a bad girl, huh?" he slurs as I climb on top of him and grab one of his wrists.

I lock the cuff around it. "You have *no* idea."

I'm about to be his worst nightmare.

He bites his lip as I fasten the other end to the headboard. "Now we're talking."

"No, actually. We're not." I quickly climb off him. "Go to sleep, asshole."

CHAPTER 26
PHOENIX

My head feels like Storm decided to use my brain as his new drum set.

Motherfucker.

With a groan, I roll over, attempting to shield my face from the sunlight streaming through the curtain so I can go back to sleep… only I can't.

Because I'm handcuffed to the bed.

"What the fu—"

"Good afternoon, douchebag. Did you sleep well?"

Holy hell. That *voice*.

Nah. There's no way that's possible. I'm still fucking high.

Only, when I cock my head toward the door…I realize I'm not imagining shit.

It's *her*.

At least, I think it is because she looks…different.

"Lennon?"

Jesus fucking Christ.

Aside from the voice I still hear in my dreams and those big brown eyes I could pick out of a lineup, this isn't the same girl from Hillcrest.

Her hair is darker and longer. The shiny jet-black tresses now end at her waist.

She's also wearing makeup. Not a lot, just enough to accentuate her eyes and those high cheekbones which are even more prominent now.

And then there's the obvious. She's thinner.

But not in a skeletal way. I roam my gaze over her hourglass figure, taking in every soft feminine curve.

Fucking hell.

And yet, that's still not the biggest change.

While I never thought Lennon was ugly and her weight wasn't a big deal to me, my attraction to her developed and grew because of who she was on the inside.

An attraction she had a hard time believing, because despite trying her best to put up a good front, deep down, her insecurities were eating her alive.

The girl standing before me doesn't have that problem anymore.

She's secure and confident. There's even a tiny smirk on her lips, as if she's thinking—eat it up, asshole, and then choke on it, because you'll never get this again.

Don't I know it.

I feel like the universe is seriously fucking with me because she isn't just my type.

She's a goddamn fantasy I wasn't even aware I had come to life.

She crosses her arms, pushing those tits that fill my hands perfectly higher. "I prefer *original creator of the song you stole*, but Lennon's fine, too."

And there it is.

I knew she heard it. There was no way she didn't. Not only because of her intense love of rock music, but we blew up seemingly overnight.

I waited for her to hunt me down and let me have it.

Hell, a small part of me *wanted* her to…if only so I could see her again.

But she never did.

"What are you doing here?"

Because Lennon Michael standing in my hotel room doesn't make any fucking sense.

Neither does me being handcuffed to a bed. *Unless…*

"Did we screw?"

No. Fuck that. There's not a drug potent enough that would make me *forget* having sex with her last night.

Placing her hand over her heart, she laughs—actually laughs—as if the thought of fucking me again is hysterical.

"Oh, God. *No.*" She saunters over to the bed and all I can focus on is the sexy way her hips move when she walks. "I'm here on business."

That makes even less sense. "Business?"

She crinkles her cute little nose. "Officially, I'm your new sober companion."

I'm trying to process this when she leans down. The close proximity, her sweet scent, and her lips touching the shell of my ear have my cock thickening.

Until she speaks.

"But unofficially? I'm here to ruin you when you least expect it… and I want you stone-cold sober when I do it."

Ice runs through my veins.

So many years went by, I figured I was in the clear and she'd either gotten over it or learned to make peace with what I did. Turns out I was wrong.

Because this is karma finally coming to collect.

There's only one problem with that.

No way in hell am I giving her the chance to ruin what I've worked my ass off for.

I don't give a fuck that what I did warrants retaliation…or how much I want her.

No pussy is worth sacrificing my dream for. *Not even hers.*

She'll have to pry my career from my cold, dead fingers.

Because without music—without that magic I get to experience on stage—I'm as good as dead.

She wrote a song—a damn good one—but it doesn't mean she's entitled to my goddamn soul.

Not that I have one of those anymore.

I grab her wrist with my free hand. "You might have gotten hotter, but not smarter."

Her eyes narrow. "I beg your pardon, asshole?"

I give her a smug smile, designed to piss her off even more. "Pro tip from someone who knows a thing or two about screwing people over? Don't expose your plans to them. It's a lot easier when they don't see it coming."

The sting from her slapping my cheek makes me groan, and it's all I can do not to slip my hand inside those skintight jeans and make her come all over my fingers again.

"Is that all you got, Groupie?"

She's looking at me like a kid who just came face-to-face with the monster hiding under their bed. *Good.*

"I am *not* your groupie."

No, she's the secret demon that's been living in my head for the past four years.

The one mocking all my success and accomplishments, because even though *my* talent crowned me the king of rock...my kingdom was built with *her* gift.

And I fucking hate it.

Which is why she needs to take her ass back to Hillcrest, where she belongs.

Lennon isn't gonna go without a fight though, because she doubles down. "And I want you to see it coming, Phoenix. Because, unlike my song you stole, I want all the credit this time."

I keep my expression neutral. "I don't know what you're talking about. I think you have me confused with someone else."

Wrath flashes in her pretty eyes. "You know damn well what I'm talking about."

I need her gone. *Now.*

So I hit her with the kill shot.

"The only thing I know is that you've always been obsessed with me, but this is pathetic, even for you. Don't worry, though. Once I talk to Chandler and tell him he mistakenly hired my high school stalker, he'll put you on the next plane home and send you back to your *daddy*."

This time, she spits in my face.

Smirking, I wipe it off my jaw and lick it. "You still taste good, Groupie. It's a shame you won't be here long."

"I fucking hate you."

That makes two of us.

"I take it things are going well?" Storm interjects before he and Memphis walk into the bedroom.

"Lennon was just leaving."

"And Phoenix was just *lying*."

My lungs lock up as I wait for her to drop the hammer. Memphis won't believe her because he doesn't even know her...but Storm might.

Lennon doesn't knock down the pins she set up, though. She goes a different route.

"He wants to tell Chandler I'm his stalker so he'll fire me."

Storm scrubs a hand down his face. "Chandler isn't going to fire you."

The hell he won't. "He will once I talk to him."

Storm glares at me. "No. Because *I'm* the one who convinced him to hire Lennon in the first place, so he knows she's not a stalker, jackass. Plus, the record label is involved now, so they're not gonna let her go without just cause."

The asshole is no longer my best friend.

"Honestly, I don't care anymore." Lennon's gaze zeros in on me. "Eat shit and die, Walker."

Memphis's eyebrows shoot up. Then he smiles and sticks out his hand. "Hey, I'm Memphis. Guitarist."

The fucker is blatantly checking her out.

"Uncuff me," I bark before her hand makes contact with his. "Now."

If looks could kill, I'd be cremated. "Kiss my ass."

With those parting words, she walks out.

And I'm reminded of what a nice ass it is.

Big, round, and shapely. It's all I can do not to bite my knuckle and chase after her.

And I'm not the only one because Storm and Memphis are practically breaking their necks to get a better look.

"Goddamn," Memphis says under his breath. "You're an idiot."

After he's looked his fill, Storm's eyes connect with mine. "You're so fucked."

I know.

CHAPTER 27
LENNON

"It's not going well," I tell Mrs. Palma as I pace up and down the hallway of the hotel, because there's no way in hell I'm going back in there. "I've already told him to die once."

"What happened?"

Closing my eyes, I inhale a breath as a flicker of pain squeezes my chest.

"The asshole won't even acknowledge that he stole—"

I stop talking when I hear the sound of a hotel door opening.

"I have to go," I tell her when I see Storm and Memphis come out of Phoenix's suite.

I find myself studying them as they approach.

While Phoenix is definitely the pretty boy of the group with his strong, chiseled jawline, piercing eyes, and gorgeous face...Storm is the complete opposite.

He's attractive, but in a scary, *intense* way.

Contrary to Phoenix, who's long and lean, Storm is built like a brick shithouse.

I'd literally piss my pants if I was walking down a dark alley and saw him.

Memphis is a combination of the two of them. Like his fellow band members, he's tall. While not *jacked* like Storm is, he's also not as lean as Phoenix. His face, albeit striking, has sharp features.

Similar to Storm, he has dark hair, dark eyes, and a few tattoos.

"Don't leave," Storm says.

He has no idea how much I want to.

And I have *him* to thank for it because me being here is all his doing.

Which doesn't add up.

"Why do you want me here so badly?"

Storm and Memphis exchange a glance before Memphis takes a step back.

"I'm gonna shower and grab a bite to eat before sound check," he drawls, and I detect a hint of a Southern accent. "It was nice meeting you, Lennon. Hopefully, I'll see you later."

As far as first impressions go, mine was *spectacular*. However, I can't focus on that because Storm takes hold of my elbow and steers me toward his hotel room. "Let's talk in here."

While smaller than Phoenix's, this one doesn't look like a bomb hit it.

He gestures for me to take a seat on the couch as he walks over to the mini-fridge.

I'm grateful when he offers me a bottle of water because the only thing to drink in Phoenix's suite is alcohol.

"Thanks."

He crosses his arms over his chest. "I want you here because you're the only person who can help him."

That nearly makes me spit up my water. "Help him? He's lucky I'm not slitting his damn throat after what he did to me."

Not that Storm knows the extent of it.

I also can't tell him because, while I don't think he would condone it, he's still Phoenix's best friend. And he's in the band.

If the world knew their favorite front man was a fraud, it would jeopardize Sharp Objects as a whole, so I have no doubt he'd suddenly be on board with me being canned.

Loyalty and all that.

"I know he hurt you."

Phoenix did more than hurt me.

He obliterated me.

"I can't stop you from leaving," he continues. "Shit, I can't even blame you if that's what you decide to do, but I…"

"You what?" I urge when his voice trails off.

"Phoenix isn't the same." Exhaling, he drags a hand down his face. "He's been in a bad place and I can't pull him out of it." Dark eyes hold mine. "I thought it was the accident, but looking back, that was just the catalyst. His head's been fucked for a while now, and he's one mistake away from becoming the person he never wanted to be."

"His father," I whisper, ignoring the pang in my heart.

He nods. "I know I had no right to make Chandler hunt you down—especially after the way shit ended between you two—but I was desperate." His massive shoulders rise in a shrug. "You helped him before when he needed it. I guess I was hoping you could do it again. Because he sure as shit ain't listening to me no more. Or anyone else, for that matter."

I feel bad for Storm because it's clear he cares about his best friend. However, I have no desire to *help* Phoenix.

"I don't care if Phoenix screws his life up." Bringing the water bottle to my mouth, I take a sip. "I'm only here because I need the money."

I don't know what to make of his expression. "Right."

I'm about to get up and leave, but his next statement makes me freeze.

"What's going on with you, Lennon?"

When I peer up, genuine concern illuminates his face.

I like Storm, so I don't have an issue confiding in him, I just don't want Phoenix to be privy to it.

"I don't want this getting back to Phoenix."

Because it's none of his damn business. He doesn't deserve to know the private details of my life.

"It won't. Whatever you tell me stays between us. You have my word."

His tone is so earnest, I believe him.

"My dad is sick." I force myself to breathe through the crushing ache gripping my heart. "Two years ago, he was diagnosed with early-onset dementia. He declined rapidly though, and I had to drop out of school to take care of him."

"Damn." His face crumples. "I'm sorry."

Me too.

He shifts his feet, looking all sorts of uncomfortable now. "You want a hug or some shit?"

A laugh breaks free because while I appreciate the offer, the poor guy looks worried that I might take him up on it.

"I'm good. Thanks."

He visibly relaxes. "Thank fuck." Stuffing his hands in his pockets, he says, "We have a show tonight and then we'll be on the tour bus. Stay in my room until soundcheck at seven."

I'm grateful he's giving me a place to hide out, so I don't have to deal with the shithead. "I appreciate it." That's when I realize. "I left him handcuffed to the bed."

Storm chuckles and I notice the tattoo on the side of his neck. It's a giant middle finger. "Yeah, you did. But let him sweat it out a little longer." A peculiar look crosses over his face. "That reminds me. I'll be right back."

He disappears into the bedroom, but returns a few moments later…carrying long black straps.

"What are those?"

"Not every headboard is handcuff friendly," he explains as he hands them to me. "This is an under-the-bed restraint system. It goes between the mattress and box spring." He gestures for me to stand. "Come on, I'll show you how to set it up."

Suffice it to say, I know *exactly* who gave Chandler those handcuffs now.

CHAPTER 28
LENNON

"*I love you!*"

"*I want to have your babies!*"

"*I'll let you stick it anywhere.*"

My belly swoops as I watch him take the stage for the final performance of the night, his slim, toned frame slithering like a snake about to devour its prey.

Cigarette in hand, despite the stadium's strict no-smoking policy, he grabs the mic in a crude gesture that earns more cheers from the crowd.

And then he just stands there—like some important biblical figure. Soaking up the energy, waiting until the tension and anticipation are wound up so tightly you can hear the frantic thumping of hearts belonging to every single girl in the crowd.

Another moment passes. Electricity buzzes through me like a live wire. I hold my breath. Clench my thighs. Silently chastise myself for the way my body responds, even though there's no one on the planet that I hate more than him.

As if sensing my thoughts, he turns his head to the right, where I'm waiting offstage.

Slowly, he peruses my body from head to toe, pausing to give every curve a thorough once-over. Like he's marking his territory.

Eyes locked on mine, he drags his tongue along his lip ring in such a lewd way it makes my knees buckle *and* my disdain for him rise to supersonic levels.

I tell myself to ignore the rush of heat that creeps up my vertebra, but I can't.

Because he's Phoenix Walker…

Rock god. Cocky asshole.

Thief.

And there's no escaping his flames.

They'll consume you long before you get a chance to snuff them out.

Despite already being burned by them once, I straighten my spine. Because although I'm on his stake and he's ready to light the match, it doesn't mean I won't put up a fight.

He might burn me, but I'll go down like Joan of Arc.

Face impassive, he turns back to the crowd as Memphis's guitar intro starts.

George—the bassist they hired to fill in for Josh—follows close behind.

A moment later, Storm hits the drums…enhancing the buildup.

They're so in sync, no one would ever know what's really going on behind the scenes. Anyone watching them perform for the first time would never guess they lost their band member a little over three months ago.

Another bolt of energy zaps me and the momentum picks up.

And then it *stops.*

Phoenix was supposed to start singing, but he missed his cue.

Unfazed, Memphis and Storm play the intro again, causing even more cheers from the crowd.

But Phoenix stays silent.

Memphis and Storm play it a third time, but the same thing happens.

Ever the polite one, Phoenix gives the crowd his middle finger.

And then he jogs off stage.

While everyone else in the stadium is confused and disappointed, satisfaction pumps through my veins and I can't help but smile.

Phoenix Walker was supposed to sing his greatest hit, just like he always does at the end of every concert…but he can't.

Because I'm here.

"I'm George," a voice behind me says before I get on the bus.

I spin around. With his red hair and scruffy beard, George isn't conventionally hot, but he has a nice smile.

I stick out my hand. "I'm Lennon."

He gives it a gentle shake. "Phoenix's new babysitter."

I'd laugh if it wasn't the sad truth. "Pretty much."

He makes a face. "Hope you stick around."

"Me too."

Only because I need the money.

Shoving his hands in the pockets of his jeans, he glances at the bus. "The other guys don't really like me, so things get kind of awkward when we're in the same room. Figured I should give you a heads-up about it so you don't peg me as an antisocial jerk."

That's…messed up. George seems sweet, so I can't imagine why they'd have an issue with him.

Other than the fact he's replacing an original band member they were all close with.

However, that's not *his* fault.

"Phoenix doesn't like me either," I tell him in hopes he'll no longer feel like a pariah.

Because I know all too well how awful that is.

A rueful grin splits his face. "Then we can be outcasts together." He jerks his chin at the bus. "We should probably get on this thing before they leave without us."

"Yeah."

Although that might not be the worst thing in the world.

My mouth drops open as I walk up the steps because it's bigger than I thought it would be.

There's a small kitchen with a table and mini lounge area...one that Memphis and Storm are currently occupying.

Along with three pretty girls, whose limbs and lips are all over them.

They're both so into their *company*, they don't look up when I pass them.

"Come on," George offers. "I'll give you a tour."

"Okay."

Then I hear it.

"Fire her," Phoenix barks loudly from somewhere in the back. "*Now.*"

"No," Chandler yells. "It's my job to do what's in the best interest of the band, and she's it."

"No, she's not. Trust me."

Holy awkward.

George places his hand on my lower back. "On second thought, maybe we should hang here for a bit."

"What's going on with Phoenix?" the girl on Storm's lap chirps as we take a seat at the table.

From the sounds of it, a temper tantrum.

The fact *everyone* on board is hearing it has me wishing I was invisible.

"She needs to go," Phoenix snarls. "Find someone else."

"She's the best person for the job," Chandler maintains.

That only makes Phoenix angrier. "No, she's not." The sound of something crashing makes the girl feeling up Memphis flinch. "How the fuck would you feel if I went digging around your past, huh? Or contacted one of your ex-girlfriends and invited them on tour? Would you like that, asswipe?"

The girl sucking face with Memphis dislodges her lips from his. "I thought Phoenix didn't do girlfriends?"

He doesn't.

Unless he wants to use you.

CHAPTER 29
PHOENIX

The noise from the Vegas crowd is deafening as I walk backstage.

Storm and Memphis follow behind me like two blood-hounds tracking a scent.

"Why aren't you singing Sharp Objects?" Storm questions.

"This is now the second time you walked off without singing it," Memphis grumbles, as if I wasn't aware. "What gives?"

Anger mixed with feelings I'd rather not acknowledge swarms in my gut. "Fuck off."

It's clear they don't like that answer, but I don't give a shit.

Fortunately, a group of chicks hanging out in the far corner gives me the perfect excuse to exit this bullshit conversation.

"Hey, Phoenix," one of them purrs. "You were really great tonight."

I'm approaching them when there's a sharp tug on my arm. "Not a good idea."

I peer down at Lennon, forcing myself to ignore the way my blood pressure and cock seem to rise whenever she's near.

"Why? Afraid you'll get fired?"

Since my dipshit manager refuses to sack her on my orders, I'm going to give him another reason to send her sweet ass packing.

Lennon opens her mouth to speak, but I don't give her the chance. "Your job isn't to control where I stick my dick."

I motion for the girls to join me in the greenroom.

Then I wink at Lennon. "But, hey. You're welcome to watch."

My statement has the desired impact because she makes a face like she smelled something rotten as the girls rush past her. "I'd rather swallow battery acid." Clearly annoyed, she huffs. "Whatever. Get your rocks off. But I'll be standing right outside this door."

Holding her gaze, I step inside the room. "In that case, I'll try not to make them scream too loud when I'm *balls deep* inside them."

I slam the door in her pretty face and lock it.

A redhead I've met a few times before saunters over to me. "You were incredible out there. It made me so hot."

The blonde and brunette close in on me a moment later.

I halt the redhead when she drops to her knees because I have more important things to focus on.

"Save that thought for later. We're gonna party first."

Unbeknownst to my new sober companion, there's another door inside the greenroom.

One of them giggles as I escort the pack out. "Well, you know what they say. What happens in Vegas stays in Vegas."

Not this time.

Smirking, I walk down the hallway that will lead to my freedom and Lennon's unemployment.

Good luck explaining this one to Chandler, Groupie.

I pound on the door. "Open up, Phoenix."

He's been in the greenroom for over an hour already.

It's almost two in the morning and I want to go back to the hotel so I can go to sleep.

I bang on the door again. Hell, I'm tempted to kick it down at this point. "Hurry up."

"What are you still doing here?" a stern voice belonging to my new boss questions.

I keep my expression neutral. "Phoenix is in there screwing some groupies."

No point in lying. Like Phoenix said, what he does with his dick isn't my responsibility. Nor is it in my job description.

Which is just fine by me, because I don't give a rat's ass. The damn thing can fall off from an incurable STD for all I care.

Heck, it probably will sooner or later.

Chandler rubs his head. "In that case, I'm heading back to my room for the night. Make sure he gets back to *his*."

"Will do."

He grumbles something under his breath as he stomps away.

When I look around, I notice most of the crew has disappeared, and the ones left seem to be shutting everything down.

If this asshole thinks I'm going to spend the rest of the night—make that *morning*—backstage when I can be sleeping in a nice, cozy bed, he's out of his mind.

Growing frustrated, I flag down a passing crew member. "Hey. Do you have a key to this room, by any chance? I'm with the band."

"I don't. But Bruce does." He gestures for another man to come over. "She needs to get into the greenroom."

"Sure thing."

Bruce produces a key from his pocket and unlocks it.

My stomach twists before dropping to the floor.

I was expecting Phoenix to be mid-thrust when I walked in...

Not *gone*.

"Where the hell did he go?"

"Who?" one of the guys asks.

"Phoenix Walker. He was supposed to be in here."

The guy points to a door on the other side of the room. "He probably went out that way. There's a long hallway that leads out to the strip."

Fuck.

I make a mental note to check all greenrooms, bathrooms, and whatever other rooms Phoenix intends to enter in the future as I walk down the corridor of our hotel.

I mutter a curse when I swipe the key card because I don't hear voices or fake moans of pleasure.

Walking past my adjoining room in the foyer, I enter his suite.

After checking every possible nook and cranny, I come up empty.

Out of options, I go to Storm's room so I can enlist his help.

I knock five times before he answers.

It's clear he's annoyed at being interrupted because he swings the door open and grunts, "What?"

"I can't find Phoenix."

He expels a long sigh. "Shit." Turning his head, he bellows, "Be a good girl and stay put. I'll be back later."

"I couldn't leave even if I wanted to," some girl replies. "But don't be gone for too long. I need that big angry monster inside me."

Big angry monster?

I file that under things I didn't need to know about Storm.

He closes the door behind him. "Where was Phoenix when you saw him last?"

"In the greenroom with some groupies."

"You know there are two doors in the greenroom, right?"

I don't miss the hint of jest in his tone.

"I do *now*."

In my defense, the one and only time I was inside it was when I realized Phoenix had vanished.

I'll never make *that* mistake again.

We stop at another room and Storm bangs on the door.

A buck-naked Memphis answers...along with a blonde whose lips are fused to his neck.

I keep my gaze trained above his waist.

Then I remember I'm young, single, curious...and he's famous, nude, and hot.

Yup. Little Memphis is the opposite of little.

Evidently, the members of Sharp Objects all have *large* objects.

Memphis gives me a sly smile when he catches me staring. "You're welcome to come inside. I've got plenty to go around."

"She can't," Storm rumbles. "Phoenix is missing. Have you seen him?"

He shakes his head. "Nah. Have you tried his cell?"

"Unless his number is the same one from high school, I don't have it."

After fetching his phone from his pocket, Storm brings it to his ear. "Straight to voice mail."

My stomach knots.

The blonde kisses her way down Memphis's stomach, drawing his attention back to her. "You're gonna have to do better than that if you want my cock again." He looks at us when she drops to her knees. "Good luck."

Then he slams the door in our faces.

Storm marches down the hall. "Let's check the casino downstairs."

Planet Hollywood is essentially one giant circle which should make it easy to spot him…

If he was here.

Exasperated, we exit the hotel and walk onto the strip. It's after two a.m., but it's a weekend in Vegas so there are tons of people outside.

Which is why I don't think twice when I notice a large crowd gathered around the Bellagio fountains.

Until we get closer and I notice a bunch of cops and firemen surrounding the area.

Storm must be curious too, because he stops walking.

"What's going on?" I ask a woman who's shaking her head as she ambles away from the crowd.

"Some idiot jumped into the fountain during the last show. Emergency services just fished him out. He's lucky he didn't die."

Damn. "That's crazy."

She nods in agreement before strolling away.

"Maybe we should split up?" I suggest.

This way, the odds of finding him are better. Because I'm exhausted.

Storm mulls this over. "I guess—"

Suddenly, he stops talking and I stop breathing.

Because twenty feet away is a dripping-wet Phoenix Walker… being dragged away by two police officers.

"I didn't pee in the pool," Phoenix slurs.

"It's not a pool," one of the officer's grits out. "It's a fountain."

"You piece of fuck," Phoenix grumbles as we race over. "Go shit yourself."

I'm so screwed.

"Calm down," the second officer says.

"Don't tell me what to do, prick. I'm Phoenix fucking Walker."

He yells the last part so loud I wince.

"I'm aware," the officer states. "My daughter's a big fan."

"Wait," I tell the officers as they lead him away. "I'm his—"

I stop talking because I don't think telling them I'm his sober companion when he's clearly trashed will work in my favor.

"Friend," I settle on, despite the way it makes my insides twist. "Please don't arrest him."

"Arrest me, pussies," Phoenix roars, trying to get out of their hold. "I don't fucking care."

I'd punch him if we weren't in front of law enforcement.

Storm glares at his friend before looking at the officers. "You said your daughter's a fan, right?"

One of the officer's nods. "Yeah. Why?"

"I'll give you four front-row tickets to tomorrow night's show and backstage passes if you let us take him back to his room."

For a moment, I don't think they're going to agree, but then the officers look at each other and shrug. "All right, but if it happens again, we're taking him in."

"It won't," I assure them as they let go of Phoenix.

"Thanks," Storm says, as we each grab one of his arms. "I'll make sure the tickets are at will call tomorrow."

They walk off and we escort a belligerent and wet Phoenix back to the hotel.

Although he doesn't make it easy because he keeps yelling obscenities and drawing attention to himself.

"Will you stop?" I grit through my teeth when we step inside the elevator, and he asks some poor old lady if she wants to suck him off.

Understandably horrified, she threatens to get security.

"I'm so sorry." The moment we reach our floor, I shove him out of the elevator. "What is *wrong* with you?"

"Too fucking much," Storm mutters under his breath.

"I just wanted a hummer," Phoenix bellows loud enough to wake the dead.

We wrangle him down the hallway as he proceeds to sing, "(I Can't Get No) Satisfaction" by The Rolling Stones. His *distinctive* melodic voice bounces off the walls of the hallway as he struggles against us.

He ends up putting up such a fight he breaks free from our hold. "Peace out, bitches."

The control I was trying to maintain snaps as Storm surges forward and snatches his arm.

"You need to shut the fuck up. Right now." I slam my hand over his mouth. "Or so help me God, I will bring you back to that fountain and drown your ass."

His voice is muffled against my palm. "What's in it for me?"

I remove my hand. "What?"

"What do I get out of it?" he slurs.

I look at Storm, who shrugs.

Annoyed, I huff, "What do you want?"

Those blue eyes languidly peruse every inch of my body before settling on my face. "You."

All his partying must have destroyed a few brain cells. "I am not fucking yo—"

"Kiss me."

That's even more appalling. "Absolutely not."

Tilting his face up to the ceiling, Phoenix starts yelling obscenities again.

Dammit.

"Fine," I concede, because I'm desperate for him to be quiet. "I'll do it."

Chances are he'll be too drunk to remember I agreed to such an offer anyway. But if he does?

I never said it had to be on the lips.

"But only if you shut up and let me take you back to the room."

"Deal," he utters as the door across from us opens...

And Chandler pops his head out.

Shit.

Anger tightens his features as he takes in a drunk and wet Phoenix. "What the hell is going on?"

Phoenix starts to speak, but Storm clamps a hand over his mouth this time.

"Nothing. Phoenix just went for a swim." When Chandler's brows furrow, I quickly add, "Don't worry. No one saw him."

Those beady eyes narrow. "They better not have. Or else."

He slams the door and we finally make our way to the suite.

"He's all yours," Storm says as we enter the small foyer separating our rooms. "I have company I need to get back to."

I'll say. His girl's been tied up for a while now.

"I really appreciate all your help."

There's no way I would have been able to convince those cops to let Phoenix go without him.

Or drag his plastered ass back to the hotel all by myself.

Storm wags a finger at his friend. "Don't give her any more shit."

"Don't tell me what to do," Phoenix spits.

Luckily Storm lets that roll off his back and leaves.

I lug Phoenix inside his suite.

I'm thankful I had the foresight to set up those restraints on his bed ahead of time.

Once we reach the bedroom, I shove him onto the mattress.

I briefly debate helping him change into dry clothes, but after tonight's *antics*, he can sleep in his drenched ones.

Unfortunately, mine end up wet too because Phoenix fights me tooth and nail when I try to restrain him.

"I believe you owe me something," he rasps as he seizes my hips and rolls us over so he's on top.

I ignore the large bulge digging into my pelvis.

"I don't owe you shit," I tell him, but then I realize it's the only bargaining chip I have at my disposal.

"If you let me put these on, I'll do it."

A muscle in his sharp jaw bunches as he moves off me. It's clear he doesn't like it, but tough shit.

If he didn't act like a feral animal, he wouldn't need to be locked up like one.

I make quick work of fastening the cuffs around his wrists, but he protests when I reach for the ankle ones. "Wrists only, Groupie."

"Fine." I check to make sure the cuffs are secure. "But I better find you just like this when I wake up."

I start to move off the bed, but he jerks upward. "Aren't you forgetting something?"

"Nope."

I already got what I needed. He can go fuck himself.

"I won't be so willing to compromise next time," he snaps to my retreating back.

Willing to compromise my ass. However, I can't afford to have another night like this if I'm going to make it to the end of this tour and get paid.

I want to slap the self-satisfied look off his face as I return to the bed.

"This doesn't change anything between us."

Leaning down, I aim for his cheek...but he turns his head at the last second, capturing my lips.

A bolt of heat punches through me, and my heart—the traitorous moron—flutters wildly. A low groan leaves him as his tongue slides inside...but I finally come to my senses and break the spell.

Backing away, I wipe my mouth, hoping to remove whatever traces of him are left, even though I feel him *everywhere*.

I hate it. *Hate him.*

"Go to sleep, asshole."

CHAPTER 31
PHOENIX

"Lennon," I bark for the hundredth time since I've been awake.

I know she's up because I heard the door to her room open and shut not too long ago.

Brat.

This is her sick way of trying to get me back for that kiss last night.

A kiss she's pissed about because she not only enjoyed it. She *felt* it.

Lennon can hate me all she wants—hell, she can scream it from the top of the highest mountain until her lungs give out—but she can't deny our chemistry.

It's fucking napalm.

I could screw every woman in the world, but no one will ever come close to making me feel even a small fraction of what she does.

She's like poison and magic rolled into one. I want to push her far away and pull her closer at the same time.

Which is all the more reason I'll be happy when she's gone.

Not only does she admittedly want to *ruin* me, she's the one and only thing on the planet that I can't fucking have.

Fortunately, the shit I pulled last night will guarantee her a seat on the next flight home.

I just need her to get her ass in here and uncuff me first.

Pressure on my bladder constricts and I yell for her again. "Come on, Groupie."

Finally, my bedroom door opens. Only it's not her who walks inside.

It's Storm.

"Why are you here?"

"I saw Lennon downstairs." Lips twitching, he walks over to the bed. "Figured you were still a little *tied up*."

The son of a bitch has jokes.

"Laugh it up while you can, fucker. It's not happening again."

"What do you mean?"

"Thanks to my drunken dip in the fountain, she'll be getting the ax."

Which probably explains why she never came in here. She's pissed she got fired.

Too fucking bad.

The hand that was uncuffing my wrist stills. "Hold up. You did that shit on purpose?"

For someone with such a high IQ, he can be dumb as a brick sometimes.

"Fuck yeah, I did. I told you, I want her gone."

Does anyone fucking listen when I speak?

Oh, that's right. They're all too busy profiting off my voice to give a fuck about the man behind it.

I'm no longer a person. *I'm a product.*

Storm's eyes become tiny slits. "You're an asshole."

"How am I the asshole in this scenario? She's the one who came here, remember?"

The vein in his forehead makes an appearance. "Because she needs the money."

That gets a laugh out of me. "Yeah, right. Are you forgetting she lives like a princess in that nice, big house?"

Unlike us, Lennon didn't have to want for a damn thing growing up. Everything was handed to her on a silver platter by her dad.

Crossing his arms, he stares me down. "Is that why she's working at Obsidian?"

The only *Obsidian* I know is the strip club back in Hillcrest.

And fuck knows Lennon would never work there.

She wouldn't even let me take off her shirt when we fucked during a blackout. Ergo, the likelihood of her taking off her clothes for a roomful of men doesn't add up.

"What the fuck are you talking about?"

Taking mercy on me, he uncuffs one of my wrists. "I heard from a buddy back in town that she's working there." He frowns. "She obviously needs the money."

And he needs to lay off the weed. "She's not—"

"It's where Chandler tracked her down, man. If you don't believe me, ask him."

A weird mixture of rage, jealousy, and uneasiness coils in my gut.

I want to ask him more about it, but the door opens and Lennon waltzes in. "Oh, you're up." Her eyes fall to my unbound wrists. "And free."

"As much as you're enjoying this, it's not cool to leave me restrained so long. A man has to take a piss every once in a while."

I'm getting ready to do just that when Chandler storms inside, waving around his phone.

"He jumped into the goddamn *fountain* last night?"

To her credit, Lennon doesn't cower like most people do when he goes on a rampage. "I told you he went swimming."

Storm snorts, which only pisses Chandler off more.

"You also told me you could handle the job."

"I can handle it." She sweeps a hand in my direction. "He's not in jail. It didn't hit the news—"

"There are pictures all over social media," Chandler shouts. "You're fired."

Her strong demeanor diminishes. "But—"

"It's not her fault," I interject.

I don't know why she's working at Obsidian, but I *do* know she wouldn't be unless she had no other choice.

As much as I don't want her here, I don't want her *there* even more.

"I lied and snuck out," I say when he whips around to face me. "She tracked me down, though. She also convinced the cops to let me go. I think that warrants another shot."

Chandler's gaze is scrutinizing. "I thought you wanted her gone?"

"It was only her third night," Storm cuts in. "And she's already doing better than the others since she didn't fuck him."

Chandler doesn't look swayed by this one bit.

"Christ. I went swimming in a damn fountain. No one got hurt or arrested, thanks to Lennon." I take a step closer. "Fire her and it will get a whole lot worse. Trust me."

My threat works because he looks at Lennon, who's eyeing me with keen interest. "I'll give you one more chance. But fuck up again, and you're *done*."

CHAPTER 32

According to Mrs. Palma, my dad is doing well. Although when I spoke to him last, he thought I was trying to sell him something and rushed me off the phone.

I'm hoping tomorrow's conversation goes a lot better.

We're currently on our way to Arizona, so I'm sleeping in the bunk below Phoenix's.

Or rather, *trying* to sleep, but I can't stop tossing and turning. A quick glance at my phone tells me it's a little after three a.m.

Given everyone else on the bus is sleeping soundly, I step out for a little quiet time.

The front of the bus has a kitchen and lounge area, the middle section is where our bunks are, and the back is where Chandler's room is. However, there's also another tiny lounge area located in the rear that has a television, so I decide to go there.

The small leather sofa is comfortable, despite the tight quarters. I'm looking around for the remote when the sliding door opens and a shirtless Phoenix walks in.

I get off the couch, but he takes several steps, cornering me. "Stay."

It's not a request, it's an order.

I shoot him a dirty look as I sit back down and he takes a seat next to me.

The close proximity makes the small space feel even more cramped.

"Why are you still up?"

The thick rasp of his voice has the tiny hairs on my arms standing on end.

"I can't sleep." I peer over at him. "Why are *you* still up?"

He has to be exhausted after back-to-back concerts.

Those magnetic blue eyes look me up and down and I resist the urge to squirm. "I can't sleep either."

Whatever hostility he was harboring appears to be gone...which is strange.

So was him telling Chandler to give me another chance.

"Why did you stick up for me this morning? That was your prime opportunity to get rid of me."

His jaw sets and some emotion I can't quite pinpoint flickers across his face. "Why are you working at Obsidian?"

I feel like I've just been dunked in a vat of ice water. I'm not sure how he knows, but my guess is Chandler told him.

Doesn't mean I have to talk about it, though. He lost the right to know anything about me or my life when he betrayed me.

"That's none of your business."

The tendons in his throat flex as he swallows. "In that case, I'm not answering your question either."

His tit-for-tat tactic doesn't surprise me one bit.

It's how we've always been with one another.

"But since you're staying," he continues. "I think we should call some kind of truce."

I want to tell him to go fuck himself, but I need the money.

Us not being at each other's throats every second of the day and night will make my job a lot easier.

"Fine." I stand. "I'm going back to bed."

His fingers wrap around my wrist. "Lennon."

There's so much longing in his tone it makes my skin heat.

"I said truce." I hold his stare. "We're not friends."

We never were.

My heart slams painfully against my rib cage when I glance down at his tattoo.

The first time I saw the clef and staff, there weren't any music notes. When I asked him why it was blank, he said he was waiting to write the song that would change his life.

Yet, the notes inked over his heart are *mine*. Not his.

Disgusted, I yank my wrist out of his grasp and walk out.

Phoenix was right.

It's a lot easier when they don't see it coming.

CHAPTER 33
LENNON

The roar of the crowd pulsates through my ears as I watch Phoenix run around the stage.

Bright lights illuminate his form, and despite it being hot as hell where I'm standing, a shiver runs through me.

He's putting every ounce of himself into this performance and it's both awe inspiring and intimidating how comfortable and hypnotic he is up there.

Like he's in his element.

Like he was born to do this.

A bitter feeling rises up my throat. I'd kill to know what it's like to not only have that level of confidence to be able to sing in front of thousands of people, but to be so incredibly talented no one can take their eyes off you.

To be him.

The song he's belting comes to an end and the stage lights dim, just like they always do when it's time for him to sing the last song of the night.

My stomach knots with equal parts vexation and intrigue.

It's our third and final show in Arizona and he still hasn't sung "Sharp Objects."

Memphis, Storm, and George don't even bother cueing up the intro this time.

Once again, you can feel the disappointment from the fans when Phoenix raises his middle finger in the air and tells them all to have a good night.

"Dammit," Chandler mutters beside me. "What the hell is his problem?"

I have to bite my cheek to keep from smiling.

Me.

Phoenix refusing to sing my song has become the proverbial elephant in the room.

Or *elevator* in this case.

It's so quiet you could hear a pin drop and the twenty floors it takes to get to our hotel room feels like a million.

Even though he's standing behind me and I'm grateful I don't have to look at him, I wish we weren't alone.

Especially when he speaks.

"You never sit in the greenroom during shows."

It's not a question, it's a fact.

One that doesn't warrant my acknowledgment.

I can feel the heat emanating from him as he moves closer, stepping into my personal space.

His breath fans the side of my neck with his next statement. "Whenever I look over, you're always standing right there… watching me."

Because I hate him.

I straighten my spine. "You know what they say. Keep your friends close and your enemies closer."

My skin prickles when his fingers skim the side of my waist. "I don't have to be your enemy, Groupie."

I'm tempted to remind him that I'm *not* his groupie, but I'm too thrown by what he said.

As long as I'm alive, he'll never be anything more than my enemy.

I turn around. "What's the matter, Phoenix? You don't like me watching you?" I take a step, but he doesn't budge so my body ends up flush against his. "Then again, it must be awfully hard to sing the words you stole in front of the person you stole them from, huh?"

There's so much venom in his stare I know I've gotten right to the crux of it.

Even though he won't admit it, deep down he knows what he did was not only wrong, it makes him nothing but a phony.

The elevator doors finally open and he sidesteps me, shoulder-checking me in the process.

"Aw, did I hit a nerve?" I taunt as I follow close behind.

Irritation bolts down my spine when he doesn't say a word. He *still* won't give me the satisfaction of owning up to what he did.

However, my annoyance for him quickly turns to annoyance for the group of girls hanging outside his door.

Not only is it alarming that they managed to find out what room he's staying in, I am not in the mood to spend the rest of my night chasing him around town again.

"Don't you have security?"

"Don't want it." He takes the key card out of his pocket. "Not for them."

I place my hand on his wrist when he goes to open the door. "Don't do this."

Those harsh blue eyes zero in on me and the corner of his lip curls.

"Why? You offering me something better?"

The slightest flicker of pain—pain shielded by the armor I've built over these past four years—spreads throughout my chest.

I would have given him everything.

"Once upon a time I did. But you fucked that up."

Removing my own key card from my purse, I stride over to the room next to his.

The rage and hurt burrowing under my skin rises to the surface when I realize Phoenix is behind me as I open the door.

I try to close it on him, but he plows through it. It shuts with a loud slam.

"Why are you in here?" Animosity spirals in my stomach as I face him. "You have a hallway full of girls. Take your dirty dick out there and harass one of them."

He stands there, glaring at me for several long seconds.

When he finally speaks, his voice is filled with acrimony. "Wow. Judgmental much? Sorry, I'm not a self-righteous prude like you."

It's downright comical that he thinks I'm still an innocent virgin.

"Prude?" Shooting him a cold glare of my own, I place a hand on my chest. "Did you really think after the *stellar* half sex you gave me, I wasn't going to go out there and find guys who could, I don't know…do a much better job and finish?"

Anger comes off him in violent waves as he surges forward. "The only reason that didn't happen is because you're a fucking liar."

This time, I do laugh. It's impossible not to after that statement. "You're one to talk. Last I checked, you were the one who pretended you wanted to *pursue* things with me so you could steal my song, remember?"

I know I've got him because he doesn't have a retort.

Then again, how could he? We both know I'm right.

His eyes drop to something on the floor. "You still have it."

When I look down, I see the Papa Roach shirt he gave me.

The one I refused to wash for a month straight because it still smelled like him and my dumb teenage broken heart kept hoping he'd contact me and apologize for hooking up with Sabrina.

I shrug nonchalantly so he won't read too much into it. "It's not the band's fault you're an asshole."

He stares at his former shirt for a few more moments before walking to the door.

I take a deep, cleansing breath; thankful he's going because I hate these conflicting feelings oscillating within me whenever we're in the same room.

He's almost to the door when he halts his steps.

"I wasn't pretending with you, Lennon." Turning, he holds my gaze. "And yeah, I've fucked a lot of women." His expression turns pained and his voice drops to a whisper. "Because after things ended between us, I knew I lost you for good."

My heart folds in on itself as he walks out.

Yeah…you did.

CHAPTER 34
PHOENIX

Lennon scowls from her new bunk. "Stop staring at me."

Apparently the one beneath mine was too close for comfort after last night's conversation, so she asked Storm to switch when we loaded onto the bus.

What she didn't realize at the time was that his bunk is directly across from mine. Which gives me a prime view of her.

She's currently sitting with her legs tucked underneath her while listening to music on her phone...trying her best to ignore me.

"Can we switch back?" Lennon asks when Storm passes us on his way to the bathroom.

The look I give him makes it clear I oppose it.

"No backsies," he mumbles before disappearing.

However, my victory is short-lived because George the wannabe climbs out of his bottom bunk. "I'll switch with you."

Asswipe. "Can't," I inform him. "Only original members of the band can authorize bunk arrangements."

It's a bullshit rule I just made up on the fly.

One Lennon calls me out on. "Oh, please. Since when?"

"Since always." I knock on the bunk above mine. "Tell her, Memphis."

"It's true," he says in a sleepy voice.

"You're being juvenile," Lennon mutters before regarding George. "Want to go watch a movie?"

"Sure."

Not happening. Not without me anyway.

I've seen the way George looks at her, and if the motherfucker values his eyeballs, he'll cut the shit out.

She might not be my *friend*, but she sure as fuck isn't his. Or anyone else's.

Exiting my bunk, I stand and stretch. "Which one do you have in mind? I prefer action flicks, but I can get down with some suspense or horror."

Lennon looks like she's about to throw a hissy fit, but the sliding door opens, and Chandler comes in.

"A word, Phoenix."

It's never just a word with him. It's a never-ending sermon.

I don't miss the taunting look Lennon gives me before she and George head toward the back of the bus.

"What do you want?" I bark as Chandler gestures for me to follow him into the kitchen.

Frustration colors his face as he takes a seat at the small table. "Did you call Skylar like I asked you to the other day?"

I don't recall him asking. I recall him *demanding* I call her because evidently some of our fans are complaining online about me no longer singing Sharp Objects at concerts.

However, talking to Skylar is the last thing I want to do. "No."

The bus comes to an abrupt stop in front of a hotel, which is weird because we're nowhere near Colorado. "Why are we stopping here?"

Ignoring my question, he huffs, "You better get a pair of tweezers, pull out the bug that crawled up your ass, and sing the goddamn song at the next show."

I can't. *Not while Lennon's here.*

"I'll call Skylar later."

That will get him off my case for a bit.

He smiles snidely. "No need."

Without warning, the bus door opens, and a familiar petite blonde climbs up the stairs.

Fuck.

"Why is she here?"

"Nice to see you too, Phoenix," Skylar chirps as she wheels her luggage on board, although she doesn't make eye contact.

I don't blame her. I can barely look at myself in the mirror these days.

Outrage and guilt coil in my gut. "You didn't need to drag her on tour because of a damn song."

"Simmer down," Chandler says. "You're not the only one giving me issues."

That's news to me. "Who else is causing problems?"

The door to the bunk area opens and Memphis—who was about to walk out—freezes when he sees Skylar.

Chandler's eyes become tiny slits. "Him."

Unlike Storm, who butts his nose in my business and brought Lennon here, I exit the kitchen.

Memphis is my boy, but—not my monkeys, not my circus.

Fuck knows I have enough of my own shit to deal with.

Like Lennon cozying up in the movie room with George when she's supposed to be here for me.

If I had any doubt George is into Lennon, I don't anymore. Not only do I catch him staring at her every couple of minutes…they're watching some romantic comedy movie.

One I'm now forced to suffer through.

I'm relieved when the credits finally start rolling.

Until he opens his big, fat trap.

"Want to watch another one?"

Fucking hell.

Lennon opens her mouth, but I cut her off before she gets a word out. "She can't. We have important business matters to discuss."

That earns me a look from Lennon. "What important business matters?"

I glare at George. "Do you mind?"

The glare he returns tells me he does, but I don't give a fuck.

He rises off the couch. "No problem. I have to give my mom a call anyway."

Jesus. What a loser.

Lennon's expression softens. "I had fun."

Liar.

The dirt on the bottom of my shoe is more appealing than this dipshit.

"Me too."

George gives her that look again. The one that makes it clear he wants to fuck her more than he wants his next breath.

Tough fucking shit.

The moment he leaves, I cross my arms and smile. "You're welcome."

Arching an eyebrow, Lennon shifts toward me. "For what?"

I jut my chin at the door. "Getting rid of him."

Irritation creeps over her features. "I didn't need you to get rid of him."

Visibly frustrated, she rises from the couch.

I figured she'd be grateful, not upset.

Standing, I grab her arm before she walks out. "There's no way you're into that guy."

He's not her type. Not only in the looks department, but the dude has the personality and merit of a used condom.

Lennon needs someone who's not afraid to challenge her and show her new things.

Someone who's not afraid to fight with her.

Snatching her arm out of my grasp, she scoffs. "Not that it's any of your business, but maybe I am."

Now, *I'm* the one who's irritated.

She goes to leave again, but I'm not finished with her. "You can't date him."

A snort rings out, filling the small room. "Why is that?"

Because she belongs to me while she's on this tour. Not that jackass.

"It's a conflict of interest." When her eyes narrow, I lean in. "It's your job to be there for me when I need you. You can't do that if you're running around with him."

A hint of challenge flickers in her baby browns. "Then I'll hang out with George whenever you don't need me. Problem solved."

The *need* I have for her sends a surge of lust straight to my groin, so no. Problem not solved.

Far from it.

I move closer, so close she has nowhere else to go because she's pinned between me and the wall.

So close, I know she feels every inch thickening in my jeans. "No."

"No?" She purses her lips. "Last I checked, Chandler is my boss. He specifically told me I was free to hook up with anyone I wanted to as long as it wasn't you...which *obviously* isn't a concern."

I make a mental note to talk to him later because that's bullshit.

"He might be your boss, but I'm the one who pays most of his salary. I'm also your client." Placing my hands on the wall on either side of her head, I brush my lips over her ear. I want her to hear me loud and fucking clear. "Sleep with him and you're fired."

She's so full of rage she practically vibrates with it. "Let me get this straight. I'm not allowed to fuck George, but fucking you is fine?"

I run my nose down the column of her throat, inhaling her. "Since you're offering..."

"I'm not." Pure contempt fills her voice. "Let me put it this way. If I was on fire, and the only way to extinguish it was to have sex with you...I'd beg someone to pour gasoline on me."

I highly doubt it.

She may hate me, but I'm positive there's still a part of me she wants.

Wrapping that long, silky ponytail around my fist, I tug her head back. "You used to love my cock, Groupie." Her breath hitches when my teeth graze the long line of her neck. "You sucked it like it was the best thing you ever tasted and swallowed every drop of my cum like you couldn't get enough of it."

Fuck knows I still think about that night, because what Lennon lacked in experience, she made up for in enthusiasm and revere... making it one of the best blow jobs I've ever received. *Despite the interruption.*

I'm about to push her on her knees so I can give her a thorough reminder, but her next words stop me dead in my tracks.

"That was before you betrayed me, and I found out what kind of person you really were."

I try to ignore the twinge of guilt now warring with my lust, but it's impossible. "Lennon—"

"Admit it," she whispers. The sorrow in her voice has me releasing my hold on her. "Fess up to what you did, and we can go back to being friends." I swallow a groan when she rubs my erection through my sweatpants. "Say it and I'll do anything you want."

The temptation, her offer, and the sexy way she's looking at me goes straight to my cock, inciting me to give in. "I—"

A peculiar feeling slams into me, and the admission gets stuck in my throat.

Something's *off*. Not only is she effortlessly offering herself up on a silver platter...there's a trace of eagerness in her tone.

Her stare peevishly darts over my face as I slide my hands up her thighs, and the intuitive feeling brewing in the pit of my stomach grows.

A tiny squeal of surprise leaves her when I grab her ass, grinding my dick against her. "That so, huh?"

My hands slither under her shirt and smooth, buttery skin meets my fingertips. It takes every ounce of willpower I have not to tear those leggings off, bend her over the couch, and fuck her senseless.

Continuing my journey, I caress her waist.

Uneasiness crosses over her features.

Which tells me I'm getting closer.

Attempting to elude me, she crushes her mouth against mine.

The move almost works because the second our tongues touch, I lose my focus.

Then I feel it.

Biting her lip so hard she hisses, I snatch the phone cradled in her bra.

Lennon goes rigid, but the beating black hole in my chest doesn't want to believe she'd do this to me.

My gut coils with dread when I look at it.

Just like I suspected, she's been recording everything.

While I didn't think she was joking about wanting to ruin me, I didn't think her heart—or our truce—would let her go through with it.

Because deep down she still gave a shit about me and we were friends.

But I was wrong.

Lennon's out for blood.

I won't give her a drop of it, though.

She tries to take her phone back, but I put several feet of distance between us and hold it out of her reach.

I pin her with a warning glare as I press the delete button and hand it back to her. "Safe to say our truce is over, Groupie."

Scathing, her upper lip curls in a cute little snarl. "You're a fucking fraud. Everything you have is because of me."

Lennon helped me get my foot in the door, but everything I have is because I worked my ass off for it.

I'm the one who put their blood, sweat, and tears into every part of this career that was once nothing but an ambitious dream too far from the trailer-park kid's reach.

I'm the one who defied all odds and crawled out of the shithole the world thought I was destined to stay in.

I'm the one who's given up parts of myself that she could never understand in order to preserve and experience those fleeting moments of magic I live and breathe for.

Even though deep down she wishes it was her.

Because just like back then, Lennon wants to be me so bad I can fucking taste it.

Which is the real reason she's standing here.

Wrath, and my craving for her, strengthen as I edge closer. "You're not here for revenge. Despite how hard you try to convince yourself that's your motive." She glares hate fire at me as I skate my palm up the length of her neck. "You're here because you want what I have. Because you want to know what it's like." I grip her chin, forcing her to look into my eyes. "Tell me I'm wrong."

She can't.

I gesture to the phone she's holding. "Attempt to fuck me over again and I'll send you back to that strip club so fast your pretty head will spin." I can practically see smoke coming out of her ears as I sweep my thumb along her parted lips. "And stay away from George."

Her eyes narrow. "You don't scare me, Phoenix."

I palm her cheek. "That may be true, but we both know the hand you're threatening to play isn't a strong one."

She can't prove shit. Ergo it's her word against mine.

And I have millions of fans around the world who'd unquestionably believe she's nothing more than a high school stalker trying to get her five minutes of fame.

"Fuck you," she grits through her teeth. "You should be down on your knees apologizing and begging for my forgiveness."

That's quite the little fantasy she has.

"I'll get on my knees for you." I flash her a smug smirk. "But it won't be to apologize or beg."

Disgust fills her expression. "You're an—"

"I need to talk to you, Phoenix," Skylar interjects.

"Knock next time," I bark.

Skylar's eyes go big and remorse hits me like a brick to the head.

I already killed her fiancé, there's no need to be a dick to her on top of it.

"Have fun with your groupie," Lennon mutters under her breath as Skylar disappears.

Biting my lip ring, I rake my gaze over every inch of that curvy body. "I plan on it."

Lennon came here to start a war…

She's got one.

CHAPTER 35

Evidently, the girl who interrupted our *conversation* isn't a groupie, because when I walk out to the kitchen, I see her talking to Phoenix instead of screwing him.

Or rather, *trying* to, because he won't even look at her.

Upon noticing me enter, he promptly gets up.

The pretty blonde twists around in her seat as he stalks away. "Come on, Phoenix. We need to figure something out."

Ignoring her, he grabs a bottle of Jack off the counter and brushes past me.

My curiosity comes to a peak and I blurt, "Who are you?"

It's probably none of my business—but seeing as she not only claimed the last bunk, she was attempting to have a serious discussion with Phoenix—it's obvious the girl is more than a hookup.

"I'm Skylar...the new publicist," she says, and I detect a hint of the same Southern accent Memphis has.

Her presence explains a lot now. "Oh."

"You must be Lennon."

"Yeah."

Giving me a warm smile, she waves me over. "Since we're the only females staying on this bus, we should get to know one another."

Thanks to Sabrina and the rest of her cohorts torturing me throughout high school, I'm typically wary of girls who look like her.

However, she seems genuine and judging her for being beautiful and thin is no better than the way those girls judged me for not being either of those things.

I take a seat at the table. "How long have you been working for Sharp Objects?"

She draws in a deep breath before she answers. "A little over four years."

That's…strange. "I thought you said you were new?"

"The new publicist." Reaching for her water bottle, she takes a small sip. "I was a merch girl before that."

"Congrats on the promotion."

"Thanks." Her cheerful expression falters, and she looks down at the table. "I was only hired because I was Josh's fiancée."

My stomach twists with regret and sadness. I feel like a monster for congratulating her now.

"I'm so sorry."

"Can we not?" she whispers, her voice shaking. "I appreciate your condolences, but being the grieving widow is…"

My chest aches because I can't imagine how awful all this must be for her.

"Draining?"

"Yeah." She clutches the large diamond ring hanging from the thin gold chain around her neck. "When Josh was alive, people only interacted with me because I was his fiancée…and now they only do it because they feel bad." Her eyes find mine again. "It would be nice to have a real friend that actually likes me for me, you know?"

I nod.

"Anyway," she says, changing the subject. "I've always wanted to be a publicist, so I'm grateful for the opportunity."

"I imagine you must have your hands full with Phoenix." I wince. "I'll try to do a better job, so things will be easier for you."

Her nose crinkles. "Phoenix is definitely a handful, but he's not the biggest problem child of the group."

That's news to me. "He's not?"

She gives me a sad smile. "Nope. That was Josh." Something peculiar crosses over her expression and her lips press into a firm line. "Now it's his brother Memphis."

Safe to say she's piqued my interest. "What's going on with Memphis?"

"Please keep this information to yourself." Sighing, she rubs her temples. "Although it's now public knowledge thanks to the TMZ article that broke yesterday."

Uh-oh. "I won't say a word."

I couldn't even if I wanted to since I signed an NDA. Besides, Memphis isn't the one I want to destroy.

"Two women have come forward claiming to be pregnant with his baby." She exhales sharply. "One is a famous reality TV star, and the other…"

Her mouth clamps shut and she recoils, almost like it makes her physically sick to say the words.

"The other is a minor," she croaks after a moment.

I get why she looks so queasy.

"Wow…that's…"

"I know." Taking the elastic from her wrist, she piles her long, blonde hair into a knot on top of her head. "Between Phoenix's intoxicated antics and the stories about Memphis surfacing, Chandler thought it would be a good idea for me to come on tour."

I can understand why. "Yeah—"

I stop talking when the door to the bunk area opens and Phoenix and Memphis stagger out.

Frustration swells inside me as I zero in on the now empty bottle in Phoenix's hand.

"Don't mind us," Memphis slurs. "We just came to get a refill."

Skylar and I exchange an uneasy glance.

And then we get up from the table and handle our *problems*.

I watch Skylar shuffle through a stack of paperwork while we sit on the sofa in the greenroom. "What are you doing?"

"Trust me, you don't want to know."

Safe to say that only piques my curiosity more.

Sensing this, she makes a face. "Given what's happening with Memphis, I decided to make a few spreadsheets with everyone's hookups and the cities they took place in. This way, I can keep track of things."

I blink. "How in the world would you know all that?"

Granted, she's been with the band for four years, but there's no way she'd be able to keep track of *every* hookup they've had.

"I don't. These are just the ones I do remember." She pulls another face. "Along with the results of everyone's most recent STD test that I had them get yesterday." She circles something with her pen. "I don't want any more surprises or TMZ articles."

Can't say I blame her.

Curiosity strikes again and I eye the pile. I can't help but wonder just how long Phoenix's hookup list is.

I'm not as stealthy as I'd hoped, though, because Skylar catches me trying to sneak a peek. "George or Phoenix?"

"What?" I say as the song the band was playing comes to an end.

Seeing as Phoenix doesn't perform *my* song anymore, they should be walking in here any moment.

"You don't strike me as dumb, Lennon." Her voice drops to a conspiratorial whisper. "Who are you interested in? George or Phoenix?"

"Neither."

While I like Skylar, I'm not fond of this trick question.

Hurt flashes across her face. "And here I thought we were going to be friends."

The last thing I want to do is upset someone who already has so much to be upset over.

"George," I fib because I don't want her to get the wrong idea about my feelings for Phoenix.

She studies me as the first few bars of "Cryin'" by Aerosmith fill the venue.

"Why are they playing *that*?"

Skylar places the cap back on her marker. "Since Phoenix is still hell-bent on no longer singing Sharp Objects, I told him he should give a nod to his favorite artists that came before him and sing one of their songs at the end of every show. This way we could spin his bout of defiance into something positive and fans will stop complaining so much."

From a PR perspective, that's a genius move, but personally, I hate it.

I was enjoying watching Phoenix suffer whenever it came time to sing my song.

"George is clean," she tells me as she places the stack inside her giant purse. "And as far as I know, the only girl he's even remotely interested in…is you."

Oh boy. "Right."

Her gaze turns scrutinizing. "Something tells me you don't feel the same, though."

I shrug, feeling all kinds of uncomfortable with her line of questioning. "George is sweet."

She snorts. "*Sweet* is the kiss of death."

Damn her.

"It is not," I defend. "Sweet is good."

"Sweet is an elderly man holding a door open for his wife. Sweet is a six-year-old boy handing you weeds he thinks are flowers. Not guys you want to have hot, dirty sex with." Her lips twitch with humor. "You're so not into him."

I *could* be.

If a certain asshole would back the hell off.

"I don't know. It's too early to tell."

I'm pretty sure there's cheese in my fridge back home that I've known longer than George.

Besides, I'd take sweet over cold-blooded thief any day.

"Phoenix is clean, too," she says as the song comes to an end.

I stay silent.

However, right before the band barrels into the room, Skylar squeezes my hand and whispers, "Safe isn't always the safer option, Lennon."

I'm about to ask her to expand on that, but Phoenix walks in.

I want to slap the mocking smirk off his gorgeous face as he walks over to the couch. "Look who finally found the greenroom."

My retort dies when the rest of the guys come in, followed by a security guard and a small group of scantily clad girls.

"Everyone's cleared," he announces before the girls sidle up beside the guy of their choosing.

I immediately recognize the blonde Phoenix slings his arm around because she's the one who made a jab about my weight when I kicked her out of his suite two weeks ago.

My focus veers to George, who's grabbing a soda from the small fridge.

I'm not sure what Skylar meant with her last remark, but I do know what's best for me.

Sweet and safe.

"Not so fast." Skylar reaches into her purse and tosses condoms at the guys before she fixes her glare on the girls. "No pictures or videos, no posts on social media, and no talking to the press. Break the rules and it will be the last time any of you ever come back here. Got it?"

They start to nod, but Memphis throws his condom at Phoenix. "I'm gonna head back to the hotel and get some sleep." One of the girls tries to follow him, but he grinds out, "Alone."

Phoenix gestures for the girl to join him, and I don't miss the venomous look he aims my way. "More for me."

I'm not in the mood for his shenanigans.

I get off the couch. "Phoenix—"

"What?" He places an arm around the second girl's shoulders. "You want to take their place?" That deep, rough voice cuts like a blade as he looks me up and down with a taunting glint. "Or would you rather take *mine*?"

My fingers curl with the visceral urge to punch him, but I hold it together.

"Don't flatter yourself." I rub my temples, attempting to thwart off the migraine he's giving me. "I'm too tired to babysit you tonight, so do me a favor and go to bed."

He flashes the girls a panty-dropping grin. "That's exactly what I'm doing."

"In that case, you're off the hook," George declares as he strolls over to us. "Want to come to my room and watch a movie?"

Phoenix's nostrils flare, and I take the opportunity to give him a taste of his own medicine.

"No." An arrogant smile lifts the corner of his mouth...but it quickly falls when I follow that up with, "But you're welcome to come back to mine and watch one."

A muscle in his jaw tics and fury sparks in those blue orbs.

Mission accomplished.

"**T**hat really sucks." George reaches for another dumpling and takes a bite. "I'm sorry."

The plan was to watch a movie and order takeout, but we've been sitting on my bed talking for the last two hours.

He told me all about his parents, who are still happily married after thirty years, and his little sister, who he adores.

I ended up confiding in him about my mom and dad.

His brows furrow as he chews. "I can't imagine how hard that must be."

While I appreciate his sympathy, talking about my dad only makes me miss him even more.

According to Mrs. Palma, he's doing great, and when I spoke to him this morning he was in good spirits, but I hate not being able to see him.

I'm hoping she can convince him to use FaceTime for our next conversation.

I pluck a piece of chicken with my chopsticks. "Not to be a bitch, but can we change the subject?"

"Sure." He wipes his mouth with a napkin. "Of course." Glancing down, he releases a breath. "Actually, there's something I've been meaning to ask you."

He looks so serious, I stop eating. "What's up?"

"You and Phoenix—"

As if on cue, there's a sharp knock on the other side of the wall, followed by a deep, "Fuck yeah."

"I'm sorry," I grit out when the headboard thumping escalates. "You were saying?"

Visibly uneasy, George looks between me and the wall. "What's the deal with you two? I know you used to date, but…" His voice trails off and the banging finally stops.

I have to bite the inside of my cheek because it didn't last long.

Averting my gaze, I focus on my chicken and broccoli again. "We had a very short-lived thing back in high school, but it was nothing."

"It doesn't seem like nothing to him." His expression falters. "I just want to make sure I'm not barking up the wrong tree here."

It's on the tip of my tongue to tell him I'm not a tree, but he looks so earnest I don't have the heart to scold him.

"There are no feelings for him on my end." Other than *extreme* animosity. "If that's what you're worried about."

Seemingly relieved now, he smiles. "Good."

Unlike a certain asshole, I value honesty, so I tell him the truth. "I'm not looking for anything serious, though. With everything going on with my dad, I just don't have the bandwidth to deal with a relationship."

"I get it. And I'm cool going at whatever speed you want." He inches closer. "I just want to keep getting to know you. Because I'm enjoying it."

"I am, too."

Not only is George stable, kind, and *normal*. He seems genuinely interested in me for all the right reasons.

Which is why I don't push him away when he leans in…

And the obnoxious headboard banging comes back with a vengeance.

I glower at the wall. "I'm gonna march over there and strangle him."

"Talk about a mood killer," George mutters under his breath. "Why don't we go to my room?"

Back to his room...where we'll kiss.

And maybe more.

Thump. Thump. Thump.

"Please don't take this the wrong way, but it's been a long day and I'm exhausted."

It's not exactly a lie. Dealing with Phoenix is grueling and I need to catch up on my sleep.

Fortunately, George doesn't get mad about me declining and doesn't push the issue. "No problem."

I walk him to the door. "I had fun."

"Me too."

Cue the awkward moment that always happens after a date... even though I'm not sure this qualifies as one.

George must think it does, though, because when I lean in for a hug, he leans in for a kiss.

And that only makes things even more awkward because we end up doing this weird half-hug thing before his lips brush mine and we exchange a very quick and *very* chaste kiss.

"Text me so I know you made it home safely," I joke in an attempt to break up the tension.

It works because he chuckles as he walks down the hallway. "You got it."

A moment later, he disappears into his room and my phone lights up with a text.

George: I had fun tonight.
Lennon: Me too.
George: Get some sleep.

After placing my phone on the nightstand, I undress so I can climb into bed.

Sweet and safe is good.

I'm slipping the Papa Roach T-shirt over my head when the impulse to join Pettyville strikes.

Gripping the headboard, I slam it against the wall as hard as I can a few times.

Then I moan. Loudly.

Take that, asshole.

Tiny bolts of pleasure course through me, rousing me from sleep. I squeeze my eyes shut as Phoenix's hot, wet mouth gently laps at my pussy, unwilling to wake up from this dream despite how much I hate him in real life.

Because in my dreams, he's not an asshole who betrayed me.

In my dreams, he'd never hurt me.

In my dreams...he makes me come harder than I ever have before.

"Phoenix."

My voice is a throaty whisper as I squeeze my breast.

I trail my hand down my torso so I can slip it between my legs and make this little fantasy more realistic.

A sharp jolt runs through me when my fingers make contact with long, silky strands.

Shock roots me to the spot the moment I open my eyes.

Turns out it wasn't a lucid dream like I thought...because some blonde's face is between my thighs.

Something hard digs into my skin as I spring up. "Whoa—"

Words jam in my throat when I realize one of my wrists is hand-cuffed to the headboard.

What the hell?

I'm about to demand this crazy bitch release me, but a tall shadowy figure on the other side of the room draws my attention.

"I figured the cuffs would help give you the *full experience*."

Phoenix's mouth curves into a cruel smirk as he takes a step forward.

The stream of light spilling in from the ajar bathroom door illuminates his shirtless, jean-clad form like he's a mythical god...but it's the dark, menacing look in his eyes that has my pulse racing.

He's like a dangerous animal cornering its prey as he makes his way to the foot of the bed.

Anger mixed with outrage twists my insides. "What the *fuck*?"

The blonde freezes.

Crossing his arms, he peers down. "You want to know what it's like to be me, don't you?"

"I...you're crazy." I bang my wrist against the steel headboard, hoping the cuff will break. "Fucking certifiable."

Phoenix's sneer is downright taunting. "What's the matter, Lennon? Can't handle it?"

His words are the equivalent of pouring salt in the wound he created.

This asshole has everything I've ever wanted.

And he used *me* to get it.

Scowling, I open my mouth to remind him of that, but he twists the knife he plunged into my back.

"There's a reason it's me on that stage and not you."

If I thought I hated him before, it pales in comparison to right now.

I can feel it pumping through my veins like a toxic venom, fueling me to provoke him too.

I want to kick him and his friend out, but I'd rather extract my vocal cords with a dull, rusty razor blade than let him think I can't hack the life I gave him.

The life he stole.

I glance down at the girl who's still hovering mere inches away from my crotch. The fact she's the same chick who made fun of my weight makes what I'm about to do even better.

Gripping the back of her head, I give Phoenix a sinister stare of my own. "Keep going."

Our hostile gazes lock as she licks me cautiously, like she's unsure which one of us is calling the shots now and who she should listen to.

Fuck Phoenix Walker.

I open my legs wider. "More."

She speeds up her movements, but it's the pure hunger stealing over *his* expression as he watches me that causes my nipples to harden against the thin, faded fabric of my T-shirt.

Those sensuous lips part on a ragged inhale as he zeros in on them…and then his stare descends.

The tip of his tongue traces his bottom lip before his teeth clamp down on his piercing…like he's in pain.

Like he wishes it was his face parked between my thighs.

Tension and wrath fill the space between us in equal measure. We don't even have to touch one another to feel sparks.

Hell, we don't even have to like each other.

A sharp breath leaves me in a whoosh when he runs a hand over the large bulge trapped inside his jeans.

His own becomes uneven as he gives me a knowing look.

Like he's fully aware of what I want…even though I'll never admit it.

The sound of him tugging down his zipper rivals the frantic thumping of my heartbeat in my ears.

A warm flush spreads throughout me and it takes every ounce of willpower I possess not to watch while he touches himself.

As if sensing that I'm about to fall off the cliff he stuck me on, a cocky glimmer enters his gaze…daring me to look down.

Lust and loathing war within me, grappling for control.

It's the very same battle he's fighting.

Because we both want something we shouldn't.

A low groan fills the room. The rough sound goes straight to my core and before I can stop myself, I break eye contact.

White fabric partially obstructs my view of his cock as he strokes himself hard and fast.

My blood heats when I realize it's my panties.

He lets out a choppy breath and I draw one in as the blonde focuses on my clit.

Pleasure is a slow roll sweeping through my body. I'm so close I can taste it.

My stomach quivers and I buck my hips.

I'm so turned on I don't even care that it's a girl who's about to make me come, or that Phoenix is getting off to the show.

I just need it to happen. *Soon.*

My grip on the back of her head constricts, keeping her right where I need her. "Don't stop."

I shoot my gaze past her, taking in the giant cock with my panties wrapped around it. The wide mushroom head is slick with precum and the thick veins running along his long length have me wishing I didn't abhor him with the fire of a million suns so I could take him into my mouth.

Phoenix must be thinking the same thing because his stare bounces between my mouth and pussy and he tightens his grasp.

The muscles in his forearms flex as he speeds up his movements, and the girl sucks harder, driving me out of my mind.

"Stop," Phoenix snarls, and her movements come to an abrupt halt.

"Are you fucking kidding me?"

I was seconds away from climaxing.

Bastard.

"Keep going," I urge, imploring her to listen to me instead of him.

Leering at me, Phoenix growls, "Who are you here for?"

Faster than I can blink, she gets off the bed and drops to her knees before him.

The tendons in his neck coil as he strokes himself a few more times and covers her face with his cum.

"That's all you're getting." Backing up, he tucks himself into his jeans. "Grab your shit and get out."

Jesus.

Her embarrassment is tangible as she stands up, grabs her dress off the floor, and scurries to the door.

I narrow my eyes. "You're a dick."

My outburst only amuses him. "I simply gave her what she kept begging me for earlier."

Slowly, he lowers himself onto the bed. "Besides, we both know she's not the one you want."

My heart punches against my ribs and I press my thighs together as he slithers toward me. "I prefer her over you."

The look he gives me makes it clear he thinks I'm full of shit as he wrenches them apart. I force myself to ignore the heat in his eyes and the vulnerability that slams into me as he zeros in on my pussy.

"Is that why you whispered my name when you were getting ready to touch yourself before?"

I hate him. *So damn much.*

"It was a dream." A tremor flits through me as he settles between my parted thighs. "Correction. It was a *nightmare.*"

Shoving my shirt up my torso, he kisses my hip bone. "Whatever helps you sleep at night." The corner of his lip curls. "Or in your case, *not* sleep because you're too busy getting yourself off while thinking about me."

My belly clenches when his mouth moves down. The stubble on his jaw tickles my sensitive skin, taunting me.

Common sense has clearly taken a back seat to basic, primal need, because even though I should stop him, I want the release.

Doesn't mean we're friends, though.

"You were right before." His lips graze the inside of my thigh and it's all I can do not to rock into his face. "She's not the one I want."

He stills, watching me beneath long, dark lashes…waiting for me to continue.

To give him what he wants.

"That would be George."

A low, threatening sound rumbles out of him before he sinks his sharp teeth into my flesh. "Liar."

The sting of pain only turns me on even more. *Damn him.*

"There's only one liar in this room."

It's something he seems to need a constant reminder of whenever we're alone.

My heart feels like it's going to pound right out of my chest when the tip of his nose skims the length of my pussy. "Phoenix—"

His teeth clamp down and he draws my tender flesh into his mouth, sucking and biting my lips like I'm succulent fruit.

I need him to do all that to the *inside* of me, though.

My frustration rises to dire levels when he shifts a mere centimeter and repeats the movement.

I drive my hips into his jaw. "Make me come. *Now.*"

But he doesn't...he continues torturing me with his tongue and teeth.

I whimper, desperate for him to alleviate all this pressure he's building.

"Beg," he groans between harsh sucks and pulls.

I'm about to tell him to go fuck himself, but then he *finally* spreads me open with two of his fingers.

I swallow the words, not wanting to give in.

"Come on, Groupie. Be a good girl and beg me to eat this tight little cunt."

He blows a stream of air on my clit, long enough to work me into even more of a rabid state, but not enough to let me come.

I'm too far gone to stop myself. "Please."

His punishing gaze sears me as the tip of his tongue flicks my aching clit. I close my eyes and buck my hips, chasing the feeling.

I'm so close.

So. Freaking. Close.

And then he stops.

Making a fist with my free hand, I punch the mattress, the back of my throat prickling with tears of exasperation.

Shark teeth flash white. "Now you know."

"Know what?" I hiss as he gets off the bed. "That you're somehow an even bigger asshole?"

Ocean eyes full of torment steal every ounce of air from my lungs.

"What it's like to be me."

With that, he walks out.

"You forgot to uncuff me," I yell, even though I'm positive it was intentional.

A choked sound lodges in my esophagus as I take in the bright-purple bruises scattered along my inner thighs and pussy.

It looks like I was attacked by a savage beast.

Or rather…a snake trying to mark his territory by covering me with hickeys and bite marks so his bandmate will know exactly who I belong to.

Too bad it won't work.

Because I'm no longer his.

CHAPTER 37
LENNON

I can't understand a word George is saying due to Storm's chaotic drumming.

I point to my ear. "I'm sorry. What?"

"I said I had a really good time last night," George screams.

A little too loudly, though, because Storm chooses that exact moment to take it down a few decibels.

"Me too." Not wanting things to turn awkward like they did when we said goodbye last night, I add, "And hey, maybe next time we'll actually get to watch the movie."

That's when Phoenix—who's a good twenty feet away talking to Chandler about something—stops mid-convo.

His eyes narrow into tiny slits and it's all I can do not to roll mine.

Squaring my shoulders, I focus on George again.

Sweet and safe.

"Maybe next time we'll actually get to kiss for real." Inching closer, he studies my lips. "Or we could do it right now."

Seeing as this is my job—and there are *lots* of people around because we're in the middle of sound check—that might not be the best idea.

"Pump the brakes, Casanova."

George spins around at the sound of Phoenix's voice.

Jaw tightening, Phoenix hikes a thumb at the stage behind him. "You're on deck."

George gives me a rueful smile. "Sorry." He smacks a kiss on my cheek and does this weird hair-ruffle thing. "See you later."

I'm attempting to fix my now disheveled ponytail when I catch Phoenix leering at me.

"I take it your little boyfriend doesn't know about us."

Gathering my hair, I wrap my scrunchie around it. "That's because there is no us."

The tip of his tongue sweeps along his lip ring, and his fiery gaze drifts down my body. "The bite marks on your pussy beg to differ."

Forcing myself to pay no heed to the rush of embarrassment his statement causes, I survey the stage where George is playing.

Sweet and safe—I tell myself again, like it's my new mantra.

"Look, what happened last night is never happening again." Peeling my stare away, I meet Phoenix's, so he knows I'm dead serious. "I like George. He's a nice guy."

Something he'll never understand because he's most definitely *not* one.

He doesn't say a word for so long, I internally rejoice.

About time the asshole finally got it through his thick skull.

I'm debating walking over to the snack table when he leans down.

His warm breath tickles my ear when he speaks. "Too bad nice guys don't make your panties wet."

A wolfish grin spreads across his lips as he pulls something out of his pocket.

The retort I was constructing vanishes into thin air the moment I see my panties.

"We need you up here, Phoenix," someone calls out.

The look he gives me is so vulgar, I'm glad Chandler walked off to take a phone call.

Relief fills me as he treks over to the stage because the more distance between us right now, the better.

However, it's short lived.

Shock roots me to the spot—followed by a torrent of dread—when he ties my panties around his mic stand.

I have to remind myself to chill the fuck out because it's not like anyone knows they belong to me.

Much like my song.

Drawing in a deep, cleansing breath, I turn on my heels.

I inwardly flinch when he starts singing "Voodoo" by Godsmack.

I try to ignore the ache ballooning inside my chest as memories slam into me, but I can't.

Once upon a time, Phoenix Walker made me believe I was special.

Then he destroyed me.

I won't give him the opportunity to do it again.

"So…" Skylar begins as she scans my hotel room over the rim of her coffee cup. "Are you going to tell me why *I* had to uncuff you from your bed in the wee hours of the morning?"

I should have known there'd be a catch when she knocked on my hotel room door with coffee and pastries.

Fueling up for tonight's show, my ass.

I eye the pattern on the comforter. "Weird. I have no recollection of that happening. Are you sure it wasn't a dream?"

Those bright eyes sharpen. "I like you, Lennon, but you're making my job harder. Start talking."

Keeping my expression impassive, I shrug. "I told you. I had company."

After placing her half-eaten danish and coffee cup on the nightstand, she stands. "Yeah, but you didn't tell me *who* the company was."

Jesus. I'm convinced she's part bloodhound.

I casually study my nails. "You're the publicist. Anything I say can be used against me in the court of public opinion."

Assessing me, she taps her chin. "So, it *was* one of the guys in the band."

Dammit. Not only is she drop-dead gorgeous…she's awfully perceptive.

Seemingly determined to get to the bottom of this, she starts pacing the carpet in front of me.

"Let's see. Handcuffs are definitely Storm's thing, but he left with the redhead last night and you don't seem like the type to have a threesome."

I wisely keep my mouth shut.

Her pouty lips press together. "George would be the obvious choice…" There's a long pause, and she bites her cheek like she's trying not to laugh. "But he doesn't have a kinky bone in his body."

No argument here.

She stops pacing. "That leaves Phoenix."

"You're forgetting Memphis," I point out.

Something I can't quite ascertain flashes in her eyes briefly before she gives me a feeble smile. "You're too smart to be baby mama number three."

Grabbing her purse off the bed, she hustles to the door.

It appears my buttons weren't the only ones pushed during this little exchange.

"Skylar?"

She turns around. "Yeah?"

She strikes me as someone who doesn't appreciate people beating around the bush, so I cut to the chase.

"Is there something going on with you and Memphis?"

I get why she wouldn't be an open book about it given he's Josh's brother. However, I'm not the type to throw stones.

Skylar can trust me.

She raises one perfectly tweezed eyebrow. "Is there something going on with you and Phoenix?"

Checkmate.

Neither of us says a word as we stare at one another.

Fortunately, the sound of my phone ringing comes to the rescue.

I smile as I see Mrs. Palma's name flash across the screen. "I gotta take this. It's my dad."

The sound of my ringtone blaring wakes me out of a dead sleep. Groggy, I quickly rummage around the bed for my cell.

Everything was fine—well, as fine as it could be, considering my dad thought I was trying to sell him life insurance—when I spoke to him earlier today.

I'm relieved when I see George's name on the screen.

After pressing the green button, I bring it to my ear. "Hello?"

"Do you want to hang out?"

I glance at the clock on the nightstand. It's a little after two a.m.

Granted, that's relatively early for a rock star and all, but I'm already in my pajamas *and* in bed.

"It's the middle of the night." Skylar's remark from earlier flits through my head. "Are you booty calling me?"

Perhaps he's not that *vanilla* after all.

"What? No?"

The spark of intrigue I had pops like a bubble.

"I mean...maybe," he quickly rattles off. "Would you say yes?"

The guy really needs to work on his confidence.

I'm conjuring up excuses in my mind when a loud thump on the other side of the wall snags my attention.

Dammit, Phoenix.

"Seriously? He's freaking handcuffed."

No way in hell am I going to let this asshole interrupt my well-deserved rest because he can't keep it in his pants.

George is saying something, but I cut him off. "Gotta go."

Clenching my teeth, I hop out of bed and charge for the door connecting our rooms.

"Listen here, ass—"

A low, tortured sound fills my ears. "Josh."

When my eyes adjust to the darkness, I see Phoenix's silhouette thrashing around on his bed.

The headboard thumps again as I run over to him.

"Josh. Wake up!"

I quickly unlock the cuff around his wrist. "Hey." Placing my hand on his shoulder, I give him a gentle shake. "It's okay. You're just having a bad dream."

"Josh!"

Shit.

I shake him a little harder. "Phoenix—"

He bolts up with so much vigor he nearly knocks me to the floor.

Forehead creasing, he takes in his surroundings. He looks so disoriented and his breathing is so erratic I briefly debate calling for help.

I flick on the light next to his bed. "Are you okay?"

God, what a stupid question. Of course, he's not. He's having a nightmare about his friend and bandmate dying.

A nightmare based on reality.

Coming out of his haze, he lurches off the bed and wanders over to the minibar. He yanks the door open with so much force I'm surprised it doesn't come off the hinges.

He surveys the various alcoholic mini bottles and reaches for the Bacardi.

I scoot to the end of the bed. "You're gonna regret this in the morning."

Chandler more or less said he doesn't care if Phoenix drinks in private as long as it doesn't become a public issue, but drinking won't make the demons he's trying to drown out disappear.

It will only create new ones.

With a snort, he twists the cap off. "Add it to the list."

Leaning down, I grab his forearm. "Why don't you switch to Coke instead?"

"Great idea. I'll call my dealer."

Talk about a *misinterpretation.*

I gesture to the Coca-Cola can in the fridge. "I meant the soda."

His throat bobs on a swallow. "Soda won't make me forget."

"Neither will getting trashed." Something tells me deep down he knows that, though, so I try a different tactic. "Do you want to talk about it?"

"I'd rather drink about it," he grunts before he downs the Bacardi.

Can't say I'm surprised. Getting Phoenix to open up makes pulling teeth seem effortless.

Even still...I try anyway.

"I know losing your friend was hard—"

"No, you don't know. Trust me." He jerks his chin in the direction of the door. "I've got it from here. You can leave."

His dismissal makes my heart sink like a cinder block.

"I want to stay."

He might not want to talk, but I don't feel right leaving him alone.

After all, it's my job to watch over him.

Cutting me a look I can only construe as 'suit yourself', he opens a mini bottle of Jack Daniels and guzzles it.

Then—as if getting drunk were some kind of Olympic sport he was training for—he plucks a bottle of Hennessey from the fridge.

"Phoenix."

I might as well be talking to a wall, though, because he finishes it.

"You should slow down."

He launches the empty bottle across the room. "You should *leave*."

Trepidation coils my stomach when he gets off the floor and makes a beeline for the small bar in the corner.

My trepidation turns to full-blown aggravation when he swipes the bottle of vodka off it. Unlike the others, it's a fifth bottle.

The composure I was trying to maintain snaps like a twig, and I spring up. "Jesus Christ, dickhead. Would you fucking *stop*!"

"No!"

I'm trying my hardest to sympathize, but he's making it beyond difficult. "I know losing your friend hurts like hell but—"

"You don't fucking know!" he screams so loud I flinch.

"Then why don't you tell me?" A bolt of sadness spikes through my chest. "And if not me...then someone. *Anyone.*"

Because trying to block it all out with drugs and alcohol will only send him to an early grave.

Nostrils flaring, he brings the bottle to his lips and turns toward the gigantic window overlooking Houston.

He's silent for so long that when he finally does speak, it nearly startles me.

"It was my fault."

Most people have a tendency to blame themselves when preventable tragedies happen to someone we care about.

Doesn't mean it's true.

"No, it wasn't," I remind him. "You weren't the one driving."

In the window's reflection, I see pure agony slash his face. "Yes, I was."

His confession makes the room spin.

So many thoughts—followed by even more questions—zip through my head, but I clamp my mouth shut.

He's finally talking and I don't want to give him a reason to stop.

The veins in his forearm flex as his grip tightens around the bottle of vodka. "But I was so high I ended up pulling over." A gut-wrenching noise escapes him. "Josh told me he was fine to drive back...but he wasn't. I *knew* he wasn't because we'd been partying together most of the night." He expels a shaky breath. "Hell, the fucker had just snorted a line of heroin off the dashboard."

Broad shoulders sag with what looks like the weight of the world. "I was too fucked up to care, though, so I handed him the keys and switched places with him." His voice dips. "Didn't even put up a fight."

I rack my brain, attempting to think of something that might alleviate his guilt...but I come up empty.

"When I woke up, Josh was still alive. He even cracked a joke."

He grips the back of his neck with his free hand. "The car was fucked, but at least we survived, you know?" Sorrow laces his tone. "Then I watched him die."

My chest tightens as I process what he's saying.

I can't imagine how awful it must have been to see his friend alive one second...only to watch him die the very next.

No wonder he still has nightmares.

No wonder he's been stuck in such a downward spiral.

Phoenix takes a lengthy sip from the bottle. "I didn't realize we hit another car until after Storm pulled me out of ours."

I remember the reporter mentioning it was a two-vehicle accident on the news that night, but he didn't give any details about who was in the other car...aside from citing they didn't make it.

His hands clench into fists. "The woman we hit was only a year older than me." The muscles in his back tense and coil. "She was pregnant...and her four-year-old son was in the back seat."

A sharp pang spreads throughout me as he continues.

"She was on her way to clean a house but couldn't find a babysitter, so she decided to take her son with her to work because she needed the extra money and couldn't afford not to." His shame is so palpable it nearly brings me to my knees. "Her mom said she was a huge fan and listened to us all the time."

An excruciating sound fills the room. "They had their whole lives ahead of them."

I wince when he launches the bottle against the wall. "But *I* ruined that."

He whips around to face me and his expression makes my throat close.

He's utterly wrecked.

Those dazed blue eyes lock on mine and his voice cracks like the broken glass on the carpet. "I'm exactly like him."

No. His father was a drunk who beat the shit out of his kid.

While Phoenix is far from a saint and God knows he's done some terrible things, the reason he's stuck in this self-destructive vortex is because he's consumed with guilt over a mistake he made.

That alone proves he's nothing like that man.

"Come here."

Grief steals over his features as he staggers over.

Peeling the comforter back, I help him into bed.

Peering down, I sweep my finger over the crest of his sharp cheekbone. "Mistakes don't define who someone is, Phoenix. It's what you do *after* that does."

I'm about to leave, but his fingers wrap around my wrist. "Stay."

God, there's so much pain contained in that single word.

Ignoring all the reasons I shouldn't, I crawl into bed beside him.

Exhaling a shaky breath, he rolls onto his stomach. "The moment I got behind the wheel, I signed their death warrant." His next words are muffled against the pillow. "The world thinks I'm a god...but I'm in hell."

Sometimes there's nothing you can say to make it better. No words of comfort or solace you can give to make it hurt a little less.

Sometimes the only thing you can do is be there...so they aren't alone.

Gently, I run my fingertips up and down his bare back, hoping to lull him to sleep.

As his breathing grows deeper, I study the large tattoo spanning his back. I've noticed it a few times since I've been here, but I never had the inkling to examine it before now.

It's a beautiful piece of art.

Vibrant colorful flames surround a resilient phoenix ascending from the pile of smoky embers below.

The bird is half black and half color...as though stuck in mid-transformation.

Trying his hardest to overcome that which destroyed him.

The little I know about Phoenix's past and everything he's told me tonight sits heavy in my chest as I trace the wings with the tip of my finger.

"I should be dead," he whispers. "Not them."

It feels like someone reached inside my chest and pulled out my beating heart.

Because if he keeps going the way he is…he will be.

"I wish it was me." The hopelessness in his voice cuts like a knife. "So fucking bad."

I know he does.

I continue tracing the lines of his tattoo as his heavy eyelids close and his labored breathing evens out.

Phoenix's are supposed to rise from the ashes…

But this one wants to burn.

CHAPTER 38
LENNON

Waking up next to Phoenix Walker is both strange and oddly familiar at the same time.

Like catching up with an old friend you haven't seen in years.

Upon rousing and seeing me, he grins. "Hey."

Holy hell, it should be illegal for someone to look like *that* when they first wake up.

"How do you feel?"

Yawning, he stretches those long limbs like a feline. The movement causes the covers to drop, exposing his flat sculpted stomach… and the scar on his torso.

"Like shit."

"Luckily, you still have a couple more hours before soundcheck."

"Yeah." Stuffing one hand under his pillow, he holds my gaze. "Thanks for last night."

Emotions run rampant throughout me as we continue staring at one another.

My chest hurts when I think about everything he told me.

But just as quickly…my self-preservation kicks in, reminding me we're not friends.

While I feel terrible for what happened, and I don't think he should spend the rest of his life harming himself because of it...it doesn't change what he did to me.

Spending the night in his bed—albeit for comfort as opposed to sexual reasons—is not only a bad move on my part, it's flat out dumb.

"I'm gonna go."

My feet have barely touched the floor when a strong arm wraps around my waist and I'm hauled onto the bed again.

Pressing the front of his body against my back, his lips find the sensitive spot under my ear. "Stay."

Unlike last night, the word isn't laced with pain...it's pure desire.

The substantial morning wood digging into my ass triggers that all too familiar war to wage inside me again. "Phoenix."

"Don't worry." My breath hitches when the pad of his thumb slides along the bare patch of skin above the band of my sleep shorts. "I'll let you come this time."

His voice is like warm honey over rust, equally caressing and abrading my insides as his hand slowly makes its way up my shirt...

Giving me just enough time to come to my senses before it's too late.

Ripping his hand away, I get off the bed. "Not happening."

"Why?" he rumbles like a toddler who's about to have a temper tantrum because their favorite toy was taken away.

The fact he even has the gall to ask *why* I'm turning him down only pisses me off more.

"Are you serious?" The confused look on his face has me straight up seething. "Just because I was there for you last night doesn't mean everything is okay between us."

It *never* will be.

He sits up "Goddammit, Lennon. I'm—"

"You're *what*?" I push when he stops himself.

Jaw ticcing, he grabs a pack of cigarettes and a lighter off the nightstand.

Come on. Say it.

Give me the acknowledgment—and the apology—I deserve.

But he doesn't.

He sits there smoking his cigarette.

"That's why."

Disgusted, I speed toward the door.

Another surge of wrath explodes inside me as I twist the knob.

"Phoenix?"

I wait for him to look at me before I utter my next words.

"Does it hurt to hear *me* everywhere you go?"

For the briefest of moments, the anguish from last night is back.

Good.

"Where's Phoenix?"

Still being a no-good rotten liar.

"Come again?" Chandler snaps.

Shit. I didn't realize I said that aloud.

I clear my throat. "Bathroom."

Chandler waves a hand emphatically. "Well, if you want to stay employed, I suggest you go fetch him. The sound engineer is having an issue and they need him out there pronto."

"Sure thing, *Dicky,*" I grit through my teeth as I stalk off.

I try the public bathroom backstage first since it's the closest.

Irritated, I pop my head inside. "Shake it and zip it, scumbag. They need you on sta—" Phoenix isn't in here, but I see George standing at the urinal. "Whoops."

George quickly zips up his pants. "Hi."

"Hey. Have you seen Phoenix?"

He strides over to the sink and washes his hands. "Um...yeah, actually." He tears a paper towel from the dispenser. "I...saw him go off with a groupie a little while ago."

What the hell?

"Dammit. The concert hasn't even started."

Heck, we're not even through *soundcheck* yet.

George chases after me. "What are you doing after the show?"

Seriously? *Focus, grasshopper.* We have a lead singer to find.

As if on cue, Chandler steps into my path. "Well?" Another impatient hand wave. "Did you find him?"

Looking between us, George hikes a thumb at the stage behind him. "I'm gonna go."

Smart move.

The big, juicy vein in Chandler's forehead makes an appearance. "Where is he?"

Freaking Phoenix.

"He's…busy." I laugh and shrug like it's no big deal. "Rock stars, amirite?"

That only makes him more irate.

"Busy with *what*?"

His dick.

But I can't tell him that because it's my job to make sure he's performing at *maximum capacity.*

Thinking fast, I utter, "Look, he has the shits. He won't be coming out for a while."

There. Now he can take it up with mother nature instead of me.

I'm about to walk away, but he steps in front of me.

"I don't care if he's shitting out of his eyeballs." He stabs his pointer finger in the direction of the stage. "We've only got five minutes left to finish sound check and get the levels right, so you better handle this or you'll be on the next plane home!"

Shit on a stick.

Given I have no idea where Phoenix and his *devoted fan* are boning, I'm not exactly sure how I'm supposed to fix this.

Unless…

Indignation billows through me as I march toward the stage where the rest of the band is gearing up to play.

"What the fuck are you doing?" Chandler booms as I lower the mic.

"I'm handling it."

Nerves coil in my belly, and my grip on the microphone tightens.

What the fuck *am* I doing?

"Check for mic one," the guy at the soundboard calls out.

My heart pounds in my chest as I look around the empty stadium.

Over twenty thousand people will be here tonight...

To hear him sing my song.

Butterflies fill my stomach, and my palms start to sweat. There's so much panic coursing through me, my voice shakes with the first few words.

"Close your eyes."

Steeling myself, I squeeze them shut and power on.

This is what it would be like.

Adrenaline spirals through me, wrapping around my body like an electrical wire as I let the music—*my* music—take over.

In this moment—I'm not the girl who's too petrified to sing in front of others.

I'm not the girl whose song was stolen by her first love.

I'm not the girl forced to stand on the sidelines while he lives my dream.

Right now? The magic on this stage is mine. *All mine.*

Unfortunately, it doesn't last long because far too soon I'm singing the very last note.

"Holy shit," Storm yells behind me. "You got a set of pipes."

"Hot damn," Memphis howls. "You been holding out on us, girl."

Oh. My. God. I can't believe I just did that.

My cheeks heat with embarrassment as I turn around. "It's really not a big—"

Words lodge in my throat when I see Phoenix standing off stage...staring at me.

Anger mixed with something that looks a whole lot like jealousy etches his features as those blue eyes pin me to the spot...sucking all the oxygen from my lungs.

"What the hell?" Chandler balks as the four of us walk off stage.

Mouth agape, he looks at Phoenix. "Did you know she could sing like that?"

He stays silent.

Beaming, George slings an arm around my shoulders. "Have any other hidden talents, beautiful?"

I find myself grinning. "Not really. Although I—"

"She sucks a mean cock." Phoenix shoots George an icy smile. "Not that you would know."

So help me God, I'd reach over and throttle the douche if there weren't so many witnesses around.

I turn my attention back to George—the guy who actually deserves it. "I play piano."

Seemingly impressed, his face lights up. "That's awesome. Ever write any songs?"

The shattered pieces of my heart stir painfully in my chest and the knife wedged into my back twists.

Writing songs was my outlet for all the pain I held inside.

It's what made me go on living when life got too hard.

My stare locks on Phoenix as we walk past him. "Not anymore."

He took that from me, too.

CHAPTER 39
LENNON

My stomach growls as I head for the greenroom. I am *starving*, and the pepperoni pizza I picked up for me and Skylar smells heavenly.

We've both had salads for dinner the past three nights, so I figured we deserve to indulge a little.

Balancing the pizza box in one hand, I push open the door. "Got us some dinner."

Skylar doesn't look up from her laptop. The deep wrinkle forming between her brows indicates that whatever she's looking at not only has her full attention, but also has her concerned.

I place the pizza down on the table in front of her. "What's up?"

She taps a few keys. "Turns out this fifteen-year-old baby mama is *quite* the stalker."

That doesn't sound good.

I scan the room for some paper plates, but come up empty. "What do you mean?"

"Well, since the articles didn't print her name—given she's a minor and all—I bribed one of the sleazy journalists for her info… then I did a little social media recon." She reaches for her coffee cup. "Her name is Quinn Moore. She's from Chicago. She'll be sixteen at the end of August and she'll start her junior year of high school in the fall."

Talk about impressive. Impressive with a side of *scary*.

"Damn. You're like a detective."

She gives me a pointed look. "All girls are detectives when they need to be."

Her pretty eyes narrow as she zeros in on the screen again.

Curious, I peek over. I see a list of dates. A *long* list of dates.

"Anyway, it turns out that this girl has been to a lot of shows." She gives me the side-eye. "Do you know what that means?"

"She has a lot of time on her hands?"

Time and money because these concerts aren't cheap. Neither is transportation.

"Not just that, but she and Memphis have obviously been in the same place before."

Right. "Oh."

She mutters a curse. "Knocking up a bimbo reality star is one thing…but it's gonna be hard to fight these allegations now."

I like Memphis. A lot actually. So much so, I—much like Skylar—really wanted to believe that this whole knocking up a minor thing was nothing more than a stupid rumor started by a crazed fan seeking attention.

Knowing there's a high probability it's true churns my stomach.

"I can't believe he slept with a minor."

Granted, he wouldn't be the first musician to turn into a creep.

I just hoped he—and the rest of Sharp Objects—would be better than that.

Skylar fixes her glare on me. "Memphis swears he never touched a minor."

Shocker. "So did a certain R&B singer who's now—rightfully so—behind bars."

She peers down at her shoes. "I get why you would assume the worst about him. But Memphis and I go way back. I *know* him, Lennon. He wouldn't lie to me."

My heart squeezes painfully in my chest.

Phoenix and I go *way back*, too.

"Sometimes the people you think you know best...turn out to be nothing but impostors."

"I'll get to the bottom of this one way or the other," she declares. "Trust me. I *always* do."

I want to ask her to elaborate, but the band barrels into the greenroom.

"There's my girl," George says when he sees me.

I get off the couch. "Hey."

Slinging an arm around my waist, he kisses my forehead. "You know, George and Lennon made a great team."

Skylar casts me a pointed look as she closes her laptop. "Aww, that's so *sweet*."

Phoenix walks over to the fridge and grabs a bottle of water. "That would be Lennon and McCartney, you bloody tampon."

I want to jump to George's defense, but you'd think he'd know that given McCartney not only wrote songs with Lennon and sang alongside him...he also played bass guitar.

The same instrument *he* plays.

Storm and Memphis snicker.

Not wanting this to devolve into another round of *everyone attack George because Phoenix doesn't like him*, I say, "Lennon and George Harrison *were* friends, though, so it still applies."

I don't catch what Phoenix grumbles under his breath as George pulls me close. "Movie night tonight?"

"She always was a cheap date," Phoenix mutters.

That does it.

"How would you know? You *never* took me on a date."

The closest thing to one we ever had was Phoenix buying me a burger after I convinced our English teacher to let him take the final with the reading pen.

Granted, at the time, I stupidly thought it was the best day of my life.

Because not only did Phoenix ditch a girl to hang out with me...it was the very first time I shared my art with someone else.

I wish like hell I could press the rewind button and tell that naive girl with stars in her eyes to run far away and never look back.

"Wait a minute. You never took your girlfriend on a date?" Skylar questions.

"I wasn't his girlfriend," I say at the same time Phoenix grunts, "I was poor."

You could hear a pin drop as everyone's eyes ping-pong between us.

Talk about awkward.

"Oh, hey, pizza." Reaching across Skylar, Memphis grabs a slice from the box.

"I'd love to take you out on a date sometime," George whispers in my ear.

I scowl at Phoenix before directing all my attention to George. "Your room or mine tonight?"

Sighing, George grabs the remote and pauses the movie we were watching.

Or rather, the movie I was *trying* to watch because it's boring as hell.

"Phoenix seems really bothered by the two of us."

Ugh. I'd much rather watch the dull movie than talk about Phoenix.

However, George seems upset.

"Honestly, what doesn't bother Phoenix? He's in a perpetual state of—I'm a dick."

As if on cue, a deep voice on the other side of the wall booms, "I'm not doing the motherfucking interview, Chandler. Get the fuck out."

I jut my chin. "See? *Dick.*"

Seemingly appeased now, George snuggles closer. "So, about this kiss…"

Where's the freaking remote?

"Lennon?"

"Yeah?"

"Can I kiss you?"

I mean, if you have to ask…

Tucking a strand of hair behind my ear, I sit up.

George is nice and all, but I need more time to see if there's a spark between us. Although even if there turns out to be, I still don't want a boyfriend.

"I'm not trying to be a tease or anything…it's just that kissing is kind of a big deal, you know? I like you, George, but I'm still not ready for anything serious."

He sprouts up. "I know and I'm not trying to pressure you, I swear. I'm just really into you and want to see where this goes, even if it's just casual."

Casual. Glad we're on the same page because I was starting to think we weren't.

"In that case…yes."

I close my eyes as he leans in.

A little too hard…because his forehead thumps mine.

"Shit."

His nervousness would be adorable if it didn't require the need for over-the-counter painkillers.

My head throbs and I brace myself for the inevitable migraine coming my way. "Ouch."

"I'm sorry. Give me another chance."

I don't think letting him take the lead again is a good idea. I don't want another injury.

"Maybe I should kiss you."

He grins. "That works."

I inch closer, but a heartbeat before our lips meet, something heavy hits the wall and shatters.

"What the hell?"

George sulks. "Sounds like someone is having another temper tantrum."

Before I can scrutinize *that* any further, my phone rings.

Happiness billows through me when I see *Dad* flash across my screen. He never calls me himself anymore. It's always Mrs. Palma who hands him her phone.

"I need a rain check. It's my dad."

Ever the understanding one, George gets off the bed. "No problem. I'll come back later. We can pick up where we left off."

Waving him out of the room, I bring the phone to my ear. "Hey."

"Hey, Sue. It's Don. I've got someone coming over to trim back the maple tree branches on my half of the property this weekend. Just want to make sure it's okay."

Disappointment sinks like a brick in my chest when I realize he thinks *I'm* Mrs. Palma.

That's definitely a new one, but as usual, I play along because this is his reality.

"Sure. No problem."

"Thanks a lot. See you at the HOA meeting later."

"Wait," I say before he can hang up. "How are you?"

"I'm good." He's quiet for a beat. "A little lonely now that Lennon's away at school, but the holidays are just around the corner and she'll be home then."

I swallow the lump in my throat. "Yeah, she will."

"I'm so proud of her," he says and I can picture him smiling as he sits by his piano. "She was so scared to go away to college, but she faced her fears." His sigh is expansive. "Granted, she has this awful math professor who she's positive is out to get her—"

"Professor Hanks," I interject before I can stop myself.

"That's the one. I guess she told you about him, too."

I trace little patterns on the bedspread with my finger. "Yeah. The guy sounds like a real piece of work."

Even though all but one of my answers were correct on the first exam he gave us, the jerk tried to fail me because I didn't show my work the way he preferred. Although he never specified we had to.

"Tell me about it," my dad says. "I offered to make a phone call but Lennon said that would only make things worse. She didn't want me babying her."

He's right. Because the only way that god-awful professor was ever going to respect me was if I put my big girl panties on and handled it myself.

So, I marched right into his office and threatened to set up a meeting with the Dean. I was petrified because fighting with teachers wasn't my thing, but he wasn't being fair.

Just because I went about getting the *correct* answer a different way than he would didn't mean I was wrong.

To my surprise, he took his power trip down a few notches and I ended up passing the course with a ninety-two.

Even though it should have been a ninety-three.

"Well, you know how she is." I bite my cheek as I recall what he used to always say about my *willful* spirit. "Stubborn as an ox."

"That she is." He laughs. "She gets it from me."

I really do.

"I'm so proud of her," he repeats, and it's both a dagger and a balm to my heart. "My baby girl is going places."

How I wish that were true.

"Only because she has a great dad."

"No. It's all her. She's so much more than she gives herself credit for; you know? So strong...and talented." A deep exhale fills the line. "She doesn't know it, but I heard her sing once. She has the voice of an angel. Just like her mama. It's a shame she keeps it hidden."

My chest cracks open like a dam and it takes everything inside me not to break down.

"I miss her," he whispers a moment later.

She misses you, too.

So damn much.

CHAPTER 40
PHOENIX

"You've been extra pissy since soundcheck yesterday," Storm grunts.

I bring the lighter to the end of my cigarette. The record label keeps harping on me to quit so I don't ruin their *investment*, but they can lick my nutsack.

"So?"

"So, you should be grateful Lennon covered for your ass while you were outside making a phone call." Huffing, he plucks the cigarette from my mouth and stubs it out. "Speaking of which, did you hear her voice? Who knew she could sing like *that*?"

Something ugly and bitter tightens my chest.

I did.

My silence only spurs him on. "Look, man. I know her hanging with George has you—"

"I don't give a fuck about George."

Aside from his involvement with Lennon.

I clench my hands until they become fists. The thought of them kissing on the other side of that wall makes me homicidal.

Bet if I slipped something lethal into his drink later, no one would suspect a thing.

Just like that, guilt sinks its sharp claws into me. *Haven't you killed enough people already, asshole?*

Storm looks at the broken whiskey bottle on the floor. "Tell me again how you're not jealous."

I flip him the bird. "I told you, jackass. It slipped out of my hand."

His stare rests on the large dent in the wall. "Right."

I'm about to kick him out, but there's a knock on the connecting door.

Speak of the devil. "What?"

Lennon ambles in. She's never been exceptionally perky or anything, but her demeanor is more serious than usual.

What's the matter, Groupie? Prince Charming's kissing technique not up to par?

"Chandler wanted me to tell you that your driver will be here at seven a.m. to pick you up for your interview on Saturday."

The driver will be here, but I won't.

"Hard pass."

Lennon pinches the bridge of her nose. "Public relations comes with the territory of being a famous rock star, Phoenix. If you keep canceling all these interviews and dodging every meet and greet, the record label will fine you for violating your contract."

Let them.

"I don't give a fuck. They could fine me a million times and it still wouldn't make a dent in my bank account."

I've got more money than I'll ever be able to spend in a single lifetime. Even after donating substantial sums of money to various charities every year.

Disgust scrunches her features. "Must be nice."

That's funny. Last I checked, *she* was well acquainted with the concept.

"It is nice." Arms crossed, I stare her down. "Not like you wouldn't know, princess. Daddy placed you in your nice ivory tower and gave you everything you ever wanted, remember?"

I relish the outrage on her face. "Go fuck yourself. Unlike you, I earn my money honestly."

In my peripheral, I see Storm's eyes bounce between us.

"I *honestly* worked my ass off for this career."

She has no fucking idea.

I've sold my soul to the goddamn devil to get where I am, and he doesn't take refunds or exchanges.

Those big brown eyes narrow in a vindictive stare, and she jabs a finger in my chest. "Being a liar isn't a legitimate career."

Christ. She's like a baby shark who's just had her first taste of blood and wants more.

Too bad I bite back.

Fisting her shirt, I pull her close. So close our noses touch.

"But taking your clothes off and shaking your ass is? Bet daddy's so proud of you."

The kill shot works because she goes silent.

But I'm not done.

Giving me shit about having money when she saw the trailer I grew up in is a dick move.

"Or not." I palm her cheek. "Come on, Lennon. Why'd daddy cut his precious daughter off?"

Her face collapses and she takes a step back, looking at me like I'm the biggest piece of shit on earth.

I suddenly feel like it.

Before I can get to the bottom of why her cage is rattled so much, she's gone, slamming the door behind her.

"You're a fucking asshole."

Pushing past me, Storm twists the doorknob and heads into Lennon's room.

What the fuck is going on?

The walls in this hotel are paper thin but I press my ear to one anyway.

"What can I do?" Storm questions, his voice uncharacteristically gentle.

"Can you get George?" Lennon rasps, and it's a kick to the gut.

This shit makes no sense. We've always pushed each other's buttons.

It's what we do.

In two strides, I'm barging into her room. "What's wrong?"

Two things immediately catch me off guard.

The first—is that Storm's hugging her.

Neither of us are huggers...unless we're trying to cop a feel.

The second—and most important—is Lennon's crying.

Her puffy, tear-stained face gnaws at my insides. "Are you fucking kidding me?"

I can't shake this feeling that I'm the punch line of a joke. One that isn't funny.

"I was a dick, but I've teased you about being a daddy's girl before and you never acted like this. What's going on?"

Indignation steals over her expression, temporarily masking the hurt. "Why would I ever trust you with my personal shit? Get out."

Fuck. Something *is* going on. "Len—"

A loud knock on the main door cuts me off.

"That's George," Storm tells her. "I texted him."

Traitor.

Lennon looks at me. "Leave. *Now.*"

I don't want to, but I don't want to hurt her anymore, either.

I'll come back after she calms down.

Storm follows me back to my room.

The second I hear the latch click; I slam him against the wall. "What's wrong with Lennon?"

We don't keep secrets—aside from the one I've been holding on to—so the fucker better tell me whatever he knows.

But then I realize that I'm barking up the wrong tree since there's no way Lennon would tell Storm.

Sure, they're friends, but Storm's not *me.*

I'm about to let him go, but his next words halt me. "It's not my shit to tell."

It's like a goddamn brick to the face.

Not only does George know something that I don't about Lennon…Storm does, too.

Then again, why would she confide in me?

I gave her every reason not to.

The muscles in my chest draw tight with regret as I back away.

I expect Storm to give me more shit, but he exits without another word.

I can't hear what George is saying on the other side, but given he's speaking so low, I assume he's consoling her.

Irritation simmers in my gut, and I punch the wall.

This is *my* fuckup.

He doesn't get to swoop in like some noble hero and fix this.

Fuck that motherfucker.

I don't deserve Lennon, but neither does he.

I twist the knob so hard I'm surprised it doesn't rip off.

George's arms are wrapped tightly around Lennon's waist while he whispers something in her ear.

Her face is buried in his neck and she's clinging to him like a lifeline.

Like she needs saving from the big, bad wolf who hurt her.

Only he didn't mean to hurt her.

Not *this* much.

"I need to talk to you."

At the sound of my voice, they break apart.

Lennon looks like she wants to rip my intestines out with her teeth and choke me with them. "I don't want to talk to you."

I look at George. "Get out."

God help the prick if he chooses this moment to find his balls, because I'll toss his ass out the window.

He doesn't get a chance to, though, because Lennon snaps, "Stay." Then she grabs his hand. "On second thought, let's go to your room."

Fuck that. The only thing worse than knowing they're in here together is them moving their little movie watching rendezvous to his room down the hall.

Then I won't be able to hear what they're doing...or interrupt.

"Lennon," I warn as she leads him to the door.

She doesn't have to speak to tell me to fuck off...but she does anyway.

Her next words feel like a dull knife slicing the cold, black thing beating inside my chest.

The one she managed to burrow her way into over four years ago, despite how much I resisted.

"He's the one I want, Phoenix. Not you."

Her mouth is saying the words, but her eyes don't back it up.

They tell me *I'm* the one she wants.

Millions of girls have looked at me like I was something special over the years.

Like I was going to change the world with my talent.

But she's the only one who ever made me truly believe it.

And I fucked it up.

"You don't even know him."

It's a weak argument, but it's all I've got.

I can't stand here and tell her I'm a better guy than George... because I'm not.

I can't offer to comfort and console her like he can...because I don't know how.

I can't tell her I'll never hurt her...because I did.

Those baby browns glare hate fire in my direction. "And yet, I trust him way more than I'll *ever* trust you."

This time, her eyes corroborate the validity of her words.

That ugly, bitter feeling in my chest is back with a vengeance the moment she closes the door.

I can't tell her to trust me...

Because she never will again.

CHAPTER 41
LENNON

Mother nature sucks big, hairy monkey balls.

Three days ago, Skylar and I got our periods…which explains why I'm more emotional than usual.

And hungrier.

In the spirit of sisterhood solidarity—and the need for copious amounts of sugar, chocolate, and tampons—I left to make a snack run during the concert while she stayed back to do some more investigation work on baby mama number two.

I rummage around the paper bag I'm holding as I enter the greenroom. "Okay, I got us some twinkies, chocolate bars, ice cream—"

"Some things never change," a familiar voice sneers.

My head snaps up at the sound of Sabrina's voice. "What the fuck are you doing here?"

This must be a nightmare. That's the only logical explanation for why the girl who made it her life's mission to torture me nonstop for years is sitting a mere seven feet away…looking at me like *I'm* the one out of place.

Then again, that's how she's always looked at me.

Like I didn't belong anywhere.

So much so, I started to feel like I didn't.

Shifting her focus to something behind me, Sabrina's face lights up. "There you are, baby. Sorry I'm late, my plane was delayed."

My stomach churns as a sweaty Phoenix strolls inside.

My mind spins as I attempt to put the pieces together.

It's been twenty-four hours since our blowout and we still haven't spoken a word to each other, which was fairly easy to do because I intentionally spent the night in George's room.

Guess Phoenix invited her here as payback.

But is it?

Because she did call him baby.

Just like she used to.

Storm walks in a moment later. His eyes go big when he spots Sabrina on the couch. Then they narrow on Phoenix.

"You just keep fucking up."

A confused Skylar comes out of the bathroom. "What's going on?"

I wish I knew.

Memphis, Chandler, and George join us next.

"Good sh—" The tension must be obvious because Memphis stops mid-sentence and looks around until his eyes land on Sabrina. "Who's the new chick?"

"Not a new chick," Storm says. "That's Sabrina."

This time, Chandler's eyebrows shoot up. "Oh, for fuck's sake."

Then he marches off, muttering something about not being paid enough to deal with drama.

Memphis shakes his head. "You're a brave motherfucker. Brave and *stupid*."

Definitely the latter.

George sidles up beside me. "You okay?"

I plaster a smile as fake as Sabrina is on my face. "Yeah. Why wouldn't I be?"

That's when it occurs to me that everyone—aside from poor Skylar who's looking more confused by the minute—knows Phoenix cheated on me with Sabrina and it's the reason things ended between us.

Visibly annoyed now, Sabrina twists around to look at Memphis. "I'm sorry. Is there a problem?"

To her credit, she appears even more beautiful than she did in high school. Her long blonde hair is even longer, she's tanner, her makeup application is flawless.

She's thinner.

"There's about to be," Skylar bites out. "Who the hell are you?"

Not one to lose her alpha-female position, Sabrina stands. "I'm Phoenix's high school sweetheart."

Oh, God. I'd laugh if I didn't think I'd end up puking instead.

Doesn't stop Storm from doing it, though. In fact, I don't think I've ever heard the guy laugh so hard in my life. "That's one hell of a delusion."

Sabrina's jaw drops. "Excu—"

"I'm gonna go shower," Phoenix interjects.

I might as well not even be in the room anymore because all his attention is on *her*.

It's that action—or rather, inaction—that makes me realize this isn't him trying to give me a taste of my own medicine.

If it was, he'd be looking at me for a reaction.

Hell, he'd be preening around the room, silently gloating.

Sabrina isn't here because of me.

She's here because he wants her here.

"After, we can grab a bite to eat."

I nearly rock back on my heels from the force of the blow.

Phoenix Walker never took me on a date.

But he has no problem taking the girl who used to mercilessly bully me to the point that I sincerely believed the things she said were true out on one.

I came here to make *him* suffer. To hurt *him*.

But if this were a contest to see who could wound the other more, he not only won...he effortlessly wiped the floor with my heart and outshined me.

Just like he always has.

Moist cake with creamy white filling infuses my taste buds as I chew.

I can practically feel the endorphins going off in my brain as I swallow, already anxious for more.

My stomach recoils as I take in all the empty wrappers scattered on the floor of my hotel room.

And just like that, an all too familiar shame surrounds me like a viscous fog as I finish my last twinkie and walk over to the mirror.

It's been years since I've binged.

Standing in nothing but a bra and boy shorts, I assess my body. Only, instead of appreciating my curves and focusing on the things I like—my old demons have come back to haunt me.

And they sound just like Sabrina and her friends.

Because if they were here right now…

They'd tell me my stomach isn't flat or toned enough.

That my thighs are still too big.

That the cellulite on my huge, jiggly ass is hideous.

That a size ten is still a double-digit…and therefore not acceptable.

That me not giving a fuck what they think because I lost weight for the right reasons doesn't matter…because I'll always be the fat girl.

Perhaps they're right.

My eyes burn and a tear escapes down my cheek as I reach for the black Sharpie I borrowed from Skylar earlier.

Walking over to the bed, I position the marker over my upper thigh and press down, writing my first word. *Fat.*

Emotions collide in my chest as my mind flits back to the pig-slop incident.

The way everyone oinked and laughed at me.

How I felt so gross I legitimately wanted to die.

How mortifying it was when Phoenix arrived and saw me like that. Because the secret world I created in my head—the one where I pretended that boys like Phoenix chose girls like me—could no longer exist.

It had been infiltrated by the real world.

And in the real world…boys like him don't want me.

They want Sabrina.

Another tear falls as I etch the second word on my other thigh. *Pig.*

Somewhere in the back of my mind, I know what I'm doing is wrong, but I can't seem to stop.

Seeing Sabrina was the equivalent of carving open an old scar you thought had healed.

But scar tissue never goes away. You just make a conscious effort not to let it define you until it fades into the background.

Kind of like an old box of keepsakes you stuck in the back of your closet.

Only these memories aren't good ones.

I angle the marker over my lower stomach. I might not be able to remember the specifics of every bullying episode clearly because it was a daily occurrence, but I remember exactly how it made me feel.

Like I wasn't good enough.

Like I didn't belong.

Like I'd never be special.

I'm penning another word when I hear the door to Phoenix's room open, followed by his deep voice.

"I'm shot. You should go back to your room."

Bile rises up my throat. *Shot from all the sex they had.*

"We can be quick," Sabrina says in a seductive, breathy tone.

One I'm sure turned him on dozens of times in the past.

"Can't. I gotta be up early. I have an interview in the morning."

I stop writing. *No, he doesn't.*

"Come on, Phoenix," Sabrina whines before her voice fills with anger. "Don't invite me to your show, act like you're gonna fuck me, and then not follow through like last time."

Hold the freaking phone. *What?*

I shake my head, feeling like an idiot. For all I know they've seen each other lots of times since then and she's referring to a different night.

"Look, I'm beat," Phoenix grits out. "I'll see you at the show tomorrow night."

The sound of Sabrina's heels clacking down the hallway fades away as I ponder what his deal is.

He invited her here so he could fuck her, yet he turned her down. It doesn't make any sense.

Without warning, the door connecting our rooms swings open and Phoenix marches inside.

I quickly reach for my shirt on the bed and shield myself. "Jesus. Do you *ever* knock?"

How the hell did he even get in here to begin with? I locked the door.

My back teeth meet with a clack when I notice the card in his hand. *Bastard.*

"You've been crying."

Springing off the bed, I point to the door. "Astute observation, captain obvious. Now get out."

"Lennon."

The way he says my name—all full of concern, like he actually gives a shit about me—is almost more than I can handle right now.

He's standing in front of me in three quick strides. "What's wrong?"

"Leave me alone."

He's already done enough.

Long fingers tip my chin, and he studies my face, as if doing so will give him the answers he's seeking. "Talk to me."

There's a weird note laden in his tone.

Something I haven't heard since that night we were fighting in his car after we had sex—well, partial sex—on Storm's futon and he realized I was a virgin.

"I ate a twinkie."

His eyebrows draw together. "So what? Twinkies are good."

I avert my gaze as shame snakes up my spine once again. "I ate the whole box."

Dammit. Why am I being so candid with him?

My heart thuds painfully against my ribs with awareness.

Despite what he did, Phoenix is the only one who didn't judge me—or make fun of me—when I let him see the ugliest parts of myself.

As it turned out, I didn't need to invent a secret world for us.

Because Phoenix Walker saw me—and for one fleeting moment—he wanted me.

Just the way I was.

Those blue eyes sear into my soul…like he already knows everything I'm feeling, but can't bring myself to say.

After what feels like an eternity, his gaze drops down my body in a slow perusal that has the tiny hairs on my arms lifting.

"Perfection is unattainable, Lennon. But from where I'm standing, you're the closest thing to it. Now and—"

Suddenly, his nostrils flare, and he brushes past me.

A moment later, I hear water running in the bathroom.

"What are you doing?"

I get my answer when he storms back out…holding a wet washcloth.

Oh. My. God.

Humiliation is a boulder rolling downhill and picking up speed.

I'm just as embarrassed as I was the first time he saw the words.

He motions to the end of the bed. "Sit."

As I do, he wrangles the T-shirt from me.

Then he kneels.

The first swipe of the warm washcloth against my thigh makes my chest cave in.

Exhaling, I look down.

His gaze is dark with intent and his jaw is tight as he attempts to scrub the ink off my skin without hurting me.

My throat prickles with tears because it's not the moments when he's an asshole that hurt me the most…it's moments like these.

I don't understand how the guy who's trying to wash away the cruel words I wrote on my body...is the very same one who caused me so much pain it put a crack in the foundation of my psyche and irrevocably changed me.

"Did you have sex with Sabrina that night?"

I don't know why I'm asking because I'm positive I won't like the answer.

The hand scrubbing my stomach freezes.

His silence stretches for so long I don't think he's going to answer.

But then I hear it.

"No."

The fingers gripping the side of my thigh twitch. "Did you fuck him last night?"

"No."

But I was so upset I probably would have if I didn't have my period.

His gaze lingers on my mouth and his stare turns threatening.

Like it belongs to him.

"Did you kiss him?"

This is my opportunity to wound him the same way he wounded me by bringing Sabrina here...

But he just gave me honesty. *For once.*

"No."

He stands up. "Get some sleep."

He's almost to the door when another thought occurs to me. Or rather, a question. One I desperately need an answer to.

"Phoenix?"

He twists around to face me. "Yeah?"

"Why didn't you have sex with her that night?"

His throat flexes, almost like he doesn't want to utter his next words.

Like he's ashamed.

"I didn't want to break my promise to you."

I'm having trouble merging what he just told me with his actions, because it's a complete contradiction.

Even though he didn't sleep with Sabrina, he still intentionally made *me* think he did so he could steal my song.

Sure, he didn't break his promise...but he still broke my heart.

Broke me.

He averts his gaze. "There's a ticket for tomorrow night's show at will call."

The abrupt change of subject nearly makes my head spin. "Ticket for who?"

"You."

That makes about as much sense as him not sleeping with Sabrina. "Why?"

I don't know what to make of his expression. "You'll find out if you come."

That's all I get before he goes back to his room.

When I look down, all the words are gone.

However, when I take a closer look, I can still see a faint outline shadowing my skin.

It's another reminder that even though pain can fade...it never really goes away.

"Why are we here?" I scream over Phoenix's melodic raspy voice as he belts the second to last song of the night.

Skylar shrugs as he runs to the other side of the stage and holds out his mic. "Beats me. Phoenix just told me I'd wanna be here for this."

Gee, that really clears things up. "Be here for what?"

Another shrug. "I have no idea."

After whipping his head back and forth with so much vigor I'm positive he now has whiplash, Phoenix saunters over to Storm, who's in the middle of an awesome drum solo. "You assholes better give it up for this motherfucker right here!"

At Phoenix's request, the crowd goes from wild…to sheer pandemonium. A girl sitting on her boyfriend's shoulders lifts her shirt, flashing the band…and everyone else. A few women throw their bras on stage.

Unfortunately, one ends up hitting Skylar.

Nose wrinkling, Skylar inspects the bright-red bra. "This one is cute, but it's too big for me." She cups a hand over her mouth. "What's your bra size?"

Even two of my boobs couldn't fill one of those cups. The owner of said bra is *lucky*.

"Won't fit me either."

Skylar tosses the bra onstage. Seconds later, a bright-yellow G-string sails over our heads.

It gets caught on the end of Memphis's guitar. *Impressive.*

He gives the crowd a sexy lopsided grin, which only makes the females in the audience go even more nuts.

"I want to have your babies, Memphis," some woman in the row directly in back of us screams.

"He has enough baby mamas already," Skylar snaps.

Oh, boy.

"Take me home tonight, Phoenix," a woman to the right of me shouts. "I want to suck your big fat dick."

I roll my eyes when Phoenix flashes her a panty-melting smile.

The song *finally* comes to an end and Phoenix grabs a bottle of water off the drum riser.

"Don't worry. It's water, guys." He winks at the crowd before chugging it down. "But now that I got your attention, I'd like to introduce you to someone."

I eye Skylar, who looks as confused as I feel.

"An old friend of mine is in town tonight."

My stomach knots as Phoenix motions to someone offstage.

I swear to God, he better not…

"Sabrina, come on out here."

What. The. Actual. Fuck.

There are a few catcalls and whistles from guys as Sabrina struts out in a skintight leather dress that clings to her perfect body.

I grind my teeth as Phoenix places an arm around her.

"We go way back, don't we?"

Sabrina giggles. "We do."

Phoenix turns his attention to the crowd. "In high school, there's always that one girl. You know who I'm talking about—the pretty, popular, bitchy chick. She gets crowned homecoming queen. She always looks perfect." He waggles his eyebrows. "She goes to prom with the quarterback but fucks the bad boy in the parking lot."

The crowd cheers.

I look at Skylar. "I'm out."

He's already hurt me enough. I'd be a masochist to stay here and let him get another sucker punch in.

I bend down so I can grab my purse off the floor.

"She bullies the girl she's secretly jealous of because she knows deep down *that* girl is smarter, sexier, and more authentic than she'll ever be."

I freeze.

"However, there's a little thing called karma." He shoots Sabrina an icy glare. "And she's an even bigger bitch than you."

Taking a step back, he gives a rope suspended above his head a sharp tug.

Less than a second later, chunky liquid pours all over Sabrina.

It smells so bad I have to plug my nose.

"Shit," Skylar mutters as Sabrina lets out a shriek.

"Sooey," Storm yells into his mic before he does a *"ba-dum-tss"* rimshot on the drums.

"What sound do pigs make?" Phoenix roars as he holds the mic out to the crowd.

On cue, everyone in the arena starts oinking.

As a blubbering, pig-slop-covered Sabrina flees the stage, Phoenix's eyes find mine.

Giving me a smug smirk, he drops the mic.

CHAPTER 42
PHOENIX

An irate Skylar paces the floor in her red stilettos. Ever since the pig-slop incident three days ago, she's been on edge, and tonight she declared an emergency family meeting in Chandler's suite so we can talk about *etiquette*.

"Where's the black sheep?" Memphis mutters as he plops down on the couch beside me.

Storm's lips twitch, and Skylar stops pacing. "Since George is the only one who can stay out of trouble, I gave him permission to take Lennon out to dinner." She makes a face like she smells something rancid. "And the World War II exhibit downtown."

"Things must be getting serious between them." Memphis elbows me in the ribs. "That sounds like a date to me."

I reach for the bowl of chips Skylar set on the table. "Not a good one."

While I was under no illusions that pouring pig slop on Sabrina would make Lennon drop to her knees and blow me, I was hoping it would make shit better between us.

Granted, she hasn't glared her usual hate fire at me in three days…but most of her free time is still being spent with *him*.

George the jackass.

Clearing her throat, Skylar reaches inside her giant purse and pulls out a stack of papers.

"First things first. Let's review dos and don'ts." Her gaze rests on Storm. "We don't leave a woman handcuffed to our bed and then forget where our room is."

"Hey." Storm takes a swig of his beer. "I knew where the room was. I just couldn't find the hotel."

Sighing, Skylar flips to the next page of her stack. "We do not use our personal credit card to send fifty-thousand dildos to a renowned music critic's home because he didn't give your last album a good review. Especially with a note that reads: 'Go fuck yourself. Love, Sharp Objects.'"

The three of us exchange fist bumps.

Pinching the bridge of her nose, her stare returns to Storm. "We do *not* offer to pee in a fan's mouth when they mention being thirsty at a meet and greet."

Storm takes his phone out of his pocket. "She complained about the lack of refreshments. I simply gave her options."

She focuses on me again. "We do not pour pig slop…" Her nose scrunches. "On second thought, I'm okay with that one." She steeples her fingers. "Anyway, now that we know better, we have to do better. I want everyone to be on their best behavior for tonight's show. Got it?"

She's packing up her things when Memphis grunts, "What about me?"

She sharpens her gaze. "*You* are beyond my help." She produces a condom from her giant purse and throws it at his chest. "If you need instructions on how to use one of these…Google is your friend."

With that, she flips her hair over her shoulder and meanders out.

"Seems like Storm's the real troublemaker here." Reaching over, Memphis swats the back of his head. "Get your shit together, brother."

Storm pays him no mind. He's too focused on his phone.

Or rather he *was*, because Memphis snatches it.

"Damn." He lets out a whistle. "Who's the hottie with a body you're talking to?"

Storm looks sheepish. "Don't know."

That gets my attention. "What do you mean, you don't know?"

Memphis laughs as he scrolls through his phone. "It appears our boy is on a hookup app."

Now *I'm* the one who's laughing. "You do realize you're a rock star who's about to have a stadium full of chicks tonight, right?"

"Yeah, but he pees on our fans, remember?" Memphis rubs his jaw. "On second thought, you're in luck. This one's into that."

Storm seizes his phone back. "We're not talking about this."

"Oh, no," I say. "We're talking about this."

The fucker's still giving me shit about upsetting Lennon and bringing Sabrina here, but he's still my best friend.

Storm scrubs a hand down his face. "Don't you ever get tired of having women throw themselves at you constantly just because you're famous?"

Memphis and I exchange a puzzled glance, because what the fuck?

"No," we say in unison.

He rises off the couch. "Never mind."

I gesture for him to sit back down. "Pull the stick out of your ass. We're gonna help you."

Memphis takes a seat next to him. "So, it sounds like you're tired of the fangirls being your willing hostages and you want a challenge?"

"Something like that," Storm murmurs.

I raise a brow. "You mean like a girlfriend?"

Horror spreads over his face. "Who the *fuck* said anything about a girlfriend? I just want a chick who doesn't make shit so easy for me all the time."

Once again, Memphis and I exchange another confused look.

"Sounds like a girlfriend to me."

"I meant when it comes to sex, you fucking idiots."

I mull this over for a bit. I never had a problem getting laid pre-stardom or post, but it was Josh who got off on making all kinds of chicks demean and humiliate themselves on a regular basis for his enjoyment. Maybe taking a page out of his book will help.

"You can always do what Josh did."

"Give them drugs?" Storm questions with a frown.

"Treat them like shit?" Memphis adds.

"I meant making every girl think they were special to him so he could get them to do anything he wanted."

And I mean *anything*. There were no lines that dude wouldn't cross…or fuck.

"That's because he was a manipulative asshole," Memphis bites out.

One who's no longer here.

A surge of irritation runs through my veins, and I stand. "In case you fuckers forgot, he's dead."

"Phoenix," Memphis grunts when I amble to the door.

"What?"

"Don't let your guilt make *you* forget who he really was."

That's easy for him to say…he wasn't responsible for his death.

My steps accelerate as we head out the back door.

The last show of the week ended twenty minutes ago and I'm fucking exhausted. The second I get on the bus, I'm sleeping till we get to Kansas.

"Tonight was a good show," Chandler remarks.

Next to me, Storm nods. "Yeah, Memphis's solo was absolute fire."

"Nah, man," Memphis says behind us. "*Yours* stole the show tonight."

Storm slaps my back. "And let's not forget the way Phoenix obliterated his rendition of 'Down with the Sickness.'"

"George was awesome, too," Lennon chimes in.

No one says shit.

We're about to get on the bus, but the security guard stops us.

"There's a woman in there who specifically requested to see you two tonight."

Storm looks at me.

"If it's Megan Fox, I call dibs. You know I got that MILF fantasy."

I'm pretty sure security is fucking with us right now because all I see when we walk up the steps is a short woman with gray hair wearing a long flowery dress and orthopedic shoes.

Memphis nudges Storm. "How about a cougar fantasy?"

Storm opens his mouth to respond, but the woman turns around. "I prefer GILF."

We all break out in smiles—aside from Storm who's now cringing —as we realize the GILF in question is none other than Grams.

Memphis pushes past us so he can give her a hug. "Hey, Grams. How's Bermuda?"

"Bermuda is fine." She fans herself. "So are the men."

Storm groans. "Come on, Grams. Don't start."

She opens her mouth, but her stare snags on Skylar, who runs over to hug her next.

Grams cups her face in her hands. "How you holding up, sweet pea?"

A heavy silence falls over the bus.

Skylar gives her a smile that doesn't quite reach her eyes. "I'm hanging in there. How are you, Grams?"

She pops a hand on her hip. "I'm fabulous. Got me a younger man."

Now Skylar's smile is genuine. "Oh. Spill the tea, sister."

"I met him on one of them dating apps. He ain't much of a looker, but Lord have mercy. Thank heavens for those little blue pills."

Storm looks like he's gonna be sick. "For fuck's sake, Grams."

She wags a finger at him. "You mind your tongue. Sex is healthy." Her gaze flicks to Chandler. "You taking care of my boys?"

Chandler salutes her. "Yes, ma'am."

"You better be—" Whatever she was going to say falls by the wayside when she spots Lennon behind me. "Oh, my word."

Lennon gives her a shy smile. "Hi."

"Don't you hi me, young lady," Grams chides as she opens her arms wide. "Get over here."

Lennon doesn't waste another second, and neither does Grams. The moment their hug ends, she's fawning all over her. "Well, look at you. And then the caterpillar turned into a butterfly."

Lennon's cheeks redden due to all the attention. Fortunately for her, Grams shifts her focus to me.

"I'm glad you finally pulled your head out of your ass and got your girl back." Finger wag. "I told you she was a keeper."

George clears his throat and sticks out his hand. "Hi, I'm George. Pleasure to meet you."

She shakes it. "Hello, dear. You must be one of the new roadies. Would you be a peach and grab my bags? They're still outside."

"I'll do it," I quickly offer since I'd do anything in the world for the woman.

Plus, I could use a breather.

By the time I come back in with her bags, everyone is discussing sleeping arrangements.

Given there are only six bunks, one bedroom, and now eight of us—we need to figure out where everyone's gonna crash.

"Lennon can sleep with me," George says, which earns him a confused look from Grams and a murderous one from me.

Over my dead body.

"Gram's is taking Chandler's room. Chandler is taking my bunk, and I'm sleeping on the couch in the lounge."

Now that *that's* settled, I make my way to Chandler's bedroom so I can drop off Gram's luggage.

She ambushes me the moment it hits the floor.

"Regardless of your aversion to romantic relationships, you never struck me as the type to share."

One of the things I love most about Gram's is that she doesn't mince words.

That's not the case right now.

"I'm not sharing Lennon."

She arches a brow. "Well, considering he still has a pulse, I assume she's his then."

Anger laced with bitterness is a virulent cocktail in my veins.

I stalk toward the door. "Night, Grams."

She grabs hold of my arm. "Still pushing the people who care about you away, I see. How's that working out for you, baby?"

Just fine.

She cradles my face, forcing me to look at her. "We all make mistakes, Phoenix. But then we have to do our penance, learn the lesson, and move on."

That's not an option.

"Innocent people died. There's no moving on from that."

Sadness etches her features. "Yes, there is. It's called forgiveness."

"The people I need forgiveness from are dead."

Except one.

"Then perhaps you need to forgive yourself."

"I should have died that night."

At least then the punishment would have fit the crime.

She sighs. "You may as well have, since you're determined to live in purgatory for the rest of your life."

"It's what I deserve."

No one can tell me otherwise.

"Nobody deserved what happened to them that night. But you're still here." She grips my shoulders. "Living like a ghost and punishing yourself day in and day out won't undo the events of that night."

"Grams—"

"Life rarely gives you a second chance. You better not screw this up or waste it."

Too late.

I kiss her cheek. "I'm glad you came to visit. Let me know if you need anything."

"Phoenix?" she calls out as I'm crossing the threshold.

"Yeah?"

"I see the way that girl still looks at you. We both know she's not his."

CHAPTER 43

I stuff my pillow over my head as the sound of a passing freight train shakes the bus.

And by freight train? I mean Chandler's snoring.

Now I understand why he has the bedroom in the back. And why everyone else put in earplugs before they went to bed.

I make a mental note to get a pair of earbuds at the next city since my headphones are too big to sleep with.

I'm debating turning the kitchen table into a bed when my phone vibrates. Assuming George can't sleep through Chandler's deafening snoring either and wants to plot out an escape plan, I feel around for it.

I grind my molars when I see a text from Phoenix instead.

Phoenix: Are you up?
Lennon: Are you drunk?

While I know Phoenix giving Sabrina a taste of her own medicine was his way of trying to right one of his many wrongs, it doesn't magically make everything better.

I let my guard down in front of him the other night and not only was that senseless…it was a mistake.

In order to ensure it never happens again, I have to set some boundaries.

He's the client and I'm the...babysitter.

Tiny dots appear at the end of my screen before it lights up with a new message.

Phoenix: Not currently. Why?
Lennon: Because that's the only time I'm contractually obligated to talk to you.
Phoenix: Last I checked, you're *contractually obligated* to be there for me when I need you.

I'm pretty sure my sigh is louder than Chandler's snoring.

Lennon: Fine. What do you need?
Phoenix: What are you wearing?

I squint as I type out my response.

Lennon: Pajamas.
Phoenix: So, my T-shirt and a pair of panties?

Darn it. I've got to throw this damn thing out.

Lennon: No.
Phoenix: No panties?
Lennon: No T-shirt, asshole.
Phoenix: Even better.

He's the freaking worst. I swear.

Lennon: Inappropriate much?
Phoenix: Very much.

On that we agree.

Lennon: Good night.

I'm about to put my phone down, but another text comes through.

Phoenix: You used to like that about me.
Lennon: I used to like a lot of things about you.

I close my eyes as memories puncture me.
I liked his crudeness and his dirty mouth.
The way he took control.
How he pushed me past my limits and the things he brought out of me.
I liked how he didn't give a fuck what anyone else thought about him.
How hard he worked to make a better life for himself.
The raw talent he has.
How he was rough around the edges, but once he finally permitted you to get a brief peek inside, you realized he was actually sensitive...and complex. *Damaged*.
Even though he refused to let his scars define him.
I didn't just like Phoenix Walker...
I loved him.
My phone goes off with another incoming text.

Phoenix: You still do.

Not anymore.

Lennon: Quite the imagination you have.
Phoenix: You have no idea.
Lennon: I'm going to sleep.
Phoenix: I imagine how sexy you looked with my cock stuffed in your mouth. How eager you were to please me and how fucking hard it was not to come.

My heart kicks up, both the organ *and* me completely caught off guard.

Phoenix: That's why I made you jerk me after we pulled up to your house that night. You turned me on so fucking much. I wanted to make it last a little longer.

A rush of heat snakes through me, coiling around my lungs.

Phoenix: I imagine teasing your little pussy with my fingers and tongue.

My cheeks burn and my chest heaves on a shallow breath.
I *have* to put an end to this.

Lennon: You can stop now. I'm not interested.

He doesn't.

Phoenix: You were so wet when I put them inside you. All I could think about was tasting you.

My nipples pull tight against my T-shirt...
And that's when I realize.
He's not typing these words.
He's *saying* them aloud.
Knowing that sends a whole new wave of arousal through me.

Phoenix: I could have your pretty cunt for every meal and it still wouldn't be enough.

Jesus.
I press my thighs together, desperate to relieve the ache.

Phoenix: I imagine the needy way you moaned my name as I made you come. How you bucked your hips, demanding more.

I no longer have the strength to tell him to stop.

Phoenix: I imagine you climbing out of bed, sneaking in here, and riding my cock.

A pulse throbs between my legs as I imagine the same thing.

Phoenix: I imagine those plump pink lips stretching around me as you slide down slowly, giving yourself time to adjust. But I can't wait any longer to have you, so I'd grab your hips and force you to take every inch of me at once.

I nearly whimper. God, it would hurt…in the best possible way.

Phoenix: I'd fuck you so good you wouldn't be able to think about how wrong it was.
Phoenix: And I wouldn't stop fucking you. Not until

Not until *what*? I almost scream.
Then my phone rings.
Do. Not. Answer.
Silently cursing myself, I swipe the green button. So quickly, I don't realize it's a FaceTime call until it's too late.
My stomach clenches and a shiver breaks free when my screen lights up with the image of Phoenix's hand moving up and down his dick.
He groans and I nearly jump out of my skin with panic as I fetch my headphones and plug them in.
This is so wrong, but I don't care.
All I can focus on is the way his thumb glides over the thick, pulsing veins of his big cock with every stroke and the ragged

breathing filling my ears as he vigorously pumps himself with skilled efficiency.

A slow tremble crawls down my spine. I'm so wet my inner thighs are slick with it.

"Lennon."

The hoarse, raspy way he says my name has me slipping my hand inside my panties.

Biting my lip so I don't make a sound, I rub my clit feverishly as I watch the muscles in his thighs clench and thick ropes of cum jet out of his pulsing cock, spilling along his stomach and hand.

I go off like a rocket as he gives himself one final stroke, squeezing the tip.

Then the screen goes black.

After catching my breath, I rip my headphones off.

Safe to say I should have no problem falling asleep now.

I roll over, intending to do just that, but my phone lights up with another text.

Phoenix: Looks like we're both liars.
Lennon: What are you talking about?
Phoenix: If you weren't interested, you could have hung up...but you didn't.

My nostrils fill with the delicious aroma of bacon, pancakes, and banana bread.

"Is this heaven?" Phoenix questions as I open the dividing door and head out to the kitchen where everyone is already eating.

Storm stuffs his mouth with a forkful of pancakes. "Nah. Heaven is when she makes biscuits and gravy."

Grams slaps the back of his head. "Are you insulting the food I just made? Be grateful you have a nice home-cooked meal instead of that stale cereal I found in the cupboard."

Storm sulks. "I'm grateful, Grams."

She smiles when she sees me. "Come on, sweet pea. Grab your-self a plate. Let's put some meat back on those bones."

Never thought I would hear *that*.

I'm happily loading up my plate when I hear, "She doesn't need more meat on her bones."

Seven pairs of eyes swivel to George.

Grams pops a hand on her hip. "Care to explain what you mean by that, young man?"

George looks like he's going to shit his pants. But I don't feel the need to come to his defense like I usually do.

"Well, you know." He visibly gulps. "She's not *that* skinny." When several jaws drop, he quickly adds, "But it's not like she's fat or anything."

I put my plate down.

Memphis points his fork at George. "Dude, you really need to quit talking."

Dismissing that excellent advice, George looks at me. "I didn't mean you were fat. You're not. You're perf—"

Phoenix pounds his fist against the table so hard the dishes rattle. "Shut the fuck up. *Now*." Cocking his head, he zeros in on me. "Eat your breakfast."

"So, breakfast was…unexpected," Skylar exclaims as we tidy up the kitchen.

"Yeah, those pancakes were the best I've ever had."

"They were delicious." Her lips quirk. "But I was referring to George putting his foot in his mouth and Phoenix almost ripping it out and beating him to death with it."

Before I can respond, Grams strides into the kitchen.

Phoenix, Storm, and Memphis are right behind her.

A pang of sadness shoots through me when I notice Phoenix is carrying her luggage. "You're leaving already?"

The woman just got here.

"Afraid so, dear. Got me a booty call in Miami, thanks to that app."

Phoenix gives Storm a shit-eating grin as he heads to the front of the bus. "Looks like Grams has more game than you."

Storm raises his middle finger before wrapping Grams up in a big hug. "Call me when you land."

"Sure thing, baby. Stay out of trouble."

He laughs. "I'll do my best."

Turning to Skylar, Grams kisses her forehead. "Make sure he doesn't get arrested."

Skylar smiles. "I'll do my best."

Her attention shifts to Memphis. "And *you*. Don't be a fool, wrap your tool."

A sheepish smile tugs at his mouth as he hugs her. "I'll do my best."

After they break apart, she folds her arms around me. "I'm so happy you're back." Face lined with worry, she cups my cheek. "Please don't give up on him."

I don't have the heart to disappoint her, so I say the only thing I can.

"I'll do my best."

CHAPTER 44
LENNON

The moment the elevator doors open, I take off in a sprint.

Phoenix isn't behind me like he should be though because—as usual—he's taking his sweet time and lagging behind.

Impatient, I tap my foot while I wait for him to catch up. "Chandler's going to kill me if I don't have you at the venue in the next ten minutes."

He meanders down the hall like one would if they were having a leisurely stroll through a park. "The venue's only nine minutes away. We got plenty of time."

So help me God…

When the sloth *finally* joins me, we make a quick left down the hallway leading to the private exit out back.

I feel him appraising me. "You know, our relationship would go a lot smoother if you'd learn to chill the fuck out."

"Easy for you to say. You're not dealing with *you*. "Also…" I gesture between us. "This isn't a relationsh—"

"Phoenix," a masculine voice slurs from behind.

Weird. Since everyone we know is already at the venue.

I'm about to chalk it up to a fan wanting an autograph, but

Phoenix's steps come to a halt and his expression turns serious. "I'll meet you in the car."

An uneasy feeling fills my gut. "Why? What's going—"

"Get in the car."

His ominous tone sends chills down my spine, but I'm not leaving.

Not until I know who this guy is and what's got Phoenix so on edge.

"Aren't you gonna say hi?" the man presses.

Phoenix spins around. "What the fuck are you doing here?"

The man staggers forward. He's around Phoenix's height, with long greasy dark hair, and the bluest, cruelest eyes I've ever seen.

The same shade as Phoenix's.

"Just came to pay my boy a visit."

The uneasy feeling in my gut intensifies.

Instinctively, I grab Phoenix's hand, giving it a sharp tug. "Come on. Let's go."

I don't know what this piece of shit wants, but we're not sticking around to find out.

His father's bloodshot eyes zero in on me. "Who's your little girlfriend?"

In a flash, Phoenix yanks me behind him. "None of your fucking business."

"Is that any way to talk to the man who raised you?" He takes another step, swaying as he does. "I taught you to have more respect than that."

This asshole didn't teach him a damn thing. *His fists did.*

"What the fuck do you want?"

"Your old man is having some money problems. I was hoping you could help me out."

And there it is.

Phoenix snorts. "Big fucking surprise."

Sneering, he rocks back on his heels. "Don't you dare take that self-righteous tone with me, boy. You lived in my house rent-free for eighteen years, remember?"

That's par for the course when you have children.

Baring his teeth, Phoenix takes his wallet out of his pocket. The look he gives him is engulfed with venom as he throws a wad of cash in his face.

"How could I forget?"

"Does he visit you a lot?"

Paying me no mind, Phoenix rolls down the window in the back seat of the SUV and lights a cigarette.

Shocker.

"Wow, the silent treatment. What else is new?"

Grinding his jaw, he brings the cigarette to his mouth and inhales. "You're one to talk."

"Are you deaf? I do talk to you."

Far more than I want to.

He laughs, but there's no humor. "Not about shit that matters."

Good Lord. He's unbelievable.

"Fine. What do you want to talk about?" I snap my fingers. "Oh, here's an idea. Let's talk about your dad."

"Let's talk about *yours*," he bites out, eyes blazing.

Ripping a page out of his book, I scowl at my window.

A harsh snicker cuts the air. "Hypocrite."

Anger brews in the pit of my stomach, and my hands itch with the urge to smack him. "Fraud."

Closing my eyes, I draw in a deep, cleansing breath.

Fighting with him all the time is exhausting.

But that's all Phoenix has ever known. Thanks to that abusive piece of shit with a vacant block inside his chest in place of a heart.

"I wasn't trying to start an argument," I whisper. "I simply wanted you to know you could talk to someone about it."

He tosses his cigarette out the window. "Maybe I should go find George then, since *that's* who we're telling all our secrets to these days."

I don't know why I even bother anymore.

"That's because George is my…"

I don't finish that statement…because I can't.

Phoenix's cruel stare burns right through me. "Your what?"

"None of your business."

My feelings for George might not be clear, but I don't owe this asshole a damn thing.

The silence stretches between us, growing heavier by the second…

Until he speaks.

"He comes around every couple of months. Begging for money."

I tilt my head to look at him. "Well, if you didn't give him any, he'd probably stop."

Remorse squeezes my heart when I see pain flicker in his eyes.

"I'm sorry. That was really judgmental—"

"He was there." His voice is a raw rasp. "Which is more than I can say for her."

Never in a million years did I think I'd ever open up to Phoenix Walker again.

But I know what it took for him to share that small part of himself and be vulnerable.

About as much as it's going to take for me to share this with him.

"My dad is sick."

"We're here," the driver announces.

I reach for the door handle. "Chandler's gonna be pissed."

His hand wraps around my wrist before I can exit. "Talk to me."

He's out of his mind. This is so not the time or place.

"There are over twenty-five thousand fans waiting inside that arena for you."

And we're already late.

The calloused tips of his fingers capture my chin. "But the only person who matters to me is sitting right here."

My heart—the traitorous organ—slams against my chest.

I know better than to believe anything he says, but it still hasn't gotten the memo.

"A couple of years ago, he was diagnosed with early-onset dementia." I close my eyes so they don't fill with tears. "Most days, he doesn't even know who I am."

The pad of his thumb skims my cheek. "Lennon."

There's so much sorrow in his voice you'd think it was happening to him.

My breath stills as he cups the side of my face, inching closer.

Even though I should push him away, I can't.

He's the sun...pulling me into his atmosphere.

He breathes me in, I bleed him out.

"Lennon," he repeats, only this time it sounds like an apology.

The soft press of his lips is like a salve to my exposed wound.

But not the one he caused.

Pain spears my chest and I tear my mouth away. "No."

I swear I hear him growl.

"Why?"

The fact he has to ask me is further proof why this not only shouldn't—but can't—happen.

I flash him a vindictive smile and toss his old words in his face so he can choke on them this time.

"It will complicate shit."

Pushing the door open, I climb out of the car.

Stupid, stupid, stupid.

There's a sharp tug on my arm before I'm shoved against the SUV.

I open my mouth to yell at him, but the pure agony cutting into the sharp lines of his face renders me speechless.

"I *hate* that I hurt you."

And then he's walking away.

That makes two of us.

CHAPTER 45

Backstage after the show, everyone gathers around Chandler, who's standing in front of a giant cake.

"In the words of Bon Jovi—we're halfway done."

A bunch of us exchange baffled looks because that's *not* what Bon Jovi said.

Phoenix cups a hand over his mouth. "We're halfway there, asshole."

"Yes." Chandler raises his glass in the air before downing it. "Yes, we are."

Phoenix and Storm shake their heads.

"Anyway," Chandler drones. "Thank you for all your hard work." He lifts a finger. "No one touch this cake until the stage is broken down."

There are groans all around as the crew goes back to work.

A frown mars George's face. "I can't believe we're midway through the tour."

Thank God.

"What is the matter with you?" Skylar screeches.

"Save some for the crew," Storm grunts.

Memphis—who's parked a chair in front of the cake—shrugs as

he shoves another forkful into his mouth. "You snooze, you lose. Shit's good."

I'll take his word for it, because I won't be having any of it now.

George turns to me. "Can we talk for a second?"

I place my cup of sparkling cider down on the table. "Sure. What's up?"

"I meant in private."

Grabbing my elbow, he steers me into the empty greenroom and closes the door.

Oh boy.

"So," he begins. "I've been thinking about us."

Shit. I'm so not ready for where this conversation sounds like it's going.

"Uh-huh."

Reaching down, he takes both my hands in his. "I really, really, *really* like you."

I swallow. "Really?"

"Yes." He blows out a breath. "A lot."

I stop him right there. "George, I told you. I'm not ready for anything serious."

"How do you know?" he exclaims. "Every time I try to kiss you, something gets in the way."

Not something. *Someone.*

"Bad timing?" I squeak.

His brows draw together. "Bad timing…or reluctance?"

"It's not…" I clear my throat. "It's not reluctance."

Who are you trying to convince here, Lennon?

He takes a step forward and I instinctively take one back, causing my spine to meet the wall behind me.

Dammit. I've trapped myself.

"Then prove it." He comes closer. "Kiss me, Lennon. *Please.* I'm begging you."

"Okay," I whisper.

Leaving him hanging isn't right. I need to sort this out.

I squeeze my eyes shut. And then I brush my lips against his.

The kiss is…fine.

He's not terrible at it, but there are no sparks.

Which makes my once unclear feelings for George crystal clear now.

I'm gonna have to figure out how to let him down gently.

"Groupie."

The sinister bite in Phoenix's voice makes the tiny hairs on my arms stand on end.

I didn't even hear the door open.

Steeling myself, I glower at him. "I'm in the middle of something."

His jaw goes tight and his steps eat up the distance between us in no time.

Without warning, he grabs my arm and tugs me out of the room, leaving a bewildered George in our wake.

"What is your problem?" I snap as we cross the threshold.

He stops walking and leans down.

His rough voice is a menacing rumble in my ear. "Bus. *Now*. Or I'll snort a gram of coke off the nearest girl's tits and force you to watch me fuck them."

The threat is the equivalent of dull razor blades slicing into my skin.

I feel Phoenix's furious stare boring into my back with every step I take, like a killer hunting their latest victim.

A flush burns my cheeks as I trek past all the people backstage, hoping they can't sense the tension mounting between us.

Butterflies swarm my stomach as I push open the back door.

Behind me, Phoenix makes a noise of impatience, like I'm not moving fast enough.

I quicken my strides, my heels hitting the pavement of the parking lot with a loud *click click click.*

My heart races as we approach the bus. The lights are off and it's completely empty.

I walk up the steps on legs that feel like Jell-O, Phoenix following close behind.

My head grows woozy as we enter the kitchen.

We'll be reaching the bunks soon.

A sharp gasp leaves me when he grips the back of my neck and bends me over the kitchen table.

"Spread your fucking legs."

So many thoughts go through my head, but I can only focus on one.

I. Want. This.

White-hot heat punches through me as he shoves my skirt up over my ass.

Cool air kisses my skin and the sound of him shredding the delicate lace of my thong assaults my ears, followed by the sound of him tugging down his zipper.

The hand on the back of my neck tightens and his other curls around my hip possessively, keeping me right where he wants me.

"Take my dick like a good girl."

It's the only warning I get before he juts his hips, filling me to the hilt in a single, painful thrust that makes me hiss.

There's no time to adjust to his massive cock because he starts fucking me in quick, brutal strokes.

Adrenaline is an intoxicating drug surging through my system, heating my blood, and sending me spiraling.

I dig my nails into his thigh. "Oh god."

Every time he withdraws, he drives back inside me that much harder.

It's both a punishment and a reward.

I whimper when he stills. "Phoenix. *Please.*"

His coarse voice snaps like a whip. "If you want it…" A sharp breath leaves me when he winds my ponytail around his fist and tugs. "Then take it."

Understanding dawns, generating a new wave of arousal.

My belly clenches as I circle my hips, working myself on his dick.

It feels so good I can no longer form cohesive thoughts. All I can focus on is the way his cock fills me and the rough, greedy sounds he makes as I grip the sides of the table and impale myself on him, taking what I want.

What I need.

The control he permitted me doesn't last long, though, because he yanks on my ponytail, pulling me upright. "Play with your pussy."

Slipping my hand between my legs, I do what he says.

His breath is a hot rasp against my neck as I work myself into a frenzy. "That's it. Rub that little clit."

Wet sounds fill the bus and sweat slicks over my skin as my body winds tighter and tighter.

I'm so close. So fucking close.

With a growl, Phoenix pushes my hand away and replaces it with his.

A desperate moan escapes me when he finds a rhythm that sets me on fire.

He thrusts faster, hitting a spot that makes me mewl and moan like a feral animal in heat. I writhe against him, demanding more.

He gives me what I want and then some. Every ruthless snap of his hips sends another bolt of pleasure whipping through me until it reaches a crest.

My orgasm is so potent, so *severe* it takes hold of me and doesn't let go until I'm crying out his name.

With a harsh grunt, he spins me around and seats me on the table.

If I thought his thrusts were vicious before, it has nothing on right now. Hand squeezing my throat, he takes what he wants from me...and I spread my thighs wider, letting him.

Pleasure contorts his face and a deep throaty sound tears out of him...

Then his mouth crashes against mine.

His kiss is so intense, so *consuming*, I lose the ability to breathe.

Phoenix takes my mouth like an enemy conquering his opponent.

Like he's won.

I swallow his savage groan as he pumps inside me one last time before pulling out. He bites my lip hard enough to draw blood as a stream of warm liquid seeps into the fabric of my shirt.

I'm dizzy when we finally break apart. All the thoughts I forced myself to ignore before come rushing back with a vengeance, sobering me.

Scrambling off the table, I adjust my skirt while he tucks himself back into his jeans.

Voices in the distance send a whoosh of panic spiraling through me. I turn so I can run to the bunks, but Phoenix fists the back of my shirt, pulling me flush against him.

He slips his hand between my legs, gathering the remnants of my orgasm on his fingers. "I told you the next time I fucked you, it would end with you coming all over my cock."

Regret pinches my chest as I twist out of his hold. "That was a one-time thing."

Now that we got it out of our system, we can go back to hating one another.

His lips curve in an arrogant smirk as he licks his fingers clean. "Liar."

CHAPTER 46
LENNON

I close my eyes as "She Hates Me" by Puddle of Mudd blasts through my new earbuds.

I'm thankful we're on the bus because not only do I get to sleep, I can easily avoid both Phoenix and George.

I'm mouthing the lyrics and drumming my fingers to the beat when my bunk curtain is yanked open.

"What—"

Skylar pulls my earbuds out. "Get ready, sleepyhead. We're going out tonight."

Ugh. George's birthday is today.

It's yet another reason I've been avoiding him like the plague.

Telling someone you're not into them when they're *really* into you is harsh enough. Telling them on their birthday? That's straight up heartless.

"I'm gonna hang back." I clutch my stomach. "My period cramps are *killer*."

"TMI, Lennon," Storm grunts from the bunk above mine.

Skylar raises a brow. "That's weird. You bought us snacks and tampons ten days ago."

Dammit. That's the last time I go on a food run for Miss Nosy Pants.

"Even *more* TMI," Storm mutters.

"I...you don't know my cycle, Skylar."

"I don't want to know your cycle either," Storm bellows.

Making a fist, I strike the top of my bunk. "Then put your head-phones on."

Skylar folds her arms over her chest. "Everyone knows girls' cycles sync up in close quarters."

I stay silent, which only makes *detective* Skylar more suspicious. "You wouldn't be hiding out because something happened with you and Phoenix, would you?"

I feign innocence because anything I say can be used against me. "Nothing happened between me and Phoenix."

Above me, Storm snorts.

I make a mental note to buy the snoop a pair of noise-canceling headphones.

"In that case, it's your man's birthday. It's pretty much your duty to be there." Walking over to her own bunk, she pops open her suit-case. "Besides, the club we're going to is awesome. You *have* to come."

"Can't." I sit up in bed. "I don't have any fancy clothes."

My only nice outfit now has a cum stain on it.

Skylar doesn't take no for an answer, though because she pulls out a tiny black dress. "You're in luck. Your new bestie has lots of fancy clothes." Her eyes narrow. "But touch my shoes and I'll peel your skin off with a rusty box cutter."

Yikes. Fortunately, I won't be touching her shoes. Or her clothes.

I couldn't even if I wanted to.

"I appreciate it, but you're like a size two. There's no way that dress or anything else of yours will fit me."

These aren't my old insecurities talking, either. It's just basic math, science...and fashion.

Hand clutching her chest, she laughs. "I'm flattered, sugar, but I never turn down cobbler or fried chicken, so I'm a five." She motions for me to stand. "No worries. The dress is spandex."

Ugh. That's the worst material for someone who doesn't have a flat stomach.

"Spandex doesn't mean it will fit."

With a huff, she pops a hand on her hip. "Yes, it will. Hell, with a good pair of Spanx, it will fit *Storm*."

"Not liking where this conversation is going," Storm gripes. "Take the dress, Lennon."

"I—"

"Oh my god," Skylar cries out. "Trust me. I have a knack for these things. You're gonna look hot as fuck."

I shake my head at my sweet, *delusional* new bestie. "Only if you think *hot as fuck* is ten pounds of shit in a five-pound bag."

Literally. Given our size difference.

Skylar peers up. "Tell her she's a hot, sexy bitch, Storm."

"You're a hot, sexy bitch, Lennon," he says dryly. "Now wear the damn dress so I don't have to hear you two yakking about it all night."

"Fine." I snatch the dress from Skylar. "But only because it's cute and ruched."

"Hallelujah. I was about to strip you down myself." Ecstatic, she tugs my hand. "Come on. I turned the back lounge into a dressing room so we can get ready. I'm even heating up wax for our kitties."

"Adios," Storm mutters as we walk away. "Wait. Not so fast." He sits up. "By *kitties* you mean…"

Skylar blinks. "Our vaginas."

Duh.

Grinning, Storm waves us back in. "Then, by all means, ladies. *Stay.*"

I turn to Skylar. "You know what really sucks? Menstrual clots."

"Ugh," Skylar agrees with a devious smile. "They're the worst. Especially when you have to sneeze—"

Storm points to the door. "Out."

The dress Skylar gave me is so short it virtually flashes my freshly waxed *kitty* to whoever's in the near vicinity every time I move.

George—who's sitting next to me at the VIP table Skylar reserved —leans over. "Do you want a drink?"

I eye the three empty glasses in front of him. For someone who doesn't drink, homeboy is racking them up tonight.

Then again, it is his birthday.

"Can't," I say above the music. "Sober companion, remember?"

Instinctively, I glance across the table at Phoenix. I'm pleased— and relieved—to see he isn't drinking either.

That relief is short lived, though, when Storm returns from the bathroom…with four gorgeous girls.

Our half-moon table in the corner takes up a decent portion of the VIP section, but it's not big enough to squeeze in so many people.

Skylar—who looks extra stunning in a short white backless dress with a *plunging* neckline—looks up from her phone. "We need to take a group photo for PR."

The guys groan, but the girls Storm brought perk up like flowers in the springtime.

Taking charge, Skylar makes everyone stand and then proceeds to position the guys for the photo.

Next, she turns to the girls. She instructs two of them to sit on opposite sides of Storm and the other two to sit next to Phoenix.

I can't help but notice how she didn't give Memphis a girl. Not that it matters. His eyes have been glued to her all night.

"Come here, Lennon." Without warning, she takes hold of my hand and escorts me over to George. "Since it's such a tight squeeze, you'll need to sit on his lap."

I'm about to decline, but George grabs my hips and places me on his knee.

Skylar snaps a few photos and the moment she's done, Storm takes off with two of the girls, freeing up the table.

I'm about to get up, but George's hold on me constricts. "Stay." He gives me a dopey grin. "After all, you're my birthday present."

I stay put because...*it's his birthday.*

"You have no idea how much I like you." Sweeping my hair to one side—hair that took Skylar a full hour to create beach waves in given the length—his fingers skim the span of my arm. "We're so good together."

Movement at the other end of the table snags my attention. When I glance up, I see Phoenix rubbing his jaw, looking highly amused.

Until his gaze descends and he notices George's hand creeping up my thigh.

Then he looks downright homicidal.

George presses his lips to my shoulder blade. Liquid courage has made him awfully bold tonight. "You're my girl, right?"

I'm *a* girl.

"It's a shame our kiss got interrupted." His hand travels higher. So high I have to clutch the bottom of my dress for dear life. "But we'll make up for that tonight."

Fuck my life. *Hard.*

The empty glasses on the table rattle, and I see Phoenix get up in my peripheral.

My gaze locks on his retreating back as he leaves the VIP section and walks up the stairs, disappearing onto the crowded dance floor.

The two girls that were sitting beside him share a co-conspiratorial look before they chase after him.

Let him go.

Yet a second later, I'm climbing off George's lap. "I'm sorry. I need to keep him out of trouble."

"Phoenix is a big boy," he argues.

"It's my job," I remind him before I take off.

My heart pounds like a drum as I climb the steep steps leading to the balcony in a pair of stilettos Skylar was willing to part with after she saw my limited shoe inventory.

Colorful lights illuminate the packed dance floor. Unlike the fast up-tempo house music playing on the lower level, the music up here is slower. *Edgier.*

Wall to wall bodies gyrate against one another, moving to the hypnotic beat.

I push my way through the jam-packed crowd, attempting to find him.

Given he's so tall and a freaking rock star, you'd think the task would be that much easier.

Warm, prickly panic crawls up my chest and I feel dizzy. *What if he's off doing drugs?*

I try to ignore the way my heart trips over itself with my next thought.

What if he's fucking those girls?

My frustration escalates with every passing minute. I'm debating giving up and going back downstairs, but a strong arm wraps around my waist.

I'm about to tell whoever it is to keep their grubby paws off me, but I'm spun around so fast I nearly get whiplash.

I barely have time to register it's Phoenix before he slams me against the back wall and his lips collide with mine.

His kiss is every bit as dominating as he is. He's not staking a claim… he's taking it.

Hand tunneling my hair, he forces my mouth open wider.

A deep groan rumbles in his chest as he feeds me his tongue in ravenous strokes, his fingers digging into my ass.

Oh god. Oh god. Oh god. This *can't* happen.

And if I don't stop him right this second…it will be too late.

Ripping my mouth away, I press a palm to his chest. "What are you doing? I told you last night was a one-time thing."

He braces his hands on the wall on either side of my head, caging me in. "Not for me." Biting his lip ring, he peruses my body from head to toe. "And not for you either. Otherwise, you wouldn't be up here." Inclining his head, he skims his nose along the column of my throat. "Does your little boyfriend know he doesn't stand a chance yet?"

Just when I think his resolve can't get any worse.

"I don't belong to you. And unlike my song, I'm not something you can steal."

"You're right."

I hold my breath. *Is he finally admitting it?*

My bubble of hope pops when his lips curve into a pompous sneer. "I can't steal something that's already mine."

Anger, hurt, and lust are a potent mixture in my veins as I shove past him. "You can't have something you already lost."

Phoenix is hot on my heels as I make my way through the crowd. I'm approaching the balcony leading to the stairs when he seizes my wrist.

"I didn't lose you, Lennon. You're right here."

Not because I want to be.

His grip tightens, like he's afraid if he doesn't hold on to me with everything he's got, I'll slip away. *He doesn't realize I'm already gone.*

"Tell him about us."

I can't look at him as I deliver my next words. "There is no us."

And he only has himself to blame.

CHAPTER 47
PHOENIX

There is no us.

She knows that's a fucking lie.

And I'm gonna prove it to her right now.

Because no matter how hard she tries to convince herself she despises me...there's still one part of me she wants.

And I'm using it to my full advantage.

Curling my free hand around her hip, I press the front of her body against the balcony.

The glass panel between the two railings is tinted black, shielding her lower half from the people below us.

To anyone else, we'll look like we're dancing, but that's not what I have in mind.

Those big brown eyes are wide when she glances at me over her shoulder. "Phoenix."

I run my nose along the side of her neck. She smells so fucking good, like virtue and temptation. I want to lick, fuck, and corrupt every inch of her.

"Grip the railing."

A sharp noise catches in her throat and she hesitates, like she wants to say no, but her body won't allow the betrayal.

"It wasn't a request."

I twist her silky hair between my fingers until she complies like the good girl she is.

Tugging down the zipper on my jeans, I release my cock. I've been hard as a fucking rock ever since that kiss and I need to be balls deep inside her.

She needs it, too.

Only unlike me, she won't admit it.

She can't handle the implication.

"I know what you want, Lennon."

"I highly doubt it," she scoffs.

Stifling a groan, I slide my hands up the back of her bare thighs.

The higher I climb...the more she trembles.

Her breath hitches as I inch her tiny dress up enough to expose the bottom of her ass. "You want a free pass to get off on my dick."

I glide the tip of my finger down her crack before pulling her thong to the side. "You want me to fuck you so good you'll forget."

The head of my cock nudges her satiny slit. She's so wet for me, she's dripping.

Fisting myself, I drag my length through her drenched lips, gathering her juices on my shaft.

"Do you get this wet when he touches you or is this only for me?"

Goose bumps break out along her flesh and she arches her back ever so slightly.

"That's what I thought."

On a groan, I sink inside her. Unlike last night, where I took her hard and fast, I fuck her in measured strokes, deliberately drawing out her pleasure.

And mine.

Looking out over the balcony, I scan the crowd. My lips twitch when I spot George who's still sitting alone.

No doubt waiting for *my* girl to come back.

I press my lips to the sensitive spot just under her ear. "Do you think he knows I'm inside you?"

Instantly, her body tenses.

Cupping her pussy, I graze her shoulder with my teeth. "Do you think he knows this is mine?"

All mine.

I suck her skin into my mouth and rub her swollen clit with my knuckle. "Do you think he knows how hard you came for me last night?"

Bucking her hips, she whimpers.

Heat licks up my balls and I rub faster. "How hard I'm about to make you come right now."

That's the only warning she gets before I grip the railing.

My thrusts pick up speed as I pump in and out of her. I don't care who's watching. The only fucks I'm giving are to her tight little cunt.

Lennon's head lolls to the side, and she hisses as she clenches around me, milking my dick as she orgasms.

It triggers my own release, summoning a low groan from me as my balls draw tight.

As if sensing I'm about to pull out, she peers over her shoulder. "Inside me."

Fuck.

My abs clench and I pulse for what feels like a fucking lifetime before filling her pussy with my cum.

Triumph surges through me and the corners of my lips rise in a smug smirk as my stare locks with George's.

The chump's been watching since the moment I shoved my dick inside her.

Hope he enjoyed the show. *I know I did.*

Oblivious to our spectator, Lennon adjusts her dress.

Without breaking eye contact, I press a soft kiss to the side of her neck. "Safe to say he knows now."

Lennon doesn't say a word on the limo ride back to the bus.

Neither does George.

However, I know what guilt looks like better than anyone.

And right now? It looks like Lennon.

Which makes no fucking sense because she didn't do anything wrong.

George isn't her boyfriend and deep down, she knows she was never into him.

If she was, her pussy wouldn't be leaking my cum.

Expression uneasy, Lennon looks at George as the limo approaches the bus. "Can I talk to you?"

Staring straight ahead, his nostrils flare. "No."

Memphis, Storm, and Skylar exchange an uneasy glance and the moment the limo comes to a full stop, they scramble out.

George exits the vehicle next.

I grab Lennon's arm when she starts to leave. "Don't you dare apologize."

It was his own damn fault for trying to claim something that didn't belong to him. The motherfucker should have paid attention to my warning signs instead of ignoring them.

Averting her gaze, she whispers, "It's his birthday."

With that, she climbs out.

So do I.

Rage swarms in my gut when she runs up to George, stopping him right before he gets on the bus.

"I'm so—"

"Fuck you," George snaps, but that's all he gets a chance to say because I shove him against the bus.

Lennon tugs on my sleeve, trying to protect him. She doesn't comprehend that I'm doing the same for her.

"Phoenix, *stop*."

Nah. If this bastard wants to take his anger out on someone, he can man the fuck up and take it out on me.

Because I know that look in his eyes. *Where it can lead.*

And the next time he even so much as glances in Lennon's direction with a hint of hostility, I'll make him swallow his goddamn teeth.

"You never stood a fucking chance with her."

Her rejection wasn't predictable...it was *inevitable*.

That's why he's so mad.

His jaw hardens. "What makes you so sure about that?"

He's stupider than I thought if he thinks there was ever a contest between us.

My fingers tighten around his shirt and I look him in the eye.

I don't need to use my fists to hit this motherfucker.

I just have to hit him with the truth.

"Because you begged her to kiss you...and she begged *me* to fuck her."

Hurt flashes across his face as the stone-cold reality of the situation sinks in.

Releasing my hold, I take a step back.

As expected, he doesn't say shit as he turns and jogs up the stairs of the bus.

Indignation crosses Lennon's pretty features. "What the hell do you think you're doing?"

I pin her with a glare that makes her breath catch.

"I'm pursuing this."

CHAPTER 48
LENNON

'm pursuing this.

For the last forty-eight hours, those words—the very same words he told me back then—have been echoing in my head like a bad song on repeat.

The door connecting our two hotel rooms swings open and the lipstick I was applying slips out of my hand, falling to the floor.

An irritated and buck-naked Phoenix storms inside. "You weren't in my bed when I woke up."

Keeping my gaze trained on his face takes a startling amount of willpower.

So does not thinking about him barging into my room in the middle of the night and ripping me out of my bed...just so he could bend me over and fuck me senseless in *his*.

It all happened so fast I had no time to object.

At least, that's the story I keep telling myself and I'm sticking to it.

It seriously sucks when the person you hate is also the very same person who gives you mind-blowing dick.

But hey, a girl has needs.

And right now? I *need* him to put some clothes on so we can leave for sound check. I'm so not in the mood to deal with Chandler's bitching…or his bulging forehead vein.

I bend down to pick up my lipstick, permitting myself one cursory peek. *Dear God.* Even soft, his size is impressive.

"Get dressed. We have to be at the venue in thirty minutes."

Turning back to the mirror, I finish applying my lipstick.

"I want you in my bed when I wake up."

I can't help but laugh, which causes my *Ruby Woo* to extend past my cupid's bow. *Damnit.* "And I want world peace." I grab a tissue from the box. "We can file both those under things that are never going to happen."

The tight clench of his jaw tells me he's not amused. "What part of *I'm pursuing this* is hard for you to understand?"

This time, the laugh that leaves me is coated with bitterness. "Those words don't mean what you think they mean, Phoenix."

Because when you *pursue* someone? You don't invite them to your show so they can walk in on you screwing their worst enemy for the sole purpose of stealing their song.

The sex might have been fake, but the pain was real.

"I know exactly what those words mean and exactly what I meant when I said them." He scans me from head to toe, his gaze downright penetrating. "Here's a hint, Groupie. It also starts with the letter G."

Sharp pain flares through my chest, singeing my lungs.

After all these years, the naive girl sitting in the passenger seat of his car handing him her beating heart finally got her answer.

Too bad he took that heart and crushed it.

Shaking my head in disgust, I grab my purse.

I'm aware of him rounding on me as I head for the door, so I speed up.

He's faster than I thought, though, because the second I open it, he slams it shut.

I press my forehead against the panel as his lips touch my ear. "It means you're mine. And I'm yours." Rough hands latch on to my waist and he spins me around. "And now that we're back together, I want you in my bed every night. Got it?"

No. I don't *got it*.

My head feels heavy with emotions and memories. "Back together?"

The hands on my waist tighten when I laugh. "We dated—and I use that term very loosely—for two days." Which is being *generous.* "That's not a relationship."

He grips my chin, looking so earnest it makes my heart skip several beats. "Then let me do a better job this time around."

Closing my eyes, I swallow past the lump in my throat.

Four years ago, I would have not only said yes without any hesitation, I'm positive I would have died from happiness.

But that Lennon doesn't exist anymore.

And this Lennon will never forgive him for being the cause of that.

The only relationship I want from Phoenix Walker is the kind that gives me orgasms.

Opening my eyes, I stare into his. "We're not together. This thing between us is just sex."

The earnest expression on his face morphs to one of vexation. "Bullshit."

"It's not. As far as I'm concerned, we're just two people getting each other off. Fuck buddies."

Only, we aren't buddies anymore.

Both his face and hold go slack. "I don't want to be *fuck buddies.*"

He spits the last two words out like they taste rancid.

Sadly, for him, this isn't about what Phoenix Walker wants anymore. This is about what *I* want.

"Fine. I mean, you offered me a free pass the other night, but if the offer is no longer on the table, it's cool."

I go to brush past him, but he pins both my wrists above my head with one of his hands. "And if it's still on the table? What then?"

Fire zips through me, and my nipples harden. "Then your cock can have me for the next four weeks…that's it."

That's all it will ever be.

Due to the choice *he* made back then.

Those thoughts fly to the back burner, though, the second his mouth finds my neck, and he squeezes my breast.

"In that case…" A warm buzz flutters deep in my belly when he drops to his knees and pulls both my leggings and panties down in one fluid motion. "I'm gonna make every moment count."

Too bad we don't have any moments to spare right now. "We're late—"

The first swipe of his tongue is a slow, languid tease along the length of my slit that makes me choke.

Groaning, he spreads me with two of his fingers. "Fuck. That's good."

The second is a ravenous lash of hunger that lights every nerve ending of mine on fire. "Holy shit."

He simply laughs between long licks that drive me out of my freaking mind.

"Don't stop," I whisper. "Don't you dare stop."

Tugging my hips forward, he buries his face between my thighs. *Feasting.*

My hands brace the door behind me for balance and I moan his name.

A little too loud.

Anxiety tightens my chest with my next thought.

"We have to keep this under wraps."

I can't lose my job.

His hungry gaze flicks up to meet mine. "No more fucking in public. Got it."

My stomach twists with remorse. "Poor George."

Safe to say he's no longer talking to me. Not that I can blame him.

A sharp bite on my inner thigh makes me hiss.

This time, when Phoenix looks up at me, his stare is downright lethal. "Do not ever say his name, or any other guy's name, while I'm playing with your cunt."

"Or what?" I challenge.

"You don't get to do this."

He sweeps a long path up my pussy that ends with a deep pull of my clit.

I quiver, turning to putty against him. "Oh—"

A loud bang on the door makes me jolt.

"Have you seen Phoenix?" Chandler bellows. "He's not answering his phone or his door."

Shit. Shit. Shit.

I motion for Phoenix to stop, but he ignores me. *Asshole.*

"He's..." *Oh god.* He's probing my hole with his tongue, stretching me. "Eating." I let out a shaky breath. "Downstairs."

"Well, tell him to hurry up," Chandler grumbles. "We have to be at the venue in fifteen minutes."

As his footsteps fade, I give Phoenix a sly smile. "Hurry up."

He lifts his head and the sight of his hooded eyes, messy hair, and sharp jaw glistening with my wetness is nearly enough to make me unravel. "You'll come when *I* decide."

Slowly, he slides one of his long fingers inside me. I draw in a sharp breath when he retreats and promptly plunges back in. "Don't stop. Please."

Pressing a soft kiss to my pussy, he gives me a dark grin. "I like it when you beg, Groupie."

I hate him.

Ugh...but his *cock.*

His *mouth.*

I dig my fingers into the back of his neck. "Please."

"Keep begging," he rasps, and the vibration makes me mewl.

"Please." He suckles my clit and I swear I see stars. "Pretty please—"

"If Phoenix is eating, then what are *you* doing?" Chandler booms from the other side of the door.

I propel into his jaw as an endless surge of pleasure engulfs me. "I'm coming." My fingers coil in his hair, gripping for dear life as I explode. "I'm coming right now."

"Make it snappy," Chandler barks, and then his phone rings. "Shit. It's Vic. I'll meet you downstairs in the lobby."

Phoenix stands a moment later. The arctic expression on his face throws me.

I'm about to ask what his problem is, but he sweeps his thumb over my bottom lip, smearing my lipstick. "I expect this mouth to be wrapped around my dick later, *buddy*."

With that, he stalks out of the room, but not before I catch a glimpse of the hurt in his eyes.

The irony of Phoenix— Mister I Don't Want Shit To Get Complicated—being upset about me only wanting him for sex is comical.

I'm yanking my leggings up to meet Chandler downstairs when it occurs to me.

If I really wanted to ruin Phoenix Walker...all I have to do is break his heart.

Just like he did to me.

CHAPTER 49
LENNON

"What's that?" I question as I enter the elevator behind Phoenix.

He's been staring at the same packet of papers ever since we left the venue.

After looking around the empty elevator, he pulls something out of his pocket.

I do a double-take when I see the reading pen I bought for him.

"It's the launch plan and recording schedule for our upcoming album." He averts his gaze. "I think. Haven't been able to read it fully yet."

My chest aches as it becomes painfully clear why he's been staring at the same document for so long.

"No one knows about your dyslexia...do they?"

Eyes narrowing, he reaches across me and slams the emergency button. "No one except Storm...and you." Annoyance clashes with discomfort on his face. "I'd appreciate it if you'd keep your fucking mouth shut."

Even though I came here for revenge, I'm still a good person with morals.

Just like my father raised me to be.

Which means there are lines I won't cross.

Telling the world Phoenix has a learning disability is one of them.

Although I do think *he* should tell people about it.

"Having dyslexia is nothing to be ashamed of. It—"

"I don't need people finding out I'm stupid," he growls.

Whoa. He's got it all wrong.

I open my mouth, but he doesn't give me the chance to speak. "People take advantage of weak people." The tendons in his neck strain against his skin as he steps into my space. "The label already treats me like a goddamn puppet. I don't need to make it easier for them to control me. I give those assholes *everything* I have so they can fatten their bank accounts." Rolling up the document, he shoves it into the back pocket of his jeans. "But I'm not giving them that part of me."

I turn this over for a bit because there's a *lot* to unpack here. On some level, I understand what he means.

People do take advantage of weak people. Especially when money and power are thrown into the mix.

But Phoenix isn't weak. Or stupid.

"You are many things." Reaching up, I cradle the side of his face. "But stupid *isn't* one of them."

My heart hammers in my ribs. Even though I shouldn't say the next words, I know he needs to hear them.

"As far as the record label is concerned, it might be their chessboard, but *you're* Phoenix fucking Walker. You get to decide whether or not to play the game. And if you don't want to? Leave the damn table. Trust me, they'll follow…because there is no one else like you out there."

There never will be.

I knew from the first second I laid eyes on him that he was special…and that hasn't changed.

My stomach flutters when he trails his fingers up the side of my neck and our gazes collide.

I feel the contact *everywhere*.

His voice is such a low rasp I almost don't hear it. "I miss you."

Before I can process what he's saying, his mouth is on mine, claiming me.

My pulse accelerates when he slams me against the wall, his hands roaming over every part of my body and his erection digging into my stomach.

A moan escapes when he shoves his hand inside my pants and rubs his knuckle against the damp crotch of my panties. "You're always so wet for me."

I'm about to remind him that half the women in the world are always wet for him—and that's an *underestimation*—but he slips a finger inside me.

"Our rooms are only two more floors up."

Provided he didn't break the elevator by pressing the emergency button.

He starts pumping his fingers. "I want you to come for me right here."

Oh god.

My head falls back and I close my eyes.

"Have you showered since the last time I fucked you?"

The last time he fucked me was in the car earlier while we were driving to sound check...and then after that, we grabbed food with everyone before the concert.

"No." My cheeks heat with embarrassment. *Do I smell? Do I feel grimy?* "There was no time—"

"Good. Then your pussy is still full of my cum."

On a ragged breath, Phoenix removes his finger and smears the wetness on my lips. "Open."

When I do, he slides them inside my mouth, making me taste *us.*

My heart rate kicks up because the move is so dirty.

"Suck."

God help me, because I listen.

"Do you like feeling my cum drip out of you after I fuck you?"

I nod.

Even though I'm on birth control, I've never had sex without a condom before that night at the club.

And the only reason I told him to cum inside me then was because I didn't want the asshole to stain the dress Skylar let me borrow.

And now? Well…you can't unring a bell.

He slips his fingers out of my mouth and shoves them inside me. "Do you like how messy it makes your panties?"

Jesus.

Inching closer, he licks my bottom lip and his movements speed up. "Do you—"

The elevator comes to life with a great big jolt.

What the hell? Isn't someone supposed to determine what the emergency is first?

Phoenix barely has time to take his hand out of my pants before the elevator doors are opening.

Anxiety floods my stomach when I see Chandler standing there.

He regards Phoenix. "Ah. There you are. I've been knocking on your door for the past five minutes."

"Problem with the elevator," we say in unison.

He looks between us before returning his attention to Phoenix. "Vic's gonna have his secretary overnight the contract so you and the rest of the guys can sign it."

"I'm not signing anything until I look over the proposal and schedule."

At that, Chandler lets out an expansive sigh. "I gave it to you as soon as the concert ended. You had plenty of time to read it."

Phoenix's jaw tightens. "I—"

"It's my fault," I interject. "I kept nagging him about going to therapy on the ride home."

Chandler makes a face. "He is a rock star. You needn't hold him close to your bosom and nurse him."

He's a fucking *person* I want to yell back, but Phoenix clears his throat.

"*He* is standing right here. I'll look it over tonight."

"Fine." Chandler pulls his phone out of his pocket and presses the button for the elevator. "I'm heading to bed. Good show tonight."

Neither of us says a word.

"Lennon?" he barks as the doors open.

"Yeah?"

"We pay you to keep him out of trouble, not keep him from his obligations. Stick to your job description."

I'm glad he goes into the elevator after that so he can't see the giant middle finger I'm giving him.

"I see what you mean about them treating you like a puppet," I tell Phoenix as we walk down the hall to our rooms.

He laughs, but it's devoid of humor. "Chandler's actually the most decent one out of all of them."

It doesn't feel right. Chandler said it himself. *He's* a rock star. Therefore, *he* should be the one calling the shots.

Phoenix must be able to sense what I'm thinking because he grinds out, "This is my dream, Lennon. The one I worked my ass off for."

Right.

I dig my key card out of my purse. "Night."

I'm opening the door to my room when his hand slips around my waist. "Where do you think you're going?"

"To bed."

The hand on my waist slides down to squeeze my ass. "Good. Then we're on the same page." Before I can protest, he sucks my earlobe between his teeth. "But the plans I have in mind for us involve my bed. Not yours."

A rush of heat envelops me. "What plans?"

After digging his key card out of his pocket, he opens the door and pulls me inside. "Tonight, *you're* gonna be the puppet."

It shouldn't sound so enticing, but holy hell, it does.

The moment the door closes, I'm pressed against it.

I close my eyes as his mouth glides down my neck. "I didn't get to make you come in the elevator." Sharp teeth nip my collarbone. "Which means I need to make you come twice right now."

Lucky me.

I rub his erection through his pants. "If you really want me to come, you—"

A scream rips from my throat when I notice a woman standing twenty feet away, *staring* at us.

Phoenix whips around, shielding me.

"Hi," the woman—or rather *girl*—says because she can't possibly be a day over seventeen. "Sorry. I didn't mean to scare you. I just… I've been dying to meet you."

I poke Phoenix in the ribs. "See? *This* is what happens when you don't use security for your groupies."

Maybe *now* he'll realize how important having bodyguards is and he'll quit telling them to fuck off all the time.

Phoenix digs his phone out of his pocket. "On it."

"No," the girl pleads as she comes closer. "Please don't call security. I can explain."

"Start by explaining how you snuck into my room," Phoenix barks.

"Easy." She lifts her shoulders in a lackadaisical shrug. "I stole a housekeeping card from one of the maids."

Yep. These fans don't mess around.

But what's even more disturbing than her breaking and entering is the way she keeps ogling Phoenix with her big green crazy eyes.

I honestly wouldn't be surprised if she pulled out a gun at this point.

I poke him again. "Get security. *Now.*"

He brings his cell to his ear. "Yeah. I need someone up here right away. A groupie snuck into my suite—"

"I'm not a groupie," she interjects. "I'm your sister."

I freeze.

Phoenix, however, shakes his head, not buying it. Then again, he's probably heard this line a thousand times before. People will do and say anything to meet a famous rock star.

Although now that I look at her…she does bear a striking resemblance to him.

Like Phoenix, she has dirty-blonde hair, only hers is long and super wavy. She shares his amazing bone structure, too. She's also lanky and tall—well, tall compared to me—given she hovers around five-five.

Not to mention…she's stealthy and likes to steal, so there's that.

"Get your asses up here now," Phoenix grunts before hanging up the phone.

"How old are you?" I ask, which earns me a look from Phoenix.

"Don't start up a conversation with the psycho fangirl. It will only encourage her."

"Hey. I'm not a psycho fangirl," she says with a scowl. "I don't even think Sharp Objects is all that great. Harvey Trinity from Steppingstone was right, your last album sucked worse than a whore on payday. You got too commercial and became sellouts."

When Phoenix's eyes narrow into tiny slits, she tucks a strand of hair behind her ear and smiles sweetly. "I *really* loved your first song, though. You guys should go back to doing stuff like that."

On second thought, I kind of like her.

Phoenix crosses his arms over his chest. "We did *not* become sellouts."

She mutters something under her breath before looking at me. "To answer your question, I'm fifteen. But I'll be sixteen in like five weeks."

Geez. She's even younger than I thought. Where the hell are her parents?

There's a loud knock on the door and Phoenix goes to answer it. "Hope you enjoy jail."

"Wait," she begs. "Please. I *swear* I'm telling the truth."

I take hold of Phoenix's arm. "Tell security we don't need them."

His jaw drops. "Are you fucking kidding me? You're the one who told me to call them in the first place."

"And now I'm telling you to send them away." I jut my chin at the girl whose lower lip is now wobbling. "Look at her, Phoenix. She's just a scared kid. She doesn't deserve to go to jail. We can handle this ourselves."

"Fine. But if she kills us, it's on you." He opens the door. "Everything's cool, guys. False alarm."

"Are you sure?" a man on the other side asks.

"Yeah," Phoenix says while glaring daggers at me.

Then he slams the door.

After digging a bottle of water out of the fridge, I lead her to the small couch on the other side of the room.

"Okay, so you're fifteen—"

"Sixteen," she corrects as she sits down.

In five weeks.

I take a seat on the other end. "Where are you from?"

"Here."

Phoenix—who's leaning against the window ledge—waves a hand. "Here meaning…"

"Chicago."

That makes sense since we're currently in Chicago. It will also make it a lot easier to take her home.

I should probably find out more info before we get to that, though.

"What's your name?"

Hesitation crosses over her face. "You guys aren't gonna call the cops on me, right?"

"Maybe," Phoenix says at the same time I utter, "Of course not."

She pulls her bottom lip between her teeth. "My name is Quinn Moore."

I stiffen. I can't recall why but that name sounds familiar.

My hands fly to my face when it hits me.

She's the girl Memphis knocked up *and* the girl Skylar says has been stalking him.

Oh. My. God. What if Skylar's right after all? Maybe she truly *is* psychotic, and she's hatched a plan to hold us hostage until she gets whatever she wants from Memphis.

I look at Phoenix. "Call security. Right now."

His eyes nearly pop out of his skull. "Jesus Christ, Lennon. Will you make up your damn mind?"

Quinn's nervous gaze darts between us. "Whoa, whoa, whoa. I thought we were past all that security nonsense?"

Dammit. I cannot trust my gut. Because my gut tells me she's an innocent girl in trouble.

Because of Memphis.

I snap my fingers at Phoenix, who's on the phone again. "Hang up with security and call Skylar. Tell her to come here...with Memphis."

This way, if *teen mom* goes nuts, all her rage will be directed at the right person.

I'm positive Phoenix is contemplating my murder as he grits out, "Sorry, guys. Looks like it's another false alarm." He snorts. "Am I sure? Who the fuck knows."

With that, he hangs up and calls Skylar. "Come to my suite ASAP with Memphis." He cups the phone. "She wants to know what's going on." He makes a face. "So do I."

I'm afraid if I tell her right now, she'll alert Memphis and he'll run away.

This is his mess. He has to clean it up.

"She'll know when she gets here."

After relaying the message to Skylar, he looks at me. "Are you gonna tell *me* what's going on anytime soon, or do we need to play charades?"

I start to, but there's a knock on the door. The moment Phoenix opens it, Skylar marches into the suite like a member of the National Guard. Memphis and Storm follow close behind.

Skylar's jaw drops to the floor when she spots Quinn sitting on the couch. "*You.*" Her gaze flicks to me. "Thanks for the warning, Lennon."

I look at Memphis. "Sorry, but I didn't want him to flee. This is his responsibility."

I am *not* going down with this ship.

Memphis—who's eating what appears to be a melting popsicle—slurps juice off his hand. "What's my responsibility?"

Good Lord. He's a whole new level of disgusting.

"Your baby that this young girl is carrying, jackass."

At that, Phoenix and Storm's eyebrows shoot up to the ceiling and the situation goes from on edge to downright mayhem.

"The *fuck*?" Phoenix barks.

"You told me it was just a rumor, shithead," this from Storm.

"What the hell are you doing here?" Skylar snaps.

"I'm visiting my brother," Quinn states. "And I'm not pregnant."

The five of us exchange puzzled glances.

Storm's the first to speak. "Who's your brother?"

Quinn blinks like it should be obvious. "Phoenix."

When everyone looks at him, he shakes his head. "No the fuck I'm not."

Quinn's not backing down, though. "It's true. My mom is Genevieve Moore, but her maiden name is Katz."

She draws in a deep breath. "Which technically makes you my half-sib, but who actually uses the term half-sib…unless you don't like the person. But you have no reason not to like me because you don't even know me. Which is *exactly* why I've been trying to meet you for the past three years, but you're incredibly hard to pin down. I've tried to go backstage a few times, but security won't let me because—"

She makes air quotes with her fingers. "'I'm too young'. I took a bus to the hospital after your accident, but they had the nerve to tell me I wasn't family, and every single freaking time I've attempted to break into your room, you were already gone." She smiles. "I'm really glad you were here this time, though…and that I was able to catch you right before you two boned."

Holy. Shit.

Phoenix looks at me. "That part checks out…well, the part about my mom's last name." He pulls a face. "Not the ramblings of a lunatic."

I can feel Skylar mean mugging me. Feigning innocence, I twirl my finger around my ear and mouth, 'she's *crazy*.'

Phoenix eyes Quinn suspiciously. "How do you know my mother's maiden name?"

Appearing exasperated, Quinn blows out a breath. "Because she's my mom, too, dummy." She points to herself. "Where do you think I got this mop of hair and these insanely high cheekbones from?" Peering up at the ceiling, she touches her eyeball. "I also have her green eyes. See? No contacts."

Phoenix doesn't look nearly as unsure about all this like he did a minute ago.

Oh boy.

While Quinn and Phoenix definitely look like they could be siblings, their personalities couldn't be more opposite.

Phoenix is locked up tight, and this girl is an open book.

A *strange and crafty* open book.

I honestly don't know what to make of her or this situation. I *want* to believe her…but there's a chance she's lying.

I'm not the only one who must be thinking this because Storm scrubs a hand down his face and utters, "Are you really gonna trust this little juvenile delinquent who broke into your hotel room?"

"Um, hello," Quinn says, her face twisting with outrage. "Weren't you listening? I had a good reason."

Memphis takes a step forward. "What was the reason you broke into mine then?"

We all turn to look at Memphis, who until now hasn't said much. Which is odd considering Quinn's his baby mama. *Allegedly.*

Skylar's eyes narrow. "You told me you never touched a minor."

Memphis pinches the bridge of his nose. "That's because I never touched her, Sky." Palms up, he looks at all of us. "Or any other minor for the record."

"Start talking," Phoenix grits through his teeth before he plops down on the chair next to the couch. "Now."

Memphis draws in a lungful of air. "The first night on tour, I came back to my room and found her there. I was about to call security, but she begged me not to and then went on and on about needing to see you immediately. She seemed a little…"

"Fucking psychotic," Storm offers.

"Hey!" Quinn screeches.

"Mentally unstable," Memphis says. "Anyway, I figured she was a stalker, but when I threatened to call security again, she broke down crying." He shrugs. "She's obviously young, and I felt bad, so I offered to call her parents..." He peers down at Quinn, who looks sheepish. "That's when she bolted out of my room."

"And then told the world she was pregnant with your love child," Skylar cuts in, unable to contain her grimace.

I'm right there with her. It seems Quinn went to a trashy tabloid and started rumors that she was pregnant with Memphis's baby... presumably so she could get *Phoenix's* attention.

That's beyond insane.

Quinn hangs her head. "I just wanted to meet my big brother." Her gaze fixes on her sneakers. "And I only told TMZ that I *thought* I was pregnant with his child. I figured that would be enough for someone in the band's camp to track me down...then I'd be introduced to Phoenix."

"You could have destroyed his life," Skylar bites out, and I don't think I've ever seen her so furious.

"I didn't mean to." Remorse floods her features. "I know I lied, but it's not like I was planning on going to the cops or anything. It was only a rumor."

"Lies still damage people," I whisper, intentionally avoiding looking at Phoenix.

Quinn turns to Memphis. "I'm really sorry. It was wrong of me to do that."

Memphis—who has every reason to be livid with the girl—gives her a soft nod. "It's cool. We've all done shit we regret."

I can't help but notice the way Skylar stiffens, but before I can read into it, Quinn pulls something out of her pocket and hands it to Phoenix. "I found this in a box stashed away in Mom's closet a couple of years ago."

Phoenix keeps his expression neutral as he stares at an image of a little blond-haired boy singing into a shampoo bottle...like he was gearing up to take the world by storm one day.

He doesn't have to confirm it's him...because there's only one Phoenix Walker in the world.

Skylar straightens her spine, jumping into work mode. "Before this goes any further, I think we should get a DNA test."

Phoenix—who's still staring at the picture—nods.

Turning on her heels, Skylar hustles to the door. "I'll set everything up."

Storm hikes a thumb at the door Skylar just walked out. "I'm gonna go do that thing."

Memphis slaps his back. "Yeah, we have that thing to do."

Wanting to give Phoenix and Quinn time alone to talk, I get off the couch. "I'm gonna go."

Phoenix grips my hand.

Even though he doesn't say it, I know what he's asking for.

Giving it a small squeeze, I promptly sit back down.

Phoenix blows out a heavy breath. "Does Mom know where you are?"

Going quiet, Quinn directs her gaze out the large window. *Must be genetic.*

"My guess would be no." Which poses a big problem since she's only fifteen. "I know you want to talk to your—Phoenix—but if your parents don't consent, he can get in a lot of trouble."

Especially if she turns out not to be his sister. Although the chances of that are growing slimmer by the minute.

Which makes talking to her mother even more crucial...because then we'll know for sure.

"We need to give them a call, Quinn."

That gets her attention. "You can't." Her eyes dart around the room nervously, like a scared animal caught in a trap. "They're...out of town."

Phoenix and I exchange an uneasy glance.

Maybe she's not his sibling after all.

"In that case, is there somewhere we can take you? Just until we can talk to your parents and make sure they're okay with you coming back here."

Quinn bolts up like a jack-in-the-box. "You know what? Never mind. I'll go."

In the blink of an eye, she makes a mad dash for the door.

Phoenix—whose legs are way longer than mine—manages to grab her arm right before she exits.

Quinn winces like she's in pain.

I sprint over to them. "Relax, Phoenix. You're hurting—"

My stomach recoils when he rolls up the sleeve of her sweatshirt —which now that I think about it is a bit odd given it's summer— revealing a nasty bruise on her forearm.

"Where'd you get this?"

"Soccer," Quinn quickly responds. "Got attacked on the field the other day." Plastering a smile on her face, she fist bumps the air. "Go Tigers."

Phoenix doesn't look like he buys it. I'm not sure I do either.

"What position do you play?"

"Goalie," she replies without hesitation.

He frowns. "Name a famous soccer player."

Quinn doesn't miss a beat. "David Beckham."

Still not convinced, Phoenix grunts, "How many players are on a soccer team?"

That's when she falters. "Ten."

Phoenix levels her with a look. "It's eleven."

Laughing, Quinn tries to play it off. "I wasn't counting myself, silly."

Despite having an answer for everything, I can't shake the anxiety tightening my chest.

Something's not right.

Phoenix feels it too, because he's not done prying. "Why would you get attacked on the field if you're a goalie?"

I can tell Quinn's momentarily stumped because I can practically see her brain constructing a story. "Attacked by the *ball*. But my team also got into a huge fight with our school rivals on the field the other day." She slaps her knee with her free hand. "You should have seen it, man. Shit got crazy."

"It's the summer," Phoenix says cynically. "School's not in session."

When Quinn's demeanor wavers, he looks back at me. "Call the police."

"Please don't."

Breaking free from his hold, she runs full steam ahead.

Phoenix manages to wedge himself between her and the door a fraction of a second before she takes off.

"Those bruises aren't from soccer. Trust me, I know. I used to make up the same bullshit stories." Crossing his arms, he stares her down. "Sister or not, there's no way I'm letting you go back to a place where someone's beating on you."

My heart constricts for two different reasons.

One—because I know this must be tearing him apart inside.

And two—Quinn's next words.

"If you really knew, then you'd understand why calling the police is a bad idea."

Dread wraps around my chest and pulls tight.

It will only make it worse for her.

"Fuck." Exhaling sharply, Phoenix scrubs a hand down his face. "Look, I'll make sure the police take this seriously and don't bring you back there, okay?"

"You don't understand," Quinn whispers, her voice quaky. "He *is* the police."

Phoenix rears back like he's been sucker punched and the dread in my chest turns to full-blown horror.

"It will be bad enough when he finds me, because he *always* finds me. But if you call the police, they'll tell my father—who's a fucking sheriff—and he's gonna lose his shit entirely." Curling her arms around herself, she studies her shoes. "He hates when I run away, but he hates it even more when I embarrass him. Not only will he make it brutal, he'll..." She swallows thickly. "He'll—"

"Hurt Mom," Phoenix interjects. "Because that's the worst punishment."

I try to take a breath past the heavy weight crushing my lungs, but it's impossible.

I don't understand how someone could abuse their child.

I don't understand how someone could stay with someone who abuses their child.

Or how someone could abandon their child and leave them all alone with the monster who abuses them.

"What do we do, Phoenix?" I croak, my brain desperately trying to come up with options.

We can't call the police because her father is a sheriff.

We can't call her mom because it's evident the woman protects him.

The only thing I do know is that we're not taking her back to that hellhole.

I don't give a shit if she's his sister or not.

Visibly frustrated, Phoenix grips the back of his neck. "There's fuck all I can do right now. Not until we do a DNA test and get the results back."

"You're my brother," Quinn insists for what must be the hundredth time since she's been here. "I swear."

"I need to have proof of that," he booms before his voice drops to a far gentler tone. "Otherwise, there's nothing I can do to help you. I'll just look like some creep harboring a teenage girl."

It's true. While I hope Quinn turns out to be his sister, his hands are completely tied until we know for sure.

"But then you're gonna save me?" Quinn exclaims and the glimmer of hope in her voice has me blinking back tears.

"Yeah. I just need the results to come back first." Glancing at me, he shrugs helplessly. "In the meantime, I guess she can stay here."

Phoenix tries to remain aloof, but the moment Quinn rushes forward and tackles him his poker face diminishes, An array of emotions illuminate his face, ranging from trepidation and shock to protectiveness.

It's obvious he needs a moment—or several—to process the bomb that's been dropped on his lap, so after Quinn detaches herself, I smile at her and say, "You can have my room. It's right next door."

Her incredulous stare bounces between us. "How come you two don't share a room?"

Shit.

I'm thinking of ways to explain what she saw between us earlier while simultaneously asking her to politely keep her mouth shut, but Phoenix says, "We'll be sharing one tonight." He glances at the expensive watch on his wrist. "It's three a.m. and we have another show tomorrow, so you should probably go to bed."

Placing an arm around her shoulders, I steer her toward my room. "I'll lend you some pajamas and wash your clothes while you sleep so they'll be clean for tomorrow, okay?"

"Are you sure?"

"Positive."

I pull a clean T-shirt and a pair of sleep shorts out of my suitcase and hand them to her. "They'll be roomy on you, but Skylar and I can get you some things before the concert."

A frown mars her face when I hand her the clothes. "Um...I don't want to seem ungrateful, but do you have anything other than shorts?"

Oh.

"Yeah. Of course." I root around for a pair of clean pajama pants. "Here."

Relief crosses her face. "Mucho appreciated."

After she's done changing in the bathroom, she pads back out. She hands me her T-shirt and jeans, but she's still wearing her sweatshirt. "I get cold a lot."

My heart lodges in my throat, but I nod anyway. I've already deduced why she wants to keep the sweatshirt on—the same reason she didn't want to wear shorts—but I don't want to make her feel self-conscious by pointing it out.

"It's the Windy City after all." I trek over to the main door so I can make a pit stop at the laundry room in the hotel. "Let me know if you need anything, okay? I'll be in the next room."

She climbs into bed. "Thanks, but no thanks. I do *not* want to interrupt you two again."

Double shit. "We're not…" I stop talking because it's late, and she needs to rest. I can broach all of this with her tomorrow. "Sleep tight."

"Lennon?"

"Yeah?"

"Is Phoenix really gonna save me?"

Oh geez. This girl has a way of pulling on your damn heartstrings.

I don't want to lie to her, so I give her the truth.

"Phoenix is the most stubborn and determined person I know and when he wants something…he'll stop at nothing to get it."

Given she has no knowledge of the appalling things he'll resort to, she innocently assumes this is a positive thing and smiles.

"You're good people," she says as I twist the knob. "My bro's lucky to have you."

After making a quick trip to the laundry room, I return to Phoenix's suite.

I find him propped up against the headboard of his bed in a pair of boxers. Both his reading pen and the documents from earlier are in his hands, but the distant expression on his face tells me he isn't focusing on any of that.

Can't say I blame him.

"Hey."

At the sound of my voice, he snaps out of his haze. "Hey. Is Quinn…" He stalls like he's at a loss for words. "Tucked in?"

I bite back a smile. "She's fifteen, not five. But yeah, she's settled. I told her to come get me if she needs anything." I gesture to one of the pillows on the bed. "Is it okay if I take one of these? The ones on the couch don't look very comfy."

"Yeah—" He gives his head a shake. "Wait. Why are you talking about the couch?"

"Because that's where I'm going to sleep."

I go to take one of the pillows, but Phoenix snatches it away. "You're not sleeping on the couch."

Yup. Should have known this would happen.

"The floor is way less comfortable."

I try to steal a different pillow, but he snatches that one, too. "You won't be sleeping on the floor either." He points to the bed. "Bring that ass."

Bring that ass?

I could stand here arguing with him all night—and were it *any* other night I would just for the sheer principle of not wanting him to control me—but he's under enough stress right now.

Sometimes you have to pick and choose your battles.

It suddenly dawns on me that while I gave Quinn pajamas, I didn't get myself any. Seeing as she's probably—hopefully—fast asleep, I don't want to wake her.

Poor girl could use the rest.

"Fine. But do you have a T-shirt I can borrow?"

He quirks a brow. "T-shirt for what?"

"For me." I toe off my shoes. "I forgot to grab myself some pajamas and I don't want to go back in there and wake her. Hence I need a T-shirt."

"No," he deadpans. "You're supposed to take your clothes *off* in my bed. Not put clothes on."

He's incorrigible.

"Whatever. I'll sleep in the one I'm wearing."

My hands go to the zipper on my jeans, and I slide them down my hips. I stop undressing when I catch him watching.

"It's rude to stare."

"It's rude that you're not already naked."

That gets a laugh out of me.

Kicking my jeans out of the way, I pull back the covers on my side of the bed. "Guess I'll be eternally rude then because you won't be seeing me naked. *Ever.*"

I inwardly curse because that was supposed to be an internal thought. Not an external one.

He winks. "Hate to break it to you, Groupie, but I've already seen you naked."

Not *naked* naked.

That time he barged in while I was writing on myself, I had on modest boy shorts and a bra, plus the room was dimly lit.

And every time we've had sex or fooled around after that, I've managed to keep at *least* one article of clothing on—typically my shirt—and the moment it's over I'm always in a rush to get dressed before someone discovers us.

So while he's seen lots of various bare body parts, he hasn't seen the whole enchilada all at once.

Truth be told, I have no objection to being naked during sex. I've been stark naked with all my prior partners and I was totally confident.

I just have an issue being fully naked in front of *him.*

Do I think he'll scream and run away? Absolutely not.

I *know* he finds me attractive.

But to me, Phoenix has always been the epitome of perfection.

Well, physically.

And the fact that I literally cannot find one single thing less than flawless on his face or body is a little—okay, *a lot*—intimidating when I know the same can't be said when it comes to me.

I'd rather just enjoy sex with him instead of ruining it by worrying if he can see my lower stomach roll or if the cellulite on my ass and thighs is too distracting.

"Yup. You're right." Climbing into bed, I fluff my pillow. "My bad."

Approximately one minute later…I hear it.

"I've never seen you fully naked," Phoenix mutters in disbelief. "How the fuck is that possible?"

Something tells me I'm *never* going to live this down.

Before I can change the subject, I feel a sharp sting from his hand slapping my ass. "Show me the goods."

I clutch the covers protectively. "I'm not showing you anything."

The look he gives me makes it clear that's unacceptable. "Wanna bet?"

I squeal when he rips the covers off me.

"Phoenix," I warn when he reaches for my T-shirt. "Can we stop focusing on me and focus on you?"

Naked issue aside, I know he's only using this as an opportunity to distract himself from dealing with his world imploding. Because *that's* what he does.

"Tonight was kind of a huge deal, don't you think? I mean, finding out you have a sister and knowing your mom's—"

"Christ." Releasing my shirt, he sits up in bed. "Talk about a fucking buzzkill."

"Sorry, I just really think we should discuss what happened. Don't you?"

"No."

Surprise, surprise.

"Where are you going?" I ask when he stands up.

He stalks toward the door. "Couch."

Oh hell no.

"Are you fucking kidding me?" I yell several octaves higher than necessary.

The asshat simply continues on his merry way, slamming the door behind him.

Anger boils inside of me because, while his rejection was expected, it still stings.

The words are out of my mouth before I can stop them. "And this is just one of the many reasons why I will *never* be with you. I get not wanting to talk about the things that hurt, but stop shutting me out."

Pot meet kettle, Lennon.

If Phoenix is the king of evading…you're the queen.

I grit my teeth, attempting to shut down the nagging thought before it can take root, but it's too late.

I'm yelling at Phoenix for doing the same thing I do—running away from anything and everything that makes me uncomfortable.

Why is it so much easier to call someone else on their shit than face yours?

Stupid glass houses.

I'm about to go out there and apologize, but he charges through the door.

"I'm only shutting you out because *you* keep forcing me to talk about shit I don't want to fucking talk about!" Face contorted in pain, he squeezes the back of his neck. "I fucking *can't*. It's too much for me to wrap my head around."

"I'm sorry," I whisper.

Typically, I don't regret pushing him, but this time I pushed him too far.

Chest rising and falling with sporadic breaths, he lifts his head. "What?"

"I'm sorry," I repeat. "It's only been an hour since your life got turned upside down. You haven't had any time to process everything, let alone talk about it. I had no right to get mad at you for not wanting to."

Unlike Phoenix, I have no problem owning up to it when I'm in the wrong.

And I was this time.

Slipping back into bed, he grabs the pile of papers and his reading pen off the nightstand.

He scans over the first few lines and from what I gather, they want the album to release at the end of January. Given this tour hasn't even ended and they still have a European tour after this one, it doesn't leave a whole lot of recovery time.

Visibly irritated, Phoenix places the pen down. "I can't concentrate on this shit."

Since I don't want him to make the mistake of not reading it and signing the contract Chandler will undoubtedly hand him first thing tomorrow, I grab the packet.

"What are you doing?"

"I'm gonna read it to you." Digging around the nightstand drawer, I find a pen. "Anything you don't like or want to follow up on, I'll mark. This way, you'll be able to address everything before you sign the contract, okay?"

He gives me a soft nod.

As I read, Phoenix makes comments. A lot of stuff he's fine with, but some he's not…like the lack of downtime.

Appearing calmer than he was earlier, he rests his head on my lap. "I'd kill to have a week where I could do nothing but stay in bed and order takeout."

"You're allowed to ask for time off, Phoenix."

I don't realize I've started massaging his scalp with my free hand until he says, "Damn. That feels good."

Continuing, I flip to the last two pages. "Okay, so it looks like all that's left is…" *Awkward.* "Song choices for the album. There are thirteen tracks listed."

"This should be interesting. Let's hear them."

"Well, they want the lead single to be a song called 'Breathe Dust.'"

Instantly he tenses. "Fuck that. None of us like that song. When the guys and I talked, we agreed the lead single should be 'Existentialism' since it's the strongest and sounds the most like *us*."

"Then you guys need to be a united front and tell them that."

He huffs out a breath. "What are the other songs?"

I rattle off the list. Phoenix stays silent until I reach the end.

"What happened to 'Don't Take Your Vitamins'"?

I scan the sheet, but don't see it. "It's not listed."

"That's bullshit." He lurches up. "That was our second favorite song. It's like Vic didn't hear a fucking word we said."

There's an easy solution to this problem. "So why don't you tell him you want it on the album?"

"Because it's Vic's label. Which means what he says goes."

"It shouldn't be that way."

He closes his eyes and sighs. "I know. It's why Josh was learning production. He was getting good at it, too. We were planning on having a meeting and telling Vic that we wanted him to produce this album because then at least we'd know it would be authentically us, but then...the accident happened, and he died. Now we're stuck with Vic's producer again." An ugly snort leaves him. "We're no longer Sharp Objects...we're dull fucking puppets."

"Well, if you guys band together—pun intended—and threaten to walk, I guarantee Vic will let you have more control."

"Fat fucking chance. Vic swears he knows best—and his track record proves it since he's a legend." Looking defeated, his shoulders sag. "I just wish he'd actually listen to us instead of placating us with his typical, *I'll consider it* bullshit."

"Once again, there's a resolution—"

"Threatening to quit isn't an option."

"Why?"

"Because if Vic calls my bluff, I'll lose *everything*, Lennon. Singing and performing a few shitty songs on an album is better than not singing and performing at all." The fear and desperation in his eyes has my chest clenching. "I'll die without it."

I get it.

Sure, I still have a pulse and I'm still breathing.

But vital parts of me are dead.

"I need that magic," he whispers. "It's not just the most important thing to me. It's the *only* thing." He breathes in deep. "It stays when everyone else leaves." The veins in his neck flex as he swallows. "It will never abandon me."

Like his mom.

My heart compresses so hard it hurts. "I still think it's worth talking to him. Maybe he can add them as additional songs on the album and then everyone gets what they want."

Only not really. Because what Phoenix wants is to have both his human and his creative needs taken seriously and implemented...as he should.

"Yeah...maybe."

A lengthy yawn leaves me as I place the proposal on the night-stand, and I glance at the clock. "It's four-thirty." Reaching over, I flick off the light. "We both need to get some sleep."

A few minutes later, I'm drifting off... but Phoenix isn't.

His unsteady breathing fills the dark room, and I can feel the tension coursing through him as he grapples with his thoughts.

Assuming his focus is still on his career problems, I murmur, "The worst Vic will say is no, but you won't know until you ask him."

"Quinn looks just like my mom," Phoenix utters unexpectedly.

Shifting, I turn toward him. "I can't imagine what you must be feeling."

"That's the thing...I don't know." His arm brushes mine. "When someone's been absent from your life for so long, all you're left with is this mental picture of them. One you base all your thoughts and emotions off of, because you don't have anything else."

He audibly swallows. "And the more time that passes, the more concrete that image becomes."

Those long fingers reach for mine. "The image I have of my mother is constructed from a seven-year-old boy's head. And in his head, his mother left him because she needed to save herself. In his head, she wanted to take me with her, but she couldn't. Maybe because there was no time, or maybe she didn't want any ties to the man she was terrified of. Maybe she didn't want the reminder every time she looked at me...or maybe she truly believed my father would kill her for stealing his kid."

I squeeze his hand when he stops talking, silently urging him on.

"Either way, the seven-year-old boy forgave his mom and made excuses for her because in his head she was perfect and beautiful, and she could do no wrong, but..."

I place my free hand on his chest, right over his heart that's beating so hard it feels like it's going to explode.

"But what?" I whisper after a moment passes.

"If Quinn is my sister—and I'm pretty fucking positive she is—

then the image I have of her…" A shaky sigh escapes him. "The one I've been holding on to is shattered."

A cold sweat breaks out over his skin and his breathing becomes rickety and shallow, like his lungs are unable to draw in enough air.

"I don't know what I'm gonna do." A tremor runs through him. "I don't know—"

I crash my mouth against his, hoping to calm him down. *To ground him.* Because he's spinning out of control. However, before long, my kiss is overpowered by his.

And his kiss is all-consuming. Like a raging, turbulent ocean you have no control over.

Every swipe of his tongue is a thrashing, every sharp nip of his teeth a jostle, and every touch a gravitational pull.

But the sun can't be volatile like the ocean…otherwise the universe becomes a dark, cold, and lonely place.

The sun needs to be in control…because the entire world revolves around it.

I pull back. "When you're spiraling, you hold on to an anchor."

Gripping my waist, he tries to kiss me again, but I turn away, which only enrages him. "What the fuck, Lennon?"

Pushing him so he's lying on his back again, I climb on top of him. "I got you."

I kiss his neck and walk my fingers down his torso until I reach the large bulge in his boxers.

Caressing his erection through the soft cotton, I slither down his body, stopping to lick and suck every inch of skin I come across.

He groans when I slip my hand inside the waistband and grip him. "I want to fuck you."

Tugging his boxers down, I stroke him from root to tip. "I want to suck you." I press an openmouthed kiss to the wide head that's slick with precum. "So much."

Situating myself between his parted thighs, I gently circle the head of his dick with my tongue, tasting the salty liquid. "Is this for me?"

"You know it is." The tendons in his throat flex with restraint, like me taking control is torture for him. "Stop fucking around, Groupie."

It comes out like a warning. One I ignore.

Batting my eyelashes, I smile coyly, goading him. "What would you like me to do with this nice cock of yours?"

I was planning on drawing out the teasing, but he wraps my ponytail around his fist. "Give me your fucking mouth."

The second my lips part, he shoves his crown inside. "Lick it."

Wanting to drive him crazy, I teasingly lap at his tip like it's a melting ice cream cone.

Cursing, he reaches down and squeezes a handful of my ass. "Lick *all* of it."

Gripping his base, I drag the flat of my tongue up and down his thick shaft, savoring him.

He pulls my hair tighter. "Suck it."

My mouth aches as it stretches, and I take him as far down as I possibly can. However, it's not enough because he wants more.

Yanking my hair so hard my scalp stings, he slides in deeper, causing my gag reflex to kick in.

"That's it," he grunts as saliva drips from my chin onto his balls. "Let me fuck that sexy mouth."

I'm in no position to protest—not that I would—when he raises his hips and starts thrusting so hard my jaw aches.

Cupping his sac, I relax my mouth as he clamps down on the back of my neck, holding me steady while he continuously pumps.

A feral sound tears out of him and he juts into my face, tightening his hold. "Swallow." That's the only warning I get before warm liquid fills my mouth. "Every fucking drop."

I willingly do. Because the sight of Phoenix's hooded eyes, clenched face, and mouth parted in pleasure while he's staring at *me* like I'm the hottest thing he's ever seen is *everything*.

A tremble goes through him when I release him and lick up the fluid that trickled out of my mouth and onto his balls. "Fuck."

I yelp when he hauls me up and wraps his arms around me, clutching me to his chest. "Thanks. I needed that."

I lightly trace the scar on his abdomen with my fingertip. I'm making a mental note to ask him about it at a later time when he rasps, "Ruptured spleen from the accident. I lost a little over three liters of blood."

Holy crap. "Jesus."

"Apparently, I coded in the ambulance. I don't remember shit, but Storm does. He said it was the second scariest moment of his life and he never prayed harder." A vitriolic laugh leaves him. "Too fucking bad. Maybe then I would have died."

My heart plummets before compressing against my rib cage. Knowing he truly wishes he didn't survive physically hurts.

"I was relieved when I heard you lived." My eyelids grow heavy as the rhythm of his pulse lulls me to sleep. "You're still here for a reason. And I hope like hell you figure out what that reason is before it's too late...because the world can't shine without Phoenix Walker."

He sucks in a sharp breath.

"Quinn was right," he murmurs into my hair. "I'm lucky to have you."

A knot of alarm twists my insides.

Phoenix and I have a mountain of history. Awful. Messy. *Painful* history.

A few weeks of great sex and a couple of nice moments like these don't erase our past.

"Only for the next three weeks and five days," I remind him and *me.*

However, when I glance up, he's already fast asleep.

Being careful not to wake him, I slip out of his arms and curl up on the opposite side of the bed.

I'm dozing off when I hear him whisper, "I know."

CHAPTER 50
LENNON

Quinn's eyes are as big as saucers when Phoenix leads her backstage. "Holy crap. I can't believe my big brother is a *rock star*."

Phoenix grins before his expression turns somber. "I can't believe I have a little sister."

"Whoa," Quinn exclaims. "Don't look so sad. The important thing is that we found each other, right?"

They share a smile, but the moment is short lived because Chandler—who's walking alongside me—mutters, "Are those DNA results back yet?"

Skylar—who's on the other side of me—sighs. "The test was done this morning. I'm having it expedited, but it's still going to take some time."

That only deepens his glower. "Let's just hope we get them back before the rascal convinces him to buy her a castle and a pony."

Halting her steps, Quinn spins around to face him. "Castles and ponies are basic bitch shit. And for the record? The only thing I want from my brother is for him to be a part of my life, you anal pore."

Quinn's managed to do the impossible, because for *once*, Chandler's speechless.

Behind me, Storm and Memphis chuckle.

"That's one way to call someone an asshole," Memphis states.

"Yes," Chandler muses. "Who knew the vagrant could be classy."

Phoenix's lips twitch. "I'll give you five bucks every time you insult Chandler and put him in his place today."

Quinn's face lights up and she gives him a fist bump. "Deal."

Something tells me Phoenix's wallet will be empty by midnight.

"Goodie," Chandler mutters under his breath. "At least now the little convict has some goals and ambitions."

Quinn's big green eyes narrow into tiny slits. "I have plenty of goals and ambitions, you colon polyp."

Phoenix hands her a crisp five-dollar bill. "Like what?"

She starts ticking things off with her fingers. "Well, for starters, I'd like to get my own apartment. I'd also like to get my driver's license and start a foundation dedicated to rescuing animals. And then, of course, there's my dream career…"

"Which is?" Skylar cuts in.

Quinn dramatically places the back of her hand over her forehead. "I'm going to be an Academy Award-winning actress one day."

I'll admit, I wasn't expecting that.

Chandler claps his hands sardonically. "Bravo. You can add fake pregnant teen and impostor sister to your résumé."

Her hands find her hips and she swivels her head. "At least I'll be making money off *my* own talents instead of being a minion who has to earn a living profiting off others."

Skylar and I share a look as she shuts Chandler up for the second time in five minutes.

If I had any doubts the girl was related to Phoenix, I don't anymore. She cuts like a knife.

Phoenix hands her a ten-dollar bill this time. "Ouch. Be easy, though. Chandler does a lot for us."

Regret washes over Quinn's face and she mumbles a quick, "Sorry."

"Don't be," Chandler says as we head into the greenroom.

"You're like a puppy. Annoying, needy, and smelly…but otherwise harmless."

With those parting words, he turns on his heel and walks out.

Her mouth drops. "I don't smell." Raising her arm, she sniffs her pits. "Do I?"

I'm about to assure her she's fine, but Phoenix takes hold of my elbow. "I need to talk to you."

"Is everything okay?"

He swiftly leads me out of the room and into a storage closet backstage.

When I woke up this morning he was already gone and then twenty minutes before sound check he texted me and asked if I could bring Quinn with me to the venue, so I have no idea what he's been up to all day.

"What's going—"

I don't get to finish that sentence because he fuses our mouths together in a scorching kiss I feel all the way down to my toes.

I'm about to scold him because Chandler is lurking around—and tons of other people—but his expression turns serious.

"This morning I rounded up the guys. And then I took your advice and called Vic."

A spike of anxiety arrows through my chest. *Oh no.*

Maybe my suggestion backfired and Vic canned him…just like he said might happen.

"I…uh…"

It's on the tip of my tongue to apologize, but then it occurs to me that *this* was what I came here to do.

Victory doesn't taste as sweet as I thought it would, though.

His hand slides to my nape, and he rests his forehead against mine. "We came to an agreement. We nixed 'Breathe Dust' and now 'Don't Take Your Vitamins' is the lead single."

I try not to smile but fail. I'm so happy he's standing up to Vic and fighting for what he wants.

"That's awesome."

"He's still not sold on 'Existentialism' being on the album, but I came up with a way to convince him."

"How?"

His grin is so mesmerizing it steals my breath. "I'm gonna sing it at the end of the concert tonight…and every other concert after that. Once he realizes I'm right and sees how much our fans love it, he'll have no choice but to give me what I want and put it on the album."

It's smart. Not to mention doing that also means he'll get everything he wants because technically "Existentialism" will be the first song people hear on the new album.

"That's a great idea." His exhilaration is so contagious I feel it pumping through me. "I'm so happy for you."

He cradles my face in his hands. "I have you to thank for it. You piss me off so fucking much sometimes, but you also push me to be better."

My heart somersaults when I look into those blue irises…because that fire is back.

He's finally giving himself permission to enjoy things again.

"I'm so proud of you."

That makes him grin wider—which makes *me* grin wider—and now we're standing in some random storage closet grinning at each other like two fools, but I don't care because I'm over the moon.

No. *I'm touching the sun.*

"Has anybody seen Phoenix?" Chandler barks in the distance, breaking our spell.

Shit.

I motion to the door. "You go out first. Tell him you were with a groupie."

Amusement dances on his gorgeous face. "In other words, don't lie?"

"Ass."

I go to shove him, but his arms lock around my waist and he tugs me against him.

"You gonna watch me sing the song tonight?"

My heart beats double time. "I wouldn't miss it for the world." I shove his chest. "Now *go* before you get me fired."

After giving me one last kiss, he slips out.

Leaning against the door, I smile so hard it hurts…until I remember.

The sun is exceptional, alluring, and mystifying…

But it burns when you get too close.

I watch in astonishment—and a little bit of envy—as Quinn wolfs down her fourth slice of pizza.

I've never seen someone so skinny eat so damn much. The girl is a bottomless pit.

"So, you and my brother, huh?" she questions around a mouthful of pizza.

Skylar stops typing on her laptop, appearing *very* interested in our conversation now.

My eyes dart around the greenroom and to the partially open door, making sure Chandler isn't loitering nearby.

"How long have you two been together?" Quinn probes before letting out a loud belch.

I reach for my drink on the coffee table, carefully considering my words. "It's…complicated."

"*Very* complicated," Skylar adds. "So complicated it's one big secret. Right, Lennon?"

I can't tell if she's helping or hurting.

However, Quinn nods in understanding. "Because it's wrong to fuck your boss. Even though it's kinda hot."

Skylar starts laughing and I choke on my water.

"Actually, Chandler is my boss," I tell her after I'm able to breathe again.

Quinn makes a face. "Gross. Please don't fuck him, too. Objectively speaking, my brother is a *way* better catch."

"I'm not fucking…" Inwardly cringing, I rub my temples. "Look, your brother and I go way back."

Quinn puts her feet up on the table. "Hence the complicated."

She's more insightful than I give her credit for. "Yes. But we're not in a relationship. We're just friends."

Skylar's lips twitch. "*Very* good friends."

So help me God, I will skin her favorite pair of heels if she keeps this up.

"Yeah." I crinkle my nose. "You know, kind of like how you and *Memphis* are very good friends."

Skylar shoots me a dirty look and turns her attention back to her laptop.

Quinn's face scrunches in contemplation. "So you're fuck buddies. Gotcha."

I seriously wish she'd stop using the word *fuck* so much, but I can't focus on that right now because there are bigger fish to fry.

"I'd really appreciate it if you'd keep this just between us girls, okay? If Chandler finds out, I'll get fired."

Nodding, she grabs the last slice of pizza from the box. "Don't worry. I ain't no snitch."

In that case, crisis averted. "Thanks."

Chandler flies into the greenroom like a bat out of hell, looking more tense than I've ever seen him. Which is saying something.

Instantly, my stomach churns. I'm assuming he overheard our conversation, but what he says next is even worse.

"The miscreant's mother is here. She was outside the venue screaming that the band is holding her underage daughter hostage." The vein in his forehead bulges. "She threatened to call the cops, which she apparently has a direct connection to…seeing as her husband's a goddamn motherfucking *sheriff*."

He screams the last part so loud Quinn flinches.

Skylar said she left out that little tidbit when she informed him about the Quinn situation so he wouldn't freak out.

I can see why.

Skylar bolts up from her chair. "Shit."

Yup. Not only is this terrible for Phoenix and Quinn, this is a PR nightmare.

"Is she still outside the venue?" Skylar questions.

Chandler starts to answer, but some woman shoves past him and barrels into the greenroom. Like Quinn, she's beautiful, lithe, and has a mass of curly blonde hair and green eyes. And like both Quinn and Phoenix—her bone structure is to die for.

She immediately zeros in on her daughter. "Come on, Quinn. We're leaving."

Quinn grips my hand like a lifeline. "Please don't make me go back there. *Please.*"

My heart folds in on itself.

Skylar and I exchange an uneasy glance. I'm in no position to stop this woman from taking her daughter, but I might be able to buy us some time.

I stand up and so does Quinn. "She's not going anywhere until we talk to Phoenix."

Something flashes in her eyes when I say his name, and I know without a shadow of a doubt that Quinn has been telling the truth. I feel bad for ever doubting her.

"Come with me, Quinn. *Now.*"

Lunging forward, she tries to grab Quinn, who recoils and squeezes my hand so hard it hurts. "No!"

"Back up, lady," Skylar growls, surprising all of us. "She doesn't want to go with you."

Indignation washes over her face as her furious stare bounces between all of us. "She's *my* daughter. Keeping her captive is a crime."

I play the only card in my deck.

"In that case, I'll call the police."

"Lennon," Quinn hisses. "You *promised.*"

But my threat works because her mom's mouth instantly clamps shut, and she takes a step back.

Disgust billows in my gut. "That's what I thought."

Making sure Quinn is on the safe side so her mother won't try to grab her again, I march toward the door.

"I'm taking her to the bus."

I expect Chandler to hem and haw, but to my surprise, he stays silent.

As much as I'd love to give Phoenix a heads-up about his mother being here, there's no way that's possible since he's on stage.

The only thing I can do is exactly what *he* would do...and that's keep his sister safe.

CHAPTER 51
PHOENIX

S creams and shouts pulsate my ears as I sing the final note of "Existentialism" and the last bars fade.

I soak up the energy like a fiend, unable to get enough. This is what I live and breathe for.

This is why I'm still alive.

However, when I look off stage, my good buzz evaporates.

I was hoping Lennon would at least be out here to catch the end because it's my favorite part of the song and I know she'd love it just as much as I do…but she's not.

I try to tell myself it's no big deal, but it's a lie.

Because it's another reminder that once the tour is over…

So are we.

I raise my middle finger in the air. "Good night, Chicago. Get home safe."

"That was fucking awesome," Storm says as we trek off stage. "Did you see how crazy they went?"

Hell yeah I did. Just like I predicted.

"Mark my words, guys." Memphis slings an arm around each of our shoulders, pulling us into a huddle. "We're getting another Grammy."

George doesn't say shit as he walks off. The fucker knows better.

"Only if Vic agrees to let us put it on the record," I remind them.

"Trust me, that fucknut will," Storm says with a grin. "Especially after the way you handled shit today." He looks around backstage, which is unusually quiet. "Where's Chandler?"

Nowhere to be found...which is weird. I figured he'd be waiting in the wings, gearing up to either curse us or praise us.

Memphis surveys the backstage area. "He's probably in the greenroom with Sky and Lennon." Tongue in cheek, he rubs my head. "And my baby mama."

That earns him a sucker punch to the shoulder. "If you want to keep that arm, don't *ever* refer to my baby sister as your baby mama again."

Memphis holds his hands up. "Relax, man. It was a fucking joke."

Not a funny one.

Plus, I'm still fucking pissed that he never told me about Quinn sneaking into his hotel room.

"You should probably focus on your *actual* baby mama, don't you think?" I stroke my jaw. "Gwen's gotta be what, two or three months along now?"

Gwyneth Barclay is the most pretentious reality star on the face of the goddamn planet and the very type I can't fucking stand.

The kind who's famous for having a rich grandpa and a few smokin' hot sisters. Not because she's actually good at anything.

Not even sex...according to Memphis. Their relationship was supposed to be nothing more than a quick fling, but apparently mother nature had other plans. The *permanent* kind.

"That chick is fine as fuck," Storm notes. "Can't blame him for dipping his wick in that a few times."

I cock my head. "*Dipping his wick*? Christ. You're starting to sound like Grams."

Memphis grinds his teeth. "Will you two shut the fuck up already?"

Aw, the whittle baby is upset we're discussing his girlfriend. Serves him right for talking about *my* sister.

Storm snorts as we turn a corner. "You better invite me to the baby shower."

Memphis flips him off. "You better suck my nut sack."

Storm grins. "Only if it's dripping with Gwen's cu—"

Storm stops talking, and I stop breathing the second we enter the greenroom.

Skylar and Chandler are sitting on the couch with grave expressions on their faces. However, it's the familiar woman sitting between them that causes my chest to cave in.

The woman who left me fifteen and a half years ago.

"Mom?"

Rising off the couch, Skylar looks at Storm and Memphis. "Hey, guys. We need a minute."

Storm squeezes my shoulder. "I'll be around."

Memphis slaps my back. "Me too."

Chandler starts in the moment they leave. "We can't keep Quinn here unless we call the cops and tell them what's going on."

My mom recoils. Even after all these years, the thought of her being scared causes something inside me to unhinge.

"We're not calling the cops," I bite out.

That's when she finally looks at me...for all of two seconds.

Like she can't bear the sight of me.

"We need a few minutes alone."

"Of course," Skylar says as they head for the door. "Come find me after you're done and let me know what you want to do."

"Wait," I call out. "Where are Lennon and Quinn?"

"Your mom tried to make Quinn go with her against her will, so Lennon took her out to the bus."

That explains why she wasn't there for the song. She was protecting Quinn...because I wasn't able to.

I'm not even surprised. That's just who Lennon is.

Last night she told me that whenever I'm spiraling, I need to hold on to an anchor.

That's exactly what she's always been for me.

I thought Lennon coming back was my karma—and while that's

still true—I also think it was serendipity. Almost like the universe knew I was going to need her in order to hack seeing the woman in front of me again.

Skylar closes the door behind her, leaving me all alone…with my mother.

I always thought I'd have a million things to say to her if we ever crossed paths again.

Turns out, I only have one.

Make that two.

"You're not taking Quinn."

Her head whips up and I'm struck by how little she's changed.

Genevieve Walker—or *Moore*—has the kind of beauty that could stop traffic.

The kind of beauty that would make a secure man appreciative she was his, but an insecure man even more insecure.

The first fight I remember overhearing involved my father ramming his fist through the wall because one of his bandmates flirted with her.

Guess the apple doesn't fall far.

Maybe that's why she left me. She could sense the evil inside me…lurking.

Waiting for the right fuse to set it off.

"I'm not letting you keep Quinn." She sits up straight. "She doesn't even know you."

"Whose fault is that?"

She shrinks back—withdrawing—just like she always did whenever she didn't want to talk about something.

Once again…*the apple doesn't fall far.*

Too bad for her, I'm no longer seven. Upsetting my mom is no longer the plight it once was.

I want an answer to the question that's been gnawing at my goddamn psyche since the day I woke up and realized she was gone.

She's not leaving this room until I get it.

"Why?"

She looks down at her shoes. "If I don't get Quinn home, there will be consequences."

Not for Quinn. Because she's never stepping foot inside that *home* again.

"The first five years you were gone, I left my window cracked open every night...hoping you'd come back for me."

But she never did.

She closes her eyes, like my words upset her.

Good.

"I made you a card every year for your birthday until I was eleven."

And every single year, my dad would snatch it off the table and call me stupid because I couldn't write or spell well.

But I *tried*. I tried so fucking hard.

Because I wanted her to know how much I loved her.

I cried when he'd tear the card into shreds and remind me that she was never coming back.

But I didn't cry when he beat the shit out of me.

I wanted the pain.

"The first week you were gone, I got it so bad I couldn't walk. I kept calling out for you, hoping you'd rescue me."

But she didn't.

She clutches her stomach, like she's going to be sick. "Don't do this."

"I'm sorry. Does it hurt, Mom?" I laugh but there's not a drop of humor. "You know what else hurts? Being a human ashtray. Being forced into a scalding hot shower. Being beaten with a bottle, a bat—"

"Stop it!" she cries out. "Stop!"

"Answer the question."

Clamping her mouth shut, she shakes her head. "Just give me my daughter so I can leave."

"What about your son?" I roar so loud she jumps. "What about the son you abandoned?" My chest coils and bile surges up my throat. "Oh, that's right. You don't talk about him." Leaning in, I get close to her face, this way she can't ignore me like she has for the past fifteen years. "You tucked me away in a closet. Just like the picture of me Quinn found."

"Phoenix," she chokes out, but I don't care about her tears.

She never gave a fuck about mine.

"Why, Mom?" I kick the coffee table a few times, sending shards of wood sailing across the room. "*Why?*"

"I didn't have a choice," she screams. "I wanted to take you with me, but he wouldn't let me."

Shocked, I stagger back. "My father?"

He never wanted me. A fact he never let me forget.

"No. The man I left your father for." She blows out a shaky breath. "He was a cop who came to our house on a domestic dispute call one night when a neighbor called the police. He was sweet and kind...asked me to meet up for a cup of coffee so we could talk."

"And then you ran off into the sunset. Leaving your kid to fend for himself."

She wrings her hands. "I didn't want to. It's why I didn't leave your father right away, like Chad demanded. I *had* to protect you." She holds my gaze. "You're my baby boy. I couldn't leave you, Phoenix."

I ignore the way the dead thing in my chest constricts. "Then why did you?"

She looks away. "Because I got pregnant with Quinn."

I stay silent as I process what she's saying.

She takes the opportunity to continue. "I was going to get an abortion, but Chad begged me not to. He was leaving for Chicago because he'd been offered a job on a force that paid more, and he wanted me to come with him. He said we could get married, and I'd never have to live in fear again because he'd take care of me and our child. There was just one problem."

A tear falls down her cheek. "He didn't want you to come with us. He didn't like having a constant reminder that I'd been with another man." She swallows thickly. "I had a choice to make. I could either give myself and the child I was carrying an opportunity to have a good life, or…" her voice trails off.

She doesn't need to say the rest. The *choice* she made is the one I live with every day.

"How'd that work out for you?"

Sadness swims in her eyes. "Same as with your father. Things were great…until they weren't. Quinn was two when Chad put his hands on me the first time." Her face screws up. "She was five when he started hitting her."

And fifteen when it stops. Because the son of a bitch will never touch her again.

"You're not taking Quinn."

The same way our conversation started is the same way it's ending.

"I have to. If she doesn't come back home tonight, he'll…"

"He'll what?" I prompt when she stops talking.

"It will be bad, Phoenix. *Very* bad."

It's like she's living in her own little delusional world. "It's already bad."

She stands up. "You don't understand. I have to protect her."

She's the one who doesn't understand.

I move so I'm directly in front of her, blocking her from leaving. "The best way to protect her is to let her stay with me."

I don't know shit about taking care of someone else and I sure as fuck don't have the lifestyle for it, but I do know the life I can give her is light-years better than the one she has right now because it doesn't involve getting beaten.

Reaching up, she touches my face. "You've accomplished so much." Another tear streams down her cheek and she kisses my forehead…just like she used to before she'd tuck me into bed. "I always knew my baby boy was a rara avis. That's why I named you Phoenix."

A sharp twinge of pain strikes my chest. *Rara avis.*

It means rare bird in Latin. A *phenomenon.* A *prodigy.*

It's what she used to always call me.

The cold, hard truth slices through my sternum…a final stab to the vestige of the organ she broke.

There's no way my mother truly believed that…otherwise she wouldn't have left.

She tries to sidestep me, but I catch her forearm.

Then I repeat the very same words Lennon said to me.

Because I know how much they sting.

"Does it hurt to hear me everywhere you go?"

Her face collapses. "Phoenix."

"Did you ever have the urge to reach out? It's not like you didn't know where I was."

I was everywhere.

And she was nowhere.

She wipes her tears with the back of her hand. "No. Chad wouldn't like it."

This woman has fucked me up more than any drug ever could, but she's still my mother. I can't stand the thought of her being abused by her husband. *Again.*

That little boy couldn't protect her, but I can.

"Mom." I wait for her to look at me before I speak. "I can help you. You and Quinn. I can set you up in a nice house somewhere. I'll hire security to be with you all the time and I'll be there whenever I'm not working. I'll make sure you never see him again."

She gives me a sad smile. "I appreciate the offer, but I need to stay with Chad."

Whatever hopes I had of patching up our relationship and having a mother again vanish.

I don't fucking get it. I'm offering her protection and a chance to live a nice *safe* life that involves having both her kids in it…but she doesn't want it.

She wants *Chad.*

I guess it's true what they say. Some people like being the victim.

Because they don't know any different.

But Quinn isn't a victim. Despite everything, she's vibrant, quirky, and strong.

She's a survivor.

Just like her big brother.

Which is why she sought me out. Quinn wants out of that hell-hole and I'm going to do everything in my power to make sure she never goes back.

Which is exactly what our mother should be doing.

But she's always chosen men, herself, and her submission to those men over us.

"It's funny. You claim you want to protect your kids, but you never do." The truth is a visceral punch to the gut, as the image I've always had of her shatters. "You don't want to leave your precious Chad? Fine. Stay and let him beat the shit out of you. But for once in your fucking life, be a mom and do what's right for your kid."

She opens her mouth—no doubt gearing up to spew some bull-shit about how she is a good mother—but Lennon barges inside.

My guts twist as I take in her glassy eyes and the panic on her face.

"Quinn's gone."

The hairs on the back of my neck stand on end. "What do you mean Quinn's gone?"

"We were on the bus watching television and then I went to the bathroom...but when I came back out, she was gone." She draws in a jittery breath. "I don't understand. Everything was fine." Her gaze flicks to my mother. "Well, as fine as it could be, considering the circumstances."

My mother brushes past me. "I have to find her before he does."

No. *I* have to find her before he does.

I race out of the room and Lennon chases after me. "I'm so sorry."

Reaching behind me, I grab her hand. I can't afford to be mad or assign blame. I have to keep my head clear and my emotions regulated so I can find Quinn.

I gather whoever's still around backstage so we can start a search party.

As I'm issuing commands and breaking everyone up into teams so we can split up around the city, I notice my mom is gone.

It comes as no surprise.

Because while that seven-year-old boy desperately wanted to believe his mom could do no wrong and thought she was superwoman...

The man I am today knows she's actually a villain.

CHAPTER 52
LENNON

The sun was already rising by the time we made it back to the hotel.

We scoured every inch of the city—even the suburbs—for seven hours straight.

Between all of us—and some crew members who offered to help—you'd think we would have found her.

But we didn't...which means Phoenix had no choice but to call the police and file a missing person report.

Or rather, *try* to file one. Because they're being less than helpful, despite Phoenix telling the officer she's his long-lost sister.

The cop clicks and unclicks his pen for the millionth time. The same pen he hasn't even bothered to use...aside from writing her name down.

"Just because she's not with you doesn't mean she's missing. She could have gone back home."

She wouldn't have. *Not willingly.*

"She wouldn't—"

"Lennon," Phoenix growls, the warning in his tone clear.

I clamp my mouth shut even though it's beyond frustrating.

Grabbing his notepad off the coffee table, the officer stands.

"Look, we'll give her parents a call and if she's still not home, we'll follow up with them and take it from there."

I can tell Phoenix doesn't like this one bit—neither do I—but there's nothing either of us can do.

Phoenix scrubs a hand down his tired face. "If you find her, can you call me and let me know right away?"

"Will do."

He begins heading for the door but stops in his tracks.

Clicking his pen, he holds the notebook out to Phoenix. "I hate to ask, but my wife's a really big fan and her birthday is next week. Can I have your autograph?"

Swear some people have no tact.

Gritting his teeth, Phoenix takes the notebook and pen from him.

There's no doubt in my mind that Phoenix wants to shove the pen through the cop's eyeball—truth be told, I'm surprised he didn't —but he's probably hoping the autograph will prompt the guy to look for his sister.

After scrawling his signature, the cop takes out his phone. "Can I get a quick selfie, too?"

I stand there gaping at the douche in disbelief because honestly, *what the hell?*

A trail of tension rides down Phoenix's neck as he stands next to the cop, raises his middle finger, and plasters a somewhat less murderous look on his face so the cop can snap the picture.

A moment later, the guy mutters a quick thank you and leaves.

Asshole.

My anger only temporarily overshadows my anxiety, though, and once again, my thoughts go back to Quinn.

I don't understand why she left. I mean, *yes,* her mother was there to take her back home, but Phoenix wasn't going to allow that to happen. Hell, neither was I.

She *knew* this.

And yet, one second, we were watching *The Barclay's*—a god-awful reality show that Quinn's obsessed with—and the next...she was gone.

It just doesn't make any sense.

Unless she realized her mother was going to refuse Phoenix's help because she'd never leave her husband.

Quinn wanted to protect her mom...even though her mom doesn't protect her.

My heart pangs. *Them.*

Dammit. I don't like this feeling of being trapped in a box with no way out.

The only way this terrible cycle stops is to bring it to light. Something Phoenix *has* to realize.

"Why didn't you let me tell the cop what happened?"

Sure, he was rather nonchalant about the whole thing and kind of a prick, but that's because he didn't know the gravity of the situation.

Would he have protected a fellow officer? Maybe. But we don't know that for sure. Not all cops are bad.

Phoenix looks at me like I'm a moron. "Because it would only make things worse for her. You know that."

But the more we stay silent, the more we enable the abuse.

"That piece of shit is already going to be infuriated once the cops call the house asking about Quinn. The way I see it, we have nothing to lose by telling them the truth."

Then again, Phoenix and the *truth* don't exactly go hand in hand.

An ugly sound rumbles deep in his chest...and then he walks over to the bar.

"How is you getting drunk going to help Quinn?" I snap when he grabs the bottle of whiskey.

He twists the top off and takes a big swig. "It's gonna help me."

Phoenix might not be an alcoholic in the sense that he drinks every day, but the fact that every time he has a problem he uses it to cope proves he has a serious issue.

"Don't take the easy way out of this like your mother does. Don't accept defeat. You have a chance to help her."

My words only anger him more because his expression darkens.

"Help her?" I jump and yelp when the bottle whizzes past my head before crashing against the wall. "I can't fucking find her."

My heart beats a mile a minute. All I want to do is calm him down. "We will."

Quinn's a smart girl. Maybe she'll realize protecting her mom isn't what's best for her and she'll come back.

"She hasn't even been gone twelve hours yet. Give her some time—"

He cuts me off with a sharp sound. "And then what? What happens? She goes back to her dad's house, where he continues beating the shit out of her." He opens his arms wide. "But hey, at least our mom didn't abandon *her*."

Expelling a breath that hurts, I press a hand to my aching chest.

I try not to judge people, although I'm human and sometimes I can't help it.

But no matter how much I try to tell myself that this woman deserves my sympathy, I just can't seem to wrap my head or heart around the fact that she left her son in a trailer with the man who abused them…and chased her daughter down so she could drag her back into a violent environment.

Parents aren't infallible, but they're *supposed* to want what's best for their children.

Sadly, that's not the hand Quinn and Phoenix were dealt.

Closing the distance between us, I palm Phoenix's cheek. I know he's hurt and scared and feeling hopeless, but he can still save his sister.

"Even if Quinn goes back, you can still get her out of there. You have a shitload of money and you have access to exceptional lawyers."

But even if he didn't, I know he'd find a way to protect her.

Like I told Quinn, he's the most stubborn and determined person I've ever met. And whatever he wants, he gets.

Rising on my tiptoes, I drag his face down and bring our foreheads together. "You've got this. And Quinn's lucky she's got you now."

Heat pounds through me, settling between my legs when his mouth claims mine.

A groan tears out of him as he deepens the kiss. One hand clamps firmly around the back of my neck and the other squeezes my ass as he walks me backward until we tumble onto the bed.

Hovering above me, he grinds his pelvis, brushing up against the spot where I'm warm and aching.

His kiss is desperate, and frantic and he tastes like cinnamon gum...

And whiskey.

I tense because up until tonight there's one emotion Phoenix has never made me feel before.

Fear.

And not the kind that's a product of emotions...the kind that comes when you feel like you're in danger of being physically harmed.

It was so close. *So fucking close.*

Phoenix lifts his head. Confusion whirls in those blue orbs as he stares down at me. "What's wrong?"

My heart beats a chaotic path up my throat. "If your aim was off by a centimeter, the whiskey bottle would have hit me."

He opens his mouth, but doesn't utter a sound. Shock steals over his features...and then shame.

"I didn't mean..." He grazes my cheek with his thumb. His touch is impossibly gentle, like I'm made out of glass. "I would *never* hurt you, Lennon."

That's not true because he already has. However, I know in my gut that Phoenix would never lay a hand on me in anger.

But warnings are warnings for a reason. They alert you that if you keep doing what you're doing...something bad will happen.

Maybe this is his.

I just hope he pays attention this time.

"I don't want to be around you if you're going to drink or throw bottles."

Granted, it's my job, so I'll have no choice…but the sexual part of our relationship will end quicker than either of us wants it to.

His expression changes from one of guilt to resolve. "No more drinking, and no more throwing bottles." His lips brush my forehead. "Promise."

I'm about to kiss him, but he rolls off me and lies flat on his back. He keeps his gaze trained on the ceiling. I'd give just about anything to know what's going through his mind.

Curling up next to him, I place my head on his chest. "Sorry for killing the mood."

Shame floods his features again. "I don't like that I scared you."

I thread my fingers with his. "I know you'd never intentionally harm me while you're raging."

I just want him to grasp that even though he would never do it on purpose, it could still happen if he's not careful.

Bringing my hand to his mouth, he kisses the inside of my wrist. "I wouldn't." He tilts his head to look at me. "I'm sorry."

Never in a million years did I think I'd ever hear those words from Phoenix Walker.

"It's okay." Not wanting to drag him over this all night, I give him a flirty smile. "If you want to be rough with me, do it during sex."

Because I definitely don't mind it then.

I expect him to make a crude remark and pick things up where we left off…but he doesn't.

He goes back to staring at the ceiling.

I place my free hand over his heart. It's beating fast and hard. "What are you thinking about?"

In the heavy silence, his gaze searches mine. As usual, his impassive expression gives nothing away…but I'd give anything to know everything he keeps bottled up inside.

Just when I've given up hope, he speaks.

"Quinn doesn't deserve this."

He's right, she doesn't.

The thought of someone hurting a girl who's so vibrant and full of life makes me want to find the asshole and dole out my own brand of punishment.

So while I wholeheartedly agree that Quinn doesn't deserve this, it seems Phoenix doesn't realize something equally as important.

I trace the curve of his brow with my finger, waiting for him to make eye contact. When he does, I whisper, "*You* didn't deserve it either."

This time when he kisses me, it's soft and gentle...like he's saying *thank you* with his lips.

Then again, Phoenix has always been enigmatic when it comes to kissing.

I wonder if there's a reason for it. Maybe he had a bad experience.

"Can I ask you a weird question?" I breathe between kisses that are quickly heating up.

"You can ask me anything." He licks my bottom lip before biting it. "Doesn't mean I'll answer."

I'm aware.

"What's your deal when it comes to kissing?"

He stills, his lips grazing mine. "Got a problem with my technique?"

"No," I quickly assure him. "I love the way you kiss."

He puts every single thing he feels into it, just like he does whenever he's on stage.

I pull back because having a conversation when we're literally lip to lip not only feels funny, it's difficult.

"I remember you telling me once that you didn't kiss your hookups. I'm just wondering why kissing is so important to you."

His gaze drops to my mouth. "Like I told you back then. It complicates shit. Makes them think it's more than what it is."

A weird twinge flits through me with the memory.

It's not that it's important to him...it's that it's important to *them* and he doesn't want women to misconstrue things.

"Yeah, I remember."

His lips find mine again, but I place a hand on his chest, halting him.

Phoenix might be onto something.

"Since we're only fuck buddies, maybe we should stop kissing."

His jaw sets. "We're only fuck buddies because of *you*."

No…because of *him*.

Which is all the more reason I need to start drawing some clear lines in the sand before they all become blurred.

"It's just…it makes sense, you know? I think we should take kissing off the table."

"Yeah." He pulls his mouth away. "You're right."

I should be happy we're in agreement about this, so I force myself to ignore the stupid pang in my chest.

The ensuing silence stretches to the point it's almost uncomfortable. *Complicated.*

I look past him to the window. The sun is fully up now, the birds chirping with the start of a new day.

"I'm exhausted and I know you must be, too. I'm gonna head to my room."

A spark of hope goes through me because maybe Quinn will be there.

I start to move, but long fingers wrap around my wrist.

"Whenever my mom would tuck me into bed at night, she'd kiss me on the forehead." Phoenix looks away, withdrawing into himself. "No matter how shitty the day was, she always ended it with, 'I love you, my rara avis' and then a forehead kiss…until she left." He exhales heavily. "I held on to those memories, though because it's the only time I ever felt loved. But that love eroded into pain. And the longer she was gone, the more it hurt."

His eyes find mine. "I didn't want to get attached to another woman, because the one woman who was never supposed to break my heart smashed it into a thousand fucking pieces."

My own heart does an excruciating flip. It makes so much sense now.

Not just the kissing. But him never wanting to have a relationship.

He doesn't want to let another woman in.

He doesn't want to get hurt.

I palm his cheek. "I'm so sorry."

I hate that this woman ruined her son so much that he's closed up parts of himself eternally.

She didn't just rob him of her love, she took away his ability to accept love from anyone.

He shrugs a shoulder like it's no big deal. "I just thought you, of all people, deserved to know the truth behind my no-kissing rule."

I run my thumb along the faint stubble on his jaw. "And here I stupidly wondered if it was a bad first kiss that put you off."

His lips curve. "My first kiss was great, actually...until I fucked it up."

Safe to say he's piqued my curiosity. "What happened?"

Those blue eyes hold me captive. "Well, she was my tutor, but we had a strong connection and ended up forming a friendship."

My stomach coils because this story sounds awfully familiar.

"She helped me pass an English final so I could graduate high school. I met her in the band room to tell her the good news, but the moment I saw her sitting at the piano...it felt like someone hit me over the head with a steel pipe."

I can't speak. Can't breathe. Can't move.

He takes the breath I'm unable to and his fingers find my hair, drawing me closer. "I thought about all the hours she spent helping me, the reading pen she bought me...her unwavering belief in me." His gaze drops to my mouth, and he leans in. "When I told her I passed, she ran over and hugged me, but it wasn't enough. I wanted more."

Oh god.

His lips ghost mine. "With her...I wanted more."

An array of emotions tangle in my chest as his mouth slides over mine.

I was his first kiss.

I almost want to laugh because I was so inexperienced myself I never would have known if he was bad at it.

My pulse skyrockets as his fingers grip my chin, keeping me in place. A breathless moan leaves me as he takes me deeper, and I can feel my resistance crack a little more with every sweep of his tongue.

He's definitely not bad at it. If anything, he's *too* good at it.

It's almost unfair.

Knowing I'm the only one in the world who gets to experience this with him makes me feel...*special*.

"Kissing is back on the table," I murmur against his lips.

He hitches my leg around his waist, and I feel his mouth twitch. "It was never off."

Dammit, Lennon. Get a hold of yourself.

I pull back slightly. "We're still temporary fuck buddies." I try to catch my breath but it's impossible because he's looking into my eyes, siphoning all the air from my lungs. "But I'd be lying if I said we didn't have an intense physical attraction to one another, right?"

The corners of his lips rise. "Right."

"And because of that, it wouldn't be fair to deny ourselves the full experience, right?"

Full experience.

My stomach twists. I just had to say *those* words, didn't I?

He's full on smirking now. "Right."

As if sensing I'm about to get stuck in my head, he slams his mouth against mine.

We kiss for so long...I lose all concept of time.

We kiss for so long...I never want to break apart.

We kiss for so long...I almost forget how much it hurts.

CHAPTER 53
LENNON

Balancing the plate of eggs, ham, and toast, I exit the kitchen and open the sliding door to the bunk.

It's been three days since we reported Quinn missing and we still haven't heard anything.

The first day, Phoenix was still optimistic we'd find her and we had another search party before and after the concert.

Day two...he got angry. Not bottle-throwing angry, but angry enough that he made a poor woman in wardrobe cry and the sound-board guy threatened to quit several times.

After that, everyone aside from me avoided him unless it was urgent.

Day three, his anger turned to misery...and he's been like that ever since.

Skylar's been messaging Quinn nonstop on social media to no avail and every time one of us calls her, it goes straight to voice mail.

We were going to stay in Chicago a little longer but Chandler threw the world's biggest hissy fit and threatened to call Vic if we didn't get our asses on the bus.

Needless to say, Phoenix isn't happy.

The moment we got on the bus, he went straight to his bunk and hasn't come out.

I know nothing I say will make any of this better but I'm at a loss, so I did what my dad has always done for me whenever I'm sad.

I made him food.

Sadly, there wasn't a whole lot in the fridge to work with and while I'm a decent chef, I'm nowhere near as good as Grams.

The curtain on his bunk is drawn closed when I walk in, so I cautiously pull it back. "Hey."

Sadness etches his features as he lies there staring up at nothing.

My heart falls to the floor as I take a seat next to him.

I gesture to the plate I'm holding. "I made you some food."

Phoenix rolls over, dismissing me and his breakfast. "Not hungry."

It was a shot in the dark. But I took it anyway because I hate feeling helpless.

In an attempt to find some ray of hope he can cling to, I utter, "Indianapolis is only three hours away from Chicago, and we'll be there for the next four days."

"Where we are doesn't mean shit when I still don't know where *she* is."

I rub his back. "I know." After placing the plate on my bunk, I curl up next to him. "If there's anything I can do or anything you need—"

The sound of his phone ringing cuts me off.

Sighing, Phoenix presses the speakerphone button. "Hello."

"Hi, this is Officer Bancroft. Is this Phoenix Walker?"

"Yes." Phoenix bolts up so fast he nearly knocks me over. "Did you find Quinn?"

I say a silent prayer.

"Yeah," Detective Bancroft states, and a giant wave of relief flows through me.

However, that relief turns to dread with his next words. "It turns out her father is actually a sheriff. Small world, huh? Anyway, she's back home with her folks."

My stomach plummets and the ground beneath me tilts.

"Where does she live?" Phoenix barks.

There's a lengthy pause before he says, "Given you're not her guardian and she's a minor, I'm not at liberty to give out that information. But don't worry, she's safe."

Then he hangs up.

Snarling, Phoenix throws his phone. "She's *not* fucking safe."

A moment later, Skylar walks in with a somber expression on her face. "I just heard back from the lab. Quinn's your sister."

What should have been happy news only makes him that much more miserable.

CHAPTER 54
PHOENIX

I raise my middle finger at the crowd of screaming fans. "It's been real, Indiana."

Real fucking stupid.

Gritting my teeth, I stalk off the stage.

I grab Skylar the second I spot her. "Did you find her address?"

She shakes her head. "No, but I'm working on it. So is the PI."

In this day and age, no one should be off the grid. What the fuck is taking them so long?

Skylar's smart enough to walk away when I snarl.

The people backstage part like the red sea as I head for the greenroom. Even Storm and Memphis pretend to be busy on their phones.

Lately everyone has been avoiding me if they can help it and muttering what a prick I am behind my back when they can't, but Lennon's face lights up when I enter, and she looks genuinely happy by my presence.

"Hey, you."

She's been going out of her way to be there for me while I deal with this shit and I'm grateful, but right now, I need her away from me.

"Get out. Now."

Visibly offended, her mouth drops open and those big brown eyes flash with that all too familiar hate fire I haven't seen in a while. I can tell she's torn between wanting to tell me to go fuck myself with a cactus and wanting to pour the soda in her hand over my head.

Fortunately for us both, she rolls her shoulders back and marches out, but not before calling me a dick under her breath.

The moment she's gone, I kick the snack table, sending whatever shit was on it scattering, and punch the nearest wall.

It's not a bottle, though, so my promise to her is still intact.

Well acquainted with my temper, Chandler simply steps over the mess on the floor.

"You have a phone interview with a journalist from K-pop magazine."

I brace my hands on the wall, debating whether or not to punch it again. "Why the fuck does K-pop magazine want to interview me?"

"Because you're Phoenix Walker," he says with a roll of his eyes. "Besides, it's free press." He shoves his cell into my hand. "Get your ass on the phone."

"I don't speak Korean," I remind him.

Walking backward, he shrugs. "In that case, it will be a short interview."

Bastard.

Grinding my molars, I take a seat on the couch and press the speakerphone button. "Hello."

The reporter says something on the other line, but I don't know what because I don't speak the motherfucking language.

You'd think they would have gotten us an interpreter.

Incompetent assholes.

I can sense the reporter is growing frustrated because I still haven't given a response. "I love my Korean fans."

The reporter asks another question, and just like the first, I don't have the faintest idea what.

For all I know, she could be asking to suck my dick and give me a rim job.

She certainly wouldn't be the first. And I'm positive she won't be the last.

At a loss of what to say, I run a hand down my face and lean back. The migraine throbbing at the base of my skull is growing by the second.

"Korea rocks."

Seemingly pleased with my response, she asks a follow-up question…one I don't fucking understand.

Dammit. I've got nothing.

"I love my Korean fans—"

All of a sudden, the door swings open and a swarm of people rush inside.

Words jam in my throat when I see Storm holding a limp girl in his arms.

I can't see her face because it's buried in Storm's neck, but her limbs are black and blue and there's dried blood caked on her clothes. A *lot* of it.

"Phoenix," the girl croaks.

My gut recoils. *Quinn.*

I bolt up. "Put her on the couch." I look at Skylar since she's the closest to me. "Call an ambulance."

Skylar fetches her phone out of her purse. "On it."

"No." Quinn moans as Storm lays her on the couch. "Please don't."

Lennon kneels down beside her and reaches for her hand. "We have to, honey. You're really hurt."

"I'll get better. I always do." Her eyes find mine and the desperation swirling in them gnaws my insides. "Please don't call an ambulance. I'm begging you."

Fuck.

I make a split-second decision. One I hope doesn't backfire.

"No hospital." I turn to Chandler. "Call that doctor you know, and set up the private plane if he needs it. I want him here as soon as possible. Tell him we'll make it worth his while."

Nodding, Chandler plucks his phone off the floor. "I'll see what I can do."

In the meantime, we'll need to get her comfortable.

I eye Storm, who looks like he's about ready to kick someone's ass. "Go grab some ice and a first aid kit." I turn to Memphis next because I know this is his area of expertise, thanks to Josh. "Go find some painkillers."

"I'll make sure the crew stays out of here," Skylar says.

Lennon blanches as she takes in her blood-stained shirt. "I'll go get her some clean clothes."

"Don't leave," Quinn croaks.

Lennon stays put. "I won't." She goes to touch her forehead but hesitates at the last second, like she's afraid it might hurt her. "I'll stay right here."

That's when it dawns on me. "How did you get here, Quinn?"

It's a three-hour drive from Chicago and there's no way she went on a bus like this.

Her eyes flutter open and what she says next has me reeling.

"Mom."

My chest tightens with a weird mixture of pain and gratitude. *She finally put her kid first.*

"She has three bruised ribs, a dislocated jaw, two wounds that needed to be stitched up, numerous contusions, and what appears to be a concussion." The doctor hands me a bottle of pills. "These are some painkillers. Don't give her more than four in a twenty-four-hour period. Call me if she has any new symptoms, although once again, I recommend you take her to a hospital."

"No," my sister protests from the couch. "They'll call him."

"Relax, Quinn." I lead the doctor out of the greenroom. "I appreciate you coming here. Skylar said she already Venmoed you the money."

A shit ton of emotions filter through me as I sag against the door, but only one emerges the winner.

Rage.

The kind that burns villages to the ground and starts wars.

As if sensing the hurricane brewing inside me, Lennon glances up with a worried expression. "What are you gonna do?"

There's only one thing I can do.

One thing that will end this bullshit for good.

I'm gonna fucking kill him.

CHAPTER 55
LENNON

I pace back and forth in my hotel room, my mind racing a mile a minute and my stomach flipping like a gymnast on speed.

"They've been gone a really long time."

Detective Skylar ended up finding Quinn's address a couple hours after Quinn was dumped in the parking lot by her mother, and Phoenix took off in a cloud of rage.

But not before instructing Storm and me to stay back with Quinn because he wanted the two people he trusted the most to look after his sister.

I was scared when he left.

But now? I'm fucking *terrified*.

Because that was over nine hours ago.

"Well, Phoenix hasn't called me to bail him out of jail yet, so that's a good sign," Storm unhelpfully supplies.

Quinn sits up in bed, wincing with the movement. "We should go there. My dad might hurt him. He's really strong."

Storm and I exchange a glance. *Phoenix is stronger.*

Which only makes the panic rising up my throat churn my insides.

Crossing his arms, Storm peers down at her. "You're not going anywhere, juvie. Lay down."

Quinn shoots him a dirty look.

Storm's right, though. Quinn isn't going anywhere.

I am.

I grab my purse off the table. "I'll be back later."

Hopefully.

Storm snatches my arm. "Do you want Phoenix to kill me, too? Because he specifically told me not to let *either* of you out of my sight."

I'm a grown-ass woman, goddammit.

"Sorry, Storm." I pat his shoulder with my free hand. "I'll send flowers to your funeral."

I'm halfway to the door when it opens.

My hands fly to my face and I gasp when I notice the purple bruise surrounding Phoenix's eye. "Holy shit."

Those lips curl into an arrogant smirk. "You should see the other guy."

Part of me wants to run into his arms and hug him harder than I've ever hugged anyone, while the *other* part of me wants to slap him for being so unfazed by all this while I was going out of my mind with worry.

"What the hell took you so long?"

Another gasp leaves me, and I clutch my chest. The entire room spins like some kind of rotating carnival ride. "Oh god. You didn't actually kill him. Did you?"

Phoenix is far too pretty for jail. Plus, I'm fairly certain they don't allow conjugal visits for fuck buddies.

"He nearly did," Chandler mutters. "Thankfully Memphis pulled him off in the nick of time."

Quinn pales. "Do I have to go back there?"

Phoenix's gaze breaks from mine and locks with hers. "No. You're staying with me."

While I'm happy to hear it...I'm also extremely confused.

"How is that possible?"

Skylar smiles wickedly. "The power of good ol' extortion." She studies her nails. "Works every time."

Quinn blinks, appearing bewildered. "I don't understand."

That makes two of us.

Phoenix grabs a bottle of water from the mini-fridge. "Let's just say I made it crystal clear that he had no choice but to let you stay with me. If he didn't, I was going to let the entire world know that the honorable sheriff was an abusive piece of shit."

Yup. That will do it.

Phoenix isn't a B-list celebrity with a small following. He's *internationally* famous.

And the internet isn't a very forgiving place. Everywhere that asshole went, someone somewhere would recognize him for exactly what and who he is.

"Does this mean we're stuck with the juvenile delinquent now?" Storm mutters.

Quinn bolts out of bed. "Whoa. Hold on. I get to stay?"

Phoenix nods. "Yeah."

Hobbling over, she wraps her arms around him. "You're the *best* big brother ever."

Chandler sighs as he ambles to the door. "Let's hope another one of these doesn't show up."

CHAPTER 56
PHOENIX

I toss and turn on the couch in the back lounge of the bus, unable to fall asleep. Not only because it's way too small to accommodate my six-four frame comfortably, but I have way too much fucking shit on my mind.

I'd text Lennon and tell her to come in here so I could fuck us both to sleep, but a—she won't because she's too afraid of getting caught by Chandler. And b—she needs the rest.

She's not only been taking care of me, but helping me take care of Quinn the past few days.

And just like that, my lungs restrict to the point it's damn near suffocating.

The closer we get to the end of this tour…the more the brick in the center of my chest expands.

We're running out of time.

I'd ask her to stay and come to Europe with us, but I know she won't.

Not only because of her dad, but because she's made it perfectly fucking clear that this thing between us is only temporary.

I'm nothing but an itch to scratch.

Something to get out of her system.

Even though she'll *always* be in mine.

Fucked-up thing about it is…it's my fault.

I made this bed—and just like the tiny couch in the lounge I took so Quinn could have my bunk—I have to lie in it.

Fuck this.

I'm restless and irritated and could use something to take the edge off. However, I promised Lennon I wouldn't drink anymore, and I want to keep all my promises to her. Which means I have no choice but to grab a sports drink from the fridge and *pretend* it packs a punch.

The bus is dark, and everyone is passed out as I make my way to the kitchen.

Everyone but Skylar, who's sitting at the table.

I should have known she'd still be up. Like me, she tends to have trouble sleeping and we've had plenty of late-night bus conversations throughout the years.

Those days are long over, though.

She looks up from her laptop when she sees me. "Hey."

Turning my back to her, I take a Gatorade from the fridge. "I'll be out of here in a second."

"We used to be friends," she says when I start to leave.

Until I killed your fiancé.

"And now you act like I don't exist."

That's not true. We aren't close anymore, but I don't ignore her.

Hell, I couldn't even if I wanted to.

I turn around. "What are you talking about? You're my publicist. I have no choice but to acknowledge you."

Leaning back, Skylar folds her arms over her chest. "And *that's* exactly how you act. Like talking to me is an obligation."

I should walk away, but for the first time since she's been back, I catch a glimpse of the old Skylar.

The one who wore her heart on her sleeve and bled out time and time again for the guy who—although infatuated with her—treated her like shit, manipulated her into doing things she probably didn't want to, and cheated on her every chance he got.

Nevertheless, it was the guy she loved with all her heart.

The guy she was supposed to marry this year.

And I stole that from her.

Expelling a heavy sigh, I drop down in the chair across from her. "You shouldn't want me to talk to you, Skylar." My gaze falls to the ring dangling around her neck. "I'm the reason that engagement ring will never turn into a wedding ring."

"No, you're not." She inspects the table like she's searching for an answer to a question she hasn't asked. "You might not remember that night, but I do. Josh made his own choices." Anguish washes over her expression and she blows out a shaky breath. "It was never gonna end any other way for him."

"That's not true. He's dead because I didn't stop him."

I should have.

We were both way too fucked up to get in that car.

And now a mother, a child, and an unborn baby are dead.

She makes a scoffing sound. "Take it from someone who spent most of her life trying to save him. You couldn't." Her eyes turn glassy. "Once he set his mind on something, there was no stopping him."

She's not wrong. But still...

They're dead because of me.

And nothing she says—nothing *I* do—will ever change that.

Reaching across the table, she steals my Gatorade and takes a sip. "Josh fucked up enough people's lives. Don't let him fuck up yours and become another one of his casualties. Trust me, the coffin is crowded enough."

Considering their toxic relationship, it would be easy to read between the lines of that statement, but I don't want to assume something I shouldn't.

Josh wasn't a saint and he sure as fuck didn't deserve a girl like Skylar, but I know he loved her.

So much so his last breath was her name.

"Lennon's an amazing girl, Phoenix." Placing the cap on the bottle, she hands it back to me. "Do yourself a favor and don't destroy the best thing that ever happened to you, okay?"

Too late.

"So," Quinn says through a mouthful of chips. "How's this gonna work? Do I have to ask you for permission to do stuff?"

"Yes."

If she thinks I'm going to give her free rein to do anything she wants, she's even crazier than I thought.

I'll be her cool older brother when she turns eighteen. Right now, I have to be her parent.

Looking out the bus window, she stuffs another handful of chips into her mouth and chews. Loudly. "Do I get my own credit card?"

Skylar tried to warn me that Quinn liked to shop just as much as her, but I was skeptical.

Mostly because *no one* likes to shop as much as Skylar.

Lennon's lips twitch as she takes a seat next to me at the kitchen table.

I snatch the bag of chips from Quinn and eat a few. "No."

I have no problem giving Quinn whatever she needs, but I'm not giving her whatever she *wants*.

I had to learn the value of a dollar when I was a kid and so will she.

Her mouth opens and closes like a fish. "Are you serious? Dude, you're *rich*."

Time to let her in on a little secret. "Rich people stay rich because they don't spend their money on frivolous shit, *dude*."

After Vic cut us our first big check, Josh bought a Ferrari and whisked Skylar away to Paris on a shopping trip.

Memphis bought himself a new guitar.

Storm took a trip back home to see Grams.

And I bought myself groceries and stocked my fridge for the very first time.

Then I paid my bills and deposited the rest of the money into my savings account.

Our second check was triple the first.

Once again, Josh whisked Skylar away on a fancy trip. Along with buying an engagement ring, a swanky mansion, and another fucking Ferrari.

Memphis got himself an apartment in LA while Storm and I moved out of the one we shared and went fifty-fifty on a villa.

And a condo for Grams...despite her protests.

The checks got even bigger after that, but I already had a sweet home, a nice car, and groceries in the fridge so I was more than content.

Josh wasn't, though. Every check he got he spent on extravagant shit for himself, over-the-top gifts that Skylar begged him to return, drugs, prostitutes, and fuck knows what else.

Despite earning more than we'd ever be able to spend in our lifetimes, guess who started having money problems by the time our second album went *diamond*?

The only positive that came from watching Josh burn his money was that it reinforced for the rest of us just how important it was not to spend it all like you were dying the next day.

Ironic, considering Josh perished so young.

The constant guilt hanging like a black cloud over my head threatens to take over, but I can't have a pity party right now because my sister—who has chip crumbs all over her face and shirt—is currently gaping at me like I sprouted another head. "What am I supposed to do for money?"

The same thing I had to do when I was her age. *Work.*

"Congrats. You're our new merch girl."

Chandler—who's entering the kitchen—shakes his head. "Absolutely not."

Quinn lets out a belch loud enough to wake the dead. "How come?"

The vein in Chandler's forehead bulges as he eyeballs me. "She's been with us for over a week now. Are we going to get our new bundle of joy an education, or are we going to leave her undomesticated?"

"Hey," Quinn exclaims, clearly offended. "I'm potty trained."

Storm, who was typing out a text on his phone, looks up. "Thank fuck for that."

While her being housebroken is a plus, Chandler's right. I need to enroll her in school.

I'm just not sure how that's going to work, given my lifestyle.

I look at Lennon. "I know a good tutor."

Plus, if she agrees, it will give her a reason to stay longer.

No dice though because Lennon says, "She's gonna need more than a tutor."

I focus on Quinn again. "What grade are you in?"

"I start my junior year after the summer."

Graduation is a long time away. Fuck.

Quinn waves a hand like it's no big deal. "Don't worry. I can get my GED."

"You can also sign her up for online high school classes," Lennon suggests.

I think about this for a bit. It's not a bad idea, but if Quinn's anything like me, she might have difficulty when it comes to learning.

"Do you think you can handle that? If not, it's okay."

"Totally doable, bro." She licks each of her fingers. "I'm one of the top students in my class."

"Must be a small class," Storm mutters.

Quinn rolls her eyes. "I'm serious. I'm actually *really* smart."

Lennon squeezes my knee under the table. "You and your brother have that in common."

CHAPTER 57
LENNON

"I heard he likes blondes."

Not anymore.

"I heard he has his dick pierced."

Negative.

"I heard he doesn't like to kiss."

I raise my phone, attempting to hide my smile.

Actually, he loves it.

"I heard it's so big you'll be sore for a week straight."

I shift my stance and that familiar ache I've become addicted to throbs between my legs.

Can confirm.

A moment later, the hoard of impatient girls standing at the meet-and-greet table scream Phoenix's name like he's their messiah when he walks backstage.

However, *I'm* the one he makes a beeline for.

His gaze turns molten when he reaches me and he lifts a hand, intending to touch my face. I give him a warning look since we're not only in public, but Chandler is lurking around.

His hand clenches into a fist as he drops it. Scowling, he stands beside me and mutters a curse …like it's taking every ounce of willpower to restrain himself.

That makes two of us.

Attempting to get a handle on things, I jut my chin at the group of girls desperately vying for his attention.

"They want you."

His mouth bends into a wolfish grin. "Everyone wants me." Dipping his head, he brushes his lips over my ear. "But only *you* get to have me."

My heart slams into my ribs.

As if knowing the impact of his words, his gaze slowly sweeps up my body, deliberate and blatant, before walking over to the group of fans.

My clothes suddenly feel like they're smothering me. I have the reckless urge to march over there, steal him away, and make him screw me in front of everyone just to verify his statement.

That's when I notice George staring at me from across the room.

Guilt is a heavy cinder block in my chest. We haven't spoken since that night at the club and he has every reason to hate me.

While you can't choose who you're attracted to, the way things ended between us wasn't right.

I owe him a sincere apology and I'm hoping he'll finally allow me to give him one.

Drawing in a deep breath, I make my way over to him.

"Hey. Can we talk?"

He snorts into his drink. "Last time we *talked,* it ended with you fucking the guy you swore you didn't have feelings for."

Fair enough. Although that's not entirely accurate. The only feelings I'll allow myself to have for him are the carnal kind.

The safe kind.

"It's not like that. I don't have feelings for Ph—" I stop myself from uttering his name in the nick of time because Chandler strolls by. "I'm really sorry. I never meant to hurt you."

Another snort leaves him. "Yes, you did."

It's on the tip of my tongue to assure him that wasn't the case, but then he says, "You knew I had feelings for you, Lennon. But instead of doing the right thing and telling me you didn't return them, you strung me along so you could use me." His face twists with disgust. "Telling yourself you never meant to hurt me might help you sleep better, but it doesn't change the truth. You're not a good person. You're a selfish one."

I'm *him*.

My heart lodges in my throat with the realization.

Although different scenarios, what I did to George is similar to what Phoenix did to me.

And to think, there was a time when I would have killed to be Phoenix Walker.

Guess I got my wish.

I've been shoving all my pain into a safe and forcing myself to *forget* so I can enjoy the sex, but George's words just busted that safe wide open and all the contents inside are searing my soul.

George isn't quite done with me yet, though. "I used to think you were a smart girl, but you're not. Smart girls don't run back to their exes who cheated on them."

He's right.

Only what Phoenix did to me was worse. *Much worse.*

And here I am having sex with him like everything is hunky-dory.

Yet, *he* still won't even admit what he did to me.

The only one who got a *free pass* in our scenario is him.

I'm not just stupid. I'm *weak* and senseless.

"I'm sorry," I choke out, the reality of it asphyxiating me. "I'm *so* sor—"

I don't get to finish that statement because Phoenix wraps a hand around George's throat and shoves him against the wall. "Say one more word to her and I *will* fucking kill you."

There's a collective gasp backstage and the girls at the meet-and-greet table start snapping photos with their cell phones.

I dig my nails into Phoenix's hand, attempting to pry them from George's throat before he loses consciousness. "Leave him alone. He didn't do anything wrong."

Phoenix looks at me like I'm insane. "He hurt you."

"No." Tears blur my vision as a mass of people rush over. "*You* did."

I grind my molars so hard I'm surprised they don't turn to dust when my phone vibrates with *another* text message.

Rolling over in bed, I peer down at my phone.

Phoenix: Talk to me.

I have nothing to say. Or rather, nothing he'll want to hear.

I'm thankful he can't barge in here like he usually does because this hotel doesn't have connecting rooms.

Won't stop him from calling and texting me all night, though.

Dots at the bottom of the screen appear and then disappear, before appearing again.

Phoenix: Come on, Groupie. You can't avoid me forever.

Ha. *Watch me.*

It's what I was planning on doing after the tour ended anyway.

Now it's twelve days ahead of schedule.

With a huff, I throw my phone across the room.

"Is my brother still pissing you off?" Quinn questions with a frown. "According to Skylar, boys get dumber with age."

Skylar's not wrong.

However, despite only knowing her big brother for a short time, it's clear Quinn thinks the world of him.

I don't want to ruin that for her.

Because I know better than anyone how devastating it is to find out the person you care about isn't who you thought they were.

Ugh. It's going to be hard hiding my disdain while sharing a room with her for the next twelve days.

I'm about to tell her everything's fine, but she starts tossing some of the clothes and toiletries Skylar recently bought her into a small tote bag.

I glance at the clock on the nightstand. It's almost midnight.

"Where are you going?"

"Last I checked, you were Phoenix's babysitter. Not mine."

She's right.

But the girl has a history of fleeing.

Dread coils my insides and I sit up. "Please don't run away."

I'm thinking of ways to bribe her to stay when her pretty face splits into a grin. "God, you should see your face right now." She stuffs a pair of pajamas into the tote. "Relax. Skylar invited me to her room for a sleepover. She's gonna teach me how to do my makeup and then we're gonna give ourselves mani-pedis." A hopeful glint enters her eyes. "Wanna come?"

As much as I don't want to disappoint her, I won't be much fun, given my sour mood.

"Can I take a rain check?"

Shrugging, she shoulders her bag. "Fine. But only if you let me borrow your Doc Martens."

It seems wheeling and dealing is one of her favorite pastimes.

"You got it."

She heads for the door, but I call her back. "Quinn?"

She turns. "What's up?"

"You swear you're going to Skylar's room, right?"

If she runs away on my watch and gets hurt again, I'll never forgive myself.

Tilting her head, she sighs. "Holy crap. *Yes.*" Her expression turns serious. "No cap."

I have no idea what that means.

"It means no lie," she calls out.

In that case, it isn't genetic.

After she leaves, I walk to the other side of the room and pick my cell up off the floor.

I'm debating if it's too late to call Mrs. Palma when I hear a knock.

I jog over to the door. "Did you forget your—"

I stop talking when I realize *he's* standing there.

As much as I want to slam it in his face, he might be here to tell me something work related.

I cross my arms over my chest, mainly because I'm pissed but also because I'm not wearing a bra under my white pajama top. "What do you want?"

He has the nerve to look at me like *I'm* the irritating one. "I've been texting and calling you for the past two hours."

I'm aware. "And I've been ignoring you for the past two hours."

Something I'm certain he's already figured out. Hence the stubborn ass is here.

I start to close the door, but he wedges his foot between it and the frame. "Friends don't ghost friends, remember?"

Oh, this motherfucker.

Swinging the door open, I get in his face. "We are not friends."

I want to cut the smug grin off his lips with a chainsaw. "Then how come you keep insisting we're fuck *buddies*?"

"*Were*. As in past tense." I flash him a vindictive smile. "Good night."

He makes a growly sound deep in his throat. "Dammit, Lennon. Let me in."

Despite knowing he's bigger and stronger and could easily push his way through if he wanted to, I stand firm. "No."

He drags a hand down his face. "I know you're pissed because I attacked George."

While I'll admit that was totally uncalled for, he's irrefutably missed the mark.

The fact he doesn't even realize what's wrong is the problem.

Phoenix is highly intelligent. It shouldn't be hard for him to figure this out.

However, I throw him a bone because the quicker he knows, the quicker he'll leave. "I'm not pissed. I'm upset."

Hurt.

He blinks in confusion and it's all I can do not to throw my hands up.

"Why? We both know you're not into him—"

"I'm upset because I'm just like *you*!" I scream so loud I'm positive someone will call the front desk with a noise complaint.

My outburst only puzzles him more. "What?"

"I knew George had feelings for me that I didn't return, but I used him anyway. Just like you used *me*."

Follow the bouncing balls, jackass.

"Jesus fucking Christ." A gruff noise leaves him, and he bulldozes past me into the room. "I told you, my feelings for you were —*are*—real."

"Which makes what you did even worse."

Because when you have feelings for someone, you don't intentionally break them.

But he did. And now we're here.

Stuck in a spot we'll never be able to get out of.

My lungs freeze when he grabs my T-shirt between his fingers and tugs me forward. "I *hate* that I hurt you."

It's the second time he's said that. Only the agony in his expression is somehow even stronger now.

So strong I find myself desperately wanting to believe him... despite my subconscious telling me I should know better.

The moment of silence between us feels like an entire lifetime before he finally releases me.

I notice the paper bag he's holding as we break apart. "What's in the bag?"

Face impassive, he reaches inside it and pulls out a bottle of Jack Daniels along with two red Solo cups.

The memory slices through me like a blade.

"You're not supposed to drink, remember?"

Something he promised me—but *shocker*—he lied.

His expression hardens, almost like he knows what I'm thinking, and it perturbs him. "Good thing I filled it with iced tea then."

Dammit. Fine. He didn't lie this time. Whoopty-freakin-do.

I watch in confusion as he walks over to the small desk in the corner of the room and proceeds to fill both cups.

Then he hands me one.

"What are you doing?"

Giving me an impish smile, Phoenix taps his Solo against mine. "We should play a drinking game for old times' sake."

I pin him with a look that makes his smile fall. "Let's not."

Some dumb game we played in high school isn't going to miraculously make us friends again.

Granted, it worked back then, but there's a world of difference between kissing a girl and ignoring her for three days...and ruining someone who was in love with you for your own selfish gain.

"Lennon."

There's an edge to his voice, but I don't care.

"I'm not playing this stupid game."

Disregarding that, he raises his cup in the air. "I'll start. Never have I ever had a curfew."

Seriously? It's been over four years. You'd think he'd have a better opener.

In spite of my enmity for him and this ridiculous game he's determined to play, I take a small sip.

"That's surprising, given Chandler and all."

"He tried once, but we both know I don't follow rules." The knowing look he gives me is an arrow through the heart. "Your turn."

Well, if he can do repeats, so can I.

"Never have I ever sang on stage." When he raises a brow, I add. "In front of a crowd."

Not like he does.

He surveys me as he drinks...and then the asshole does it.

"Never have I ever had pig slop thrown on me at a party."

He's lucky this iced tea is good or else he'd be wearing it.

Raising the cup to my lips, I hold up the pointer finger of my free hand. "Still too soon."

That gets a laugh out of him.

One I make sure to cut off with my next statement.

"Never have I ever cheated on a test...or a girl."

His expression turns accusatory. "Test yes. Girlfriend, no. I told you, I didn't fuck Sabrina that night."

"Doesn't matter." Wanting to strike him where it hurts, I lift my gaze to his. "Because I was never your girlfriend...and I never will be."

I can tell my comment hit the bull's-eye because he looks like he's been kicked in the nuts. I *almost* feel bad.

But, hey. He's the one who wanted to play the game and trudge down memory lane. I can't help that our path is paved with pain, flooded with heartache, and obstructed by deceit.

After all, it's the one *he* chose.

His nostrils flare on an indrawn breath and he gives me a punishing look. "Never have I ever lied to myself about just being fuck buddies with someone when I wanted more."

I start to take a sip, then intentionally stop myself from drinking at the last second. "You'd know all about lying. Wouldn't you?" A burning sensation grips my heart like a fist. *His* fist. "Never have I ever stolen a song from someone."

The tendons in his throat flex as he drains the rest of the liquid in his cup.

This is the closest he's ever come to admitting what he's done.

And this time...victory tastes sweet.

It gives me a small kick of satisfaction; one I'm riding high on until his next words.

"Never have I ever gotten paid to take my clothes off."

The bite in his tone is unmistakable, and I know this was payback for my last one.

Too bad for him it doesn't work, because I don't have to drink.

His features twist with confusion. "What were you doing at Obsidian then?"

Placing my cup on the desk, I give him a cold look. "We'd need to play truth or dare for that."

He meets my icy expression head-on. "Truth or dare it is then."

"Great." My lips purse. "I'll go first this time. Truth or dare?"

There's only *one* question I want to know the answer to.

But Phoenix dodges it like a pro. "Dare."

My eyes narrow. "I dare you to go fuck yourself."

Directing a shit-eating grin my way, his hands go to the zipper on his jeans and he walks toward my bed. "I'd much rather fuck you, but—"

"Stop," I shout before he whips his cock out. I want the truth from him tonight and I won't let *that* distract me. "I dare you to…" I look around the room, trying to think of something. It comes to me when I spot his cell on the desk. "Send a dirty sext to the last person who called you."

His face contorts with amusement as he rakes his gaze up and down my body. "How dirty do you want it, Groupie?"

"Very." I grab his phone and hand it to him. "And make sure to use their name in the message. This way, they'll know it was meant for them."

Biting his lip ring, he states, "Trust me, they'll know."

It's obvious he assumes I'm going to be on the receiving end since he's been blowing up my phone the past two hours. However, I rarely call Phoenix seeing as we're always attached at the hip—and other body parts.

I give him a cheeky smile. "Remember, it has to be the last person who called *you*. Not the last person you called."

The sexy look wipes clean off his face as he stares down at his phone. "The last person who called me was Chandler."

This just keeps getting better and better. "Come on, Walker. Time's a wastin'. And don't forget, it needs to be *very* dirty."

Since he uses speech-to-text, I get to hear every word of his love note.

Shooting me a look of annoyance, he holds his phone a few inches away from his mouth, "I want to…" He looks like he's going to be sick and I love every minute of it. "Rip your clothes off."

I level him with a look because we both know he can be *much* dirtier than that.

Wanting to inspire his creativity, I slowly trail a hand between my breasts before squeezing one. My other hand slips inside the waistband of my pajamas.

Phoenix's eyes track the movement, causing my nipples to pucker against the thin fabric.

"And then I'm going to tie you up, spread you open, and taste you until you come all over my fucking face." He crooks a finger. "Get over here."

Shaking my head, I mouth, 'Chandler.'

Phoenix looks like he wants to straight-up murder me before he grits out, "Chandler."

"Do you want to send this text to Chandler?" a robotic voice asks.

"Yes," I say.

"Message sent."

He tosses his phone on the bed. "Just for that, I'm gonna dare *you* to let me do everything I just said."

As tempting as that is, I'm on a mission. Sadly, I have to endure one more round before I can accomplish it.

"It's your turn."

Phoenix starts to speak, but then *my* phone rings.

I blanch when I see Chandler's name flash across the screen.

I clear my throat before I pick up. "Hello?"

"Phoenix is drunk again," Chandler gripes, sounding extra crabby. "Keep an eye on him tonight and make sure he stays out of trouble."

It takes everything in me not to crack up. "Sure thing."

"And take his goddamn phone away," he bites out. "The last thing I need is him texting Vic Doherty that he wants to tie him up and *taste* him."

Bringing his fist to his mouth, Phoenix bites his knuckle, stifling a snicker.

"Got it."

The moment Chandler hangs up, I can't contain my laughter, and neither can he.

The husky sound fills the room and, just like his voice, it's hypnotic and magnetic. I could listen to it on repeat every day and never get sick of it.

"Guess being a drunk has its perks after all."

I wipe the water leaking from my eyes as I picture Chandler's face reading that text. "Evidently."

After a beat, Phoenix's demeanor turns serious. "Truth or dare?"

I steel myself because I know what's coming. "Truth."

"What were you doing at Obsidian?"

Here goes nothing.

"Three weeks before the end of my second year at Dartmouth, I received a call from Mrs. Palma. My dad was acting strange, and they took him to the hospital. Long story short, they ran a bunch of tests and diagnosed him with early-onset dementia."

I tuck a strand of hair behind my ear. "I ended up leaving college early to take care of him. However, being a freelancer meant he—we —had to pay for his medical expenses out of pocket."

"I used what was in his savings account and retirement fund to take care of most of the medical debt and pay off the house...and cover my last semester's tuition because my dad forgot to send them a check. Anyway, I got a job at a restaurant, but I wasn't making enough money to cover our living expenses. So, I started working at Obsidian...as a bartender."

His expression morphs to one of sadness. "I...shit."

I don't want or need his pity. "It's fine."

He inhales through his nose before exhaling sharply. "I wish you had reached out."

I can't hold back my laughter, although unlike before, it's devoid of any humor.

"And say what? Hey, Phoenix. Remember me? The girl you screwed over. Mind cutting me a check for that song you stole?" Anger races over my skin, followed by a sharp kick of sorrow to my rib cage. "We both know you never had any intention of seeing or talking to me ever again, let alone helping me. The only reason I'm standing here now is because of Storm and Chandler."

Falling silent, he plucks the cigarette tucked behind his ear and lights it.

"This is a non-smoking room," I remind him, but as usual, he doesn't give a fuck.

Because he's Phoenix Walker.

He does whatever he wants without consequence.

Must be nice.

Gritting my teeth, I open the window, hoping to get some of the smoke out. "Truth or dare?"

"I went to Dartmouth," he rasps, his voice barely above a whisper.

His admission nearly knocks me off my feet. "When?"

Bringing his cigarette to his lips, he takes a long drag. "A little over a year and a half after I left Hillcrest." A trail of smoke leaves him in a harsh exhale. "Sharp Objects blew up, and I knew there was no way you hadn't heard the song. Part of me kept hoping you'd hunt me down and scream at me...but you didn't."

I wasn't going to give him the satisfaction. Especially since there was nothing I could do about his betrayal.

It would have been the equivalent of punching a brick wall.

The only one who gets hurt is *you*.

The smoke from the lit cigarette hanging out of his mouth wafts through the air and his gaze turns inward, as if getting lost in his thoughts.

"It was snowing like crazy by the time I reached the campus, and I froze my nuts off searching for you. I was beginning to think I wasted my time and debated leaving when I saw you come out the door leading to the courtyard." A faint smile spreads across his lips. "You were wearing this big puffy coat, a purple hat with a fuzzy ball on it, and earmuffs. Your nose and cheeks were red from the cold. You looked so fucking cute I had to stop and catch my breath."

He stubs his cigarette out in his cup. "You kept walking, though, and I didn't want to lose sight of you, so I did too. I called your name as I got closer...and you stopped. It took me a couple seconds to register that it wasn't because you heard me. It was because of the guy handing you a cup of hot chocolate."

Harry.

I remember that day. There was an impending snowstorm—which was normal for winters in New Hampshire—and I was meeting my boyfriend during the twenty-minute break I had between classes.

The earmuffs I had on were a Christmas present from my dad. They had an option to connect to your phone so you could listen to music.

It's why I didn't hear him call my name.

Even though I felt him.

Phoenix's gaze locks with mine. "He bent down to kiss you, and after, you smiled at him." Emotions flicker across his face. "It was the same smile you used to give me…and that's the moment I knew."

"Knew what?"

His low, rough voice wraps around me like a thread, pulling tight. "The reason you never came to see me wasn't because you were too nervous or upset to confront me. It was because you were happy…and I had lost you for good."

A knot forms in my chest and my eyes sting with tears I won't ever let him see.

But I will give him this.

"I did come to see you once."

He looks just as surprised by my admission as I was his. "When?"

"During your first tour. You were playing a few towns over from my school and I decided to buy a ticket to the show last minute." A lump fills my throat and I swallow it down before I continue. "I wanted to experience what it would be like to have a venue full of two-thousand people listen to my song."

Even though it wasn't me who was singing it.

His chest rises and falls with quick, uneven inhales, and his expression shatters.

He looks like he's drowning…

But I'm the one he tossed overboard without a life preserver.

"Why?"

It's the question I've asked myself every day for the past four years.

He bows his head, like he can't bear to look at me.

He's quiet for so long, I'm positive he's not going to give me an answer.

But then his deep, tortured timbre fills the space between us. "Words have always been my biggest obstacle. No matter how many instruments I teach myself to play, or how good I can sing and perform...I've never been able to do the one thing an artist is supposed to."

Lifting his head, his gaze collides with mine. *"Create.* The only thing I can do is take their art and replicate it—maybe modify a few notes and change it up a bit. But even if I make it sound ten times better than the original and put everything I've got into it when I sing, it still doesn't make it mine. I was born with a great voice and an inherent love of music...not a gift."

Rising off the bed, he closes the distance between us. "The industry is cutthroat and the odds of ever getting discovered are one in a million. At least." His features twist with indignity. "I had the voice, the looks, and the drive to chase my dreams...but it wasn't a guarantee that I'd ever succeed. I needed something original. Something rare and unique." His fingers graze my cheek. "Something *special.*"

A swell of agony rips from my soul, engulfing me in a violent wave that makes everything around me spin.

All I've ever wanted was to be special...

And he stole it.

I shove him with every bit of strength I possess. "Get out."

He tries to wrap his arms around me, but I won't let him.

I need him gone.

Phoenix was already all those things he said he needed and then some, he didn't have to take the only thing *I* had.

When he refuses to budge, I charge over to the door and open it. "If you ever truly cared about me, you'll leave. Right now."

It's the only thing that gets him to move.

He grips my forearm as he crosses the threshold. "I'm sorry."

Sorry doesn't change anything. *It doesn't fix us.*

"You didn't have to steal it."

Just when I thought there was nothing inside me left for him to break, something deep inside my chest smashes.

I loved Phoenix Walker. So much so I would have willingly sacrificed and done whatever he needed just to make sure all his dreams came true.

He didn't have to stab me in the heart to get what he wanted.

"I would have given you the song." My vision blurs and my voice cracks. "I would have given you *everything*, Phoenix."

My heart, mind, body, soul, and art.

Whatever I'm made up of, it was all his.

Sheer torment slices the sharp angles of his face, almost like he's hurting as much as I am, but there's no way that's possible since he's the one who did this.

"Give it to me now." His hand slides to the nape of my neck. "I won't fuck it up this time."

There's no way I can trust that. *Trust him.*

All-consuming agony breaches the wall of armor I put up, crippling me. My forehead hits his chest and I inhale him into my system. I don't have to experiment with drugs to know he's the most lethal one out there for me.

The organ beating in my chest pleads with me to pull him closer, but self-preservation takes over and I push him away.

"I can't."

I give him one last shove before slamming the door.

A sob shreds from my throat as I slide down to the floor.

All the tears I've been holding on to for the past four years spill over and the words from my song reverberate throughout my head…taunting me.

I'm tough as a nail
Sharp as a blade
But I'm still lying here...
In the mess you made.

Jagged and broken
Dull and washed out.
Everywhere I turn...
I breathe you in and bleed you out.

CHAPTER 58
LENNON

I freeze when the sliding door of the bunk opens, but relax once I see Skylar.

I haven't spoken to Phoenix since last night and I have no intention of talking to him unless absolutely necessary.

There are only eleven days left on tour, so while it will be difficult, it's doable.

I turn off the music I was listening to and remove my earbuds when she plops down on my bunk.

"Want to talk about it?"

I would, but unfortunately the two friends I have on this bus—Skylar and Storm—are the two people I can't tell—given it would be a conflict of interest and all.

I just need to get through this tour so I can get my money and go back home to my dad.

I shake my head, internally cursing myself when my eyes water.

A frown mars Skylar's face. Then, to my absolute surprise, she wraps her arms around me. "I won't make you tell me anything you don't want to. But I'm here—strictly as your friend—if you ever need to talk."

She wipes my tears away. "Want me to kill him?"

That gets a small laugh out of me. "If you did, I'm pretty sure seventy-five percent of the females on the planet would call for your beheading."

She lifts a shoulder in a shrug. "Eh, I've been threatened with worse." She studies me intently. "I don't know what the asshole did, but whatever it is, I know it's hitting him hard because he won't speak to anyone and he won't come out of the lounge."

I have nothing to say to that.

Her brows crash together. "On a scale of one to ten, how bad is it?"

"A million."

She sucks in a sharp breath. "In that case, he's screwed." She looks away. "Promise you won't get mad at me for saying this?"

Talk about a trick question. "That depends on what you say."

Her teeth saw along her bottom lip. "Okay, but just know that this doesn't mean I'm sticking up for him. Trust me, I am *firmly* team Lennon."

Despite not liking the sound of this, I silently urge her to continue.

"Phoenix is an asshole."

"On that, we agree."

"But he's got a good heart. And while it's not fair that in order to get to the good stuff you'll have to trudge through a mountain of abandonment issues and damage…once you finally reach the gooey center, you'll realize that underneath all that crap is a guy who not only wants to be loved but will give that back to you tenfold." She makes a face. "Once he pulls his head out of his ass."

She raises a hand. "But again, team Lennon. If he's screwed things up with you indefinitely and you're done, I know it's only because whatever he did was unforgivable."

"What makes you say that?"

I mean, her assessment is spot on. I'm just curious how she arrived at that conclusion without knowing the details.

"Because we're a lot alike. Which means you're not the kind of girl who gives up on people. Not until you truly believe with your entire being that there's no longer any good in them and there's nothing inside them that's salvageable or worth fighting for anymore."

I blow out a breath. Damn her and her perceptiveness.

However, I can't help but wonder if she's also speaking from experience.

"Is that what happened with you and Josh?"

She averts her gaze. "Something like that. Only I held on *way* longer than I should have. Which caused me to lose the best thing that ever happened to me...permanently." Her face scrunches. "I'm Phoenix."

I'm pretty sure I know who she's talking about. And if that's the case, I don't think it's as *permanent* as she thinks it is. I've caught him staring at her numerous times when he thinks no one's watching. Not that I can blame him. Skylar's easily one of the most beautiful women on the freaking planet.

"I don't think—"

"I hurt him a lot, Lennon," she interjects. "Like *a lot*. And not just once or twice...so many times I lost count." She wipes a tear from the corner of her eye. "Now he's having a baby with someone else."

I'm not so sure I believe that.

"You don't know that for a fact. She could be lying." I lower my voice because I don't want Quinn to think we're in here talking shit about her. I simply want to prove a point. "Just like Quinn."

She shakes her head. "No, he's the father. It was confirmed this morning. And because I know him better than anyone, I know he'll step up and be there for her and his baby." Her eyes close. "I had *years* to make the right decision and I never once chose him, so I have no one else to blame but myself. I'm not a good person, Lennon. If you knew the things I've done, you'd be disgusted, and we wouldn't be friends anymore."

My heart twists. I'm sure she's made some mistakes. Who hasn't? However, Skylar's being way too hard on herself. It sounds like what she's going through right now is punishment enough.

"That's not true."

Her nostrils flare and she grips the ring on her necklace so hard her knuckles turn white. "If there's even a small chance you can forgive Phoenix and give him another shot…do it. I'd hate to see him end up like me. Because the only thing that hurts worse than a broken heart is watching someone walk away with everything you ever wanted…because you fucked it all up."

Sadly, I know all about what it's like watching someone walk away with everything you ever wanted.

Because he stole it.

"I—"

The door to the bunk opens and Chandler pops his head inside. "Emergency staff meeting. Now."

Composing herself, Skylar clears her throat. "Be right there."

Arching a brow, Chandler looks between us. "Do us all a favor and leave this Ya-Ya Sisterhood bullshit at the door."

"Sure thing, Dicky."

Mumbling something under his breath, he leaves.

Skylar and I scramble off my bunk. "The last name sure fits him, huh?"

Raising her chin, she heads for the door. "Trust me, his actual dick isn't nearly as big as his attitude."

My mouth drops open.

How the hell would she know the size of *Chandler's* dick?

Then again, she's been with these guys for years. I'm sure she's seen lots of stuff she wishes she could forget.

When I pad out to the kitchen, mostly everyone's already out, and either seated at the table or on the bench.

Everyone except Phoenix.

I breathe a sigh of relief because it will be much easier to focus without him around.

As if on cue, the universe flips me the bird because Phoenix appears.

Skylar wasn't kidding. He looks like shit.

I mean, gorgeous shit…but still.

He has bags under his eyes like he hasn't slept in days, his hair is a mess, and his jaw is covered with stubble.

Not that I'm looking any better with my puffy eyes and blotchy face.

As if sensing I'm thinking about him, he leans against the counter and zeros in on me.

I quickly divert my attention to Chandler, who looks like he's playing a game of Clue in his head.

"What's this meeting about?" Quinn inquires before stuffing a cookie into her mouth.

Chandler rips the package of cookies away from her. "Would it kill you to stop eating for two seconds?"

She burps and snatches the cookies back. "Yup."

Rubbing his temples, Chandler looks at all of us. "We only have three more stops before the end of this tour."

Thank God.

"Now is not the time for things to fall apart. Got it?"

When we all give him a blank look, he sighs and starts ticking things off with his fingers.

"Phoenix and George are fighting backstage in front of fans. Phoenix is still getting drunk." He sweeps a hand in Quinn's direction. "We have that one to deal with." He looks at Memphis. "You're knocking women up left and right." He eyes me and Skylar. "And you two are sneaking off to go braid each other's hair and cry."

I can feel everyone's eyes on us.

"We were not crying," Skylar defends.

Chandler makes a face. "Don't bullshit me—"

"I was talking to Lennon about Josh. You know, my dead fiancé. Sorry if I got a little emotional."

At that, everyone goes silent and Chandler pales.

"Shit," Chandler whispers, and I don't think I've ever seen him look so *human*. "I didn't…I'm sorry, Skylar. Truly."

While what she told him isn't *entirely* accurate, she did just cover for both of us.

I give her hand a small squeeze.

Chandler peers up at the ceiling and pinches the bridge of his nose. "Look, there's been a shift ever since the last concert and I don't like it. So, whatever is going on with you people. Fix it before we get to Florida."

I nearly choke on my tongue. "We're going to Florida?"

I asked where our next stop was when we got on the bus, but everyone acted like they didn't know.

"Storm and I wanted it to be a surprise," Phoenix says while glaring at Chandler. "Thanks."

Chandler throws his hands up. "Whatever. I have enough shit on my plate." He turns to Memphis. "Anyway, I believe congratulations are in order."

Beside me, Skylar stiffens.

"More like *condolences*," Phoenix mutters and Storm snorts.

"Why?" Quinn asks innocently. "What's going on?"

"Memphis is having a baby. You know, with a girl who didn't lie about being pregnant," Chandler answers dryly.

Oblivious to the tension brewing, Quinn's face lights up. "Oh shit. So, it's true? You're really having a baby with Gwyneth Barclay? Man, that's so cool. She's like my *favorite* Barclay—"

"May I have a cookie?" I cut in because I can practically feel Skylar's heart breaking into a million pieces.

Blinking, Quinn hands me the package. "Sure." She turns back to Memphis. "Is Gwen gonna come on tour with us?"

Memphis shakes his head. "Nah. Tours can be stressful, and I want her and the baby to be safe." When Quinn deflates, he adds, "But she'll be in the UK with me for a few days, so you'll meet her then."

Quinn practically does a cartwheel. "Awesome—"

"Hey, Chandler?" Skylar chimes in. "Given everything with Memphis is settled and Phoenix seems to be doing better, it won't be an issue if I hang back here for the European tour, right?"

Chandler looks at her like she's sprouted another head. "We need you on tour, Skylar. Phoenix is still getting drunk—"

"No, I'm not," Phoenix interjects, and I don't miss the look of sympathy he shoots Skylar. "I haven't had alcohol in over two weeks. The only reason I sent that text last night is because of a dare."

Chandler stops drinking his coffee. "A dare? From whom?"

Oh fuck.

He slaps Storm's back. "This guy."

Despite looking flummoxed, Storm doesn't miss a beat. "What he said."

Chandler crosses his arms. "Why the fuck would you dare Phoenix to send me a text telling me he wants to rip my clothes off and then tie me up and taste me?"

Memphis spits out his beer and Quinn chokes on her cookie.

Storm's eyebrows shoot up and he gives Phoenix a *what the fuck* look. "I..."

"Phoenix dared me to send a dick pic to Gwyneth's sister, so Storm was getting him back for me," Memphis cuts in.

Storm shrugs. "My bad, Chandler. Thought you might be into it."

I'm not even surprised they're sticking up for each other.

Chandler makes an irritated noise in his throat. "Aren't you three a little old for childish games? Grow up."

"Which Barclay sister did you send the dick pic to?" Quinn asks with a grin. "Was it Jessica—"

"Hey, Juvie," Storm says. "Come with me. I want to show you something."

She pops up. "What?"

Placing an arm around her slim shoulders, he leads her to the bathroom. "It's in here."

When she steps inside, he closes the door and leans against it, blocking her from exiting.

"What the hell?" Quinn yells. "Let me out!"

Skylar takes the opportunity to slip out of the kitchen. I don't miss the way she briefly squeezes Storm's arm when she passes him.

"Anyway," Chandler says, even though we've all tuned him out. "We should be in Florida tomorrow morning."

Upon realizing no one is paying attention anymore, he throws his hands up and heads for the back of the bus. Looking down at his phone, George follows suit.

"Will we be passing through Hillcrest?"

I figure I should ask before getting my hopes up.

Phoenix nods. "More than passing through. Tomorrow night's show is there."

"Oh."

I'm thinking of ways to convince my asshole boss to give me a few hours free so I can see my dad when Phoenix adds, "Storm and I talked to Chandler. We told him about your father, and he agreed to give you the day and night off."

I'm so stunned I can't even speak.

Storm looks at Phoenix. "As long as Phoenix is on his best behavior."

Dammit. I knew I shouldn't have gotten my hopes up. "Well, there goes that."

Storm walks over to Phoenix and clamps a hand on his shoulder. The move makes poor Quinn, who must have been mid-push, fly out of the bathroom like a cannonball. "He'll be a good boy for one night. *Right?*"

"Lick my nut sack," Phoenix grits out before focusing on me. "Go spend time with your dad. Everything will be fine."

Scowling, Quinn gets off the floor and glares at Storm. "You're *such* an asshole. Skylar was right. Boys are only good for one thing."

Storm and Memphis exchange a glance and Phoenix looks positively horrified. "Oh really? And what's that?"

She bats her eyelashes. "Lifting heavy stuff. Duh."

I swear there's a collective sigh of relief from all three guys.

They're starting up a different conversation when she glances at me, cups a hand over her mouth, and mouths, "The D."

Once again, Skylar's not wrong.

CHAPTER 59
LENNON

"Thanks."

I quickly give the Uber driver a tip on the app and grab my luggage from the trunk. Seeing as I'm off duty today, I asked if I could sleep here instead of the hotel. In typical fashion, Chandler hemmed and hawed before reluctantly agreeing... as long as I promised that my ass would be back on the bus by nine a.m.

I was going to tell Mrs. Palma I was coming home when I spoke to her yesterday, but I wanted it to be a surprise.

After placing my suitcase on the porch, I stick my key in the lock. Given my dad tends to sleep in, he probably isn't up yet, but I can't wait to see him.

Mrs. Palma—who was watching television on the couch in the living room while crocheting—screams and then jumps up when she sees me.

"Oh my god!" Running over, she wraps her arms around me. "I wasn't expecting you home for another ten days."

"I wanted it to be a surprise."

"Well, it worked. I nearly had a heart attack." She cradles my face as we break apart. "You look...is everything okay? How come the tour ended so early?"

"Everything's great," I lie. "The tour isn't over, though. They're performing at a venue in Hillcrest tonight, so Chandler gave me the day and night off."

Smiling, she waves me into the kitchen. "Seems he's not so terrible after all."

I huff out a laugh. "Oh, he is. But Phoenix and Storm convinced him—" I stop talking when I catch myself.

I've been vague about my relationship with Phoenix. *Not* that there is one anymore. After yesterday's meeting, I made it a point to return to the bunk, and he went back to the lounge. We haven't spoken since.

Which suits me just fine.

"Phoenix convinced Chandler?" she questions as she fills a teakettle with some water.

Whenever she asks about him, I skate over the issue by telling her we've fallen into a professional relationship. Then I switch topics.

Do I hate not being honest with her? Yes.

But she's the only person who knows the truth, and she was the one who convinced me that I was strong enough to handle this.

I don't want to disappoint her.

"It's not a big deal. Plus, it wasn't just Phoenix. It was Storm, too."

She simply nods.

"Is Dad awake?"

She takes two coffee cups out of the cabinet. "No, he's still sleeping. Last night was a…" her voice trails off, but she doesn't have to finish.

It was a bad night.

Which means today will most likely be bad, too.

Probably best I let him rest a bit longer.

"Lennon," she begins as she places a tea bag in each of our cups. "You know you can tell me anything, right?"

Guilt infiltrates my chest. "I know."

I'll fill her in after I'm back home for a bit and Phoenix has been purged from my system.

She urges me to have a seat at the table. "You never have to be embarrassed. I won't judge you."

Both her compassion and words have me fighting back tears.

Evidently not well enough, though, because she hands me a tissue. "Honey—"

"No. I'm fine." I steel myself. "I almost made a bad decision, but I came to my senses. Nothing's going on between me and Phoenix."

It's done. Over. Kaput.

"How's George doing? I haven't heard much about him lately. Are you two still...getting to know each other?"

Her and Skylar would get along famously.

"It didn't work out."

"Oh, that's a shame." She takes the lid off the cake holder and cuts two slices of crumb cake for us. "He seemed sweet."

"He is. He's just...not my type."

Because apparently, I have a thing for assholes.

"I see." She dishes out a slice of cake for each of us. "Well, tell me all about the tour. I want to hear everything."

I tell her something safe.

"I met a friend. Her name is Skylar."

"That's a pretty name. What's she like?"

"Gorgeous. And strong and really smart. Her um..." I push the cake around the plate with my fork. "Her fiancé was Josh. The one who died in the accident."

She clutches her chest. "Oh, how awful. I'm surprised she's still touring with the band."

"They hired her as their publicist, so she has to. She's also really good at her job. When Phoenix...never mind. Not important." I shove a forkful of cake in my mouth and take my time chewing. "How's Dad been?"

"You know how it is. Some days are better than others. But health-wise he's doing great. His doctor said his cholesterol is much better now."

That makes me smile. "I'll never be able to thank you enough for taking care of him."

"You never have to thank me. I'm happy to do it." She takes a bite of her cake. "It's a little dry, huh?"

Nope. It's delicious. Her and Grams should open a bakery. "It's perfect."

"So, aside from meeting Skylar, are there any other interesting things that have happened over the last six and a half weeks?"

Most of my *interesting* experiences involve Phoenix.

"Nope."

She blinks. "Oh."

I can tell she's waiting for me to follow that up with something, so I add, "It's just your standard tour. You know, sex, drugs, and rock and roll." I shovel another forkful of cake into my mouth and chew. "Although there won't be much of that anymore, given Memphis is having a baby and Quinn's still a teenager."

"Who are Memphis and Quinn?"

Oh. Right.

"Memphis is the lead guitarist. He's having a baby with Gwyneth Barclay."

Her face lights up. "Oh, I love that show. Richard always makes fun of me, but it's a guilty pleasure of mine. Don't much care for that Gwen girl, though."

I'm sure Skylar would appreciate that. Especially since Quinn— who doesn't know any better—is all but ready to throw Gwyneth a parade whenever someone mentions her.

That's when I realize my blunder. "Don't tell anyone. We only found out yesterday that Memphis is the father, and I don't know if it's gone from rumor to official public confirmation yet."

Skylar will kill me if she finds out I leaked this before it was time.

Mrs. Palma makes a zipping motion across her mouth. "My lips are sealed. Now, who's this Quinn you mentioned earlier?"

"Quinn is Phoenix's—"

The sound of the doorbell ringing cuts me off.

"That must be my grocery delivery. I've been having everything sent here since it's easier."

"I'll help."

I start to get up, but she shakes her head. "No. It's only a few essentials. Sit and relax."

While she answers the door, I take another bite of cake....

And choke on it when Phoenix comes waltzing into my kitchen like he owns the place.

"I didn't know you were expecting company," Mrs. Palma says behind him.

That makes two of us.

The sound of the teakettle whistling mimics my rising blood pressure.

"What the hell are you doing here?"

Phoenix merely smirks.

"Would you like some tea?" Mrs. Palma questions, her wide eyes ping-ponging between us.

"No," I say at the same time Phoenix says, "I'd love some."

"You don't drink tea."

He takes a seat next to me. "I do now."

"Don't you have to be at sound check?"

Reaching over, he plucks the remaining cake off my plate and eats it. "Not for another three hours. This is good cake."

"Thank you," Mrs. Palma says. "I made it yesterday."

Dang it. Her manners have always been impeccable. The woman could loathe someone and still wave and smile at them.

"Stop eating her cake." I glance at Mrs. Palma, who looks like she's getting ready to serve him his own slice. "Don't let him eat your cake."

He might steal the recipe and make a fortune off it.

She places the plate on the counter and busies herself with our tea instead.

"Why are you here?"

"I miss you."

Mrs. Palma drops a spoon on the floor. "Don't mind me. Keep talking among yourselves."

I have no doubt she's eavesdropping. Which is all the more reason to keep this conversation brief.

"You'll see me tomorrow morning." I spring up from my chair with so much force it almost topples over. "Let me show you the door."

He stands, towering over me like a tree. "I know where the door is. But I won't be using it."

Holy hell. The asshole is out of his damn mind.

"Why are you doing this now?" *Here.*

"We've been stuck on a bus for the last fifteen hours. There was nowhere to talk without someone overhearing."

As far as I'm concerned, we have *nothing* to talk about. Everything we needed to say to one another has already been said.

"You need to leave. I made it perfectly clear the other night that our arrangement was over."

Those piercing blue eyes study me like I'm a puzzle he can't quite figure out. "Let me get this straight. You'll let me fuck you six ways from Sunday, and suck my dick like it's your new favorite pastime, but you won't have a conversation with me? What kind of shit is that?"

I jump at the sound of glass shattering behind me.

Mrs. Palma grabs the broom. "Darn teacup just slipped out of my hand."

I want to crawl in a hole and die.

Grabbing his arm, I escort him out of the kitchen and to the front door. "Do you have any idea how rude you're being?"

Then again, rude is practically Phoenix's middle name.

Right after *thief.*

"Rude?" His eyes narrow. "Rude is when two people have an arrangement and then one of them ends it abruptly, without just cause."

"We were fuck buddies, Phoenix. It's not like we had a freaking contract." I poke him in the chest. "And I had just cause."

"Bullshit. I finally admitted what I did just like you wanted, and you threw me out of your room." He steps closer, eclipsing my space. "I never should have acknowledged shit. It fucked everything up."

"No. *You* fucked everything up!"

Behind him, I see Mrs. Palma's head popping in and out of the kitchen entryway.

I point to the door. "Leave."

"No. We still have ten days."

"Left on tour. Not *that*."

My mouth hangs open when he crosses into the living room and sits on the sofa. "I want my ten days."

He's like a petulant toddler who's not getting their way. "No."

"Kate?"

I turn my head in time to see my dad rush down the stairs. "Dad —um...hey."

My dad wraps me up in a hug. "You're home from work early."

"Yeah."

"Why is there a rock star in our living room?"

Seriously? The man thinks I'm a woman who's been dead for over twenty-two years, but knows who *Phoenix* is?

Phoenix gets off the couch. "Hi."

I cut him a warning look. The last thing I want is to disorient my father more than he already is.

Clearing his throat, Phoenix shakes his hand. "Nice to meet you."

My dad enthusiastically shakes it. "I'm a big fan of your work. Your voice is undoubtedly one of the most unique voices I've ever heard."

Shock roots me to the spot. As far as I know, he's never even listened to a Sharp Objects song.

A pompous smile curls his lips. "Coming from you, sir, that means a lot."

My dad's eyes gleam. "'Dream On' is one of my all-time favorite songs. I'm envious I didn't write it myself. Absolute brilliance."

I bite my cheek. I can't believe he thinks Phoenix is *Steven Tyler*.

Phoenix looks like he doesn't know whether to be offended or honored. "Thanks."

And just like that, I'm back to wanting to deck him in the face.

"Of course, you'd take credit for a song that's not yours."

"Hey, Don." Mrs. Palma flounces into the living room carrying a tray of food. "I made you some lunch. Why don't we go upstairs and let these two talk for a bit?"

"All right. As long as it's not egg salad on that tray."

They start to walk upstairs. "No worries. Turkey and cheese."

"I'll be right there," I call out after them. "Phoenix was just leaving."

"No. Phoenix is *staying*."

Exasperated, I throw my hands up. "Fine. Whatever. Enjoy being down here by yourself."

I turn to go up the staircase, but he catches my arm. "Who's Kate?"

"My mom."

I can tell he wasn't expecting that because he rocks back on his heels.

Then the ass moseys back over to the couch and sits.

I pace the floor of my dad's bedroom while he eats his sandwich.

"He's insane."

"Not you, dear," Mrs. Palma reassures my dad before turning to me. "I can't believe I'm going to say this, but he seems to care about you. Not that it changes what he did."

"It doesn't."

It comes out way more curt than I intended.

Nodding, she rises from the chair. "Do you mind if I run a few errands? I shouldn't be more than an hour or two at most."

The woman never has to ask me for a favor again. I'm eternally indebted to her.

"Of course not." I look around. "Is there anything I can do in the meantime?"

She shrugs. "Not really. There's a small load of laundry that needs to be put in the wash and another load in the dryer that has to be folded and brought upstairs."

"Consider it done."

She pats my hand. "I'm gonna run to the grocery store and grab some things so I can whip up your favorite for dinner."

I should turn her down since she does more than enough for me, but my mouth salivates when I think of her awesome stuffed chicken and baked mac and cheese.

"Thanks," I tell her as she ambles toward the door.

Her steps come to a halt. "Should I get enough food in case our guest downstairs decides to join us for supper?"

I bristle. "Absolutely not."

"All right, then. We'll let him starve."

With that, she leaves.

My gaze falls on the mahogany piano on the other side of the room.

Last year—with help from Mrs. Palma and her husband—I moved it from my dad's studio to his bedroom. This way he'd be able to play whenever he wants because I know how much he loves music.

I also read once that it's supposed to help people who have dementia.

However, he rarely listens or plays anymore.

It's yet another thing this horrible disease took from him.

Plastering a smile on my face, I turn to my dad. "How are you?"

"Eh. Could be better, could be worse." He blinks up at me. "Who are you?"

That all too familiar ache pierces my chest. "I'm—"

"Just kidding," he says with a smile. "I know who you are."

The ache eases.

"You're my new nurse."

And it's back.

He places his tray on the chair beside his bed. "That sandwich made me tired. I'm gonna close my eyes for a bit, okay?"

"Okay."

Remembering the laundry I told Mrs. Palma I would handle, I grab the hamper out of his room and head to the basement.

After starting the washing machine, I take the clothes out of the dryer and begin folding them.

I woke up feeling stupidly optimistic that today would be a good day, and he'd remember who I was.

But at least I get to see him.

Even though he's a mere shell of the person he used to be.

And just like that, guilt overshadows my frustration.

This isn't his fault. My dad never asked to have dementia and I have no doubt that if he had prior knowledge that this would happen to him, he'd be utterly heartbroken.

Just like I am.

I don't have any memories of my mother. So, while losing her was hard in the sense that I never got to form a relationship with her…the things I grieve most are the experiences and memories I'll never get to have.

But with my dad, it's the exact opposite.

He wasn't just my only parent…he was my best friend.

The man has been by my side since the moment I took my first breath and I have a lifetime full of memories with him.

Memories he can no longer access.

Given our memories shape all facets of who we are…seeing a man who looks like my dad but doesn't act like my dad is a brand of psychological torture I wouldn't wish on anyone.

No matter how tight I hold on, my best friend is slipping away—a little more each day—and there's *nothing* I can do about it.

Every night before I close my eyes, I pray for just a few moments where he remembers that I'm his daughter.

But those are so few and far between these days.

After taking a few cleansing breaths to collect myself, I place the folded clothes into the basket and head back upstairs so I can put them away.

A dark, melodic sound fills my ears when I open the basement door.

It's a sound I'd recognize anywhere...

Because it came from my soul.

CHAPTER 60
LENNON

I'm going to kill him.

Heart racing, I rush up the stairs as Phoenix belts out the last few notes and the song comes to an end.

I can't believe the asshole had the audacity to go into my father's room, put his grubby fingers on my father's piano, and play him the song he stole.

I'm gearing up to run in there and kick him out, but what I hear next roots me to the spot.

"That was incredible," my dad says. "Did you write that?"

My heart thumps hard in my chest.

"No," Phoenix says softly. "Your daughter did."

Regret and sorrow expand inside my chest until it becomes a crushing weight compressing my lungs.

I never told my dad I wrote songs. I didn't think my talent ever came close to his and was convinced he'd secretly agree.

Then after Phoenix stole my song, I stopped writing altogether.

Now he'll never know.

I'm building up the strength to go in there when I hear it.

"Lennon wrote that?"

"Yeah." Phoenix exhales heavily. "She did."

Excitement surges through me, and I rush into the room. "Dad?"

Smiling, he turns to me. "Hey, monkey face." Confused, he looks around. "Aren't you supposed to be at Dartmouth?"

"We're on break for a few days, so I came home."

He processes this for a moment before he speaks. "The song you wrote was terrific." He winces. "Got a little vulgar toward the end there, but I loved it."

I don't know whether to laugh or cry because he's *here*. "Thanks."

"I'm proud of you." A smile creases the corners of his eyes as he meets mine. "I mean, I'm always proud of you, but this…you've got something special."

Embarrassment creeps up my cheeks. "It's nothing."

Phoenix gets up from the piano bench. "I have to head to sound check."

Emotions swing like a pendulum inside me.

Stealing my song is inexcusable…but he just gave me the greatest gift.

"Thank you," I whisper as he passes me.

My heart rate kicks up when he bends down and kisses my forehead.

"I still don't like him," my dad says after he leaves.

I half snort, half grumble. "I still don't like him either."

He makes an irritable noise. "Seems like he wormed his way back in your life again, though."

"Only because we temporarily work together." That's when I realize. "You know who he is?"

Frowning, he gets off the bed. "A father never forgets the man who broke his daughter's heart." He makes a face like he smells something rancid. "You were right, though. The son of a bitch has one hell of a voice."

That he does.

Another smile spreads across his face as he sits in front of the piano. "Enough about him. I want to hear you sing that wonderful song you wrote."

My throat locks as I take a seat next to him on the bench. "Phoenix sings it much better than I do."

And *millions* of people would agree.

"Let me be the judge of that."

It's on the tip of my tongue to decline, but this moment we're having is like a shooting star. There's no guarantee when I'll see another one, so I have to make it count.

Close your eyes.

With Phoenix's voice guiding me, I squeeze them shut, press down on the ivory keys, and begin playing my song.

And I don't open them until the very last note leaves my mouth.

"Beautiful," my dad whispers. "So much so I didn't even mind the cussing this time."

I roll my eyes and we exchange a smile.

His hand covers mine, and he grips it tight. "I'm sorry, Lennon."

"For what?"

His eyes harbor so much sadness it's a visceral punch to the gut. "I know something isn't right with me." He points to his head. "Up here."

My heart cracks. The only positive in all this was that he was blissfully unaware of his dementia.

Tears well in my eyes, but I don't want to lie to him or waste however long we might have talking about a disease that's already stolen so much time.

I'd rather stick to the important stuff.

"I love you, Dad."

Leaning over, he kisses my cheek. "I love you more, monkey face. Don't ever forget that."

I won't.

Even when he does.

"You know why I named you Lennon, right?"

"Because you love The Beatles and John Lennon is the best song-writer who ever existed."

His eyes crinkle at the corners. "Yes. Although he's now second best in my book." His fingers tap the keys, filling the room with the chords of, "In My Life."

The meaning behind the song holds a significance it didn't before.

"Lennon was a musical genius," he says above the melody. "But just like the rest of us, he too had moments of insecurity. Imagine— no pun intended—if John let them win? What a travesty that would have been for the world, huh?" He levels me with a look. "Don't let your insecurities overpower that which makes your soul come alive. Otherwise, you'll walk this earth never feeling whole...and that's no way to live."

Easier said than done, Dad.

Frowning, he sighs.

"What's wrong?"

"I didn't know why that Phoenix guy was in my room when I woke up...but I think I get it now." Appearing lost in deep thought, he expels another sigh. "I still don't like him, but perhaps there's some good in him after all."

My heart thumps a painful beat.

"Do me a favor and humor your old man for a bit." His fingers flutter across the keys. "I'll play and you sing."

And that's how we spend the rest of the afternoon and early evening.

Creating memories I'll keep with me forever.

Just like we used to.

I'm enjoying my second helping of Mrs. Palma's stuffed chicken when my phone rings.

I stifle a groan as Chandler's name flashes across my screen. It comes as no shock that my boss doesn't understand the meaning of the words *night off*.

"Sorry. I have to take this."

After pressing the green button, I bring it to my ear. "Hello?"

"Do you know where Phoenix is?" he gripes. "I haven't seen him since sound check."

I glance at the clock on the oven. Given it's almost eight p.m., there's only one place he *should* be right now.

Gearing up to go on stage.

"No."

"I *knew* this would happen," Chandler mutters as I get up from the table. "This is why I don't give people days off. Everything falls apart—"

"Calm down."

Rising off my chair, I search the kitchen for my car keys. It's been a while since I've driven, but Mrs. Palma says she's been taking it out for a spin once a week to make sure it doesn't sit for too long.

"Don't tell me to calm down. Phoenix is *your* responsibility and now he's gone."

"Call the hotel and ask someone to check his room. He might have overslept."

My stomach knots. *Or worse.*

"Already did."

Shit.

"I'll find him," I assure him, sounding way more certain than I feel.

"Fine. I'll tell the opening act to stay on longer, but so help me God, Lennon. He better be inside this venue within the next forty-five minutes or you're fired."

Before I have a chance to respond, he hangs up.

"I'm sorry." I grab my purse off the kitchen counter. "Phoenix is missing."

Mrs. Palma and her husband exchange a worried look. "Does this happen often?"

"Let's just say it's not the first time."

That does nothing to ease their concern, but I can't focus on that because I need to track down a rock star.

I sprint out the front door. "Be back later."

Hopefully.

Hillcrest is a small town, so there aren't many places one could wander off to...and virtually zero where a person of his caliber can hide.

After confirming with the hotel three different times that Phoenix isn't in his suite, I drove around town looking for him.

I checked our high school, Gram's old house, a few local hangout spots, some convenience stores, his favorite burger place...even Obsidian.

But he's nowhere to be found.

Pulling over on the side of the road, I bang my head against the steering wheel. It's been forty minutes since Chandler called and the odds of me locating Phoenix within the next five are beyond bleak.

"Think, Lennon. *Think*."

He seemed fine when I saw him earlier today. Demanding and pushy as ever, but otherwise normal.

Chewing my thumbnail, I mentally run through his day.

He got off the bus, came to my house uninvited, played my song for my dad, and then left so we could talk...

Oh god.

Shifting my car into drive, I peel off the side of the road.

I'm losing my father piece by piece, but I was and still am fortunate to have an amazing dad.

Phoenix has no idea what it's like to have an amazing parent *period*.

He has no idea what it's like to be loved or cared for.

The small dose he had was ripped away when his mother abandoned him in favor of her other kid.

Hearing my dad tell me how proud he was of me might have triggered something within him.

It's dark out by the time I pull into Bayview trailer park.

Dirt and gravel crunch under my tires as I make a quick right and pass the line of run-down trailers.

My heart drops to my stomach when I pull to a stop in front of the one at the very end—which is somehow even shoddier than it was four years ago.

The muscles in Phoenix's back flex underneath the dark fabric of his shirt as he braces both arms against the front of the trailer... almost like he wishes he could use every ounce of his strength to shove it out of his life for good.

Nerves coil in my belly when I notice the large bottle of vodka on the porch, but when I get closer, I see it's unopened.

For now.

The dilapidated staircase creaks under my feet as I make my way up the steps.

"Go away."

His voice is rough, the warning in it unmistakable.

I don't know what to say. I'm not sure there's anything *to* say.

I just don't want him to be alone right now.

I reach for his hand, but he yanks it away like he's been singed.

"Get the fuck out of here."

This time there's a lethal edge to his voice. *A threat.*

One I choose to ignore.

"Goddammit," he roars when I make no move to leave. "Are you fucking deaf? Get in your goddamn car and go."

"No!" I scream back, finding my voice.

An icy laugh leaves him, chilling me to the bone. "You're just as stupid as my mother is then."

I flinch when he punches the trailer.

"Phoenix."

His sneer is downright homicidal. "What's the matter, baby? Are you scared? Or do I have to kick things up a notch so you'll take a fucking hint and run?"

I stand firm. "Do your worst."

Maybe that makes me an idiot considering the state he's in, but I trust my intuition.

He *won't* cross that line.

With a growl, he rushes toward me—a wall of rage ready to

pummel me into the ground—but at the last second, he turns and kicks the trailer instead.

"Fuck off."

He can try to push me away with everything he's got, but I'm not budging. I refuse to amplify the demon in his head.

No matter how much he wants me to.

"Why? So I can make it easier for you to feed into this bullshit concept that you're worthless because that's what he made you believe? That everyone you let in will abandon you like she did? That because you made a careless, awful mistake that night you deserve to suffer every single day for the rest of your life? Fuck that and fuck you. I'm staying."

He gets so close to my face we're nearly nose to nose. "You're fired."

Like that's supposed to scare me. Chandler threatens to fire me on a weekly basis.

"I don't care." I poke his chest. "The only way I'm leaving is if you physically make me." I peer into his eyes. "So, go ahead, Phoenix. Do it."

It's the equivalent of poking a starving tiger at the zoo, but I have a point to prove.

Fisting my sundress, he yanks me against him like I'm a rag doll. He's so angry he shakes with the force of it.

"I told you I would never fucking hurt you."

He releases me so abruptly, I stumble back.

Phoenix is more furious than I've ever seen him. Yet, he still won't go *there*.

"I know you won't. Because you're not him."

He kicks the trailer again. "Oh yeah? Then why did she leave me too?" There's another sharp kick followed by a punch. "Why wasn't *I* the kid she chose?" A tortured sound rips from his throat. "Why did she leave me here with *him*?" He punches it again. So hard his knuckles split open and blood oozes out. "Why does he hate me so fucking much?"

I tell him the truth. "She left you because she was selfish. And he was so miserable and full of hatred for himself it seeped out and infected you." A tremble runs through him when I press a hand to his back. "But you didn't deserve any of that. Stop letting their demons become yours."

Earlier, my dad told me not to let my insecurities overpower that which makes my soul come alive. Phoenix needs to apply the same notion when it comes to his past.

Chest heaving, he turns around. He looks so broken it crushes my heart. I wrap my arms around him, holding him tighter than I've ever held anything in my whole entire life as we collapse on the porch.

Clutching the back of my dress, he buries his face in my neck.

I hug him harder. "It's their loss."

Because his mother was right about one thing. He is a *rara avis.*

However, neither her nor that monster she left him here with can take credit for it.

It's all *him*.

My heart plummets as I think about all the abuse that occurred inside this trailer.

All the times that little boy cried and wished someone would love and care for him.

All the times his father made him feel like he wasn't worthy of it.

But Phoenix rose from those ashes.

"That piece of shit tried to destroy you, but he couldn't. Because you're so much stronger than he will ever be. He thought you'd be stuck here and remain his victim for the rest of your life, but you proved him wrong." Cupping the back of his neck, I bring my lips to his ear. "Don't you *dare* let him win now."

He closes his eyes and trembles, like my words are bullets puncturing him. "Lennon?"

"Yeah?"

"Go to your car. I need a minute."

I brush the dirt off my knees as I stand up. "Okay."

My eyes burn and my hands shake so bad my phone slips out of my grasp as I head back.

I pick it up off the ground so I can call Chandler, but a guttural sound cuts through the air.

When I spin around, I see Phoenix doubled over on the porch, shaking like it physically hurts.

My heart knocks against my chest like it's trying to break free so it can fly right into him.

I've always wanted to know everything he kept bottled up inside...and right now I have a front-row seat.

It's pure torture.

My phone rings, but I press the ignore button.

I want to run back over there, but I know he needs his space.

I just wish his pain wasn't ripping my own heart to shreds, because watching him fall apart like this is cutting me wide open.

"Fuck you," Phoenix snarls as he stands up.

He brings a cigarette to his lips, his chest rising and falling with deep inhales and exhales.

Then he grabs the vodka bottle.

Bile rises up my esophagus as he unscrews the top.

I open my mouth to stop him, but the words get stuck in my throat because he smashes a window in.

I watch in bewilderment as he takes the vodka bottle and pours some through the broken window before dousing the outside with the rest of it.

"What are you—"

He lights a match and drops it.

In a matter of seconds, bright orange flames ignite the mobile home.

Holy. Shit.

He takes one more drag of his cigarette before flicking it at the trailer.

Panic spirals through me, and I run toward him. "Come on. We need to go!"

At the sound of my voice, he barrels down the stairs.

We meet in the middle and I reach for his hand, but he grabs my face…and then his lips are on mine.

His kiss is so deep—so *intense*—my knees buckle.

Gripping my hips, he attacks my mouth, feeding me his tongue in a hot, vulgar rhythm that makes my blood heat and my head spin.

He kisses me like that for so long my lips feel bruised and I don't realize we've been moving backward until I'm shoved against the hood of my car.

A tremor goes through me when his hand locks around my throat and his teeth nip at my bottom lip.

The flames behind him grow bigger. "There's a fire—"

He pulls my panties to the side with his free hand and shoves two fingers inside me. The invasion robs me of air, and I clamp down, my need overriding any other emotions.

My eyes roll back, and I gasp for air as he finger fucks me into oblivion.

The stirrings of my impending orgasm curl my toes and I writhe against his palm…and then his fingers are gone.

"Please," I croak out.

His teeth graze my ear. "Nah. You want to come, you're gonna do it on my fucking cock."

Desire and need wind through me and I part my thighs as far as they'll go. I faintly register the sound of a belt buckle followed by a zipper and then he's buried inside of me.

My mouth falls open and I pant against his lips while he takes me rough and fast.

A husky sound leaves him, and he tightens his grip around my neck, holding me steady against the hood as he fucks me so hard it's equal parts pleasure and pain.

Shoving my hands inside his jeans, I claw his ass, trying to push him deeper with every thrust.

A throaty groan rumbles in his chest, and he attacks my mouth again. This time, his kisses are needy and messy and violent.

It's too much. Every lick, touch, and thrust chips away at the barrier I keep building between us.

My body goes slack as he laps my tongue and pumps viciously, siphoning everything he wants from me.

He groans against my neck and the fingers digging into my hip constrict so much I know I'll have bruises. *But I want them.*

His features go taut as he withdraws and plunges back in, hitting a spot that feels so good it sets me off.

A scorching wave of pleasure sweeps through me and I desperately rock my pelvis, meeting him thrust for thrust.

I don't care who might be watching. I don't care what anyone else thinks.

I don't care about anything but how good it feels when he's inside me.

It's addicting. A drug I can't help but chase. A high I never want to come down from.

My whole body spasms and my hoarse moan blends with the sirens in the distance. I come so hard it dribbles out of me and onto him.

His muscles tighten. "*Fuck.*" Those blue eyes grow dark, and his fingers grip my jaw as he pulses inside me. "I'm getting my ten days."

"Ten days," I breathe as liquid heat fills me. "But that's it—"

A sharp bite to my throat makes me cry out, and then he's sucking my skin, soothing the sting and leaving his mark.

I close my eyes as the flames flicker around us and we both burn until we're nothing but ash.

CHAPTER 61
PHOENIX

A helpless whimper pushes past Lennon's lips. "Oh god."

I pinch her nipple. "Be quiet." Suppressing a groan of my own, I fill my hands with her tits. "Chandler's bedroom is on the other side of this wall." I run my tongue over the pulse point on her neck. "We wouldn't want him to hear all the naughty things I'm about to do to you, now would we?"

Not that he will. Fucker sleeps like the dead.

Defiance wars with the hunger marring her face. "But *you're* talk—"

"Be a good girl, or I'll stop what I'm doing."

I finally convinced Lennon to sneak into the lounge while everyone else is fast asleep on the bus.

And now that she's here, I plan on having some fun.

Shoving my hand inside her little shorts, I run my knuckle over the damp crotch of her panties. Her mouth parts and her chest heaves, pushing her tits against my chest.

Dipping my head, I suck her nipple through the thin fabric of her shirt and tug her panties aside.

She hisses when I trace the outline of her smooth pussy with the pad of my fingertip, teasing her.

"Next time you make a sound, I'm gonna stuff your mouth with my cock. This way, you'll have no choice but to be quiet."

Her breathing picks up and my cock throbs, loving that idea.

However, I'm not done toying with her yet.

We only have eight days left, and I don't want to waste a single second.

Ignoring the way that thought has my chest tightening, I drop to my knees and bury my nose between her thighs, inhaling her.

Her hand goes to my head. "Pho—"

She jerks when I bite her pussy through the fabric of her shorts. "Last warning." I slide them down her hips. "You gonna be good?"

She pulls her shorts back up.

'I have to stay dressed,' she mouths when I narrow my eyes. 'What if someone walks in?'

Fucking hell. That's not gonna work for what I have in mind.

I need skin. Preferably every inch of hers.

But I know Lennon will fight me tooth and nail on that.

However, since I'm a goddamn fiend for her pussy—among other things—I'm willing to compromise.

I snap the string of her thong against her skin. "Take these off."

She shakes her head.

Brat.

"Fine." Yanking her shorts and panties to the side, I give her cunt a little kiss. Then I stand. "You don't get to come."

Shooting me an icy glare, she shimmies out of them.

Then she drops to *her* knees.

Lips twisting, she tugs on the waistband of my sweatpants. My dick eagerly bobs out, slapping against my navel.

After licking her palm, she grabs my base, giving me a slow jerk before sealing her mouth around my head.

Fuck. She wins.

Or rather, I do.

Wrapping her ponytail around my fist, I drive my hips into her face, forcing her to take more of me.

I groan as she swallows me so deep she gags. I don't miss the sassy glint in her eye as she relaxes her throat as if to say, *challenge accepted.*

Christ.

Chills break out when she cups my balls. But as great as it all feels, I have to put an end to this battle of the wills we're having.

Lennon's the one who decided we could only be fuck buddies, and she's the one who's ending this in eight days.

I'm not about to let her run shit in the bedroom, too.

That's *my* motherfucking domicile.

Yanking her ponytail, I slip out of her mouth with a wet pop.

It's adorable how she chases my dick, trying to wrap her lips around it again.

"Get up. *Now.*"

My harsh tone has the desired effect because she rises off the floor without protest.

In a flash, I grab her hips and slam the front of her body against the wall. Which leaves her pert bare ass center stage.

I shove her T-shirt up because it's blocking my view. "Keep this fucking thing out of my way."

Goose bumps graze her soft flesh as I kneel.

I've never worshiped anything before, but this right here?

I'd build a goddamn shrine for *this*.

I've always been an ass guy, and Lennon by far has the best one I've ever seen.

Big, plump, and curvy. Fucking perfect.

She yelps when I sink my teeth into it.

I slap her ass in warning. My dick twitches as it ripples under my palm. "Shut up."

She glares hate fire at me over her shoulder.

Smirking, I squeeze her cheeks and spread them apart. "Want me to kiss it better?"

Instantly, she tries to swat me away, which puts me on edge.

"What's the problem?"

The playful inflection in my voice is long gone.

"Nothing," she whispers.

Something.

I don't want to assume the worst, but she's not giving me anything to work with here.

"Did someone hurt you?" I try to quell the rage creeping into my voice, but fail. If someone laid a fucking finger on her, I'm spending the rest of my life in jail.

"No."

Her one-word answers aren't putting me at ease. "Start talking."

"No one hurt me." A faint blush creeps along her face as she peers down at me. "It's just...no one has ever...you know."

"Played with your ass?"

Her silence is all the confirmation I need. My cock's back in the game, ready to get the party started.

However, Lennon's quick to pump the brakes.

"There's no way in hell I'm letting you put your giant dick in my ass. I do *not* want a rectal prolapse."

I can't help but laugh. "Your rectum isn't gonna prolapse, Groupie."

I like it rough, but not obliterate your asshole rough.

Those baby browns go wide with panic. "Do not put your dick in my ass." She gulps. "*Please.*"

"Well, since you asked so nicely..."

Her pretty face screws up. "I'm serious, Phoenix."

I kiss her bottom. "No dick in your ass."

Tonight.

Doesn't mean I won't ease my way into it, though. "Bend over."

"What part of—"

Gripping her hips, I tug her with so much force she has no choice but to brace her arms against the wall and stick her ass in the air.

I run a finger down the length of her exposed pussy. She's so wet she's glistening.

My voice is a gravelly rasp against her slick flesh. "Trust me."

Directing all my attention to the hole she's used to, I sink my tongue inside her.

Her arms shake and she pants my name as I stretch and fuck her sweet cunt.

Warm silky walls squeeze. "Holy shit."

Grinding against my mouth, she moans while I continue eating her from behind.

"Don't stop."

I nip her, reminding her to be quiet, but she's too far gone to care.

Just the way I like it.

Reaching around, I rub her swollen clit…then I change things up and circle a different hole with the tip of my tongue.

She tenses for a second. Then it happens.

A desperate whimper breaks free, followed by a curse.

I know she's almost there, so I keep up the tempo with my fingers and swirl my tongue against her puckered asshole.

"Oh god." Reaching behind her, she grips my hair and writhes against my face. "I'm gonna die."

No, she's gonna *come*.

And she does. So hard it runs down my hand.

I give her a second to collect herself before I wrap an arm around her waist and drag her over to the couch.

I take a seat, but when she goes to sit next to me, I yank her on my lap.

Lennon's been fighting me since the moment she walked in here.

It's only fair she puts her money where her mouth is.

"You wanted all the control tonight." I push my sweatpants down and my cock springs out. "Now ride it until we both come."

Licking her lips, she straddles me. She tries to ease me inside her bit by bit, but I'm an impatient asshole.

Lifting my hips, I drive into her with a hard thrust that makes us both groan.

Her eyes flutter closed, and she places a hand on my chest for support.

I spank her ass, urging her to hurry the fuck up.

"Sorry. I'm just...I need a second." A tiny shudder rolls through her. "You feel so good."

Any hope I had of making this session last all night is long gone with those words.

Slowly, she moves, rolling her hips in a lazy cadence that feels as awesome as it does torturous.

I suck the hollow of her throat. "Take your hair down."

My request surprises us both. However, she reaches up and pulls the elastic tie out without protest.

A river of shiny black strands cascade down her back. It feels like silk as I thread my fingers through it and look at her.

Her pretty face is glowing with a light sheen of sweat, her lips are pink and swollen, and her doe eyes are hooded with want.

How this girl could ever think she's anything less than perfect is beyond me.

Barbed wire invades my lungs, making it difficult to draw in air.

The only thing worse than knowing I'm going to lose her...is knowing some lucky bastard is going to have her one day.

Delicate fingers coil around my wrist. "You're checking out on me. What's wrong?"

I clench my teeth. Force myself to snap out of it. "Christ, Groupie. Are you gonna ride me, or do I need to take over so we can both get off sometime in the next decade?"

Edging forward, she bites my lip ring. "Asshole."

I give her a cocky grin. "I enjoyed playing with yours."

Her gaze meets mine, and she circles her hips, eliciting a low grunt from me.

I grip her ass with one hand and tunnel my other underneath her shirt so I can squeeze her tits.

My pulse hammers when she speeds up and the hand clamping her ass flexes.

"I'm close," she breathes.

I know. I feel her clenching. Which means she's nice and relaxed.

I bring my middle finger to her lips. "Get it wet."

Although confused, she opens her mouth and accommodates my request.

After there's enough moisture, I remove my finger and slide it between her ass cheeks.

Her eyes sharpen and she goes stagnant. "Phoenix—"

I repeat the same thing I told her before. "Trust me."

When I reach the entrance, I lightly circle the tight hole, getting her used to the feeling.

Exhaling a shaky breath, she begins moving. When she finds a rhythm she likes, and her eyes flutter closed, I push the tip of my finger inside.

Her motions pick up, and I go a little deeper. "How does it feel?"

"Different," she says with a tight breath. "Not in a bad way." Her face twists with pleasure. "I kind of like it."

"Good." My lips rise. "Now shut up and cream my dick."

Looping her arm around my neck, she works herself up and down my cock. Each time she does, I notch in a bit more, until I'm as far in as I can go.

Her breathing becomes ragged and her body curves over mine. "I'm gonna come."

Fuck yeah she is.

I love the way Lennon does it, too.

Her mouth parts in the shape of an *O* and her brows furrow like she's in deep concentration before a low moan erupts from her and she clamps down, gripping me like a vise as her juices drip down my sac.

Breathless, she sags against me. "You didn't come."

I was too busy concentrating on her to focus on my own needs.

Which, I'll admit, isn't something that happens with any other chick.

Only her.

Her teeth graze my earlobe. "I got you."

White-hot heat licks up my balls as she begins riding me fast and furious, like she's on a mission to drain every ounce of jizz from me.

"Goddamn."

Heat licks across my skin and my head lolls back as the sounds of our skin slapping together fill the room.

My cock pulsates and my abs clench.

Lennon clasps the back of my head and fuses our lips together, giving me what I want.

What I need.

Gripping her hair, I slip my tongue inside her mouth, kissing her with so much vehemence her breath catches and her heart beats against my chest like a drum.

And then she's kissing me back with just as much intensity.

Groaning into her mouth, I come inside her.

Expelling a little sated sigh, Lennon slumps against me. "We should have no problem sleeping now."

Sleeping is the last thing on my mind. That round was just foreplay.

Those long eyelashes flicker against my skin. "Um…Phoenix?"

"Yeah?"

She peers up at me with amusement. "Your finger is still in my ass."

A slow grin stretches my mouth. "I know."

And that's when it hits me.

She'll trust me with her body.

But not her heart.

CHAPTER 62
LENNON

"I don't understand," Quinn says. "Why is me talking about Gwyneth bad?"

Fuck. My. Life.

I told myself I wasn't going to get involved, but yesterday, while we were driving to North Carolina Quinn, went on a whole hour-long tangent about how beautiful and perfect Gwyneth is and how everyone on social media is *so* excited for Memphis and her to have this baby.

Skylar tried to hide it well, but when I walked back to the bunk, her red puffy eyes told me all I needed to know.

I tried to console her, but she made a beeline for the bathroom and locked it.

And that's where she stayed …until Storm threatened to piss on her bed.

It's bad enough watching the guy she's harbored these forbidden clandestine feelings for have a baby with someone else…she doesn't need Quinn twisting the damn dagger every two seconds.

Not that Quinn means to, given she has no idea what's going on under the surface.

Hell, I don't even know most of the details.

Which is why trying to broach this conversation with her is so hard.

"I did not say it was *bad*." Getting off my bed, I pace the floor of our hotel room. "It's not. You're totally entitled to like whoever you want."

I'm not trying to start a mean-girl pact that makes Quinn hate her idol.

I just want my friend to stop hurting.

Quinn pops her gum. "Then what's the problem?"

"It's just…you talk about Gwyneth a lot."

Quinn looks at me like I've just committed a cardinal sin. "That's because she's *Gwen*. Everyone talks about her. Plus, Memphis is going to marry her so—"

"Hold up. What do you mean Memphis is going to marry her?"

The guy only found out *last week* that he was the father.

"Never mind." Whistling, she looks out the window. "I know nothing."

Which means she most definitely *does*.

Staring her down, I place my hands on my hips. "Spill it."

Her voice drops to a whisper. "Okay, so according to the conversation I overheard Memphis having with Storm, Gwen's PR company wants him to pop the question soon since it will look bad for her if he doesn't."

Oh boy.

Without stopping for air, she adds, "Memphis wants to do it too, since they're having a kid and stuff." She rolls her eyes. "Even though Storm told him it was a terrible idea."

I wholeheartedly agree with Storm.

This whole thing seems to be going from bad to worse for poor Skylar.

Which is all the more reason I need her to take her fascination with *Gwen* down a few notches. I'm leaving in six days, which means I can't run interference when Quinn starts going all fangirl…or be there for Skylar afterward.

"Listen, Quinn. I really need you to stop talking about Gwyneth so much."

She huffs in irritation. "Why?"

Ugh. How the hell am I going to make her understand without telling her the actual reason?

"Sometimes people just don't click, you know? And hearing someone else talk about them incessantly in front of you can be a little…frustrating."

Her mouth drops open in shock. "You don't like Gwen? Who wouldn't like *Gwen*?"

Shit on a stick.

"Uh…well—"

"I don't," Phoenix interjects as he breezes through the door connecting our rooms.

I could kiss him for coming to my rescue.

Quinn turns her frustration on her brother. "Why? What did she ever do to you?"

Phoenix crosses his arms. "She's a snob and a bitch. She's also fake as fuck."

Quinn stomps her foot. "She is *not*."

"Have a conversation with her when the cameras aren't around." His gaze sharpens. "So, do us all a solid and shut the fuck up about her. It's creepy and annoying."

"Phoenix," I hiss when Quinn's face falls.

I mean, he's not wrong, but he didn't have to be so mean about it.

Then again, *that's* Phoenix.

Remorse flashes across his face and he tousles her hair. "Come on, weirdo. There's a Waffle House next door. I'll buy you breakfast."

Quinn's intrigued, but she isn't quite ready to cave just yet.

She's waiting for her big brother to sweeten the pot.

"And some of that shit for your face," Phoenix grunts.

Makeup. He means makeup.

Quinn smiles from ear to ear. "Deal." She looks at me. "You coming?"

I hold up my phone. "Can't. I want to call Mrs. Palma before the concert tonight."

Quinn grabs her purse off the bed. "More for us."

Phoenix follows her to the door, but the moment she's out of the room, he turns back.

I barely have time to blink before his lips are on mine, kissing me like I'm the air he needs to breathe.

"What was that for?"

Not that I'm complaining.

"You looked like you wanted to do that when I walked in." The corner of his mouth tugs up. "You're welcome."

My scowl is playful. "Ass."

He starts to leave, but I pull him back. "Hold on. I need a favor."

"I'll give you my dick when I get back. I need some sustenance first."

I roll my eyes. "Not your dick, jackass. A real favor."

His brows knit. "What's up?"

I'm in a tough spot since I can't disclose much to him either.

"I need you to look after Skylar while I'm gone. She's going through some stuff and I'm worried about her."

"If you're that worried, you should come to Europe with us."

I break eye contact. "You know I can't."

For *so* many reasons.

"Right," he bites out.

A knot forms in my chest. "Don't ruin what little time we have left, okay?"

It will be easier to expunge him from my system if I don't hate him with every fiber of my being again when we say goodbye.

"I'll look after Skylar." His knuckles drift along my cheekbone. "And I'll bring you back breakfast."

Instinctively, I lean into his touch. "Thanks."

"But I want something in return."

Of course he does. "Let me guess, a blow job?"

"Yeah, but I'll be getting one of those from you later anyway."
His expression grows serious, and he tips my chin. "Kiss me."

Rising on my tiptoes, I press my lips to his. In a matter of
seconds, his tongue is slicking over mine and we're breathing heavily, like we can't get enough of each other.

The knot in my chest grows bigger.

"Phoenix?" Quinn calls out.

Shoot.

We break apart just as the door opens. "Did you forget about
me?"

"No," Phoenix says. "Let's go."

Quinn walks out a second time...and Phoenix takes the opportunity to attack my lips again.

"She's gonna kill you," I breathe between kisses that make my
head spin.

I squeal when he grabs a handful of my ass and sucks my bottom
lip into his mouth. "Worth it."

"*Seriously?*" Quinn yells from the other side of the door.

I can't help but laugh when she stomps inside and snatches his
arm.

"I am *starving*," she whines as she leads him out of the room.

Turning his head, Phoenix gives me a vulgar smile. "Me too."

I cradle my phone between my ear and shoulder. "I didn't book my
flight home yet, but I'll do it tonight after the concert."

"All right. No problem," Mrs. Palma says. "Just let me know your
flight details so I can make arrangements to pick you up at the
airport."

"That's okay. I'll take an Uber home."

"Nonsense," she starts to say before her husband yells something
that sounds a whole lot like '*four*' in the background. "I have to go.
Your father and my husband are golfing."

That's...surprising. "Golfing? Dad doesn't golf."

"I know. But today he was recalling the one and only time he did, and Richard convinced him he should try it again since it's *his* favorite pastime. Next thing I know, Richard's lugging his clubs over here and now they're golfing in the living room. I'm pretty sure one of them just broke the television."

Yikes. "Well, if they did, don't worry." I'll be getting six figures in less than a week. "I'll buy a new one when I get home."

"Ok, dear. I'll call you back later. Richard, what is wrong with you? Take your balls outside—"

And *that's* the last thing I hear before the line goes dead.

I check the clock on the nightstand. They've only been gone a half hour and with Quinn—and Phoenix's—appetite, I'm sure they'll be there for a while.

I'm looking around for my shoes so I can meet them when there's a knock on my door.

I find Skylar on the other side of it...looking absolutely miserable.

My stomach drops. Poor thing must have heard about the upcoming nuptials.

"Come here." I pull her into a hug. "I'm so sorry. This situation sucks so bad."

She goes rigid. "Yeah, it does." She rubs my back. "But you have nothing to be sorry for, Lennon. This isn't your fault."

I'm not sure why she'd think it was *my* fault, but hey, heartbreak can do a number on the brain.

She hugs me tighter. "I've already made some calls. I'm hoping they'll be buried by tomorrow."

Now, *I'm* the one who goes rigid. I didn't think she was being literal when she asked me if I wanted her to kill Phoenix...but apparently, she was.

Anxiety coils through me. I know she's hurting, but *Jesus.*

The woman is with child, for crying out loud.

This brings a whole new meaning to the term—*hell hath no fury like a woman scorned.*

And *friendship*...because now I'm a freaking accessory.

I untangle from her. "Whoa. Don't you think that's a little extreme?"

Evidently not, because she looks at me like I'm the crazy one. "Are you for real right now?" Anger colors her expression. "This shit is beyond fucked up. It's absolutely *despicable.*"

I back away slowly. "I totally get that you're upset, but putting a hit out on Memphis and Gwen is so not the right way to deal with this."

Her jaw drops. "Wait...*what*? What are you talking about?"

I blink, thoroughly confused. "You're not planning on having Memphis and Gwen murdered?"

Shock has her rearing back. "Yeah...no." Her eyes close. "Shit. That means you don't know."

You'd think finding out my friend didn't hire a hit man would squash all my anxiety, but nope.

"Know what?"

Frowning, she walks over to my bed and sits.

Then she takes her laptop out of her bag. "I'm really sorry, Lennon, but there's something you need to see."

My anxiety turns to full-blown panic as I take a seat next to her...

And then absolute horror when I peer at her screen because there are pictures—*intimate* pictures—of me and Phoenix.

In the first photo, Phoenix has me up against a wall and he's kissing my neck.

That wouldn't be so bad, but in the second photo, his hand is inside my shorts and the expression on my face makes it clear that I'm *really* enjoying myself.

Then there's the final photo, which is a close-up. Phoenix's eyes are hooded, and his face is strained in pleasure like he's about to come...while I straddle him on the couch.

The only advantages to this one are that I have a T-shirt on, it's cropped so you can't see the lower halves of our bodies, and my face isn't in it. Not that it matters. Anyone can tell it's the same girl from the other two photos.

"I'm trying to get them taken down," Skylar whispers.

Humiliation courses through me as I flick through the online magazines and blogs with glaring headlines like:

'Who is Phoenix Walker's curvy new girl?'

'Phoenix Walker gets hot and heavy with a full-figured beauty.'

'Check out Phoenix Walker's plus-sized love interest.'

There isn't a single caption that doesn't reference something about my weight.

And when I make the mistake of scrolling down to read the comments…it's even worse.

–I knew he was on drugs, but I didn't think he was that strung out.

–Dayum. Phoenix likes 'em big.

–Phoenix can have any woman he wants. Why would he screw that chubster?

–It's those thunder thighs for me.

–He should take a cue from Memphis and bang hotties like Gwen.

–Someone call the cops. He's been crushed to death.

–He's definitely punching above his weight class.

Technically, that last one is a compliment, but I don't think they intended for it to be.

"Okay, enough." Skylar steals her laptop back. "People are jealous dickheads. Ignore them. You're beautiful."

As much as all those comments sting, I can't throw myself a pity party quite yet because I have far more important things to worry about.

"Those pics are from the other night…while we were on the bus."

Which means someone very close to us took those pictures and then gave them to the fucking tabloids.

Skylar blows out a heavy breath. "Yeah, I thought it looked familiar."

My voice cracks. She was right before, this is beyond fucked up. "Who would do this?"

Who would betray not just mine, but *Phoenix's* trust?

These aren't just his people…they're his family.

Her face scrunches. "Well, it's definitely not me, Storm, or

Memphis. We would never do that to him or you. Quinn can be cunning, but Phoenix is her hero, and she adores you, so I doubt it's her. Chandler obviously wouldn't." Her eyes narrow. "My money's on George."

Yeah, she's probably right, but I can't focus on that because she just reminded me of something even more alarming.

Nausea barrels into me and I lurch up. "Chandler." If this is all over the internet, it's only a matter of time before he finds out. "He's gonna freak."

The expression on Skylar's face tells me she's just as anxious as I am about this. "I know. I'm trying my hardest to have them taken down before he sees." Standing up, she grips my shoulders. "Breathe. Seeing as he hasn't barged in here screaming his head off, I'd say you're sa—"

The sound of my phone ringing cuts her off.

My stomach twists itself into even more knots when I see Chandler's name flash across my screen.

"He might not know yet," Skylar says as I reach for it. "Play it cool."

I answer on the third ring. "Hey. Good morn—"

"My room. *Now.*"

Then the line goes dead.

"Shit," Skylar murmurs.

Then she smooths my hair. "Okay. Here's what you're gonna do. You're going to walk in there with your head held high, and then when he starts screaming, you're gonna muster up some tears. Chandler can be a jerk, but blubbering women make him skittish. Use that to your advantage."

I'm thankful she has a game plan because I don't. "Okay."

"Good luck."

Gripping my hand, we walk out of my room together.

"You got this," she assures me before we separate and she heads down the hall to her room.

I go to knock on Chandler's door, but it opens before I have the chance.

"Get in here."

The knot in my stomach constricts to the point of pain as he stomps over to the kitchen area of his suite.

He stops in front of a small table and spins his laptop around… on his screen are the photos of me and Phoenix.

"Go pack your things," he says, his tone unusually calm.

The fact he's not screaming or raging anymore is unnerving.

I open my mouth, ready to rattle off an excuse…but there isn't one.

Disappointment and shame sit heavy on my chest. "I'm sorry."

Chandler is a grade-A asshole, but out of all the rules he gave me, he made it abundantly clear that one in particular was the most important.

And I broke it.

So even though I can stand here, produce some tears, and try to justify what I did…I won't.

Because that would make me no better than *him*.

Humiliation courses through me as I turn on my heel and head for the door.

However, my steps come to a halt with my next thought.

I messed up, there's no disputing that. But I *did* keep Phoenix out of trouble like he wanted. Hell, he's not even drinking anymore.

Not that I can take credit for that—that's all him.

But still, I fulfilled the key component of my job description.

While I deserve to get fired for my mistake, I should be entitled to some compensation.

Especially since I not only gave up my job, but Mrs. Palma has been covering all the expenses for me back home these past two months.

I don't just owe the woman my lifelong gratitude and appreciation; I owe her money.

I spin around to face him. "Will I still be paid?"

Chandler looks up from his laptop. "How long have you been fucking him?"

Another wave of embarrassment courses over me.

I don't even have to tell him the truth, because the way his features harden tells me he's already figured it out. "That's what I thought." The muscles in his face tense. "The fine print of our contract explicitly states that if you violated any of the rules, you wouldn't receive a single penny. So, no, you will not be paid." He slams his laptop shut. "Hope it was worth it."

My throat prickles as I head for the door.

I came here with one purpose in mind, but in the end, I did the one thing I swore I'd never do.

I got too close to the sun.

And it burned me. *Again.*

"I thought you'd be stronger than this," Chandler utters to my retreating back. "Clearly I was wrong."

His words feel like a slap across the face.

That makes two of us.

CHAPTER 63
LENNON

I press the ignore button on my cell as I continue cramming things into my suitcase. I know Skylar wants to talk, but as much as I'd love to say goodbye to her and the others—aside from that bastard George—I can't.

The only thing worse than being fired is the walk of shame that comes with it.

I've already lost my money. I'd like to at least hold on to a bit of my pride.

But then I think of how upset I'd be if the shoe was on the other foot and Skylar left without saying a word.

I don't want her thinking our friendship didn't mean anything to me, so I pick up my phone to text her.

I'm in the middle of typing out a message when the connecting door opens and Phoenix strolls inside, clutching his stomach.

"I just got my ass whooped by a fifteen-year-old in a waffle eating contest. Who knew someone so tiny could eat so much?"

Despite looking stuffed to the point of being uncomfortable, he's smiling like he just won the lottery.

A sharp pang radiates my chest. I'm happy he's building a relationship with his little sister.

Hopefully, it will be enough to deter him from going down that dark path again.

Groaning, he removes his sunglasses and baseball cap—otherwise known as his *incognito* props. Not that they work all that well.

It's impossible not to notice Phoenix Walker.

I stuff a small pile of folded T-shirts into my suitcase. "Where's Quinn now?"

Our last conversation was basically me implying that she was doing something wrong, and that's not how I want to leave things with her.

He snorts out a laugh. "She's still at the restaurant because Storm's convinced *he* can beat her."

In that case, maybe I'll just write her a note.

"Want to go watch him get his ass handed to—" Confusion spreads across his face as his stare flicks between me and my suitcase. "Hold up. Why are you packing? We still have another show tonight."

Not *we*.

I fold a pair of jeans. "You do. I don't."

That only makes him even more dumbfounded. "What do you mean?"

Brushing past him, I head to the bathroom so I can grab my toiletries. "I'm fired."

Phoenix catches my arm. "Fired? For what? Why?"

There's no point in keeping it from him since this affects him, too. "There are pictures of us." I twist out of his grasp. "All over the internet."

He follows me into the bathroom. "Pictures of us? What kinds of pictures?"

Opening the shower door, I collect my shampoo, body wash, and razor. "Someone took photos of us in the back lounge the other night...and then sent them to a bunch of online gossip blogs and news magazines. Chandler saw them and canned me."

Although *many* things can ruffle Phoenix's feathers, not much can shock him. This does, though, because he stumbles back like the rug was just pulled out from underneath him.

That makes two of us.

A homicidal look enters his eyes…and then he's bolting out of my room in a cloud of rage.

Heart pounding, I chase after him. I do not want him beating up Chandler. Not only will it cause issues for him with the record label, his actions will also impact Storm and Memphis.

Chandler wasn't the one in the wrong here. *I* was.

However, Phoenix bypasses Chandler's room and goes to one farther down the hall.

Oh crap.

I'm trying to catch up to him when he kicks the door open.

"You *motherfucker*."

Everything happens so fast it turns into a tornado of chaos.

Skylar, Chandler, and Memphis rush out of their rooms at the same time Storm and Quinn step out of the elevator.

There's this bizarre moment where we all stop and look at one another…

Then we hear the sound of knuckles cracking against bone, followed by an agonizing howl.

We all race inside the room and my jaw hits the floor because Phoenix is beating the *absolute* crap out of George.

"You piece of shit."

Hand around his throat, Phoenix continues utilizing George's face as his personal piñata.

He stops abruptly, and for a moment, I think he's going to let him go.

And he does…but only so he can send a sharp kick to George's stomach.

Instinctively I take a step forward, but then come to my senses.

I thought George was a nice guy, and I truly felt sorry that I hurt him.

But what he did in the name of resentment went too far. The

pictures he took of us are not only virtually pornographic and a complete invasion of privacy…they're *everywhere*.

No matter how many takedowns, emails, or favors Skylar calls in, they'll never truly go away because the internet is forever.

As of today, the entire world will only know me as the *fat girl* Phoenix Walker hooked up with.

It's a stain I'll never be able to get rid of.

One that's going to follow me everywhere.

The anger brewing in the pit of my stomach rises and I clench my hands into fists. I'm tempted to get a few punches and kicks in myself, but Chandler gets between them, attempting to stop it. Or rather, stop Phoenix, because aside from the one punch he landed, George isn't putting up much of a fight.

Chandler isn't faring much better.

Exasperated, he looks at Storm and Memphis. "A little help here, guys."

Crossing his arms over his chest, Storm turns to Memphis. "Did you hear something?"

Memphis matches his stance. "Nope."

Chandler eyes Skylar next. "Get security."

Skylar taps her chin, pretending to think about it. "You know, I probably should." Her nose wrinkles. "On second thought. Nah."

Desperate, he glances at Quinn, who's sitting in a chair on the other side of the room…eating what appears to be popcorn.

"Make yourself useful and call the front desk."

Happily munching away, she fist-bumps the air. "Go, big bro. And don't forget, if it bleeds, you can kill it!"

The four of us exchange a look then. Not because of Quinn's words—although daunting—but because Phoenix is coming danger-ously close to doing just that.

So much so, George no longer has a recognizable face.

Trepidation coils my insides. If this continues, he'll no longer have a pulse.

Fortunately, security dashes inside a moment later. It takes three big guys to pull Phoenix off. When they finally do, I notice his lip is split and bleeding from where George landed his one punch.

Upon realizing this is *the* Phoenix Walker, the security guards trade unsure looks, like they have no idea how to proceed.

Fortunately, Skylar steps up and handles it like a pro.

She gestures to George, who's in a ball on the floor. "How much to drop this guy off at the nearest hospital and claim you found him in an alley behind a bar?" She hikes a thumb at Phoenix, who spits blood on the carpet. "And how much to forget whatever *this* guy did?"

Shrugging, they swap another unsure look.

"I don't know," one of them says. "A thousand?"

"Five thousand apiece," the guy in the middle declares. "And maybe tickets to the show tonight?"

"Consider it done." She flutters her fingers at George. "After you take care of him."

"Hold on," Chandler says when they lift George off the floor. "He's our bassist. You can't just *dispose* of him."

"Him or *us*?" Memphis growls, the threat in his baritone crystal clear.

Chandler balks. "Don't be ridiculous."

"Then it's settled," Storm says. "Get a fill-in for the show tonight. If you can't find one, it's no sweat off our balls. We'll make it work."

Digging inside his pocket for his phone, Chandler hems and haws before leaving.

I take the opportunity to do the same since I still have to finish packing.

I'm halfway down the hall when someone grips my arm.

"Groupie."

His deep, gruff voice swirls around me like smoke from a wildfire.

"Are you okay?" I whisper, willing myself not to turn around.

Because once I do, my mistake will be staring me in the face and it's gonna hurt like hell.

Still gripping my arm, he comes around to me instead. "Not if you're leaving."

As much as I want my job back—even though there are only six days left—there's nothing either of us can do.

Chandler's made up his mind.

"I have to pack."

"Stay."

"Can't. I've been fired, remember?"

"Stay the next six days anyway." His voice drops to a husky whisper, and he steps closer, invading my space. "I'm not ready to say goodbye yet."

Even if I wanted to—which would be insane on my part after all this—I couldn't afford it. No longer being an employee means no more free room and board.

"Without pay."

I try to sidestep him, but he won't let me.

"Then I'll pay you." The pad of his thumb glides along my jaw. "Whatever he offered you to come on tour, I got it covered."

My shoulders tense and my stomach buckles as I process what he's saying. There's no way I can accept his proposition.

I was fired for having sexual relations with him, so him offering to pay me for *that* is all kinds of wrong.

I'd much rather go back to bartending at Obsidian.

"I'm not a prostitute."

"I didn't..." He makes a sound of frustration. "I know you're not."

"Good. Glad we're on the same page."

I try to walk away again, but he won't let me. He's like an impenetrable wall I can't break through.

His determined stare drills into me. "Don't leave."

My throat works through a tight swallow. He's making this ten times harder than it has to be.

"Maybe it happened this way for a reason," I whisper.

I obviously didn't learn my lesson the first time around, so perhaps this is fate's way of making sure I do now.

"Goodbye, Phoenix."

CHAPTER 64
PHOENIX

It's not goodbye.

Not yet anyway.

I wouldn't let Lennon cut my time with her short, and I'm sure as fuck not about to let *Chandler* do it.

But before I can deal with him, I'm gonna need to call in the calvary.

Everyone—minus Chandler and that trifling motherfucker George—are still in the room when I get back.

Skylar glances up at me. "Hey. Now that you have a minute. How do you want me to run with this whole thing? Do you want me to ignore it, or address—"

"I want you to make sure Lennon doesn't leave." I look at all of them. "Chandler fired her so she's in her room packing. I need you guys to go in there and distract her while I get her job back."

"How the fuck are we supposed to distract her?" Memphis asks.

"I think he means hold her hostage," Storm notes.

Whatever it takes.

Quinn pops up from the chair. "On it." Wandering over, she addresses the three of them. "I'll pretend my appendix burst, and you guys will all freak out about it. Then I'll beg Lennon to stay with me."

I've gotta hand it to my baby sister because that's a much better plan...especially since it doesn't involve Storm cuffing *my* girl to a bed.

Storm, however, appears skeptical. "You really think that's gonna work?"

"Trust me. I'm a great actress and improv is a specialty of mine."

Skylar ushers everyone out. "Let's go before she's gone."

They start to leave, but Quinn halts her steps and pokes Storm's arm. "I'm gonna need a lift."

He looks at her like she's crazy. "For what?"

She rolls her eyes. "Because I'm dying, dummy. Lennon's never gonna believe it if we don't make it look real." She beckons him like she's a princess and he's a mere peasant. "Now hurry up and carry me to my room."

Glaring at me, Storm lifts my sister off the ground. "You fucking owe me."

"Oh my god. It hurts so *bad*," Quinn wails like she's in actual agony.

"Just make sure she's still here by the time I'm done."

With that, I dip out and make my way to Chandler's room.

He answers after the second knock. "Come in."

I push past him. "I needed you to open the door, not an invitation to walk through it."

Sighing, he pinches the bridge of his nose. "Evidently beating the snot out of George wasn't enough for you to decompress. What's the issue now, Phoenix?"

"There isn't one." I get in his face. "Because you're gonna give Lennon her job back."

"I'm most certainly not." He strolls into the living room of his suite. "I hired her to keep you out of trouble. Not play with your dick."

And that's his second mistake of the day.

In less than three seconds, I have him pinned against a wall. "You better watch it."

He curses under his breath. "And *this* is exactly why I fired her."

The hand gripping his collar constricts. "Then you're not half as smart as you think you are."

"I beg your pardon?"

We rarely get along, but Chandler knows me. He knows I don't do relationships.

I stab his chest with my finger. "You knew she wasn't just some chick I screwed. You knew we had a past and bringing her here would stir up old feelings. What the fuck did you expect?"

The prick has the audacity to look me in the eyes when he says his next words. "I *expected* her to be more intelligent."

And that's his third mistake.

My knuckles crunch against his nose. The back of his head hits the wall so hard the people in the hotel lobby probably heard it.

"*Fuck!*"

"Are you putting two and two together yet, asshole? Or do I need to continue spelling it out with my fists?"

Glaring, he holds his now bleeding nose. "I won't insult your girlfriend anymore, okay? Still doesn't change the fact that she's fired."

It takes every ounce of willpower not to punch him again.

"Why? You hired her to take care of me, and that's exactly what she did."

"No, she took care of your—" He cowers when I raise my fist. "She broke the most important rule."

That shit doesn't make any sense.

"If you hired her to look after me, shouldn't *that* be the most important rule? Who cares what we did behind closed doors. I'm a fuck of a lot better than I was before she got here."

The girl I ruined saved me. How's that for irony?

He laughs bitterly. "Yes. So much better. You're beating up band members, missing concerts, arguing with Vic about song choices, *assaulting* me. And that's just in the last two weeks."

Adrenaline surges through my bloodstream.

"First of all, George wasn't a band member. And me missing the concert that night wasn't Lennon's fault. Hell, she's the one who talked me off the fucking ledge. And you're goddamn right I'm arguing with Vic because I'm tired of him making all the decisions. *I'm* the lead singer. It's *my* voice people come to hear. *My* voice lining his, yours, and everyone else's pockets."

A frown bends his lips. "And it's your voice that will be forgotten and your career that will go up in smoke if you don't pull your damn head out of your ass. You think you would have learned your lesson after the accident, but no. Here you go, following someone else blindly down whatever path they steer you."

And that's when it clicks. "You're threatened by Lennon."

He doesn't like that she's urging me to call the shots and take control of my life and career.

He doesn't like that she's encouraging me to sing the music I believe in.

He doesn't like that with Lennon by my side, I remember my value. *My voice.*

"I'm threatened by anyone who has the power to influence you to the point you can no longer decipher between what's right and what's wrong." He punches his chest. "I'm the manager. It's *my* job to look out for you all and make sure this band doesn't turn into a steaming pile of shit. Josh died on my watch, at my party, in my fucking car." He thrusts a finger in the air. "I will not let it happen again. She needs to go."

I take a step back and then another. It feels like a pile of bricks just got dumped on me.

"The accident wasn't your fault. However, I know better than anyone that me saying that won't do shit to alleviate your guilt." I hold his stare. "I'm sorry you're going to spend the rest of your life feeling responsible because of my actions that night. Trust me, I wish I could go back and change it…but I can't."

Anger rises in my chest, burning my throat. "You don't have to be scared of Lennon, though."

I've allowed my guilt to destroy me, but I'm not going to let it or *him* destroy what little time we have together. She's too important.

"You have to be scared of *me*." I move closer. "Because if you don't hire Lennon back, I'm done with this tour and the next one, and the next."

His mouth drops open in shock before his expression turns hard. "I will not."

I dig my cell out of my pocket and hand it to him. "You want to make the phone call to Vic then, or should I?"

He looks at me like I'm a stranger. "You're not serious."

His shirt rips as I lug him toward me. "Do I look like I'm kidding?" I bring my lips to his ear because I want this dickhead to hear me loud and clear. "Don't fuck with me, Chandler. Hire her back, or I will not only end your career, I will end *you*."

Despite looking like he wants to argue, he's too petrified to call my bluff. "Fine. But I hope you know what you're doing. Relationships based on sex and volatile emotions rarely work out. It's not healthy to be so preoccupied with another person."

My laughter is mocking as I release him. "That's awfully hypocritical coming from you, don't you think?"

He bristles. "What on earth are you talking about?"

Firing Lennon was the equivalent of getting kicked in the nuts right before you're about to bust one. It's only fair I return the favor.

"You might be upset about the accident, but you sure as fuck aren't broken up about losing Josh. I wonder why that is."

I might not be able to read or write well, but I'm not dumb. I know and observe a lot more than I let on.

Sizing him up, I take a cigarette out of my pack and light one. "Probably the same reason I heard you on the phone with the Barclay's PR person the other night, hinting that Memphis and Gwen should get married."

I know I've got him because he looks like a deer caught in headlights before he recovers.

"Yes, I suggested they get married, but it was simply from a PR standpoint. Nothing more."

Bull-fucking-shit.

"PR is Skylar's department." Studying him, I rub my chin. "Then again, we both know why she'd never go for that." My eyes narrow.

"But *you,* on the other hand. It works out real well for you, doesn't it?"

His face turns red with irritation and what looks a whole lot like embarrassment. "I have no idea what you're talking about."

Oh, but he does.

"One brother was already eliminated, so all you had to do was get rid of the second one." I take a long drag of my cigarette. "Now that you've lined your shot up, I'd tell you to man up and shoot it, but we both know Skylar would turn your ass down in a heartbeat."

"The baby is his," Chandler bites out. "Married or not, they are still tied together forever. Besides, Memphis is in agreement. He wants to do what's best for his child."

He's right about that. Storm and I tried to convince him that marrying Gwen would be a big mistake, but he doesn't want to hear it.

He wants to give his kid everything…because he had nothing.

"I know. Which is the only reason I'm not telling him about the convo I overheard."

Not only would Memphis shrug it off, it wouldn't change anything. His mind is already made up.

Chandler's relief is tangible. "I appreciate that. And really, Phoenix, I'm simply doing what's necessary. Josh already did a number on Skylar. She shouldn't have to play second fiddle to another woman and child. You may not agree with my methods, but I promise I'm doing what's best for both of them. Sometimes applying pressure isn't enough to stop the bleed…you have to cauterize the wound."

He's not wrong.

I've watched Memphis battle his demons over the years, but his biggest one by far is that he's been secretly pining over his brother's girl since they were kids.

But now he's finally moved on.

While I personally can't stand Gwyneth, he deserves to be happy.

So does Skylar.

The last thing any of us want is for history to repeat itself and watch her bleed out over another guy who can't put her first.

The two of them together would be the equivalent of an atomic bomb and we'd *all* suffer the fallout.

But while I agree with Chandler, I also know his motives aren't as virtuous as he claims.

"I get why you did it. But a word of warning?"

His brows lift high. "What's that?"

"Memphis lost Josh, but he still has two brothers left. Don't *ever* let me catch you pulling the strings behind his back again. Same goes for the rest of us."

He swallows. "I give you my word."

"Good." I stub my cigarette out on the wall next to his head. "Now that *that's* squashed, get yourself cleaned up so you can formally hire Lennon back." I snap my fingers. "Oh, and one more thing…"

"Yes?" he grits through his teeth.

I pat his cheek. "Throw in an apology too, while you're at it."

CHAPTER 65
LENNON

"**W**hat the hell is taking the ambulance so long?"

One moment I was packing, and the next Storm was carrying a hysterical Quinn in here.

"I don't know," Storm says, although he doesn't appear to be nearly as worried about Quinn's ruptured appendix as I am.

Or Skylar, who's been pacing. Or Memphis who's...what the hell is Memphis doing?

I look across the room. He's drinking a beer and smoking a cigarette. *Lovely.*

Quinn grips my hand so hard I'm positive she fractured it. "It hurts so bad."

"I know, sweetie. I know." I sweep my uninjured hand along her forehead. Poor girl is in so much pain she's sweating and thrashing on her bed. "They're coming, okay? Just hang in there."

"I don't think I can." Tears leak out the corners of her eyes as she stares up at the ceiling. "I'm gonna die. I feel it."

My stomach bottoms out. *Holy shit.*

"You're not going to die, Quinn." Panic claws up my throat and I look at Storm. "She's gonna die if we don't do something."

"You just told me I wasn't," Quinn wails.

Crap.

"You're not," I assure her before I regard Storm again. "Call the front desk and ask if there are any guests who are doctors. Tell them it's an emergency."

"I don't think that's necessary." Storm glares at Quinn. "Are you sure this isn't just a stomachache from all those waffles you ate today?"

Quinn sniffles. "I'm positive." Clutching my other hand, she peers up at me. "Will you tell my brother I love him?"

Oh my god. *This can't be happening.*

Storm's jaw tics. "Dial the dramatics down, Juvie."

Storm isn't the warm and fuzzy type and I know Quinn annoys the shit out of him, but that's just plain heartless.

"What the hell is the matter with you? Her appendix burst. Do you have any idea how much pain she's in?"

"So much," Quinn cries out.

Considering her father beat her to a bloody pulp and she never so much as batted an eye, this has to be excruciating.

"I know, baby. I know." I look around. "Where the hell is Phoenix?"

"I already told you," Storm grunts. "He's taking a shit."

"While his sister is dying?"

"You said I wasn't gonna die!" Quinn screeches.

The high-pitched sound is a million times worse than nails on a chalkboard and there's a collective wince.

"Will you shut the fuck up?" Storm roars so loud the windows rattle. "Some of us need our ears to make a living."

Then maybe *he* shouldn't be screaming.

Quinn pales and a tremor racks her small frame. "S-s-s-orry."

If Quinn wasn't holding both my hands, I'd use one of them to bitch-slap the hell out of Storm. "Are you forgetting what kind of house she grew up in, dickhead? There's no need to yell at her. *Ever.* Especially while she's having a medical emergency."

His expression softens. "I...fuck. My bad, Juvie."

But Quinn won't look at him. Can't say I blame her. I don't want to look at him either.

"It's gonna be okay, honey," I whisper. "The ambu—"

The door swings open and Phoenix charges inside.

I spring up. "Where have you been? Quinn is—"

I don't have a chance to finish that statement because he seizes my face and kisses me.

What the hell?

His hand slips to the back of my neck and he runs his tongue along the seam of my lips, urging me to part them for him.

That's when I shove him.

"Are you and Storm smoking from the same bong? Your sister's appendix just burst. The ambulance is taking forever to get here and instead of worrying about that, you're kissing me?"

Phoenix's lips twitch. "Quinn's fine."

"What are you talking about? She's not fine. She's—"

"Actually, I am. Phoenix told us to distract you so you wouldn't leave." Quinn gets off the bed. "Sorry."

I recoil as a slew of emotions filter through me. Obviously, I'm relieved Quinn isn't dying, but I was really scared.

Sensing this, Quinn wraps her arms around me. "Please don't hate me."

I hug her back, even though I'm still on edge about the whole thing. "I could never hate you. I'm glad you're okay, but please don't ever do that to me again."

"Our little actress deserves an Oscar," Skylar says. "I had to keep reminding myself she was fine."

Quinn smiles, but it doesn't reach her eyes. "Thanks. I'm gonna go downstairs and get a snack."

Before anyone can stop her, she bolts out of the room.

Skylar starts to go after her, but Storm beats her to it. "I got this."

As he should. Because I wasn't the only one who was scared during this whole ordeal.

I smack Phoenix's arm. "I can't believe you made your sister fake a medical emergency just so I'd stay."

On second thought, I can. He's relentless.

He lifts his hands. "Trust me, that was all Quinn. She concocted that plan by herself."

That I can also believe.

I walk over to my suitcase and zip it. "Well, since most of you are here, I should probably start saying my goodbyes now."

"Not so fast," Chandler says as he zips into the room. "After careful consideration, I've decided to renege my previous request for your dismissal."

"English, motherfucker," Memphis grunts.

Irritation crosses over his face. "Lennon, or should I say *Yoko*. You're no longer fired."

Phoenix clears his throat.

"And I sincerely apologize for insinuating you were stupid, weak, and not an asset to this team."

Needless to say, we're all floored. However, it's Memphis who says what everyone's thinking.

"Damn. Did it hurt when Phoenix ripped your balls off and handed them to his girl?"

Okay, so I wasn't thinking *that*, but it's clear this was all Phoenix's doing.

"Are you gonna stay?" Skylar questions, her pretty face filled with hope.

I start to answer, but Phoenix curls his hands around my hips.

"Yeah, she is."

Then he closes the distance between us and kisses me.

Making a low noise in his throat, his fingers thread my hair and he parts my lips with his tongue. My pulse spikes as he delves inside my mouth with fiery strokes that make me feel like I'm floating. A gruff sound leaves him, and his hands travel down my back until he's squeezing my ass.

"Don't forget to use one of these," Memphis says before something hits the back of my head.

That's when I remember we're not alone.

"Wow, would you look at that?" Skylar bites out. "Someone finally discovered condoms."

"Six days," I whisper as Phoenix and I break apart. "But that's—"

He silences me with another kiss.

CHAPTER 66
LENNON

"Holy crap, I have to crap," Quinn announces before she makes a mad dash for the bathroom inside the greenroom.

Given she just wolfed down an entire meatball sub in the time it takes most people to brush their teeth, I'm not surprised.

Shaking my head, I go back to my bowl of veggies. Ever since the pictures came out five days ago, I've been trying to eat super healthy. I've already lost two out of the five pounds I gained on tour.

"Shoot."

I'm reaching down for the fork I just dropped when my fingers brush against something smooth and familiar. It must have fallen out of Skylar's bag when she left to go run an errand.

My stomach erupts in a flurry of anxiety as I pick up the black Sharpie.

I haven't been having the greatest time mentally since I read those comments, despite reminding myself to ignore them like Skylar said.

Unfortunately, the bad stuff has always stuck inside my psyche like glue. Theoretically, I could receive a hundred compliments, but it still wouldn't be enough to bury one cruel remark.

At least that's how it *used* to be for me. Although that voice has been getting louder and louder these days.

Because the worst thing about those articles isn't the nasty criticism, it's that it seems to have negated all the rewiring to my self-esteem that I've spent years working on.

I finally got to a place where I was comfortable with who I was and even though my body wasn't perfect, I was happy with it.

My heart twists against my rib cage, drudging up all those old feelings I've tried to abandon as I continue staring at the marker.

It would be so damn easy to relapse and write all their words on my skin...pour salt in the wounds they created.

But doing that has never made it hurt any less.

Because it isn't Sabrina, or the people at school, or the trolls online that are my greatest enemy.

It's this thing.

It's *me*.

My dad once posed a question in which he asked me whether I would be nasty or kind to an overweight person I'd encountered on the street.

Of course, I said the latter.

To which he responded—"*then why wouldn't you extend the same compassion to yourself?*"

As usual, my dad was right.

So, while it would be easy to mark my skin with all those hurtful words, I don't want to go back to that dark place.

I don't want to let those people or my old self win.

I'm placing the Sharpie down when Skylar charges in like a woman on a mission.

After a quick look around the room, she closes the door.

That's when I notice the papers in her hand.

"What's that?"

She shoves the stack at me. "You've been letting those assholes' words live rent-free in your head all week, so I wanted to show you these."

By *these* she means various comments she printed out. Only, unlike the others…they're nice.

My chest swells as I flip through them.

—*Sheeesh. She's thicc AF and hella cute.*
—*Some of y'all need to stop hating. I think she's beautiful.*
—*Phoenix knows wassup. Curves in all the right places.*
—*Slay girl.*
—*Thick thighs save lives.*
—*She can ride me any day of the week. No cap.*
—Yaasss. *We stan a curvy queen.*
—*It's nice to see someone like him with a regular girl. Gives the rest of us some hope.*
—*Dayum. That ass is valid. Phoenix understood the assignment.*
—*He's obviously into her and that's all that matters. People need to quit being jealous.*

The fact Skylar went digging for these and printed them out to show me means more than she'll ever know.

"You didn't have to do this," I whisper through the lump in my throat. "Thank you."

She walks over to the mini-fridge and grabs a bottle of water. "I just wanted you to see the flip side of it. Don't let some keyboard warriors make you feel less than and screw up your confidence."

If only it were that simple. While I appreciate what Skylar did, she'll never truly get what it's like…because she's flawless.

"Easy for *you* to say." I place the papers on the coffee table in front of me. "You're legit perfect."

Therefore, she's never struggled with low self-esteem.

I'm about to walk out so I can catch the end of the concert…but Skylar whips off her shirt.

And her bra.

"Uh…what are you doing?"

She points to her awesome perky rack. "These are implants. I got them done six months after I turned eighteen. Before that I was barely an *A*, and it's something I used to be *really* self-conscious about, especially since Jo—" She shakes her head. "Never mind. That's not important."

Undoing the button on her jeans, she slides them down, revealing her skimpy purple underwear. She drags her red fingernail across her skin, gesturing to some tiny white streaks on her hips. "These are stretch marks." Turning around, she slaps her ass. "And feast your eyes on my magnificent butt dimple, sprinkled with some cellulite."

I can't help but laugh because she's crazy. Crazy and *beautiful*.

She turns back around. "No one is perfect, Lennon. But what you think are flaws aren't to those who love you. So, be one of those people who love you, okay? Because I don't want my friend thinking bad things about herself when she's gorgeous inside and out."

I was thankful for Skylar's friendship before, but it's nothing compared to right now. My chest is practically overflowing with how much I cherish her.

I'm about to run over and give her a hug, but Quinn comes out of the bathroom.

Her jaw drops when she sees a half-naked Skylar. "Whoa. Those are *nice*."

Skylar laughs. "Thanks."

Intrigue colors Quinn's face. "Can I feel?"

Skylar shrugs. "Have at it, sister." She looks at me. "You can too if you want."

I mean, I *am* curious.

I bite the inside of my cheek as Quinn starts asking questions in rapid fire while we feel her up.

"What size are these? What kind did you get? How come you don't have any scars?"

"They're saline. And they're four hundred cc which took me from an *A* to a small *D*. And I don't have any scars because they did it through my belly button. Josh didn't want me having sc—"

"Well, this is definitely one way to celebrate our last concert," Storm utters.

Shit. We were so invested in our conversation, none of us heard the door open.

Chandler stops moving and his face takes on a tomato color.

"It's nothing we all haven't seen before," Memphis sneers as Skylar scrambles to put her clothes on.

"Some a lot more than others," Phoenix retorts, which causes my stomach to do a weird flip.

I look at Skylar, who's slipping her shirt over her head. It's none of my business and I'd have no right to be mad if her and Phoenix hooked up in the past. I'd just like to know.

Which is stupid because tomorrow will be my last full day here and after that, Phoenix and I are done for good.

As if sensing my internal struggle, Skylar mouths, 'Never. Promise.'

Coming up behind me, Phoenix locks his arms around my waist. "What's the matter, Groupie?"

"Nothing."

"*Something,*" he teases before his lips graze the side of my neck. "I wasn't referring to myself when I made that comment. I was just trying to piss off a certain guitar player."

Memphis—who's walking over to the small bar in the corner despite already having a beer in his hand—flips him off.

"Looks like it worked."

His laugh is a low rumble in my ear. "Everyone has a weakness."

No argument here.

"How much merch would I have to sell in order to afford breast implants?" Quinn asks Chandler.

I feel Phoenix's entire body tense. "I'm gonna kill Skylar."

"How the hell should I know?" Chandler snaps. "Do I look like I have a pair?"

Skylar shoots Phoenix an apologetic look before turning to Quinn. "You don't need them, baby girl. Trust me, you're good."

"Real tits are better anyway," Memphis grunts as he pours himself a glass of whiskey. "No one likes a fake bitch."

Wow. I'm about to lay into him, but I don't have to.

"Then I guess you don't like your baby mama very much." Skylar's red stilettos click against the floor as she heads for the exit… and then they stop. "Also, I love my fake tits…and last I checked, so did *you*."

My mouth hangs open for two reasons. One, the obvious: Go Skylar. And two: aside from that brief conversation on the bus, I've never once heard either of them acknowledge there was anything between them.

It's like a big family secret that everyone knows about, but no one ever talks about.

Memphis brings the glass to his lips. "Things change. So do people."

Skylar turns to face him. "Well, I hope you enjoyed the show, because it's the last time you'll see them."

No one says a word, because it's clear Skylar just got the last one.

Until Memphis speaks.

"You were wrong before, Sky." The corner of his mouth crooks up and the look he gives her is so cold it chills me to the bone. "Gwen isn't my baby mama. She's my soon-to-be fiancée."

My heart catapults to the floor, and I feel like the worst friend in the world.

Given I didn't hear anything about Memphis and Gwyneth getting married after Quinn told me about the convo she overheard, I figured he came to his senses and it was no longer a thing.

Therefore, I didn't tell Skylar.

I really wish I had, because even though she tries to play it cool, pain splashes across her face before she walks out.

"Have another drink, motherfucker," Storm grumbles as Chandler chases after her.

Memphis downs the liquid in his glass. "Shut the fuck up."

"Why don't *you* shut the fuck up?" I blurt before I can stop myself. "You insulted her for no reason, not once, but twice. For someone who's having a baby and getting ready to propose, you seem awfully fixated on another woman."

Memphis looks past me at Phoenix. "You better control your girl."

Phoenix moves in front of me. "You better take her advice. Or the only thing I'll be controlling is the way my fist rocks your jaw."

I nearly jump out of my skin when Memphis launches his glass at the wall and it shatters. "Fuck this. I'm out."

"Awesome way to celebrate the last show, guys," Storm mutters as Memphis leaves.

A ball of anxiety lodges in my esophagus. "He didn't mean he was out of the band, right?"

Phoenix and Storm exchange a look. "Nah. He's just dealing with some shit."

So is *my* friend.

"I'm gonna go check on Skylar."

"I'm coming with," Quinn says.

Leaning down, Phoenix gives me a quick kiss. "Don't take too long. We have to be up early tomorrow."

That's...strange. "Why?"

"Come on. Let's go." Quinn yanks my arm so hard she nearly rips it out of the socket. "I need the tea."

CHAPTER 67
LENNON

Everything hurts and I'm dying.

Something digs into my back, only it's not *the* something I've come to look forward to in the mornings.

It feels like…a foot.

My mind spins as the events of last night come rushing back to me in one big blur.

Skylar told me she'd forgive me for not divulging what Quinn overheard if I went back to her hotel room and got drunk with her.

So, I did.

Quinn naturally wanted to join us, even though she didn't drink.

I think. I *hope*.

One thing led to another and our bay breezes soon turned into tequila. *Lots* of tequila.

I vaguely remember Phoenix coming in to check on us.

Then Storm showed up shortly after…because Phoenix needed backup.

And then at some point Chandler came in and started yelling at us…which really upset me.

Oh god.

I'm pretty positive I told him that his dick wasn't big enough for his attitude.

I crack an eye open, but immediately close it because the blinds aren't shut and holy hell, it's way too bright.

Probably because Skylar was flashing the people of New York her tits from the window…while I was mooning them right alongside her.

My brain pounds against my skull as I remember what happened next.

I told—or rather *demanded*—Phoenix do anal.

Given my ass is still intact, I think it's safe to say he didn't take me up on it.

After that, things are super fuzzy, but I do remember Quinn—the responsible one, bless her—ordering us pizza and putting us to bed.

Although I'm not quite sure which one I ended up in.

"Morning, party animal."

I pry my eyelids open at the sound of Phoenix's voice.

He's standing over me with a cup of coffee in his hand.

Pushing up on my elbows, I peer down.

Yup, definitely a foot poking my side. Quinn's foot.

I try to sit up fully, but I can't because Skylar's arms are locked around me…like I'm her personal teddy bear.

I have no idea how the three of us slept tangled up like this in one bed.

I glance around the room. A big body is lying on the floor…it takes me a second to realize it's Storm.

"You guys slept on the floor?"

My voice comes out ten times raspier than usual.

Phoenix snorts. "I wouldn't exactly call it *sleeping*." He glances at his watch. "Think you can be showered and ready in the next thirty minutes?"

Ugh. That's a tall order.

"Ready for what?"

My flight isn't until ten a.m. tomorrow and the final concert was last night. Which means I have the whole day to recover. Thank the Lord.

A slow, sexy smile unfurls. "Ready for our date."

Say what now?

I sweep my gaze over him. He's dressed in a pair of jeans and a crisp black T-shirt that does spectacular things to his veiny arms.

Unlike me, he's also freshly showered and shaved.

I blink up in confusion. "Date? What kind of date?"

"The one I'm taking you on." He peers at his watch again. "We were supposed to leave for brunch two hours ago, but we can still do the other thing I had planned."

I must still be drunk because Phoenix doesn't do brunch, plan, or *date*.

"Fine. But only because you brought me caffeine."

Stretching, I try to reach for the coffee cup, but freaking Skylar and her octopus tentacles are holding me hostage.

There's an impish glint in his eye. "I got this."

He walks to the door, and a moment later Chandler strolls inside...with a megaphone.

"Everybody get the fuck up. We leave for Europe in three hours."

Wait...what? I didn't think they'd be leaving until tomorrow.

Evidently our *date* will be a very short one.

Skylar springs up like a jack-in-the-box. "I'm up." Seconds later, she slinks down, clutching her head. "I take that back."

Quinn rolls over...a little too much though, because she falls on the floor with a loud thud. "Ouch. My perineum."

I have no idea how she managed to hurt *that*.

"Fucking hell," Storm mutters. "I hate you people."

Digging in his pocket, Chandler pulls out a bottle of aspirin and hands it to Skylar. "Figured you might need this."

And here I thought Chandler didn't have a considerate bone in his body.

"You're an angel." She grabs the coffee Phoenix was attempting to hand me. "Don't ever let anyone tell you any different."

Clearly, Skylar's still intoxicated.

After she pops her aspirin, I snatch the cup back.

And carefully guard it because Skylar, Quinn, and Storm are eyeing me like they're hungry vampires and I have a paper cut.

"Get your own," I grumble before taking a lengthy sip.

"Twenty-five minutes," Phoenix grits through his teeth while looking at his watch.

My, how the tables have turned.

I climb off the bed. "I'm going."

Never in a million years did I think Phoenix would be the one babysitting *me*.

"Where are we going?" I question as we trek through the streets of New York City. "And why are they with us?"

By *they* I'm referring to the massive guy walking ahead of me and the two following close behind.

Phoenix hates having security, so having them come along for our date is a bit peculiar.

He pushes his black aviators up his nose. "I wanted additional safety measures in place."

That's *alarming*. "Why? Where exactly are you taking me?"

I nearly ram into a woman passing us. Her eyes widen when she sees Phoenix, but then she shakes her head, as if telling herself there's no way it's actually him.

He's wearing a dark sweatshirt—with the hood drawn up—in the middle of freaking August so he has to be sweating his ass off.

"You'll find out when we get there."

I don't like the sound of that one bit. "Just so you're aware, I hate surprises."

I'm not saying that to get him to spill the details, either. I truly despise them. I'm a planner and the idea of having to deal with any curveballs or bombshells puts me on edge.

I can probably thank *him* for that.

Phoenix simply smirks.

"Fine. You don't have to tell me where we're going, but can you at least tell me why you suddenly felt the need for *additional safety measures*?"

He keeps his focus ahead, his expression indecipherable. "For you."

Those words have my stomach twisting. "For me? Why?"

"The pictures only came out six days ago. It hasn't fully hit you yet since you're still in my bubble, but we're everywhere. Hell, we're even trending on Twitter...along with Memphis and Gwyneth fucking Barclay." The muscles in his face tighten. "Most of our fans are cool, but some are batshit. I can't take the chance that one of them would hurt you."

As much as I hate to admit it, he has a point. While I'm well aware of the photos being splashed everywhere, they haven't really impacted my life because the people I associate with daily are either famous or members of the crew.

It's going to be different when I'm back in the *real world* again.

Just yesterday, Mrs. Palma told me three reporters showed up at the house asking to speak with me.

I open my mouth to tell him thank you, but his next words send me reeling. "Which is exactly why they'll be escorting you wherever you go after you're back home."

Hold. The. Phone.

"No, they won't. I don't need bodyguards tracking my every move."

"Relax. It will only be for a month..." A hint of a smile teases his lips. "For now."

I glare at him. "No."

A weird thought occurs to me then. While I do believe Phoenix's intentions are good, I also can't help but wonder if this is his sick way of keeping tabs on me.

Which will only make it harder for us to sever ties.

"I don't want your security following me around."

Amusement flickers across his face. "It's cute how you think you have a say in this."

I bump into another woman on the street…only this time she promptly snaps a picture with her phone.

Awesome.

In a flash, she rushes toward us while calling out Phoenix's name, which draws *lots* of attention.

"Shit." He moves in front of me. "I knew we should have driven."

Nerves creep in as more people gather around us. "Why didn't we?"

"Because *someone* had a hangover which set us back several hours. And it's quicker to walk than drive in the city." I don't miss the irritability in his tone, despite using his body to shield me from the flock of women trying to close in with outstretched hands… reaching for him.

The bodyguards quickly usher us into a nearby building.

"One week," I concede as we wait for the small crowd outside the deli we were shoved inside to wane. "That's it."

Eventually this will all die down and I'll be old news. I just have to ride it out for a bit.

Phoenix thanks the staff for letting us take cover and quickly poses for some photos.

"There's an exit out back," one of the bodyguards tells us.

Phoenix finishes scribbling his signature on the wall—via the owner's request—and takes my hand. "Let's go."

After slipping out the rear door, we walk down some alley until we have no choice but to return to the main street.

Reaching into the pocket of his hoodie, Phoenix takes out an extra pair of sunglasses and hands them to me. "Put these on."

I do without protest, even though we're back to being inconspicuous people again.

A few minutes later, his steps come to a halt, and he looks up. "We're here."

I glance around and my stare snags on a street sign that says *Central Park West.* "Central Park?"

I've never been here before, so I'm excited.

That excitement fades, though, when Phoenix shakes his head. "Nope."

Lacing our fingers again, he leads me to some Victorian Gothic-looking building.

Don't get me wrong, it's a beautiful piece of architecture—in a mysterious and haunting kind of way—but I have no idea why he brought me here.

Maybe it's a museum or an art gallery?

Dear God, please don't be another World War II exhibit. I came dangerously close to falling asleep at the one George took me to on our date.

I'm even more baffled when Phoenix stops in front of a gate under an archway. I also notice another sign. *Authorized Personnel Only Beyond This Point.*

And an angry-looking doorman.

"No loitering."

Given I don't want to spend the rest of my afternoon in a jail cell, I tug on his hand. "Let's go."

Phoenix juts his chin at one of the security guards who walks over to the doorman and whispers something in his ear...then he slips him some cash.

The guy looks a lot friendlier after that.

"Ten minutes," he tells Phoenix. "But I'm not allowed to let you go inside. You'd have to obtain special permission for that, and it's above my pay grade."

"It's cool," Phoenix says. "I appreciate it."

Okay, this is just getting weird now. I have no idea why we're standing outside of what appears to be the entrance to whatever building this is.

"Where are we?"

"This is The Dakota." His lips part on an inhale. "It's the place—"

"John Lennon was killed," I finish for him as a spike of uneasiness flows through me.

My father told me he came here once, and it was so upsetting for him he shed a tear and vowed never to return.

I can understand why.

"*This* is your idea of a date?" I point to myself. "You realize I'm Lennon, right? Why on earth would you take me to the place in which the person I was named after was shot to death?"

Phoenix really didn't think this one through. Or maybe he did… the asshole.

His lips turn down and his brows pull in, as if *he's* the insulted party here. "This isn't just the place he died. It's also the place where he *lived* and *created*."

My uneasiness turns to horror when I realize we're standing right where the horrible event happened.

I drop my voice so as not to draw attention to us or the conversation we're having. "He was murdered right here. What the hell is the matter with you?"

His jaw flexes, and even with his sunglasses on, I can feel his glare. "This is the main fucking entrance, Len—*Groupie*. We can't go beyond this point." Visibly rattled, he waves a hand in the direction of the doorman. "Right?"

Pity flashes in the man's eyes and he gives him an affirmative nod. "Yes, sir."

His face falls. "I've never done this dating shit before. But, hey, fuck me, right?"

A laugh bubbles out of me before I can stop it. He's so endearing right now, it trumps my frustration.

As *eerie* as this date of ours is, it's obvious he put a lot of thought into it.

It's also something I'll never forget…so there's that.

Phoenix scowls. "And now you're laughing." Removing his glasses, he drags a hand down his face. "Christ. Let's g—"

He doesn't get to finish that sentence because I rise on my tiptoes, grip his shirt, and kiss him. Taking him—and me—by surprise.

My pulse races as his tongue teases and coaxes mine. Cupping my face, he tilts his head and kisses me deeper. All I can feel is the thud of my heart against my ribs as I lose myself in this moment. In *him*.

Evidently a little too long, though, because the doorman clears his throat. "Your ten minutes are up."

"We need another ten," Phoenix murmurs against my lips before backing me into one side of the archway.

He's like quicksand, pulling me under and I'm helpless to stop it.

Ten minutes later, there's another throat clear. "Okay, sir. You really have to go now. Some of the residents are beginning to complain."

My cheeks flush with embarrassment as we break apart. "Sorry."

My eyes swivel around, taking everything in.

"We need another minute," Phoenix says behind me.

A weight filled with longing settles in my chest. It's been so long since I've written.

Since I've *created*.

So long I probably lost the ability to do it even though my mind and soul yearn for that outlet.

I miss it so much it hurts.

Like a phantom pain from losing one of your limbs.

My heart beats slower—*weaker*—as though it were slipping away.

I peer down at the ground. *Like dying.*

Phoenix stands in front of me...eclipsing me.

Just like he always does.

"We can't stay any longer. Not unless I buy an apartment here."

I hike my purse up my shoulder. "Where to now?"

Slipping his shades back on, he points to a nearby hot dog stand. "Food." His throat dips. "Then the airport."

My heart beats even slower and my next breath is a struggle. "Oh."

This is it.

He holds out his hand, and I take it.

"I thought you weren't leaving for Europe until tomorrow?" I utter as we walk over to the stand.

It's nuts that they're already starting another tour so soon.

"What do you like on your hot dog?"

"Ketchup, mustard...and sauerkraut."

His lips quirk. "Same."

He quickly rattles off our order and gives the guy some cash.

"I thought you weren't leaving for Europe until tomorrow?" I repeat as he hands me my hot dog.

Phoenix takes a massive bite…dodging the question for a second time.

I'm about to chew him out for not answering, but then I realize there might be a reason for it.

Like some beautiful European model.

Nonetheless, his whereabouts are no longer my responsibility.

It's time to sever the ties.

Bringing the hot dog to my lips, I take a bite.

Phoenix stills, watching me. His eyes are obstructed by his shades, but I'd be willing to bet all the money I'm going to make from this tour that they're clouded with lust because he's picturing me blowing him.

"You're such a perv."

He gives me a knowing grin. "Not my fault you give great head."

I nudge him in the ribs because the security guards are standing less than five feet away and they most definitely heard him. I know this because the third guy's ears are turning pink.

Phoenix starts to respond, but a black SUV pulls up.

It suddenly occurs to me that even though I'm saying goodbye to him, I never got a chance to say my farewells to everyone else.

"Can I go with you to the airport?" Realizing how clingy that sounds, I add, "I want to say bye to Skylar, Quinn, and Storm."

I don't know what to make of the expression on his face as he polishes off the rest of his hot dog. "Let's go."

I'm silent during the whole ride there, which is weird because I'm usually chastising him for being the quiet one.

I'm just afraid if I start talking I might spill things I'm better off keeping to myself.

Like how I hate that we didn't have sex last night…because it means our last time was yesterday morning, while Quinn was relentlessly pounding on the connecting door because she was hungry.

While it was good—because it *always* is—it was quick and disruptive.

And I didn't know it would be the final time.

Bile hits the back of my throat.

Kind of like how I didn't know when I walked into Voodoo that night my heart would be obliterated.

Closing my eyes, I focus on the music coming through the speakers.

It's upbeat, cheery pop. The fact Phoenix hasn't requested for it to be changed tells me he's just as lost in his thoughts as I am.

Memories break through the surface...both good and bad.

Now that it's over, all the abhorrence I've harbored for him should be back with a vengeance.

But the moment we pull into the airport, all I can think is that even though I hate what he did...

I can't bring myself to hate him.

"Phoenix?"

He peels his focus from the window. "Yeah?"

Since these are going to be my very last words to him, I want to make them count.

Even though they might not make any sense to him.

"You do have a gift," I whisper. "You're the sun." My throat goes tight and a range of emotions swell within me. "So, you never needed anyone else in order to shine."

Those blue depths hold my gaze.

He doesn't utter a single word and neither do I...but we don't have to.

Because no one knows the other better than we do.

And right now, we're both hurting because neither of us will get what we want.

He wants forgiveness.

But there's no way I can give him that because what he did destroyed parts of me I can't get back.

I want to forget him.

But there's no way I can because he's still in my veins...all the ones leading to the organ in my chest.

The war is finally over, but there's no winner.

We'll both suffer until we eventually move on with other people...because it's the only option we have.

The SUV cruises down the runway until it comes to a stop in front of a private jet...and the group I've spent the last eight weeks of my life with.

A bittersweet feeling erupts inside me as I get out of the car.

I came here for money and to make their lead singer pay, but I'm leaving with a block of sadness inside my chest because I'm truly going to miss every single one of them.

Memphis is the first to hug me. "Sorry about last night."

I don't like that he hurled insults at my friend, but I know underneath those cruel words was a lot of pain.

"Take care of yourself, okay?"

"I'll do my best," he drawls with a smile.

Storm is the next to hug me...which is shocking because Storm doesn't hug. "Don't be a stranger."

Sadly, I'll have to be.

"I mean it," he tells me as we break apart. "If you need anything, give me a call."

My vision becomes glassy, so I deflect with humor. "Look at you being Mr. Softy."

He snorts.

"Yeah, but once you point it out, he turns into an asshole again," Quinn says behind me.

The second I spin around, she ambushes me with a hug so tight it knocks the wind out of me. "Don't leave."

Jesus. This kid is going to kill me.

I wipe the tears from her eyes. "You're one of a kind, Quinn. Don't ever change." Leaning down, I whisper the same words Storm just told me. "If you ever need anything, please reach out to me."

She's the one person I'll break my no-contact-with-Phoenix rule for if necessary.

She sniffles. "Okay."

The moment Skylar and I hug is when the tears break free...for both of us.

"Tell me we'll still be friends," she chokes out.

I hug her tighter. "Always."

I can't imagine not having her in my life.

As long as she doesn't bring certain parts of hers into mine whenever we catch up.

But I know she won't, because she understands.

I press my forehead to hers. "You'll get through this."

It's going to hurt like hell, but she's far tougher than she realizes. And a man who no longer wants her isn't one who deserves her.

"Not this Ya-Ya Sisterhood shit again," Chandler mutters beside us.

Ugh. Might as well get this over with.

"It's been real, Chandler."

Real fucking exasperating.

"It certainly has." He pulls an envelope out of his jacket pocket. "This is a check for my half. Vic will be sending his to you sometime this week...since I gave him a good report and all." His eyes narrow. "You're welcome, by the way."

I pluck the envelope out of his hand. "It's not going to bounce, is it?"

"You'll find out soon enough, won't you?"

Swear to God if it does, I will fly my ass to Europe and rip out his spinal cord with my teeth.

I hold out my hand. "Bye, Dicky."

He shakes it. "Bye, Yoko."

It's on the tip of my tongue to point out that Yoko never left John.

Because even though their love story ended up a tragedy...John never would have betrayed her like Phoenix betrayed me.

He chose her over everything.

I try to ignore the agony cramming my chest as I face him.

He'll always be my hardest goodbye.

"At least we're parting on better terms this time around, right?"

Expression impassive, he stays silent.

I didn't expect a sonnet from him or anything, but I figured we'd share one last hug and a few parting words.

"Takeoff is in three minutes," Chandler announces, and everyone loads onto the plane.

With the exception of Phoenix, who's still staring at me...not saying a word.

It's really starting to piss me off.

"Seriously? You're not even going to say goodby—"

His lips crash against mine and he gives me a kiss that makes my head light and my knees weak.

On second thought, maybe goodbye was a bad idea. My drug just gave me another hit...which will make the withdrawals that much harder.

"Bye—" My words fall by the wayside when I notice the plane moving in my peripheral.

Without Phoenix.

Waving my arms, I run toward it, attempting to stop it before it takes off. "Wait! You're missing someone!" Anxiety rises up my esophagus. "Call Chandler...or the plane company people. They're leaving without you."

How the hell could anyone forget Phoenix?

I sure as hell can't.

Peeling my gaze away from the rolling jet, I look at him. Unlike me, Phoenix isn't freaking out.

Quite the contrary. He seems highly amused by the whole thing.

Then again, he's been acting strange all day.

"What is *wrong* with you? You don't even say goodbye to me. Then your freaking plane takes off without you and you're *smiling*. What—"

"I didn't say goodbye because it's not goodbye yet." He moves closer. "And I'm not worried about the plane taking off because it's not my plane." He points to another jet that's a little farther down the runway. "That's my plane. Or should I say, *our* plane."

Once again, I'm beyond confused. "What are you talking about? What do you mean, that's our plane? Plane to where?"

I already told him I can't go to Europe, and he's well aware that after today we're done for good.

"Our date isn't over yet." Reaching for my hand, he begins escorting—or rather, dragging me—to the aircraft. "You told me six days, five days ago, which means I get you until tomorrow. And believe me, I'm cashing in on every fucking second."

I plant my feet and yank my arm away because he's insane. Plus, I have no idea where he's even taking me, but given it involves a damn plane, I assume it's not close.

"My flight home departs from JFK tomorrow morning, which is in New York. Plus, my luggage is still at the hotel."

"I had Skylar book you a new flight. One that leaves from LAX tomorrow. I also had her pack your suitcase, which is already on the plane." His fingers tighten around my wrist and he starts tugging. "Problem solved."

Hardly.

"First of all, why are we going to California? Secondly, why didn't you tell me any of this? We spent the entire afternoon together."

"I didn't tell you because I wanted it to be a surprise, but I also didn't want to lie to you." He shrugs. "I had no choice but to ignore you."

I don't even know what to say to that.

I plant my feet for a second time when we reach the plane steps.

I already mentally prepared myself to say goodbye before, but now I'll have to do it all over again tomorrow.

Maybe it's best we go our separate ways now.

"Come on, Groupie." He cradles my face, his eyes imploring me to extend our time. "Spend one last night with me."

"Where?"

"My house."

His house.

The tour consisted of nights spent in either a hotel room or a bus. It helped maintain a clear distinction between tour world and real world. It also made things easier because every place we went was temporary.

Like us.

Going to his home makes things deeper…more personal.

The tie that much tougher to sever.

However, the pull of the sun is too mesmerizing. Too powerful.

"Okay," I whisper. "One more night…but that's it."

CHAPTER 68
LENNON

I ended up sleeping for half the duration of the six-hour plane ride…after joining the mile-high club.

Fortunately, California is three hours behind New York, so we didn't lose all that time.

My eyes widen when the driver turns into a gated community with very beautiful and very *large* houses.

"Didn't think this was your style."

If I offended Phoenix with my comment, he doesn't show it. "Me either. But when you grow up having nothing…"

"You want everything," I finish for him.

I'm torn because on one hand, I'm happy for him.

But on the other? I can't help thinking about what he did to get his *everything*.

Falling silent, I look out the window at the sunset. It's vivid and beautiful, especially among the backdrop of all these stunning properties.

We turn down a quiet street and continue past a row of houses, each one bigger than the last, until we come to a stop in front of a two-story farmhouse-style villa with a big palm tree in the front.

The driver pulls the SUV up far enough so Phoenix can punch

the security code in. A moment later, the gate opens, and we pull up a large circular driveway.

After Phoenix opens the front door, he places our suitcases in the large foyer.

"Come on." Taking my hand, he leads me toward the living room. "I'll give you a tour."

On the outside, it looks light and cheerful, but on the inside, it's darker.

Not in a depressing way, but in an intense way.

A very *Phoenix* way.

The color scheme consists of black and gray...with accents of white here and there. The twelve-foot ceilings make the already large house feel even more spacious.

I'm speechless as I take everything in.

The formal dining room with a long black table that looks like it's never been used.

The expansive gray and white gourmet kitchen that makes me want to whip up a twelve-course meal.

The outdoor patio leading to an in-ground pool.

I have no doubt Quinn will love this place, but knowing her, she'll want to add some brightness...or at least pull up the black blinds obscuring all the windows.

Phoenix guides me down a hall, pointing out a bathroom and a movie room along the way. However, when I head for the door at the very end, he gently steers me away. "Let me show you the upstairs."

I don't press the issue since I'm a guest in his home and he's entitled to his privacy.

"Storm and I share it," he informs me as we trek up the wooden staircase leading to the second floor of the house.

That makes sense. This place is beautiful, but it would be awfully lonely living here all by yourself.

He points out another bathroom and two guest bedrooms—one of which will be Quinn's. Knowing her, she'll take the one with a bigger closet.

His steps falter as we reach the door at the end of the hall. "Storm and I flipped a coin for the master suite." His grin is cocky as he turns the knob. "Guess who won?"

I'm about to remind him no one likes a bragger, but my brain goes on the fritz when we enter.

A California king bed with black silk sheets and a leather headboard sits in the middle of the room, facing a large flat-screen television that's mounted to the ceiling. There's a walk-in closet, and a luxurious bathroom attached. However, it's the panoramic view of the Hollywood Hills from the wrap around windows that makes this room go from beautiful to *holy crap.*

"Wow."

That's all I can manage.

Waking up and falling asleep to *that* view every day must be quite the experience.

I'm not sure I'd ever leave.

His gravelly timbre reverberates inside me as he locks his arms around my waist and presses a kiss to the crook of my neck. "You like it?"

"It's stunning. This place feels nothing like you and exactly like you at the same time."

Warmth unfurls when one of his hands slides down, cupping me through my leggings. "I want to fuck you against this window."

I'm assuming that's what we're about to do—especially since it's the reason I'm here—but he removes his hand. "And I will…later." He swats my ass. "Come on. Our date isn't over yet."

I can't imagine what else he'd have planned after all this.

"What's next?" I joke as I follow him back down the stairs. "Dinner on the Eiffel Tower? Perhaps a helicopter ride?"

His lips twitch as we cut through the house. "Even better."

"A tour of your cars?" I question as he leads me to a solitary door on the opposite end of the house.

"Nah. My car's in the other one."

My heart slams against my chest as we enter a garage. Immediately, I'm transported back in time because it's set up identically to the one at Gram's house. Old instruments included.

"I can't believe you kept everything."

"It's where we started."

I assumed he meant him and Storm. However, he's looking directly at *me* when he says it.

My heart thumps heavy and my stomach churns as he walks over to the futon.

"I racked my brain for the past four weeks, trying to figure out what a perfect date for Lennon Michael would entail. I thought about dinner at a fancy restaurant or hiring a world-renowned chef to come cook for us." He exhales sharply. "But that's not your style."

He's right. I don't need fancy dinners or chefs.

I just need honesty.

Someone who wouldn't steal from and hurt me.

Plopping down on the couch, he gestures to the upside-down crate with what appears to be two fast-food burgers wrapped in foil on it.

The room spins and my chest feels like it's caving in. This is what we were doing right before I sang him my song for the first time.

It's like he intentionally replicated that day.

Like he's trying to go back.

"Because perfect to you is this...how it was between us before everything changed." His voice drops to a raw rasp. "It's who I was...not who I became."

He's right.

My fascination with him developed the first moment I saw him, but I fell in love with Phoenix Walker in this garage.

And that Phoenix is the one my heart will always belong to.

The heart in question constricts to the point of pain, and my feet stay rooted to the spot.

I've always wished I could press rewind on that day...but only so I could make a different decision.

Not so I could relive it.

"I'm not the same person either."

"I know." His tempestuous stare locks on me. "Just like I know how our story ends." The groove in his forehead deepens, and he averts his gaze, like he can't look at me when he says his next words. "It ends with you hopping on a plane tomorrow morning with no intention of ever seeing me again." He drops his head. "I just want a few hours where I'm not the villain in it."

He lifts his gaze to mine and something unspoken passes between us.

"Okay."

He begins unwrapping our burgers as I sit down next to him. "I asked my housekeeper to pick these up from one of my favorite places in LA. They're really good."

They smell and look amazing.

I'm about to dig in, but a morbid thought occurs to me. "I know the instruments are the same and stuff, but this isn't *the* futon, right?"

He takes a big bite of his burger…avoiding the question.

Narrowing my eyes, I reach for the Styrofoam cup of soda at my feet. "You can't use that tactic twice in one day, Walker. Answer the question."

His words come out muffled due to his mouth being stuffed. "I plead the fifth."

I poke him in the ribs. "Phoenix."

He strokes his thumb along his bottom lip before licking ketchup off it. "It is." He laughs at my horrified expression. "You asked."

Disgusted, I shake my head. Sure, I threw the sheets out and I was beyond grateful to discover that the mattress underneath was black, but it's still gross.

"I…it looked like a murder scene." I take a bite of my burger as another thought occurs to me. "Poor Storm. He's been unknowingly sitting on a mattress full of my…hymen." Bringing the straw to my mouth, I take a sip of my soda. "You're a terrible friend."

Phoenix laughs. "Relax. I washed it later that night." His expression turns sheepish. "And Storm knows."

That's news to me. "What do you mean, he knows?"

His tongue finds his cheek. "You left the sheet in his garbage can, and Grams made him take out the trash every night before he went to bed. Plus, he walked in on us during…" He shrugs. "It wasn't all that hard for him to put two and two together and figure out that I popped your cherry that night."

"Half popped," I maintain. "Sex doesn't count unless you finish."

A smirk plays on his lips. "That's not how it works, sweetheart."

I stop eating. "Okay, first, don't *sweetheart* me. Ever. Secondly, I don't make the rules, so don't get mad at me."

He reaches for a napkin. "Who made these rules then, huh? Because I'd like to put in a complaint and request a revision."

Damn him. He looks so genuinely upset it's adorable.

I'm sticking to my guns, though.

"Wow. For someone who had their own *rule* about not screwing virgins, you seem to really want to take credit for the job."

"Damn right. And the sooner you admit it, the sooner we can put this argument to bed for good."

Nope. I refuse to let him win. "I lost my virginity to you and Doug Goldstein at the end of my freshman year at Dartmouth. You both share the title."

His nostrils flare and his jaw hardens. "I don't share, Lennon. Not when it comes to you. This Doug Goldstein douchebag can go fuck himself. He doesn't get to take credit for something *I* did."

Sucks, doesn't it.

"I—"

"You told me you didn't regret it," he says gruffly, his features going slack. "It was the very last thing you said to me…before I fucked everything up."

I should tell him that's no longer true, but then I'd be lying.

Despite what happened after, at that moment I wanted to give it to Phoenix, and nothing will ever change that. Not even my stubbornness.

"Technically, I didn't finish with Doug, either." I tuck a piece of hair behind my ear. "Fine. Virginity, yes. Girlfriend, no. Happy?"

Phoenix watches me carefully, so much so I'm beginning to think there's sauce on my face.

"Do you ever think about what would have happened with us if I didn't fuck everything up?"

A sharp wave of pain impales me. I've thought about it more times than I care to admit, but I won't give him the satisfaction of knowing that.

"No."

He looks taken aback by this. Sighing, he pushes his half-eaten burger away. "I think about it all the time." His eyes cut to mine. "We'd still be together."

He says it like it's an indisputable fact.

But as much as I'd like to believe that, there's this little thing called reality...and even if he hadn't stolen my song, we never would have worked out.

No matter how much I loved him.

"Fine. Let's play pretend." Grabbing a napkin, I wipe my hands. "You really wanna know what would have happened if you pursued things with me?"

He nods.

"You would have visited me at Dartmouth once or twice and I would have fallen even more in love with you..." My chest collapses as I continue. "But then we would have grown apart as you rose to stardom, the phone calls would become less and less frequent...and then I would have found out that you cheated on me with some gorgeous girl."

Outrage illuminates his face. "Never."

Denial isn't just a river in Egypt. "You say that now—"

"I say that *always*," he snaps, his tone harsh and his eyes sharp.

If I didn't know better, I'd believe him. Wholeheartedly.

"You're a rock star. You have millions of girls ready and more than willing to let you do whatever you want to them on the daily. Maybe not right away, but at some point you'd cave." I get off the futon. "Which is why I don't let myself think about *what if*. Because whether or not you stole my song you still would have obliterated me in the end. Only, the method you ended up choosing was exceptionally brutal. Thanks for that."

"Lennon—"

"Just *stop*. Stop lying to yourself. And for fuck's sake, stop lying to me." I sweep a hand around. "Trying to recreate how it used to be for our date was sweet, but it doesn't change what happened between us. You might have gone to my school once because your guilt led you there, but you sure as hell didn't cry yourself to sleep thinking about me like I did for *years* whenever I thought about you."

I walk to the door, so I don't break down in front of him. "You might be sad for a couple days after I leave, but your heart won't break like mine did when *you* left. Because you never loved me."

And that's the cold, hard reality of it.

Phoenix Walker doesn't love me. Not in the past, not now, not even in a pretend world.

Because if he did?

I'd be able to forgive him.

CHAPTER 69
LENNON

I force myself to breathe through the pain as I wait for the tears to subside.

Phoenix must have realized he pushed me past my breaking point because he hasn't knocked on the door once in the ten minutes I've been holed up in his bathroom.

Maybe he thinks I left.

Maybe I should.

I still have a credit card that hasn't been maxed out yet, so I could call an Uber and crash at a hotel for the night.

Wiping my puffy eyes and mascara streaks with a tissue, I peer at myself in the mirror.

Get it together.

I inhale a few more cleansing breaths, feeling much better now that I have a plan of action.

The only reason I'm still in his atmosphere is because I'm choosing to be.

As of right now, there's no longer anything holding me hostage aside from my dumb heart.

I need to get out while I still can.

Because my walls aren't nearly as strong or as high as they used to be.

As they *need* to be.

Squaring my shoulders, I turn the knob and exit the bathroom, relieved he's nowhere to be found.

It will make my escape that much easier.

The wood floor creaks under my shoes as I close the door behind me and my gaze drifts to the top-secret room he steered me away from before.

Stubbornness has always been my worst quality, but curiosity comes in a close second.

Whatever's in that room is none of my business. I *know* this.

But the longer I stare at it, the stronger the urge to pry becomes.

What other secrets is he keeping?

Skylar once told me that all girls are detectives, and I'd have to unequivocally agree.

However, if a tree falls in the forest and no one is around to hear it, does it make a sound?

And if someone betrays you and they're not around to see you snoop, does it give you the right to?

Of course not. Two wrongs don't make a right...but I can take it up with my conscience later.

I glance around the hall a final time to make sure I'm in the clear before creeping toward the room.

Given it isn't locked, there must not be a whole lot of skeletons hiding in here.

A twinge of disappointment twists my chest as I push open the door.

The expensive black baby grand piano in the corner is gorgeous, but hardly something to keep a secret.

Talk about a bust.

I'm about to walk out and grab my things, but my stare locks on the pile of papers scattered on top of the piano.

Was he writing something?

Songs?

Anger rises and boils like a cauldron inside me.

Maybe I should pilfer one of his and see how *he* likes it.

A sickening feeling crawls up my spine, incapacitating me.

Phoenix knows I wrote all my songs in a notebook, and I brought that thing with me everywhere.

Seeing as he already stole one of them, who's to say he didn't sneak a peek at it while I was in the bathroom one day?

Marching over, I mentally prepare myself to have my heart annihilated once more...only these aren't songs.

They're words. Specifically, letters. Handwritten ones.

Addressed to me.

His penmanship isn't the neatest, and he spells a lot of words wrong, but I can still make out what he's written.

Lennon,
It's been two weeks since I last saw you.
Two weeks since I betrayed you.
Two weeks since I fucking lost you.
I should be happy. We're in negotiations with Vic Doherty, the other day we met and jammed with Memphis, who's a killer guitarist, and his brother Josh, who plays bass and the four of us sound awesome together.
It's all coming together.
But inside I'm unraveling.
Every time I sing the song I want to puke, because they aren't my words.
They're yours.
Everything I have is yours.
Including the fucked-up thing in my chest.
I don't know how I'm supposed to enjoy any of this without you.

I'm still lying here...
In the mess I made.

Drawing air into my lungs, I quickly turn to the next letter.

Lennon,

It's been a month since I lost you.
I signed a deal with Vic. Me, Storm, Memphis, and Josh are officially Sharp Objects.
Guess what they want the first single to be?
I want to confess everything. Sometimes the urge is so strong I have to dip out and go to the bathroom so I can get my shit together.
I'm pretty sure Vic thinks I'm on drugs.
Hell, maybe I should be.
I want to spill everything, but today Vic told me that even though I have a phenomenal voice and the look he wants—whatever the fuck that means. It was my words—your words—that tipped the needle and made him decide to sign me.
And it's not just my dream on the line anymore. It's Storm's and the other guys.
They come from nothing, just like me. We're all rejects with parents who didn't want us…but we're still alive today because of music.
This is the only shot any of us will ever have, Groupie.
I won't just fuck up my life, I'll fuck up theirs.
I know it doesn't excuse what I did, and I know you'll never forgive me.
I just hope someday you'll no longer hate me.

Because I'm supposed to be the cutter...
But you're the one who cut me.

My throat goes tight as I read another one.

Lennon,
It's been two months since I lost you.
Every night before bed I pick up the phone and dial your number…only to stop myself from calling you at the last second.
We finished recording your song last week, and it sounds great.
It's nothing compared to the way you sing it, though.
Because they're your words. Not mine.

The other night, Vic invited us to a party. He wanted us to socialize and network. There was a girl there.
In the past, she would have been everything I'd want for a night.
But I got up and walked away.
I'm pretty sure Memphis, Josh, and a few other people think I'm gay now.
But if I fucked her, then you'd no longer be the last girl I slept with and right now, at least I still have that.
I want you to call me, but I don't think you will.
Because you think I fucked Sabrina.
But I didn't.
What I did to you is worse.
Jagged and broken
Dull and washed out.
Yeah, sounds about right.

My vision blurs as I pick up the next one.

Lennon,
It's been four months since I lost you.
A couple days ago, the song came out on the radio, YouTube, and, well, everywhere.
I know you heard it.
I also know from this point on there's no going back and what's done can never be undone.
I'm sorry, Groupie.
So fucking sorry.

Everywhere I turn...
I breathe you in and bleed you out.

My tears fall faster as I flip to the next one.

Lennon,
It's been six months since I lost you.
Our album is out, and it's doing really well.
But I can't enjoy it.
The fucking irony. I have everything I've ever wanted…except you.

Fuck the memories I'll never have.
Fuck the pain of your knife.
Fuck these feelings you left me with.

My tears fall so fast they smear the ink on the page.

Lennon,
It's been a year since I lost you.
Your song's been nominated for a Grammy.
Why aren't you calling me?
Fucking call me. Yell at me. Scream at me.
Tell the world what I did.
Tell them I'm a fraud.
Tell them I'm a piece of shit.
Put me out of my goddamn misery before I do it myself.
Fuck you, Lennon.
I stole your words, but you stole my heart.

There's only one letter left. And the sinking feeling in my chest tells me I already know what will be on this page.

Lennon,
   It's been one year, six months, and eleven days since I lost you.
   I couldn't take it anymore, so I got in my car and kept driving.

I drove all the way to Dartmouth so I could see you.

And I did.

With another guy.

You smiled at him, like you used to smile at me.

You kissed him, like you used to kiss me.

I told myself not to pursue you.

I told myself not to get attached to you.

I used to joke that I'd never have a broken heart because that would require me having one of those to begin with and my mom took it with her when she left.

But I think whatever remnants she didn't take belonged to you.

But now those remnants are extinguished.

Jesus fucking Christ.

I thought you didn't call me because you were angry or too scared to confront me or some shit.

But it's because you moved on.

Which means I didn't just lose you temporarily, like I've been telling myself.

I lost you for good.

Guess it's time I move on, too.

This is the last letter I'll write.

The last letter I won't mail.

The last night I'll let myself think about you.

My brain immediately jumps into self-preservation mode, desperately trying to convince me that it doesn't change what he did.

That he could have written these recently and placed them here for me to find.

That I shouldn't trust him.

But the organ inside my chest reminds me that he's been on tour for the past eight weeks, and he had no idea I'd be joining him so there was no way he could have planted these before he left.

Hell, he didn't even want me to come into this room.

This whole time, I convinced myself that Phoenix only thought about me when he sang or heard my song, because he didn't have a choice.

But that's not true. He thought about me a lot.

And he not only felt remorse…he felt pain.

My mind flits back to something Storm told me at the beginning of tour.

"He's been in a bad place and I can't pull him out of it. I thought it was the accident, but looking back, that was just the catalyst. His head's been fucked for a while now, and he's one mistake away from becoming the person he never wanted to be."

"What are you doing?"

His tone isn't aggravated or threatening.

It's jagged and broken.

I turn around, attempting, but failing, to get a handle on my emotions.

Everything I feel is pouring out of me in one big tidal wave. "Why didn't you mail any of the letters?"

If he had mailed even one, it would have changed things. Maybe not everything, but at least I wouldn't have hated him so much.

I would have been open to possibly having a conversation with him at some point.

At least I would have known he cared.

Closing his eyes, he scrubs a hand down his face. "How do you make someone believe you're sorry when you're living your dream because you stole it from them?"

I've never been in that position, so I haven't a clue.

"I don't know." My voice cracks and my heart rises and sinks. "But I don't want to spend our last night like this."

I don't want to think about what he did.

I don't want to think about how much it hurts.

I don't want to think about what his letters mean or how they change things.

I just want him.

I take a step and then several more, until I'm closing the distance between us and peering up at him.

His knuckles brush my jaw as he searches my face. "What do you want?"

Just one thing.

And he's the only one who can do it.

"I want you to burn me."

Raw hunger fills his expression before he grips the nape of my neck and slants his mouth over mine.

His kiss steals the air from my lungs and the strength from my knees.

My nails dig into his biceps as his tongue slides against mine, claiming me, owning me.

Our choppy breathing fills the air as he leads me through the house and up the stairs, kissing me like there's a clock we're racing against and we're running out of time

Because we are.

Before long we reach the bedroom, only instead of tumbling onto the bed, we end up near the window.

I assume Phoenix is going to make good on his promise and fuck me against it like he said he wanted to earlier, but he doesn't.

His mouth moves to my collarbone, and his hands slither inside my leggings, kneading my ass. Sharp teeth graze my skin as he pushes them down while I toe out of my shoes. The moment they reach my ankles, I kick them to the side, nearly tripping in the process, which makes us both laugh...until Phoenix's lips find mine again.

His kiss is softer now, our tongues moving in a languid tempo. Nerves coil in my belly when his fingertips glide along the side of my waist, pushing my shirt up. Instinctively, I place my hand on top of his, halting him. He cups the side of my face with his free hand and his kiss turns even more tender, as if he's imploring me to be vulnerable while also assuring me that I can trust him with my body.

My heart beats like a drum as I break contact and raise my

arms, allowing him. The air between us shifts as he lifts my shirt over my head, the tension between us becoming more charged. *Profound.*

Pulling my bottom lip between his teeth, he unclasps my bra. It slips down my arms before falling to the floor. My fingers find the zipper on his jeans and I tug it down, wanting to see and feel him. However, when I shove my hand inside and wrap it around his erection, he stops me. Frustrated, I pry my mouth from his, but he clamps his hand around my neck, keeping me there while his other hand squeezes my breast.

My nipples are so hard they hurt, and when he pinches one, I cry out, desperate to feel his mouth there.

Making a gruff sound, he dips his head, planting a soft line of kisses down my chest as he drops to his knees. A needy sound escapes me when he plumps my breast in his hand and flicks the taut bud with his tongue, teasing me, before drawing it into his mouth. My panties grow wetter, the fabric sticking to me as he continues his ministrations, giving my other nipple the same attention.

A jolt of electricity shoots through my chest and my blood heats. Every part of me is aching for him.

His mouth descends to my stomach, painting my flesh with his lips and tongue like I'm a beautiful work of art.

He moves lower, summoning a breathy whimper from me. Hands curled around my hips, his lips trace the wet spot on my panties before he buries his nose between my thighs and inhales me…like he's breathing my scent into his lungs and memory, so he'll never forget.

Groaning, his fingers hook onto the sides of my panties and he peels them down my legs, stripping me bare.

His heated stare roams over every inch of my body, taking me and all my flaws in. "Every part of you is perfect." The tendons in his neck flex and his Adam's apple dips. "I know whenever you think about me, all the bad shit will be at the forefront…but promise me you'll remember that."

My heart pangs and emotion clogs my throat. I can't speak. *Can't breathe.* All I can manage is a soft nod.

Our gazes collide. The pure hunger etching his expression and the longing in his eyes—for me—only makes my ache and need for him build.

Chills ripple through me when he inclines his head, mapping kisses along my inner thighs and pussy.

The tip of his tongue darts out, striking my clit before delving inside me. My legs shake and I have to clutch his shoulders for support because it feels so good. My heart beats between my thighs as he continues spearing me, extending his tongue as far as it will go before circling my hole.

I glance out the window, taking in the dark sky and bright lights...the reflection of Phoenix Walker on his knees, pleasuring me.

My orgasm is so close, a slow roll sweeping through my system. "Oh god."

He sucks my clit with precision, maintaining the perfect amount of pressure and giving me exactly what I need. I shudder against his face, gripping his hair as I come.

I'm fighting to catch my breath when he stands and steers me toward the bed.

Our lips fuse together as he settles on top of me, grinding his pelvis against mine. The denim against my sensitive pussy generates a friction that's too much to take and a damp spot forms on his jeans.

"I need you to fuck me."

He lowers his head, his sharp teeth grazing my throat before sucking and biting hard enough to leave marks.

"Please."

My heart stammers as he moves down, raining kisses all over my body...worshiping every inch of my skin.

It's the sweetest kind of torture.

A keening sound leaves me when he wedges his shoulders between my thighs and shoves his hands under my ass, angling my pussy over his mouth.

The first strike of his tongue has me pulling away because I'm still so sensitive, but he tightens his grip, keeping me in place so he can feast.

It's too much. Too *intense*.

"Phoenix," I plead.

But he doesn't let up. He continues licking me like a fiend.

Like he's memorizing my taste.

The thought sends my chest plummeting, and I have the sudden urge to do the same to him. "I want you in my mouth."

I look down to find him watching me. He sticks his tongue out—intentionally taunting me with the explicit visual of him flicking my glistening pink flesh—before sinking between my lips.

I grip the bedsheets. "Holy…*God*."

His mouth forms a suction over my clit…so hard I cry out and my legs shake.

I mewl and writhe, propelling into his jaw as he wrenches another orgasm from me. One that's so intense a choked sound rips from my throat and a gush of liquid trickles out, saturating the sheets beneath me.

I have no time to be embarrassed though, because Phoenix spreads my legs wider, lapping every drop before he grips the undersides of my thighs, pinning my legs to my chest.

Trembles and spasms rack my body as he attacks the delicate area between my pussy and butt before spreading my cheeks. And then his tongue is there, circling my puckered hole. A garbled noise flies out of me and I squirm, my breath coming out in short, quick pants as I struggle for oxygen.

Phoenix Walker is going to kill me tonight. I'm sure of it.

The second he rises up on his knees, I spring up, gripping his shirt. "You have one minute to put your dick in my mouth or I'm leaving."

It's a threat I don't mean, but one that works.

A cocky smile spreads across his face before he closes the distance between us, giving me another kiss that makes my brain scramble.

My need for him eventually breaks through the haze, though. I jerk his shirt over his head and push his jeans down, freeing his erection.

A rush of heat spreads throughout me. His cock is every bit as perfect as he is. Thick, huge, veiny...beautiful.

Giving himself a languid stroke, he lies down on the bed and I situate myself between his legs.

The white bead of liquid on his tip trickles onto his stomach and my need to taste him rises to dangerous levels.

However, Phoenix is the one in control because the moment I lower my head, he wraps his hand around his base and smears the precum along my lips.

His eyes turn hooded as I lick it, savoring his flavor.

That rich gravelly voice reverberates in my chest. "Open."

When I do, he gradually feeds me his cock.

My mouth stretches so wide it hurts as I glide my tongue along the underside of his length.

He raises his hips, hitting the back of my throat.

Increasing my suction, I gag on his dick, taking him in deep pulls that have his face twisting with pleasure.

The groan that erupts from him sends little shivers up and down my spine. Ignoring the discomfort in my jaw, I fervently suck him harder and faster, unable to get enough.

The muscles in his thighs contract and he growls. "*Fuck.*"

Another growl leaves him and he pulls out abruptly.

I'd ask why he stopped, but the carnal look he's giving me, along with the way his chest rises and falls, tells me everything I need to know.

He crooks a finger. "Get the fuck over here. *Now.*"

When I don't move fast enough, he tugs me until I fall on him.

His lips claim mine, his tongue devouring every inch of my mouth as he rolls us over so he's on top. His cock nudges my entrance, and he rubs himself against my slit, coating his shaft with my slickness.

My heart revs into overdrive and I'm about to reach between us so I can put him inside me, but he grabs both my wrists, securing them above my head with one of his hands.

His gaze darkens, and I expect him to start fucking me...but he doesn't.

Those blue eyes search my face, like he's trying to store every feature in his database so he'll never forget.

I find myself doing the same, taking in those ocean pools of depth, the sensual shape of his lips, his structured jawline and sharp cheekbones...for the very last time.

A sharp sting punctures my rib cage and I squeeze my eyes shut before a tear has the chance to fall.

Losing him shouldn't hurt this much.

His voice is a painful rasp I feel in my marrow. "Lennon."

He presses his mouth to mine, threading his fingers through my hair as his tongue parts my lips.

Our tongues tangle, our kiss a potent mixture of anger, regret, and sorrow.

As though we're both acknowledging the clock we're racing against is about to end...

Because it has to.

After freeing my wrists, he props himself up on his elbows, hovering above me.

I exhale and he inhales as he slips inside me inch by painstaking inch.

Our gazes lock as he fills me to the hilt. My chest contracts because I know nothing will ever feel as good as when he's inside me.

Our bodies fit perfectly, like we were made for each other...which only makes this even more tragic.

On a strangled groan, he withdraws ever so slowly before pushing back in. My fingers skim his back, and he buries his face against my throat, his thrusts a gentle rhythm...like he's trying to make time stand still.

That makes two of us.

Every time he pushes inside me, I clench around him...my body unwilling to let him go despite my mind knowing it's the right thing to do.

His mouth claims mine again and I kiss him back with every single ounce of hate and love I've ever felt for him.

Our kiss turns messy and sloppy and he laces our fingers, picking up the pace. My hips snap against his, meeting him thrust for thrust as we consume each other.

Our breathing accelerates, and he breaks the kiss. Anguish slashes his face as he stares down at me and I cling to him with everything I've got because neither of us is ready for this to end… even though it has to.

His tongue dips inside my mouth one last time before he ruts against me. My core tightens as he drives inside me again and again, my muscles tensing and my body begging for release.

Sweat slicks our skin and our fastened fingers constrict, desperately trying to hold on…even though we can't.

Pleasure builds inside me as we move as one—our cadence in perfect harmony, like a flawless song—until it becomes too overwhelming and I have no choice but to let go.

A range of emotions fill my chest—each one penetrating me with the force of a bullet—as my inner walls squeeze him and I whisper his name for the very last time.

His lips part and his brows draw together as pleasure washes over his face. His intense gaze never strays from mine as hot liquid fills me.

We stare at one another for what feels like an eternity and I feel my heart shatter into a thousand tiny pieces…just like it did that night at Voodoo.

The reminder has me setting my armor in place again, though it feels substantially weaker now…like papier-mâché.

"I need to get some sleep."

My tone is intentionally cold and distant, and I can't bring myself to look at him.

His lips gently brush my forehead and he lingers for a moment… silently telling me goodbye.

I squeeze my eyes shut and the void I feel as he slips out of me is pure agony.

The mattress dips and I hear his footsteps pad toward the door.

I curl into a ball once I'm sure he's gone, unable to stop the tears from rolling down my cheeks and soaking his pillow. Only this time, my pain isn't because of what he did.

It's for what we could have been.

CHAPTER 70
PHOENIX

Lennon's been asleep for the last three hours…and I've been watching her for the last two.

The wet spot she left on my pillow is dry now and I can't decide if knowing she was in here crying while I was trying not to destroy everything in my fucking house makes me feel better or worse.

I glance at the clock on my nightstand. The sun will be up soon… and shortly after that, she'll be gone for good.

Which means I better do this now.

She doesn't stir as I peel the sheets back, and I have to remind my dick not to react as I rake my gaze over her naked body.

Letting me see all of her tonight was a consolation prize, but one I appreciate.

That suffocating feeling rears its ugly head again—tightening like a noose around my neck.

She's leaving me. And there's not a fucking thing I can do to stop it.

The muscles in my chest draw tight as I take the cap off the black Sharpie.

Given my flight leaves two hours before Lennon's, I won't have a chance to say any last words to her.

I'll have to write them instead.

Thinking about all the times she marred her perfect body—branding herself—with the cruel words of others fucking kills me.

I take my time dragging the marker across her stomach, hoping I don't fuck this up because it's too important and I only have one shot to get it right.

Five minutes later, the word *beautiful* is etched on her skin…right where it belongs.

Drawing in a deep breath, I press the marker to her sternum.

The next words are a lot harder to write. Not because I don't mean them, but because it will never undo what I did to her.

A few minutes later *I'm sorry* is inked on her flesh and the suffocating feeling turns to full-blown pain.

After my mom left, I vowed I'd never give another woman the power to destroy me.

But Lennon didn't destroy me…I destroyed her.

Her hopes. Her dreams. The ability to trust and open her heart again.

It's gone.

All the things my mother took from me, I took from her.

Chest full of lead, I walk around to the other side of the bed.

I knew Lennon was special, and we shared a connection I've never had with another person before, but I didn't realize the full magnitude of what that meant until it was too late.

I've always been a selfish bastard, so I assumed the distress I was experiencing was due to missing all the things she did for me. Like the way she took care of me. Her unwavering belief in me. How she looked at me like I was something special, even though I was just a dumb kid living in a trailer park chasing a dream. How she made me strive to be better.

But while I did miss those things, I missed *her* more.

Her stubbornness. The way she'd get under my skin whenever we'd argue. Her passion. Her loyalty. Her smile. Her big brown eyes. Her sarcasm. Her voice. Her heart.

I told myself not to get attached. Tried to convince myself that she was just some chick with a crush, and she didn't mean shit to me.

That stealing her song was okay, because it's not like she was gonna do anything with it, and she should be thanking me for having the guts she didn't and putting it out in the world.

But after she was out of my life...I wanted her back in it.

Because no matter how much fame or money I accumulated, every night before I closed my eyes, the sinking feeling in my chest would return and I'd hear her voice.

I thought it was guilt, but that was only part of it.

The other part was something I didn't think I was capable of feeling for anything other than music.

But it was too late. I'd already chosen my path, and she'd moved on with some prick she met in college.

It made me angry and bitter, but not enough to forget her.

I run my fingertips down the length of her back, battling my visceral need to bury myself inside her.

Earlier, Lennon told me I was the sun, and I never needed anyone else to shine...but she was wrong.

The sun can't shine when it gets too dark.

I drop a kiss to her shoulder blade. *But the moon can.*

Which is what Lennon is for me.

My only source of light when everything turns black.

Positioning the marker over her upper back, I proceed to write my last words where she'll never see them.

I stare at her as I wait for the ink to dry. Once it does, I run my finger across the words I'll never say...but the ones I'll always feel for her.

After draping the blanket over her body, I get off the bed.

Lennon Michael is my biggest craving and my biggest regret.

And if I was a better man, I would have known what I had when I had it all those years ago.

If I was a better man, I never would have hurt her.

If I was a better man, I wouldn't be losing her for a second time.

I'm almost out the door when I turn my head, giving her one last look.

I don't deserve her, but I don't want to let her go either.

I want to fight for her. For *us*.

I want to do what I should have done all those years ago and choose her.

That's when it hits me that choosing her means giving her what *she* deserves.

The career.

The acknowledgment.

The *truth*.

Dragging a hand down my face, I amble back over to the bed. I know she can't go on another tour because she has to take care of her dad, but I *need* her to be there for our first show tomorrow night.

I don't give a fuck what I have to do to make it happen.

"Lennon."

She doesn't budge, so I give her a soft shake.

When that doesn't work, I shake her harder and bark, "Get up."

Her eyes pop open. "What happened?" Panic spreads across her face and she bolts up. "Did I miss my flight?"

"No. It's only four a.m."

Confusion spreads across her features. "Oh. Are you okay?"

"You need to go to Europe with me."

She looks at me like I sprouted several heads. "You already know I can't."

"It'll only be for five days."

That does jack shit to tip the needle in my direction.

"No."

Crossing my arms, I stare her down. "It wasn't a request."

I don't care if I have to drag her on that plane kicking and screaming. She's going.

Clutching the sheets to her chest, she scoffs. It's clear she hasn't spotted my handiwork yet. "You can't *order* me to go to Europe."

The fuck I can't. "I just did."

Visibly exasperated, she presses the heels of her hands to her eyes. "You knew the deal, Phoenix."

Yeah, but I also know her stubbornness is no match for my fortitude.

Time is of the essence, though, so I pull out the big guns.

"If you don't go, I'll tell Vic and Chandler to put a stop payment on their checks."

Her mouth drops open in shock before she glares hate fire at me. "What the fuck is your problem, asshole?"

"I don't have one because you're going to Europe. End of story."

She pounds the mattress with her fist, and I revel in the way it makes her tits bounce. "Why?"

I don't want to ruin my plans or lie to her, so I snap my jaw shut.

Glancing up at the ceiling, she shakes her head, laughing without humor. "You're unbelievable."

"Four days."

Those baby browns narrow. "One."

She's adorable when she's being difficult. Like a baby shark testing out their teeth for the first time.

"No one can go to Europe for one day, Groupie. The flight alone is over ten hours." Leaning down, I cup her cheek. "Three."

Despite my compromise, she swats my hand away. "No." Sadness flickers in her eyes and she frowns. "I need to go home. I miss my dad."

An uninvited spasm hits me square in the chest. I know she does. But I also know he'd want this for her.

I pull out the only thing I've got left in my arsenal.

"Three days and I'll never bother you again. Promise."

Expression softening, she searches my face, no doubt trying to decide if I'm being genuine or if I'm under the influence. "What's going on?"

She'll find out soon enough.

Knowing she won't get anything out of me, she sighs. "Fine. But you better keep your promise." She makes a face. "Actually, I can't. My passport is at home."

Fuck. That's gonna be an issue, but I can still make it work.

Money is the universal language, and I have a fuckton of it. I'll offer some courier in Florida a few grand to grab the passport and hop on a plane to Cali. Problem solved.

"I'll arrange for someone to pick it up and we'll leave later."

A *lot* later.

I'll be tired as hell by the time we get there, but I can sleep—and fuck—on the plane.

Lennon chews her bottom lip, pondering. "I'll call Mrs. Palma and run it by her, but if I sense any hesitation on her end, I'm not going."

I don't foresee an issue there. They might not be blood, but it's clear they're family.

She reaches for her phone but freezes when she notices the clock. "I can't call her now. It's four fifteen in the morning."

"Which means it's seven fifteen in Florida."

Me and words don't get along, but I've always been good at math.

Pinching the bridge of her nose, she brings her cell to her ear.

"She's probably still sleep—oh, hey, Mrs. Palma. I'm sorry to call you so early." She rubs her forehead. "No, my flight is still on time, but…" She glares at me. "Look, you can totally say no, but is there any way I can go to Europe for three days?"

There's a long pause. I'm gearing up to offer the woman anything she wants, but I don't have to, because Lennon says, "Are you sure it's not a problem?" A smile spreads across her face. "Thank you so much. I seriously owe you. Oh crap. Before I forget, can you grab my passport out of the filing cabinet in Dad's office?"

While she finishes her phone call, I step out of the room. I don't have a personal assistant despite everyone telling me I need to crack down and hire one.

However, I do know a sly teenager who wants to make some money.

God fucking help her—and Skylar—if she uses any of it to buy herself breast implants.

A half hour later, Quinn's somehow managed to arrange everything. It's costing me double the amount I was prepared to shell out, but it's worth it.

Lennon's reading something on her phone when I walk back into my bedroom.

"Everything's set. The courier should be at your house in ten minutes."

Yawning, she places her cell on the nightstand. "In that case, I'm going back to sleep."

Climbing into bed, I wrap my arm around her waist, tugging her to me. "Good idea."

I nuzzle her neck, filling my nostrils with her scent.

I've just extended our clock again, and I'm taking full advantage.

Lennon's still pissed though, because she wiggles out of my arms.

Clutching the sheet, she bolts from the bed. "I can't do this."

"Too late. I've already set everything up." I crook a finger, summoning her back. "Bring that ass."

"No..." Her voice cracks like crystal and when I cock my head, I notice her eyes are glassy. "I meant this. Us."

It's a direct blow to the center of my chest. One I wasn't prepared for.

I get up and walk over to her, but she retreats to the other side of the room, like being close to me physically hurts.

"Why?"

"Why are we going to Europe?" she counters. "And don't lie to me or avoid the question. Tell me the truth."

I *can't*. Not right now.

I just need her to trust me.

But it's obvious she still doesn't because her features twist with anger. "Fuck you."

She charges for the bathroom, but I grip her arm as she passes me. "Lennon."

I could push the issue of her not wanting to screw and I know she'd cave. Not because she's weak—hell, she's the furthest thing from it—but because this thing between us is too strong.

However, I want more than her pussy.

I want every part, every piece, every goddamn inch of her.

I want her trust. Because once I have that...I'll have everything again.

My fingers trace the curve of her cheek. "Look at me."

But she doesn't. Hell, she doesn't even attempt to. "I can't." A tear falls down her cheek and she backs up. "It hurts too much."

The hollowness in my chest spreads the more the space between us grows.

We're only five feet apart, but she might as well be in Guam.

Lennon's fixed me twice now, but I'll never be able to do the same for her.

Because I'm the one who fucked her up.

I took a masterpiece and ripped it to shreds.

I turn, watching as she makes her way to the bathroom...where she'll wash every trace of me off her skin and stick me in a box marked, *do not open.*

This way she can move on and find happiness.

Like she deserves.

Suddenly she stops walking and peers down. "What is this?"

It's me...letting you go.

T he flight to the UK was quiet, but far from pleasant.

Phoenix and I avoided each other. Like two ships passing in the night.

Which means my suspicions about why he dragged me to Europe were spot on.

Phoenix Walker doesn't like to lose. But instead of accepting defeat, he bulldozed and manipulated me into extending our time, because he knows the longer we're together, the harder it will be for me to get out of his atmosphere.

For the briefest of moments, I thought his intentions might not be based on sex, pride, or guilt.

That maybe he…

I mentally smack my brain, willing myself not to go down that path again.

I know he wants me, and while that might be enough for some people…it's not enough for me.

I need something he's not capable of giving me.

My heart thumps as his low, raspy voice envelops me in a thick fog, sending everything inside me spiraling.

I had no intention of watching him perform tonight, but Sharp

Objects is playing at Wembley Stadium, which is proving to be every bit as iconic as everyone claims.

Even from where I'm standing—all the way in the wings—it's massive and overwhelming. I've never seen so many people in the same place at the same time.

I don't know how he's not freaking out because I'd be pissing myself and passing out from fear.

Then again, he's Phoenix Walker. *He was born for this.*

I stand utterly hypnotized as he commands the stage, taking everyone hostage…stealing our souls.

He wrote on your skin—my stupid heart taunts as he belts out the last verse of Existentialism.

While penning *I'm sorry* and *beautiful* on my skin was incredibly sweet, it doesn't change anything.

He's still a rock star living his dream, and I'm still the girl whose song he stole.

He lives a life that involves frequently traveling around the world. A world where millions of women will eagerly give him anything he wants—things I wouldn't be able to—because I'll be home taking care of my father.

But even more important than that? I can't risk him breaking me again.

I barely survived it the first time.

The booming roar of the crowd pulsates my eardrums as the song comes to an end.

Just as Phoenix predicted, people are obsessed with it and even though it's not on the scheduled album, it's quickly becoming their new hit.

He beat Vic at his own game and took control of the chessboard.

I'm proud of him.

"Holy shit," Skylar yells beside me. "This is insanity."

I can't help but smile. "I know."

The fact Skylar's watching the show when she's attended almost every concert for four plus years is a testament to how epic this is.

Then again, her being out here might have more to do with *Gwyneth Barclay* sitting in the greenroom.

She was pleasant enough, I suppose, but there's something about her that rubs me the wrong way. And it has nothing to do with her having Memphis's baby, even though it's tearing my friend's heart apart.

It's the way she treats her assistant. How she's always on her phone taking selfies and videos. The satisfied glint in her eye whenever she looks at Memphis...like she's trapped him in her web and he's official *Barclay* property.

Then again, it's really none of my business. I'm not the one who has to spend the rest of my life with her. Heck, I won't even see her again after tonight.

The next song cues up and the crowd goes wild. My heart skips several beats, unable to tear my gaze away.

Phoenix always puts on one hell of a show, but tonight there's an energy emitting from him that I can't explain.

It's even more passionate and emotional than usual. *Poignant.*

"I don't think she likes me," someone who sounds a whole lot like Quinn says behind me.

"Who?" Skylar asks.

"Gwen. This afternoon she told me we could take some pictures together, but when I went into the greenroom and asked, she acted like she couldn't be bothered."

Skylar and I trade sad looks.

"She's probably tired or having a bad day," Skylar offers.

Defending the woman who's having the baby of the guy she loves can't be easy, but I know Skylar doesn't want Quinn to feel like she has to choose between her and her idol.

Quinn frowns. "I guess."

As if on cue, Gwyneth saunters by. I'm assuming she's going to keep walking, but she sidles up beside me, peering out onto the stage.

"How hot does my future husband look?" she coos while taking a picture of him with her phone. "We're gonna have such gorgeous babies."

I feel Skylar tense on the other side of me. Reaching down, I grip her hand and bite my tongue so as not to point out that Memphis hasn't even proposed yet and she should focus on her current baby before planning any additional ones.

"Yeah," I say instead. "Everyone's on fire tonight."

She crinkles her nose. "It's pretty surprising, given Phoenix's *issues.*"

Now I'm the one who's tense. "What issues?"

Tossing her bleached-blonde hair over her shoulder, she laughs. "Please, honey. Everyone knows he's a crackhead."

It's not okay to hit a pregnant woman.

"Quite frankly, I'm surprised he's not dead yet." A smirk twists her shiny pink lips and she shrugs. "Not to be a bitch, but the band will be much better off once he finally ODs." Her eyes swivel to her baby daddy. "Memphis can be the lead singer then."

Oh hell no.

My vision turns red and I face her head-on.

I'm about to unleash a string of insults and threats that will make her cower, but Quinn taps her on the shoulder. "Excuse me, Gwen?"

Gwen spins around. "Ye—"

A wave of orange liquid sails through the air before drenching Gwen's shirt…

And mine.

"You better keep my brother's name out of your mouth, cunt," Quinn sneers before she stalks off, nearly plowing into a flabbergasted Chandler in the process.

Safe to say Quinn's obsession with Gwyneth is officially over.

Thank the Lord.

Gwen's jaw drops. "That little bitch."

"Watch it," Skylar growls at the same time I sneer, "You deserved it."

Scowling, she swivels her head. "*Excuse* me?"

I take a step closer and I know my expression is murderous

because it's exactly how I feel right now. "The next time you talk shit about Phoenix or wish for him to overdose, it won't be juice all over your face and shirt. It will be your blood."

Outraged, Gwen starts flapping her hands and squawking for her assistant.

The poor girl quickly comes to the rescue and gives her a roll of paper towels.

"I need a new shirt, not paper towels, you idiot," she squeaks.

Shooting her a dirty look, Skylar grips my hand and we make a beeline for the greenroom.

We're supposed to go out to dinner after the concert, but we'll have to make a quick pit stop at the hotel before that now.

"Is Memphis aware his baby will be half demon?" I mutter as I walk over to the snack table and grab a wad of napkins.

"According to Storm, he's *well* aware." Skylar rummages around her giant purse. "Evidently, he's claiming it's pregnancy hormones."

That tells me two things.

One—Memphis is in denial. And two—Skylar and Memphis are no longer on speaking terms.

Quinn—who's sulking on the couch—grimaces. "I can't believe I was her biggest fan."

I'd give her a hug, but my shirt is covered in sticky orange juice. "I'm sorry."

Skylar hands me a pair of jeans and a top. "Here. Put these on."

I'm about to remind her that her clothes won't fit me but then I notice the tags. Not only are they new. They're *my* size.

Talk about convenient. Convenient and peculiar.

"How come you have a brand-new outfit for me in your bag?"

Skylar and Quinn exchange a look. "I went shopping today."

"Shopping for me?"

Skylar smiles. "Not specifically, but I saw this and figured you'd love it. I was going to mail them, but here you are."

"It's fate," Quinn supplies.

"Exactly."

Given Skylar loves to shop, it makes sense.

I'm about to walk into the bathroom, but Skylar grips the bottom of my shirt and carefully raises it over my head. "Let me help you change. It will speed up the process."

Okay, *now* she's definitely acting strange.

However, I can't focus on that because I'm too busy batting her hands away so I can have some autonomy. "I got it."

I quickly tug on my new jeans, and I've got to hand it to her because they fit perfectly. The top isn't necessarily something I'd pick out for myself, but the turquoise V-neck with a scoop back is really cute.

This outfit is way better than the one I was wearing, so I'm not mad about it. "Thank you."

I wince when Skylar digs her thumb into my upper spine. "What are you doing?"

"Stay still. I'm trying to get this mark off you."

"What mark?"

"I love you," she says, although it comes out like a question rather than a statement.

"I love you, too, but you're being *really* weird right now."

"I meant the words on your back."

"What wo—"

Oh. My. God.

The room tilts, and it's a struggle to draw air into my lungs.

Quinn gets off the couch and walks over. "Relax. It's pretty faded already and if you take your hair down, you won't even see it."

"I don't think that's what she's freaking out about," Skylar whispers.

My heart knocks against my chest like it's trying to break free.

Why didn't he tell me? Why didn't he...

"Shit. We gotta go," Skylar announces before she pulls my ponytail out of my hair and sifts her fingers through it.

"Go whe—"

Quinn swipes some gloss over my lips.

I rear back because this just went from strange to downright bizarre. "Why are you two *primping* me?"

Ignoring my questions, Skylar yanks my arm so hard I'm surprised it doesn't pop out of my socket.

"What the hell is going on?" I demand as she drags me out of the room with Quinn in tow.

Everything is happening so fast, and none of it makes any sense.

"One of you better start talking," I snap as Skylar steers me toward the side of the stage.

"I didn't do nothing," Quinn defends.

Which most definitely means she *did*.

When I give her a look, she raises her hands, feigning innocence. "Don't be mad at me. I simply saw an opportunity to get the job done, and I took it."

"Saw an opportunity to get what job done?"

It's like everyone's speaking a language I can't understand.

I turn to Skylar, who's motioning for Quinn to be quiet. "Will you please—"

A knot of panic strangles my throat when the current song comes to an end and Phoenix addresses the crowd. "I'll be right back, guys. There's someone special I want you to meet."

And then he jogs offstage…heading straight for me.

CHAPTER 72
PHOENIX

Lennon's visibly shaking by the time I reach her.

"It's gonna be okay."

That only makes her take several steps backward.

Christ. I know she's scared, but she doesn't have to be.

I'll be her anchor this time.

My stare locks with hers. "Trust me." I hold out my hand. "Please."

Her petrified gaze bounces between my outstretched hand and my face for several agonizing beats.

My chest recoils because I'm positive she's going to turn around and flee...

But then she takes it.

I don't break eye contact as I bring her out on stage, because I know once she gets a glimpse of the massive crowd, her fear will take over and she'll bolt.

The closer we get to the mic stand, the more she trembles.

"Trust me," I repeat as I maneuver her so she's the one in front of the mic.

Then I move behind her.

Another wave of panic courses through her body, and she peers at me over her shoulder. "I c-can't do this."

I lock my arms around her waist, keeping her right where she's meant to be. "Yes, you can."

The intro cues up and the excitement and energy from the crowd is so tangible it buzzes through me like a current of electricity.

Like magic.

Five minutes before the concert started, I told Storm, Memphis, and the fill-in bassist that we were doing Sharp Objects for our last song tonight.

I just didn't tell them Lennon would be the one singing it.

At least that was the plan...but she doesn't make a sound.

She squirms in my arms, no doubt trying to run off, but I squeeze her tighter.

She's got this. I know she does.

My lips brush the shell of her ear. "Close your eyes." After they squeeze shut, I press a soft kiss to her temple. "And no matter what happens, don't you fucking stop."

The intro cues up again and I hold my breath for the first four bars, willing her to trust me...and her gift.

Then I hear it.

I'm tough as a nail
Sharp as a blade

Her hoarse, sultry tone reverberates through the speakers, filling the stadium. The first verse is a little shaky, but by the time she hits the chorus, her nerves dissipate and it's goddamn perfection.

She grows stronger with every note, transforming into a fucking powerhouse.

A mixture of pride and exhilaration swells in my chest. She's dominating the stage. Keeping us all prisoner.

I know without a doubt that every single person witnessing this realizes what I've known for years.

She's special.

The tiny hairs on the back of my neck stand on end and goose bumps graze my arms as she belts the final verse.

She didn't just kill it. She fucking slaughtered it.

Just like I knew she would.

The outro hasn't even finished when the crowd erupts in cheers before rising to their feet...giving her a much-warranted standing ovation.

"Open your eyes."

I don't want her to miss this.

Because she deserves it.

A shiver runs through her and she audibly gasps.

I smile, soaking up the last few moments I'll have with her in my arms. "You wanted to experience what it would be like to have a venue full of two thousand people listen to your song...but how's ninety thousand?"

Her eyes are glassy when she turns to face me. "Thank you."

No. I'm the one who should be thanking her.

I got to experience this magic and live my dream for over four years.

Because I stole it.

"I'll never forget this," she whispers. "It...that was incredible."

Leaning down, I press my lips to her forehead. *That was a solar eclipse.*

Tonight will be the end of my career...but the beginning of hers.

Exactly how it should be.

CHAPTER 73
LENNON

Holy. Freaking. Shit.

I can't believe *that* just happened. Singing my song in front of ninety thousand people surpassed even my wildest dreams.

My legs are shaky as I walk off the stage and there's so much adrenaline pumping through me it makes my head spin.

That's why he brought me here.

Skylar and Quinn are jumping up and down with excitement and I'm getting ready to join them…but Phoenix's voice comes over the speakers.

"She's an amazing singer, right? Almost like she was the one who was meant to sing that song."

The crowd cheers, but I freeze.

Oh god.

The realization of what he's about to do slams into me like a Category 5 hurricane.

I quickly turn back around. "Phoenix!" When he looks at me, I shake my head and mouth, 'No.'

He doesn't have to do this.

I don't want him to do this. *Not anymore.*

This could very well ruin his career. Vic might drop him from the label.

He'll be canceled and branded a thief. A has-been.

His phenomenal talent—*his* gift—will be nothing but a punch line.

Stealing my song was a terrible thing to do, but he doesn't need to destroy his dream over it. He *can't*.

He's the sun. He needs to keep shining.

Phoenix turns his attention back to the crowd.

I sprint across the stage, desperate to stop him...but it's too late.

"That's because she's the one who wrote it." He blows out a heavy breath. "And I stole it."

Silence falls over the entire stadium...with the exception of Chandler who's screaming his head off in the wings, and a few people in the audience who call out things like, "Are you taking the piss right now, mate?" and, "Bloody hell."

Phoenix cocks his head, his intense gaze holding me captive. "Four years ago, I had to choose between all of this and you." Emotion slices his face, and he drops the mic. "I made the wrong choice."

My heart stops cold and time stands still.

He didn't have to write those three words on my skin, because right now I *feel* them.

However, I won't let him destroy everything he's ever wanted— everything he *is*—just to be with me.

I won't let him break himself like he broke me.

My feet move on their own accord, and I head backstage.

I have to figure out a way to fix this. I'll need to sit down with Skylar, so we can come up with a plan to save his career.

Skylar's expression is full of alarm when I reach her, but her attention is solely fixated on something behind me.

I barely have time to register that Phoenix is following me before a mob of people rush over and swarm him.

"What the fuck?" Chandler bellows.

Skylar points a finger at him. "Shut up." Her eyes swivel to

Storm and Memphis, who are noticeably livid. "No one say a single fucking word to anyone until I figure this shit out. Got it?" Her glare centers on Phoenix. "Greenroom. Right now."

It suddenly occurs to me that Phoenix didn't just screw himself… he screwed the people he considers his family.

Phoenix looks around the backstage area, but the moment his gaze lands on me, Skylar and Chandler usher him into the greenroom.

"Goddammit," Chandler snaps, gesturing to his cell. "Vic's already calling."

And then the door slams shut.

I don't know what I can do, but there has to be *something*.

I make a mad dash for the greenroom, but there's a sharp tug on my arm.

When I glance up, I find Storm peering down at me. He looks so appalled—so upset—I want to wrap my arms around him.

"I didn't know he stole your song."

"I know—"

The sound of my phone ringing cuts me off.

I raise a finger when I see Mrs. Palma's name flash across the screen. "One sec. I have to take this."

For all I know, *she* might have gotten wind of what Phoenix did given how fast news gets around on social media.

After pressing the green button, I bring it to my ear. "Hey. I guess you he—"

"Lennon, honey," she interjects, her quavering voice filled with dread.

My heart stops cold for the second time in ten minutes. "What's wrong?"

Storm—who was about to walk away—stays put.

"Your dad…he had a stroke about twenty minutes ago. I called an ambulance and we're here at the hospital." Her voice cracks. "It… you need to come home right away."

Blood drains from my face and the fear I felt before is nothing compared to right now.

"What happened?" Storm questions as I disconnect the call.

"My dad…I. He's…hospital." I can't form cohesive thoughts or sentences. The only thing I know is that I have to get to him as soon as possible.

I brush past him, running as fast as I can out the door.

CHAPTER 74
LENNON

The steady hum of machines filter throughout the small hospital room and every time I hear one beep, my head snaps up.

I've only been here for three hours, but it feels like an eternity.

I was foolishly optimistic during the plane ride home and figured he'd be up and talking by the time I got here.

My heart folds in on itself as I zero in on the ventilator covering my dad's face and the various tubes sticking out of him.

My dad was eating dinner at the kitchen table when he started complaining of a headache. Mrs. Palma went to get him some acetaminophen, but when she came back, his speech was slurred, and he started vomiting.

She was already dialing 911 when he collapsed.

The stroke he had was severe, and the doctors informed Mrs. Palma that his condition was critical and the outcome wasn't favorable.

But they don't know my father.

He's gonna pull through this. He has to.

Come on, Dad. Wake up.

Mrs. Palma takes a seat next to me. "I'm so sorry."

She keeps saying that, but this isn't her fault.

It's mine.

I should have been here. *But I wasn't.*

Because once again, I got too close to the sun.

Only this time it was my own damn fault I got burned.

I try to inhale, but the guilt crushing my chest is asphyxiating me.

I should have refused to go to Europe. Then we would have had more time together.

My eyes sting and I swallow back tears. *I shouldn't have gone on tour.*

Maybe then my dad wouldn't be lying in a hospital bed, fighting for his life.

Reaching over, Mrs. Palma grips my hand. "You should try to get some sleep, sweetie. You must be exhausted."

She's right, between the time difference and the nine-hour-and-fifteen-minute flight home, I should be.

But there's no way I can rest until I know he'll be okay.

I shake my head. "I need to be here when he wakes up."

Because he *has* to wake up.

And the more I repeat it, the more I'll believe it.

Shifting in her seat, she frowns. "Honey—"

"Sir," a feminine voice yells from the hallway. "This is the ICU. You can't be back here."

"What room is Lennon Michael's father in?" Phoenix rumbles, that unmistakable melodic voice bouncing off the walls.

What the hell is he doing here?

"I'm not at liberty to give you that information. Please leave."

Her refusal doesn't sit well with Phoenix though, because he barks, "Fuck off."

Shit.

Mrs. Palma and I swap flabbergasted looks before I get out of my chair. "I'll handle this."

When I step out of the room, I see him roaming the hallway with his hands cupped around his mouth. "Lennon!"

"Don't make me call security," the nurse warns at the same time Phoenix spots me.

Before I can blink, he's barreling toward me.

I planned on sending him away, but the second his arms are around me, something deep inside me ruptures and I crumble.

Phoenix doesn't try to cheer me up, encourage me to stay strong, or make false promises that everything will be okay.

He just holds me tight while I fall apart.

My muffled sobs soak through his T-shirt as he runs his fingertips up and down my back.

Moments later, the nurse comes over. "I'm very sorry but you need to leave."

I lift my head. "But—"

"I know it's an incredibly difficult time for you," she interjects. "And while I sympathize, I've already given you a lot of leeway." She flicks her hand at Mrs. Palma, who's coming out of the room. "Not only is it well before visiting hours, but it's only supposed to be one person at a time." She narrows her eyes at Phoenix. "Three is pushing it."

I hate these stupid hospital rules, but I know it's not her fault. Plus, she's right, she has been incredibly accommodating.

"If I leave, will you allow him to stay with her?" Mrs. Palma questions, surprising me.

"No," I quickly say. "I don't want you to leave."

My chest caves in as I peer up at Phoenix.

"I...um."

I don't want him to go either.

Leaning down, he kisses my forehead. "I'm staying, Groupie." He turns to the nurse. "Get the CEO on the phone. *Now.*"

Peeved, the nurse raises an eyebrow. "I beg your pardon? Who do you think—"

"I'm Phoenix fucking Walker," he snarls.

The nurse must not be a rock fan because that doesn't seem to faze her one bit.

However, the two women in scrubs making their way to the

nurses' station damn near trip and fall on their faces when they notice him.

"This can go one of two ways," Phoenix continues. "One—you can put me in touch with the CEO so I can make a very generous donation to the hospital and tell him what a wonderful employee you are. Or two—I can tell the entire country what a terrible experience I had here and do everything in my power to get your ass fucking fired."

His threat works because she turns on her heel. "I'll be right back."

I shouldn't condone Phoenix throwing his weight around like that, but I'm too fixated on my dad to object.

It's almost eight in the morning, so the doctors should be starting their rounds soon. I'm hoping they'll give me a better update than the last one they gave Mrs. Palma.

Uneasiness etches Phoenix's face as we walk into the room and I feel bad for not preparing him because it's a lot to take in.

I'm about to apologize, but he pulls me into his arms. Placing a hand on the back of my neck, he gently guides me to his chest.

"I'm gonna run down to the cafeteria and get us all some coffee," Mrs. Palma whispers.

Emotions get the better of me again and before I can stop myself, a sob breaks through the surface.

Don't leave me an orphan, Dad.

I clutch his shirt for dear life, my tears falling like rain as sobs of agony escape me.

I can't lose him. I *can't.*

However, thinking such miserable things isn't doing him any favors.

My dad needs to be surrounded by positive energy, which means I have to keep it together and not let myself go down that dark road.

"He's gonna make it." Standing upright, I clear my throat. "He's a fighter."

Giving me a soft nod, Phoenix brushes my tears away with his thumb.

Irritation billows through me when I catch the sorrow in his expression. I don't want or need his pity, because everything will be okay.

It *will* be.

"He'll be fine," I bite out before I walk over to my dad.

There's no way he'd leave me here all by myself.

He always joked that he'd stick around to bother and embarrass me until he was at least a hundred.

I take hold of his hand, gripping it as hard as I can. So hard his fingernails dig into my skin, but I don't care.

"You always said it was me and you, Dad. So, I really need you to keep your word and wake up soon, okay?"

Don't leave me.

Because even though his mind wanders off most days, there are still times when he comes back to me.

I need those times.

I need *him*.

A knock on the door startles me out of my thoughts and a short, older man wearing a white lab coat enters the room.

"Hello, I'm Dr. Gannon. The attending physician." He briefly glances at Phoenix but doesn't appear upset over us breaking the rules. "Do you have some time to talk?"

Some time to talk. I breathe a sigh of relief because that's good news. If he needs time to talk, that means there must be a treatment plan in place. It will most likely involve physical and occupational therapy and I might have to hire a private nurse to come to the house temporarily...which won't be an issue because I have the money to do so now.

"Sure."

I kiss my dad's cheek before making my way over.

The doctor looks at Phoenix. "I'm going to have to kindly request that you step outside."

"I'm going to have to *kindly* request that you fuck off," Phoenix grunts, shocking the doctor, but not me because this is par for the course when it comes to him. "I'm staying."

Appearing annoyed, Dr. Gannon looks between us before his gaze settles on me. "Is that okay with you?"

I nod.

"All right then." He gestures to the two chairs near the wall. "Why don't you have a seat?"

A weird knot twists my stomach, but I shrug it off. "I'll stand."

Blowing out a breath, he takes a seat. "Tell me what you understand about what happened to your father."

While his tone isn't exactly condescending, I don't particularly care for it or the question.

"My dad had a stroke."

"That's correct." He studies my face and whatever he sees has him frowning. "Your father's condition is quite serious."

No shit. He's lying in a freaking hospital bed.

However, he's strong.

"I know, but with the right medication and some rehabilitation, he'll recover."

That weird knot is back, and I look at Phoenix.

He gives me a soft smile, but sorrow flickers across his face again.

"I'm afraid that won't happen," the doctor says, and I snap my attention back to him. "The stroke caused your father to be without oxygen for too long."

"Mrs. Palma called an ambulance right away, though. And she gave him CPR."

"Yes, but unfortunately, the damage he suffered was too extensive." His frown deepens. "I've contacted the neurologist. He'll be doing a final consult shortly, but he doesn't think there will be any improvement. I concur."

They're wrong. These guys might have medical degrees, but it doesn't mean their assessment is infallible.

"Then you don't know my dad," I fire back and Phoenix moves closer.

Features pinched, he rises from the chair. "Lennon, I'm very sorry, but your father is not going to make it."

That's not true. "Yes, he will."

"No. He will not. The ventilator is what's keeping him alive right now."

Then I guess he'll just have to stay on a vent.

He takes a step forward. "Many people in your situation see organ donation as a way of turning tragedy into something good. When you're ready, there are some people from the donation center who would like to speak with you."

Organ donation? *What?* Isn't he jumping the gun? It hasn't even been twenty-four hours.

"I'm not giving up on him."

The doctor regards Phoenix. "I'll send a grief counselor to the room shortly." He gives me a sympathetic smile as he heads for the door. "If there's anything else I can do or anything you need, please let myself or the nurses know."

I need you to do your job and save my dad.

The weird knot in my stomach becomes a violent wave of pain. It's so intense my knees buckle and everything around me spins.

He's dying.

The tears come again…only this time they're wails that shake my entire body.

"Breathe," Phoenix whispers and it takes me a second to register that I'm in his arms.

I try to take a breath past the agony, but I can't. It's pummeling me into the ground, stealing every ounce of strength I possess.

This pain is unlike any I've ever experienced.

The harder I sob, the tighter Phoenix holds me.

I don't know how long this goes on, but eventually my tears run dry, leaving me completely drained.

I don't remember Phoenix sitting down in a chair or pulling me onto his lap, but he's rubbing gentle circles up and down my back and his lips are pressed against my forehead.

"Where's Mrs. Palma?" I croak.

"She went home to get you a change of clothes, but she'll be back soon. Do you want me to call her?"

"No, it's okay."

Once she's here, I'll have to say the words aloud and I'm not ready for that.

I peer up at him. "I really appreciate you coming, but you should go back to Europe."

He's in the middle of his own shitstorm right now and the last place he needs to be is here with me.

Emotion slashes the sharp lines of his face, and he palms my cheek. "I'm not going anywhere."

I want to argue, but I don't have the stamina for it.

Sliding off his lap, I maneuver into the empty seat next to him.

Whatever was left of my heart shatters as I stare at my dad. You'd think it would be easier given I've been losing him in pieces these past two years, but it's not...because I can't stop thinking of everything I'm going to miss out on.

The things we'll never get to experience.

"He's never gonna see me get married," I choke out as another wave of grief swallows me whole.

He once told me that my wedding day would be the best and worst day of his life. When I asked him why, he said it was because he'd be giving me away to someone who loved me just as much as he did...but it also meant he'd be losing me.

But I'm the one losing him.

I feel another loose thread of my broken heart pull with my next thought.

"He's never gonna meet his grandkids."

My dad said I'd never understand just how deep love could be until I had children of my own one day.

But I don't need to have kids to understand it, because my love for him runs deeper than an ocean.

Which is probably why I've already cried enough tears to fill one.

This wasn't supposed to happen.

He wasn't supposed to abandon me like this.

"I'm all alone now."

Phoenix's voice is raw rasp. "No, you're not."

I am, though.

My dad used to say I was his whole entire world...but he was my world, too.

Now my world is cold and dark.

Phoenix grasps my chin, tilting my face so I have no choice but to look at him.

Leaning in, he closes the distance between us, kissing me with such tenderness a rush of warmth engulfs me.

And then he whispers two words against my lips...two words that make the universe come to a screeching halt before bursting into flames.

"Marry me."

CHAPTER 75
PHOENIX

"No," Lennon exclaims as she leaps out of her chair. "You're insane."

Funny because I've never felt saner.

Lennon's it for me.

I knew it when I wrote that first letter and I know it even more now.

And while I can't undo what's happening, I can give her this.

Proof that she's not alone. That she has a family.

That even though she's losing the first man who loved her…she still has another man who loves her just as much.

"Marry me," I repeat.

Her shocked gaze flies to mine. "No. Stop ask…" She scowls. "*Demanding*."

Fuck that. I'll keep demanding until she agrees.

She takes several steps backward and I take several forward. "Marry me, Lennon."

A gasp of surprise rings out behind me and I don't need to turn around to know it's Mrs. Palma.

Lennon glares hate fire at me. "You're crazy. We're not even together."

That's my fault.

Sometimes you want something so bad you'll give up everything to get it, but I learned my lesson.

I know what it's like to lose her and *nothing* is worth that.

I just need her to realize that what we have is worth fighting for.

"Would you have wanted to spend the rest of your life with me if I hadn't fucked up?"

I don't give a shit what she *thinks* would have happened between us. I want to know what the thing inside her chest felt.

What it still feels.

She retreats again, only this time her spine meets the wall.

I close the space between our bodies, trapping her. If she wants to run away, she'll have to get through me, but she won't be able to because I'm never letting her go.

"Yes," she whispers, averting her gaze. "I told you, I loved you—"

"Do you still love me?"

The question is heavier than osmium, but I already know the answer.

I fucking feel it. This girl is burrowed so deep in my soul the best surgeon on the planet couldn't cut her out.

And I know it's the same for her when it comes to me. She's just afraid of getting her heart broken again.

But I'll spend the rest of my life not only putting the pieces together but making it even stronger.

Appearing defeated, her pretty face crumples. "Yes."

I plant my hand on the wall next to her head. "Good, because I love you."

Her gaze searches mine. I know she sees the truth in my eyes because her walls are down and she's finally looking.

But love alone isn't enough, it needs something else—something essential—in order to thrive and get you through all the fucked-up tests life throws at a relationship.

"Do you trust me?"

I hold my breath. A minute can feel like an eternity when you're waiting for the woman you love to decide if you're worthy enough of her.

And while I could stand here, pound on my chest, and shout that even though I'll piss her off at least once a day for the remainder of our lives, I'll never hurt her again…it won't mean shit unless she truly believes it.

That in her heart she knows without a shadow of a doubt that if I could turn back time, I'd choose her.

Her sharp exhale is my only response for a while.

Then she lifts her chin. Her gaze darts over every inch of my face before colliding with mine. "I do now."

My hand snakes around her waist and I kiss her.

It's honest and vulnerable. An apology for the mistakes I've made and a pledge that I'll never destroy what she's given back to me.

It's an oath. A *vow*.

"Marry me," I repeat.

This time, she finally gives me what I want.

"Okay."

As much as I'd like to stay here worshiping her mouth, we don't have a lot of time.

I saw how devastated she was when she realized her father wouldn't be there to watch her get married, but I'm gonna make it happen.

"I'll be right back."

Confusion clouds her expression. "Where are you going?"

"To find a priest." I turn to Mrs. Palma, who's still standing by the door…sniffling. "They have one of those here, right?"

She dabs her eyes with a tissue. "Yes, there are hospital chaplains."

"Wait," Lennon squeaks. "You want to do this *now*?"

"I want to spend the rest of my life with you, Lennon. The sooner it starts, the better."

I start to head out, but then it hits me that I'm missing a crucial step.

One that would be important to both Lennon and her dad if the circumstances were different.

My chest constricts as I look at him.

I won't be able to sit down man-to-man and get his blessing to marry his daughter.

Hell, he'd probably tell me to fuck off, and I can't fault him for that.

But I make him a promise anyway.

One I'll never break.

I'll always take care of her.

CHAPTER 76

PHOENIX

Approximately ten seconds after the chaplain pronounced us man and wife Lennon's father passed.

It was almost as if he knew I'd honor my promise and she'd be in good hands.

Consoling my new bride while she fell apart in my arms on what would typically be the best day of someone's life wasn't easy, but there's a reason we stuck to the traditional vows that included the words, 'for better, for worse.'

Although I did make an addendum to mine. 'To love and to cherish…and to never steal from again', which confused the minister and made Lennon shake her head before the faintest hint of a smile peeked out.

That was four days ago.

Today…is the funeral.

Lennon tried to pull herself together as best as she could to plan it, but when it came time to pick out caskets, she completely crumbled.

And she hasn't been the same since.

Fortunately, Mrs. Palma and Skylar took over the arrangements.

I've only gone to one of these things before—Josh's—but the service was nice.

The burial part? Not so much.

We were supposed to leave the cemetery a half hour ago, but Lennon keeps staring at the coffin...while everyone else keeps staring at me. No doubt wondering what the fuck to do since we're supposed to be having an after-party—or *gathering,* according to Mrs. Palma—back at the house. Which is pretty fucking stupid if you ask me because why the fuck would you throw a party for someone who can't attend?

"I'll be right back," I whisper.

She doesn't say a word. I'm not even sure if she's aware I'm here.

I glance at Skylar, who nods before coming over and taking a seat next to Lennon. As my publicist, she's still pissed, but as my friend—and Lennon's—she's been nothing but supportive.

Which is a hell of a lot more than I can say for Storm and Memphis.

The only reason they're here is because of my wife.

I can't blame them, though.

Not only did I drop a bomb that might also ruin their careers, I canceled the rest of the tour.

Which is why *Chandler's* currently here.

"We need to talk," he says as I make my way over to the cluster of people waiting for someone to direct them.

"I'm not changing my mind," I grunt before closing in on Mrs. Palma, who's conversing with some of the guests.

She politely excuses herself when she spots me.

"I'm not making Lennon go until she's ready, so I think everyone should head out without us."

She looks at Lennon, who hasn't budged. "No problem. I'll let everyone know they can follow me to the house and hold down the fort there."

"Thank you."

She touches my shoulder. "You don't have to thank me."

Grams approaches me after she leaves. "How are you, sweet pea?"

My face must convey how I feel because her brows furrow and her hands bracket my cheeks. "A rainbow always comes after the storm."

Interesting analogy given her grandson—my best friend—fucking hates me.

"He won't stay mad at you forever, and neither will Memphis. Brothers fight but at the end of the day, you're still family." Her eyes fill with sadness as she glances at Lennon. "Right now, you need to take care of your wife. Trust me, they'll understand."

I'm not so sure about that.

She nudges me. "Go on and talk to them before they leave."

I'd rather stick a rusty screwdriver through my jugular, but she gives me another nudge. A harder one that draws the attention of a few people standing nearby. "Go on."

I wouldn't put it past the woman to grab me by my ear and drag me, so I save myself the trouble—and the embarrassment—and go over there myself.

Like me, they're dressed in all-black Armani suits. The same ones we wore to Josh's funeral.

I shove my hands in the pockets of my slacks. "Hi."

Pushing his sunglasses up his nose, Memphis regards Storm. "Do you hear something?"

"Nah," Storm grunts. "Unless you mean the backstabbing piece of shit who used to be our bandmate."

The words sting, but at least I know exactly where they stand now.

I gave up everything to get the girl I love back, and that includes them.

"Thanks for coming," I mutter before walking away.

"Jesus fucking Christ," Memphis snarls. "*That's* all you have to say to us?"

"I don't know why you're surprised," Storm scoffs. "He's always been a selfish prick."

That does it.

Turning around, I glare at him. "Fuck you."

Some woman placing flowers on a headstone the next row over casts me a dirty look.

Memphis narrows his eyes. "You've already fucked us enough, asshole."

"Without lube," Storm adds.

Dragging a hand down my face, I exhale sharply. "I didn't mean—"

"Bullshit," Storm interjects. "You know exactly what you did. You've known for *years*."

He's got me there. "I should have told you."

Memphis lets out a humorless laugh. "Or maybe you could have just—I don't know—*not* stolen our hit fucking song."

"Last I checked, they don't make time machines."

"Too bad," Storm states. "Maybe then I'd let you die instead of pulling your sorry ass out of that car." He salutes me with his middle finger. "But hey, enjoy the rest of your life with your new bride. Gotta hand it to you, man. Manipulating the girl whose song you stole into marrying you was a genius move. I'm sure Chandler and Vic are thrilled."

I expected his anger and hostility. It's Storm, it would be weird if he *wasn't* having a bitch fit.

But wishing he left me for dead and thinking I married Lennon as some kind of PR stunt is a special kind of low.

I considered this asshole my family. My brother.

And he knows damn well that I love Lennon because three minutes before I coded in that goddamn ambulance, I *told* him.

"You know I'd never do that to her."

The corners of his eyes crease as he scrutinizes me. "The only thing I know is that you're a snake." His expression turns hard. "A worthless scumbag, just like your pops."

Indignity surges through me...and then comes the rage.

He's hit below the belt, not once, but *twice* now. Fuck this motherfucker.

I launch my fist into his face.

Storm stumbles back in disbelief. Then he punches me in the

stomach.

I cough a few times. Getting hit in the stomach fucking sucks, but this shit is far from over. "You hit like a bitch, *Reese.*"

He hates being called by his first name because it's *his* father's. The only one who's allowed to use it without meeting the wrath of God is Grams.

Storm puffs out his chest like a peacock and rolls his shoulders back, like a boxer getting ready to fight.

Bring it on.

"Good thing we're at a cemetery because you're a dead man."

I motion for him to hit me again. "And you're a fucking pussy."

"Better than being a liar. I hope Lennon takes you to the cleaners before kicking your ass to the curb."

White-hot rage surges once more and then I lose my shit...and so does he.

Snarling curses and slinging punches left and right, we pummel the shit out of each other.

Commotion rings out behind me, and a few people gasp. One of them being Skylar and the other Grams.

"I told you to talk to them, not start a brawl. What is the matter with you boys?" She whacks us with her purse. "Stop attacking each other. This is a *funeral,* for crying out loud."

It's about to be Storm's.

"I'm not sure which one to put money on," Quinn exclaims. "Storm's bigger, but my brother's scrappier."

"Nothing to see here, folks," Memphis says to the horrified onlookers. "Just a little family discussion."

Memphis tries to get in the middle of us then, but we end up taking him down with us as our rumble moves to the ground.

"Fuck," he grunts, kneeling beside us. "I'll give you assholes another minute to get this shit out of your systems and then *I'm* gonna start throwing punches."

My former best friend is a big oaf, so he gets the upper hand and climbs on top of me. "Why didn't you tell me the truth?"

I plunge two fingers into his eye sockets. When his hands fly up, I take the opportunity to slam him into the ground. "I wanted to, but I didn't know how."

Blinking, he tries to toss me off him, but he's weaker than he was before. "With your fucking mouth, you idiot."

I punch him again, but it doesn't have much force behind it because I'm losing steam, too. "And *that's* exactly why I didn't, you oversized dildo."

Gripping the collar of my shirt, he gets the upper hand once more. "What the fuck are you talking about, you anal pore?"

I give him the truth because I'm man enough to admit it now. "I tried to write a song for years, but I *couldn't*…because I'm an idiot." Embarrassment courses through me as I continue. "We only had one shot with Vic. Our dream was right fucking there. I didn't want to blow it."

Rolling off me, he catches his breath.

I peer up at the gray clouds. It's gonna rain any second.

"You're not an idiot," he says after a few moments.

I might be good at some things, but can't read, write, or spell well because my brain doesn't work the way brains are supposed to.

I fucking hate it. But it's still no excuse.

"What I did to Lennon—and to you guys—is beyond fucked up. I wish I could take it back." Tilting my head, I eye Storm and Memphis, who are on opposite sides of me. "I'm sorry you both got caught in the cross fire of my mess. You guys are my family and I not only stole and lied, I ruined everything you worked for."

Closing my eyes, I take a deep breath. I don't know what the future holds, but there's no longer a crushing weight on my chest.

The truth—the horrible thing I did—is out there.

But my newfound freedom comes at a heavy price. These guys.

Storm snickers, catching me off guard. "Did you call me an *oversized dildo*?"

My lips twitch. I guess I did. "You called me an *anal pore*."

"He got that from me," Quinn calls out somewhere in the distance.

Memphis snorts. "Guess Phoenix isn't the only one who steals."

"Yeah. I stole an insult; Phoenix stole a song..." Storm's tongue finds his cheek. "And *you* stole your brother's girl."

"Foster brother," Memphis mutters under his breath. "And she was never my girl."

Storm and I exchange a glance. *Bullshit.*

Sighing, Memphis gets off the ground. "What happens now?"

Storm's the next to stand. "I don't know." His gaze swings my way as I rise to my feet. "That's up to this anal pore."

My focus drifts to Lennon, who hasn't moved a muscle. She didn't even come over here during the fight, which only further confirms that her head's in a bad place right now.

She's always been there for me. It's time I take care of her.

"I don't know," I tell them truthfully. "I need to be with Lennon."

I don't give a fuck about anything else.

Memphis's stare snags on Skylar, who's talking to Quinn and Grams. "I think we all could use a break."

Gripping the back of his neck, Storm blows out a breath. "Agreed. I'm looking forward to kicking back, smoking a few blunts, getting my dick sucked, and relaxing."

I asked Lennon if she wanted to go to my house in California a couple of days ago, and the death glare she gave me was my answer.

She's not ready to leave and I won't make her.

"Well, you'll have the entire house to yourself now. Go nuts." I point a finger in his face. "Don't fuck in my bed."

I didn't ask Lennon, on account of her grieving and shit, but I don't foresee her having an issue with Quinn staying with us. In fact, I think it will be a good thing since I know how much she adores her.

As if on cue, Quinn moseys on over.

"This weather sucks," she whines as the sky opens up and it starts drizzling.

"Don't worry," I assure her. "Rain in Florida is like wind in Chicago. You'll get used to it. Besides, it never lasts long."

She gives me a smile that doesn't quite reach her eyes. "Yeah."

"What's the matter?"

She looks away. "Nothing…it's just…" She shakes her head. "Never mind."

"Quinn—"

"There's this *incredible* class taught by a prestigious acting coach that I really want to sign up for, but it's in Los Angeles so I can't attend if I come to Florida—"

"You're staying with me."

She's my responsibility, which means she goes where I go.

"Please, Phoenix. I swear I will never ask you for anything ever again."

"No." Goddammit. Now her lower lip is quivering. "I'm sorry, but you're still a kid. I'm not letting you stay in a house across the fucking country with no adult supervision."

"I'm *not* a kid. I'll be sixteen in nine days. Heck, in the Middle Ages, girls my age were already married and pushing out babies." She crosses her arms. "And I'll have *adult supervision* because Storm will be there."

Storm snorts. "Not to babysit you."

Batting her eyelashes, she turns to face him. "Please, Storm. *Please*. If you say yes, Phoenix will too, because he trusts you. I swear I won't bother you. I just…I want this *so* bad. It's my dream."

"Not happening," Storm says.

Quinn deflates. "But I need this. I'm literally begging you." Her gaze ping-pongs between us. "How you guys feel about music is how I feel about acting. It's everything to me. It's the only reason I'm still alive."

Fuck. Our personalities are vastly different, but that drive to pursue her dreams—because they saved you when all the bad shit nearly killed you—is clearly something we both share.

I don't want to take that away from her.

I took away Lennon's and I'll never fucking forgive myself for it.

Storm and I exchange a glance and I know he's about to cave.

So am I.

"Don't expect me to cook for you or pick up after your shit," Storm grunts.

"And you better get straight C's in school," I add. "I don't care that you're doing it online. It's no excuse."

Quinn blinks. "But I get straight A's in school."

Right. *She's* the smart sibling.

"Then I better not see any C's. The first time I do, your ass will be on the first plane back to Florida."

Her face lights up. "Does that mean I can stay in LA?"

"I guess."

Quinn lets out a squeal loud enough to wake the cemetery before throwing her arms around me. "You're the best big brother in the whole entire world. Thank you so much."

Technically, she should be thanking Storm. Aside from Lennon, he's the only one I'd trust to look after her when I'm not around.

That's when it occurs to me. "How are you paying for these *prestigious* acting classes?"

In other words, how much is it gonna cost me?

"With the money you gave me for being your personal assistant last week. It will be enough for five classes."

At least she's not spending it on implants.

But fuck, a *thousand* dollars per class? She better win an Oscar one day.

Letting out another squeal, she runs over to Skylar and Grams. "It worked. Phoenix is gonna let me stay."

Memphis—who's been busy on his phone—frowns. "I have to head back to LA. Gwen has a doctor's appointment tomorrow, but she wants me home tonight."

Storm makes the sound of a whip cracking.

"Moving into the Barclay mansion, huh? That's gonna be…interesting."

And by interesting? I mean, fucking horrifying.

Unlike his baby mama, Memphis values his privacy and lives a modest lifestyle. Shacking up with a reality show star that lives for drama and loves having cameras in her face twenty-four-seven is his worst nightmare.

His lack of response says more than any words can.

"When are you proposing?" Storm inquires with a smirk.

Dodging the question, he slaps a hand on my back. "Tell Lennon I'm sorry—"

The sound of people arguing has us whipping around.

"Leave me alone," Lennon yells before slapping Chandler across the face.

I don't know what this motherfucker did to upset her but whatever it was, it will be the last thing he ever does.

Memphis and Storm snatch both my arms a second before I pummel him into the ground. "What the fuck did you do?"

He rubs his bright-red cheek. "I simply tried to have a conversation with your *wife* and asked if she'd be willing to do an interview."

"Interview for what?" Skylar questions.

"To set the record straight about..." He flicks a hand in my direction. "I'm trying to save the band. Something their PR person should be focusing on instead of planning funerals."

He's lucky I'm being restrained because I want to snap his goddamn neck like a fucking twig.

"There's nothing to set the record straight about, and Lennon's not doing any interviews on my behalf."

The fact he would even ask Lennon, let alone at her father's *funeral*, makes me want to bash his skull in.

No wonder she bitch-slapped him.

Skylar appears equally agitated. "I told you I was handling it."

"No, you're not," Chandler booms. "Being eye candy for Josh isn't going to cut it anymore. You have an actual job to do."

Memphis takes a step back, releasing me. Storm follows suit.

Chandler raises a hand. "Before you three beat me to a bloody pulp, hear me out. I may seem like the bad guy, but it's only because I give a shit. If you drive this band into the ground, that's it. You only get one shot at the top and the fall down is brutal." His shoulders slump. "Individually, the three of you are exceptionally talented, but the three of you together? You blow any other band out of the water. Don't fuck this up."

I get what he's saying, but Lennon's more important than music.

"We're taking a hiatus."

"For how long?"

I shrug. "Until further notice."

Staring him down, I take a step closer. "Don't harass my wife again. Because they won't be able to hold me back next time."

It's his one and only warning.

Frustrated, he drags a hand through his hair. "You're making a mistake."

No. My mistake was losing Lennon.

"Phoenix is taking some time off for his mental health," Skylar says. "That's the statement we're putting out."

Works for me.

However, it's clear Chandler doesn't like that one bit. "What about his marriage to Lennon? You need to tell the press."

Skylar shakes her head. "No. Not yet."

Chandler makes a face. "What do you mean *no*? That's the only angle we have—"

"My marriage isn't an *angle*," I interject.

"I came up with a better approach." Skylar straightens her spine. "We're going to take the heat off Phoenix by diverting everyone's attention to someone else."

Chandler's eyebrows shoot up to the sky. "Who?"

Her gaze lands on the guy standing next to me. "Memphis and Gwyneth." She turns her attention back to Chandler. "I'll plan the proposal on the plane ride home and then we'll set up a meeting with the Barclay's publicist and get the ball rolling. As long as Memphis and Gwen are center stage, it keeps the band relevant and it will buy us some time. At least for a little while."

Nodding his approval, Chandler strokes his chin. "I like it."

Of course he does.

"You should get started on it right away," Chandler states. "We can't afford to waste any more time." He looks around. "The jet is fueled up and ready to go, so anyone who'd like to go back to California tonight better get their asses in the car."

After exchanging goodbyes, they leave.

And then it's just me and my wife…who's back to staring at her father's coffin.

The grave diggers lingering close by swap uneasy looks. They need to get started, but it's clear they'd prefer not to have a family member watching them.

Walking back over, I take a seat next to Lennon. There's a reason they don't want people to stick around for this part.

"We should go."

She keeps her gaze trained on the coffin. "No."

Fuck. I don't think her being here is a good idea, but whatever she wants, I'll go along with.

"Then we'll stay."

Only, the moment they begin lowering the casket into the ground, Lennon starts crying.

The workers glance at each other, then at me…waiting for me to take control of the situation.

But I'm at a loss because I've never been in this position before.

When Josh died, I got drunk before the funeral and high immediately after.

And then I went on a bender for a week until Storm eventually found me partying in some hotel room I have no recollection of ever walking into.

But Josh was my friend, and even though I tolerated him more than most—mainly because he fed me drugs and supported my downward spiral—he wasn't a good person or a good friend to me.

My grief for him was based on my own guilt.

It's completely different for Lennon, though. Her dad was a great father, and her grief is so intense because she loved him so much.

My eyes drop to the headstone next to his soon-to-be grave. The name *Kate* is scrawled on it. Along with the words beloved wife and mother.

Because he was her everything.

For the first time, I find myself in the position of not knowing what Lennon needs. I don't want to push her because that would be selfish and cruel. But I also don't want to give her too much space because I don't want her to feel like she's all alone.

This is her process. I'm just here to offer support while she goes through it.

"You can continue," I tell the workers, despite Lennon's sobbing.

Pulling her into my arms, I do the only thing I can think of.

I start singing "Let It Be" by The Beatles.

And I don't stop.

Not until after her father's casket has been lowered into the ground, his grave has been filled with the earth, the workers have left...

And Lennon decides it's finally time to go.

CHAPTER 77
PHOENIX

Frustration claws up my throat when I spy the tray of uneaten food sitting on the nightstand.

I brought Lennon lunch two hours ago and just like breakfast, she hasn't touched it.

It's been three weeks since her dad died and while I didn't expect her to get over it, I thought she'd be better by now.

Mrs. Palma—who I'm certain was a bona fide saint in another life—has tried to coax her into getting counseling, but Lennon doesn't want to.

The only thing she wants is her dad.

Which is the only thing I can't give her.

"You have to eat something."

Rolling over in bed, she burrows under the covers, ignoring me.

I plop down on the mattress. The little I actually do manage to force-feed her daily is hardly sustainable for life and the sweatpants she's been living in are getting looser.

While I love my wife for what's on the inside, I'm also highly fucking attracted to her. Lennon losing her curves isn't something I'm down with.

"Pick something off this tray. Or so help me God, I will strap you down to a chair and make you finish every last crumb."

I'm contemplating begging at this point—which is something I never do—when her hand thrusts out from underneath the covers.

Head buried beneath the blankets, her hand blindly roots around the tray. Bypassing the sandwich and banana, she settles on the granola bar.

I breathe a sigh of relief because we're making progress. "Thank you."

I'm halfway to the door when something strikes the back of my head.

I don't even have to look to know it was the granola bar.

My lips twitch because if Lennon's assaulting me, it means she's still in there somewhere.

I just need to ride this out a little longer.

Hitting the speakerphone button, I rest the phone on the counter so I can finish loading the dishwasher...something I haven't done in years.

"How's Quinn?" I ask when Storm picks up.

I talk to my sister regularly, but she claims everything's fantastic and there are no issues.

I want the uncensored report and I know Storm will give it to me.

"Quinn's fine," he grinds out. "Me, on the other hand? Not so much."

"What's wrong?"

"Nothing, it's cool. But your sister's a goddamn handful, man."

I stiffen. "Is she getting into trouble?"

"No. It's just...I need a break. She's annoying the shit out of me."

I had a feeling this would happen. Those two are like oil and water. Frankly, I'm surprised the arrangement lasted this long.

"I'll book a flight—"

"Not necessary," he interjects. "I called in reinforcements."

I close the dishwasher. "Reinforcements?"

"Grams," he tells me with a laugh. "Her plane will be landing in an hour and she'll be staying here for one whole glorious week. Which means I'll finally have some time to…you know."

"Fuck?"

"Exactly." He sighs. "Having a kid around all the time really messes with a man's sex life."

So does grief.

Not that I'm expecting Lennon to take care of my needs. I just hate how we've gone from fucking like animals twice a day to…jack shit.

Unless you count all the jacking I've been doing in the shower.

As if reading my mind, Storm says, "How's Lennon?"

"She's fine."

"Out of bed fine? Or…"

"Throwing a granola bar at my head fine because she doesn't want to eat."

"Ah," he says. "So the *still not okay* fine."

Scrubbing a hand down my face, I take a seat at the table.

The same table her father was sitting at when he suffered his stroke. No wonder Lennon hasn't stepped foot in the kitchen.

"She needs to get out of the house."

"Yeah," he agrees. "Some fresh air would be good for her."

"I mean permanently. How the hell is she supposed to move on when she's stuck in the place where everything is a reminder of him?"

It's like pouring salt in a wound that won't ever heal.

He sucks in a breath. "It's not a bad idea. There's just one problem."

"What?"

"If she's throwing granola bars at your head and refusing to leave her bed, how the hell are you gonna get her to leave the house?"

I have no fucking idea.

CHAPTER 78
PHOENIX

Four days later, I'm calling in some reinforcements of my own.

Skylar.

Mrs. Palma's great, but Skylar knows exactly what Lennon's going through because she recently went through it herself when she lost Josh.

I'm also hoping she'll be able to sway Lennon to move to California, because when *I* broached the topic, Lennon locked me out of her bedroom for twenty-four hours.

"You know what to do, right?"

Skylar nods. "I'll try my best to complete the mission, but I make no guarantees."

"Tell her we can buy a new house." I rub the knot of tension forming in my neck. "I'll do and give her anything she wants."

I just need to get her out of *here*.

"Got it."

Squaring her shoulders, she heads up the staircase, and I call Storm.

He picks up on the third ring, sounding out of breath. "Emergency?"

The sound of some chick moaning in the background fills my

ears. That's when I remember he's fucking his way through Los Angeles because Gram's is still in town for a few more days.

"Nope."

After hanging up with him, I dial Memphis.

Unlike Storm, he sounds…bored.

"Hey," he drawls. "I was just about to call you."

"Why? What's up?"

"Nothing." He makes an irritated noise in his throat. "Aside from dodging the camera crew because they're filming today."

I stifle a laugh. To be a fly on the wall of the Barclay mansion right now.

As if on cue, he snaps, "Get that thing out of my goddamn face. I told you not to fucking film me."

"Calm down, babe," Gwyneth whines in the background. "It will only be for a minute."

There's a loud crash.

"He just broke my camera!" some guy shouts.

"You're lucky it wasn't your fucking face," Memphis bellows before a door slams shut. "Sorry about that, man. I'm back."

I grin. "How's engagement life?"

Two weeks ago he popped the question and just like Skylar said, it took some of the heat off me. I owe him.

He snorts. "How's newlywed life?"

Touché, motherfucker.

"I'm trying to convince Lennon to move to California. Or rather, Skylar is."

"Shouldn't be an issue." I hear him light up a cigarette. "Sky's good at getting whatever she wants out of people."

I don't miss the venomous edge in his tone.

Opening the back door to the patio, I light my own cigarette. "You two on speaking terms yet?"

"Only when we have to be." The edge in his voice intensifies. "She's talking to *Chandler* a lot, though."

No surprise there.

Memphis doesn't strike me as stupid. Far from it—given the way he tends to sit back and observe shit—but maybe he doesn't realize what I do.

"Chandler wants Skylar."

"Yeah, no shit."

He goes silent for several beats…and then.

"I don't give a fuck," he barks, which means he definitely does. "I have a baby on the way, and I'm engaged. Let her be someone else's problem for a change."

"Right."

"Vic called me the other day," he states, changing the subject.

The hairs on the back of my neck rise. "What did he say?"

"Not much. Aside from reminding me that we have a contract for a five-album minimum and if we don't adhere to it…he'll sue."

Shit. I knew he'd force his hand sooner or later.

Although I expected it to be later since it's only the middle of September.

We'd still be in Europe if I didn't cancel the tour so I'm not sure why the asshole is trying to steamroll us already.

I take a long drag of my cigarette. "The next album isn't scheduled to come out until January."

The songs have already been chosen so it would only take us a couple weeks to record.

"I know." He blows out a breath. "Look, Storm didn't want to tell you this on account of everything you're dealing with, but I think you should know…"

"Know what?" I urge when his voice trails off.

"Vic said he'll find a guy to replace you if necessary."

Replace me? What the fuck?

"I'd like to see him try."

"That's what I told him, but apparently he's got someone in mind. Some new kid he saw perform a few weeks back. Said he's got a phenomenal voice."

It's what he said about *me* four years ago.

Chandler warned me this would happen if I didn't play my cards right.

I might be rare…but not insurmountable.

Somewhere in the world, there's another guy out there with a nice face and a great voice.

One who'd give up anything to take my place.

But *my* place is with Lennon.

I chose music over her—over everything—for years. There's no way I could go back to living my dreams when I can't even get her out of bed.

Music sets my soul on fire, but she makes my heart beat.

I can't have both, though.

And this time I'm making the right choice. *Her.*

"You should have Vic set up a meeting. See if it's a good fit."

Memphis says something, but I don't register what because I disconnect the call.

I find Skylar standing in the kitchen when I walk back inside. "That was quick. How'd it go?"

Averting her gaze, she worries her bottom lip between her teeth. "She wants an annulment."

The words hit me like a freight train and my chest pulls so tight it physically hurts. "What?"

"I'm sorry, Phoenix. But she seemed really adamant. She asked if I could contact a lawyer and have the paperwork drawn up by the end of the week."

Fuck that. "No."

Skylar opens her mouth, but then her phone rings.

"Sorry, I have to take this," she says before answering it. "Calm down, Chandler. What's wrong?" She pinches the bridge of her nose. "I don't know why they keep trying to force him. He made it perfectly clear that he doesn't want to be on camera. Yes, I know." Glancing up at the ceiling, she sighs. "I'm leaving Phoenix's house now. I'll go over to the Barclay's as soon as I get back to LA and see if I can work something out."

After hanging up, she looks at me. "I have to go."

"We're not getting an annulment."

Nodding, she squeezes my shoulder.

The moment she walks out the door, I sprint up the staircase.

I expected Lennon to still be in bed, but I find her waltzing out of the bathroom. Her hair is wet and there's a towel wrapped around her body, so she must be feeling better.

Which makes this annulment bullshit even more perplexing.

"We're not getting an annulment."

Sidestepping me, she heads for the bedroom. "Skylar told me you'd give me anything I want. *That's* what I want."

Her tone is cold, detached...indifferent.

I follow her into the bedroom. "I thought you loved me."

Only then do I see the evidence of it on her face. "I do."

I don't get it. "Then what's the problem?"

Making a noise of disgust, she walks over to her dresser and takes out some clothes.

"Answer the question, Groupie," I growl after a minute goes by. "If you love me, then why the fuck—"

"Because *you* dragged my friend here to try and convince me to leave my home so I can be pulled back into your atmosphere again." She tugs on a new pair of sweatpants. "I told you the other day that I didn't want to, but as usual, you have to keep pushing until you get your way. Just like you pushed me to go to Europe when I wanted to go home and see my dad."

I rear back from the force of the blow.

I thought she realized that making her go to Europe was only so I could do the right thing and give her what she deserves.

I had no idea her dad was gonna die.

Guilt—my old companion—rears its ugly head. Along with shame.

If I didn't fuck up to begin with, I wouldn't have had to make things right...and she would have had more time with her father.

"I'm sorry."

It seems the only thing I ever give this girl is heartache.

"I don't blame you." A scowl twists her features. "I blame *myself* because I can never say no to you." She pulls a T-shirt over her head and climbs back into bed. "But I am this time because I'm not leaving my home. I can't."

"Then we won't."

I'll stay in her atmosphere. Problem solved.

Only it's not because she snaps, "Which is exactly why I want an annulment."

And we've circled right back to where we started. Her wanting to end this and me not understanding why.

"I just told you we can stay."

"But it's not what you want," she yells, bolting up. "And why would you? You're a rock star, Phoenix. Music isn't what you do, it's who you *are*. I'm not letting you throw your life away just to watch me grieve for the rest of mine. It's not fair to you."

She doesn't get it. After everything, she *still* doesn't fucking get it.

"You're what I want, Lennon. I love music, but I love you more."

She wipes away the tear sliding down her cheek. "And I love you. So much so I refuse to let you give up your dream for me."

Round and round we go. The harder I try to hold on, the more she pushes me away.

"Fuck you."

Her head snaps up. "I'm never gonna be the same, Phoenix. This pain. This fucking *agony* that's taken up residence in my soul...it will never go away." Her eyes fill with more tears. "I'm trying to save you from a lifetime of misery. Don't you get that?"

I grab her face. "Don't *you* get that we're not something you can throw away or end? I don't care if you stay in this fucking bed for the rest of your life and cry every goddamn day. I'm not leaving you."

Because I'd rather be miserable with her than happy with anyone else.

CHAPTER 79
PHOENIX

I thought we had a breakthrough, but two days later Lennon's still lying in bed and barely eating.

According to Mrs. Palma, that's how grief works. It comes in stages and waves and it doesn't follow a set pattern.

One second you could be smiling and the next? The pain strikes and you're right back to square one.

Problem is, I can't seem to get my wife out of *square one*.

I haven't seen Lennon's smile in over a month. I'm beginning to think I might never see it again.

Mrs. Palma told me I should give her some space, and not the kind that involves me closing the door to the bedroom and going downstairs.

The kind that involves me leaving the house for a few hours. This way Lennon has no choice but to take care of herself.

I didn't like the idea, but I'm running out of options. And things to do because there's nothing interesting in this shit town.

I find myself at a diner eating a bland burger for dinner and talking to Storm on the phone.

"Have you met him?"

My *replacement*.

"No. The meeting isn't until next month."

"Why so long?"

"We're giving you time to change your mind."

I take a bite of my burger. When I swallow, it feels like sawdust going down. "I won't."

"You're—"

"How's Quinn?" I ask, changing the topic of discussion to something that doesn't make me want to throw myself off the nearest bridge.

"She's fine. Moody as fuck, but fine."

"She's a teenager. It comes with the territory."

Shit, we're twenty-three and we're still moody bastards.

"True, but this isn't typical teenage angst bullshit. She seems mad at me about something."

No surprise there. Storm isn't the easiest person to get along with.

But Quinn's not the type to let anything get her down for too long. "I'm sure she'll be fine in a few days. Just go easy on her. She's…"

"Crazy?" Storm cuts in. "Dramatic? Annoying as hell?"

"Sensitive."

He makes a grumbling sound. "Yea—oh, hey, Juvie. Phoenix is on the phone. Wanna say hi?"

A moment later, Quinn's voice comes over the line. Although there's no pep in it like usual. "Hi."

"What's wrong?"

"Is it okay if I stay with Skylar for a couple of days?"

I don't have an issue with it, but I want to know why she feels the sudden need to flee the scene. Given she has a history of being a runaway, it's not a good sign. "What happened?"

"Nothing," she whispers. "I just…I really want to see Skylar."

"Okay." I take a sip of my water. "You can stay with Skylar for a couple days. But after I think you should come to Hillcrest."

"No. I'm fine. I swear," she says, even though I hear her voice crack.

"Quinn—"

"I have my period," she blurts out. "And I need to go to the store to buy tampons, but I don't want to ask Storm to drive me because he gets weird about that stuff."

That makes two of us. However, this I can handle.

"Hang tight. I got you."

After disconnecting the call, I pull up my speech-to-text app and order ten boxes of tampons and ten pounds' worth of chocolate to be delivered to my house within the next thirty minutes. I figure that should be enough to hold her over for a while.

It's nice to actually be able to solve a problem for a goddamn change.

"Is there anything else I can get you?" the waitress asks.

Yeah. *My wife.*

Because I really fucking miss her.

I'm pleasantly surprised to find Lennon dressed in something other than sweatpants and standing in the kitchen when I get home.

Maybe Mrs. Palma was right, and giving her some space was what she needed.

"Hey."

My smile falls when I see the bottle of booze in her hand. But then I remind myself that aside from our *never have I ever* game in high school and the night she and Skylar got trashed, she never drinks.

Hell, she could probably use one.

Bridging the space between us, she folds her arms around my neck and kisses me.

It's like a shot of epinephrine to the heart. Immediately, my arms find her waist and my tongue parts her lips.

Judging by the alcohol on her breath and the overpowering taste I get of it, she's had more than one drink.

Giggling, her fingers go to the zipper on my jeans. "Want to have some fun?"

My dick says *fuck yes*, but my mind says *pump the brakes* because she's slurring her words.

"You're drunk."

"Drunk and horny."

Then she drops to her knees.

"Lenn—"

Fuck. And now my cock is in her mouth.

Groaning, I grip the counter, my mind and body on two vastly different trains. I crave her, but something about this feels fucking wrong.

Not for my cock, though, because he's rock hard and having a great time.

But if Lennon was sober right now, she wouldn't be sucking me off.

She'd be upstairs in bed crying.

Christ. Sometimes doing the honorable thing really fucking sucks —or in my case doesn't suck—because I stop her.

"You can blow me when you're not trashed."

"You don't..." She sways—a little too much—because she falls back on her ass and her head hits the oven. "You don't want me?"

I gesture to my dick. "Does it look like I don't want you?"

She reaches for me again, but I stop her. "You're drunk." I run the pad of my thumb over her cheekbone. "Trust me, if you weren't, I'd fuck you so good you'd beg me not to stop and so hard you wouldn't be able to walk for days."

Her lower lip sticks out in an adorable little pout. "Baby, *come on.*" She shakes her head emphatically. "I'm not dru—"

And then she pukes. All over my shoes, herself, and the floor.

After tucking my cock away, I ease Lennon to her feet. "Let's get you cleaned up."

"I'm sorry," she whispers as I lead her out of the kitchen. "I'm such a mess."

She is.

But she's my mess.

CHAPTER 80

LENNON

Wiping the steam from my shower off the mirror, I stare at my reflection. I look different and it's not because of the ten pounds I lost…it's because I feel different.

Empty.

There's a void inside me again, only this time nothing can fill it.

Skylar said it won't always hurt this much. Mrs. Palma told me it will get better with time.

They're wrong.

I don't know how I'm supposed to live in a world without my dad. I don't know how I'm supposed to ever laugh or smile again, knowing I'll never see *him* laugh or smile again.

I don't know how I'm supposed to get over this and move on.

Blowing out a shaky breath, I try to inhale past the crushing agony in the center of my chest, but I can't.

This pain has taken me hostage—drowning me in a sea of misery—and I can't seem to escape from its clutches.

Two nights ago, I got drunk. I thought it would numb me and I'd get a reprieve, but it didn't happen.

The only thing it made me do was force myself on my husband and throw up.

My husband.

I should be ecstatic that my wildest fantasies came true and I'm married to Phoenix Walker.

But I'm not...because I'm too busy grieving the first man I ever loved.

I find Phoenix curled up on the bed sleeping when I walk into my bedroom. A quick glance at the clock on the nightstand tells me it's just after two a.m.

Evidently grief makes you lose all concept of time.

I don't even know what day of the week it is.

I'm a mess. And the Lennon BDD—before Dad's death—would be positively mortified.

I'm too sad to care, though. About myself. About anything.

The broken thing in my chest squeezes, reminding me that's not true because there's still one thing I care about.

Him.

Phoenix doesn't deserve this, though.

I know he wants to spend the rest of his life with me, but it won't be a happy one. Because ten seconds after I became his wife, I turned into a different person. One he's stuck with.

It's not fair to him.

But the harder I try to push him away, the harder he holds on.

Despite me hating him at his worst...he loves me at mine.

Opening my dresser drawer, I pull out a pair of pajamas and get dressed.

I might be a ghost, but one with a heart that still beats for him. He hides it well, but not being able to sing or perform has to be eating him alive.

I know exactly what it's like to lose that thing that makes your soul come alive—the thing that heals you—and even though he took it away from me, I don't want to do the same to him.

Problem is, I have no idea where his career stands or what's been going on in public or behind the scenes.

Chandler—that no-good rotten bastard—told me I needed to do an interview and tell the world he didn't steal my song. It's something I would have agreed to do at some point—once I felt like I was no longer drowning—if only he stopped there.

But no, the asshole kept talking.

He told me that just because my father was dead, it wasn't an excuse to kill everyone else's career. That even Yoko still wanted John to make music. That I should *want* to do this interview because Phoenix and I don't have a prenup and it meant I'd get more money when we inevitably divorced within the next year.

But I don't want Phoenix's money. I just want him to keep shining.

Grabbing my cell, I pad downstairs into the living room. Not only is Skylar my friend, she's his publicist.

I wasn't up for talking much the other day—aside from asking her to find me a lawyer—but I know she'll tell me the truth about what's been going on with Phoenix from a public relations standpoint.

Then I'll know how bad the damage is and can figure out a way to fix it.

Fortunately, California is three hours ahead, so even though it's late, she'll still be awake.

She answers after the third ring. "Hey."

I plop down on the couch. "Hey. Do you have a second?"

"For you? Always. What's up?"

Drawing my knees to my chest, I cradle the phone between my neck and shoulder. "What's going on with Phoenix?"

I can tell this throws her because there's a brief pause before she says, "What do you mean? Isn't he with you?"

"Yeah." I rub my forehead. "I meant public image and career-wise...after Europe."

She sucks in a breath. "Phoenix wouldn't want you to worry—"

"You're supposed to be *my* friend too, Skylar," I remind her. "Tell me what happened. Please."

"Hold on," she says. "You need friend Skylar right now, which means I can't talk to you about this here. I'll call you back in five minutes, okay?"

Safe to say *I'm* the one who's thrown now.

"Okay."

As promised, my phone rings approximately five minutes later.

"Hey."

"Hey. Where were you?"

There's a long pause. So long I almost think she hung up.

"Skylar? Are you th—"

"Chandler's house," she whispers.

My jaw drops because I was not expecting that. "Why are you at *Chandler's* house?" I glance up at the clock on the wall. "At eleven twenty at night?"

"I'm not in his house anymore," she defends. "I'm sitting in my car outside."

That's a dodge if there ever was one. "Why?"

"Because I don't want him to overhear our conversation."

"I meant, why are you at Chandler's house?"

There was a time where we skirted around each other's questions —unsure if we could trust one another—but we've broken that wall down.

At least, I *thought* we did.

She clears her throat. "We were going over some PR stuff for Memphis."

"PR is your job, though. Not his."

"Yes, but he's the manager. Technically, PR falls under his jurisdiction, too."

That makes sense, I guess, but still. There's something fishy going on. I can feel it.

"You and Chandler aren't…" I let my sentence trail off because it sounds ridiculous to my own ears. Not only is Skylar light-years out of Chandler's league, he's sixteen years older than her.

"No," she says, although she doesn't sound very convincing. "He's my boss…sort of."

"Which is all the more reason he shouldn't be summoning you to his house at eleven at night."

"He didn't. I've been here since this afternoon."

My mouth drops open for a second time. "What the hell is going on with Memphis that requires you to spend *that* much time with Chandler?"

"Do you want to know what's going on with your husband or do you want to keep speculating about my love life?" she snaps.

Fair enough. "Option one."

But we are *definitely* circling back to option two at some point.

"Okay, so obviously, Phoenix canceled the rest of the European tour."

"Right. That much I know. Tell me what I don't know. Like how bad the fallout was after...you know."

He told the entire freaking world that he stole my song.

She exhales sharply. "Okay, so at first it was really ugly. Cancel culture was in full effect and revenue crashed. Like nearly flatlined crashed."

I wince. No wonder Chandler wanted me to do that interview sooner rather than later.

"I sent out a public statement declaring that Phoenix was taking some time for his mental health," she continues. "And then I diverted people's attention to someone they love."

"Who?"

"Gwyneth Barclay," she says dryly. "It's hard for people to hate Sharp Objects when the entire world loves Gwyneth, who's now officially engaged and having a baby with Memphis. Revenue still isn't what it used to be, but it's picking up."

My stomach rolls. This must be killing her.

I wish I did that freaking interview like Chandler wanted.

"You didn't have to—"

"Memphis and Gwen are having a baby." Despite trying to keep her tone indifferent, I catch the trace of emotion in it. "The white picket fence was bound to happen. At least now it's mutually beneficial for everyone."

Except her.

"I'm so sorry."

None of this is fair to her.

"It is what it is." She clears her throat. "Anyway, that's where we stand at the moment. Phoenix is canceled but Sharp Objects isn't."

"Well, considering Phoenix is a big part of Sharp Objects, I'm sure people will come around, right?"

They *have* to.

"Yeah, about that…"

There's a different emotion lacing her voice now. Dread.

"What?"

"Phoenix isn't part of Sharp Objects anymore."

I jump up so fast I get light-headed and have to sit back down. "*What?*"

"I mean technically he is…but he won't be."

"What do you mean he *won't* be?" I gasp when I realize. "Vic fired him?"

"Almost."

It's like she's speaking in riddles.

"I need you to give it to me straight, Skylar. Right freaking now."

Another heavy exhale leaves her. "Okay, so from what Chandler —and Storm—have told me, Vic is livid about Phoenix canceling the tour and outing himself as a thief just because he stuck his dick in some small-town pussy from back home—those are his words, not mine."

"Duly noted."

"Bottom line? Vic doesn't like his money being fucked with and from what Chandler disclosed to me the other night, he makes a lot of money. Like a *lot*."

Not surprising, since Phoenix and the rest of the guys make a lot of money as well.

"Anyway," she continues. "Vic was ready to drop Phoenix, but Chandler convinced him not to and promised he'd turn this whole thing around. That's why he approached you at the funeral and asked you to do an interview. Even though he had no right to."

It makes me hate Chandler less now. But only by a little bit.

"After my Gwen and Memphis strategy went into effect, Vic was a little calmer because sales went up and he started focusing on the upcoming album. However, when he mentioned moving up the scheduled studio time since they're no longer in Europe, Chandler had no choice but to tell him that Phoenix declared he was taking a hiatus and he didn't know when—or if—he'd be back."

Uh-oh. "Shit."

"It gets worse." She audibly swallows. "Vic called Memphis and Storm and reminded them that they had all signed a contract for a five-album commitment and if they didn't want him to sue the shit out of them, they needed to either convince Phoenix to get on board...or he'd be replaced."

I'd almost laugh if it wasn't so serious. "There's no replacing Phoenix."

"That's exactly what they told him, but evidently Vic's got some guy in the works. Chandler showed me a pic and let me hear a demo tonight. He's cute, and he has a good voice, but not a *Phoenix* voice. I think that's why Vic's so livid and on a power trip. Deep down he knows no matter how many pretty-boy singers he finds, they'll never be Phoenix. Same with Memphis and Storm. They're all diamonds in the rough, you know? That's what makes Sharp Objects incomparable to any other band out there."

She's right. "Agreed." I tuck a strand of hair behind my ear. "But Storm and Memphis have nothing to worry about because Phoenix would never let Vic replace him."

Not without one hell of a fight.

"Actually," she says. "Phoenix encouraged the guys to have a meeting with Vic's new protégé to see if they have chemistry."

My stomach drops. "He can't...they're not..."

Holy fucking shit.

"They don't want to," Skylar says. "But Vic will sue them for breach of contract too if the next album isn't made. Their hands are tied."

As scary as that sounds, there's something even more alarming in that statement.

"What do you mean sue them, *too*?"

If Vic wants to *replace* Phoenix so bad it's not a breach of contract.

"Please don't repeat this to anyone because Chandler will kill me, but today he told me that Vic's planning on taking Phoenix to court in February. Not only for breach of contract in regard to the albums, but for every cent they made off Sharp Objects...the song."

My heart folds in on itself and my chest knots. That's insane.

"He can't do that." My shock quickly morphs into outrage. "For fuck's sake, it's not even his. It's *mine*."

"I know, but Phoenix publicly admitted that he lied about writing it and Vic signed and financed them based off that song. It's his reputation and label at stake. Chandler's hoping Phoenix will agree to come back and they can work something out and do damage control, but Phoenix doesn't want to."

"I'll convince him."

Hell, at this point, he doesn't have a choice.

"I don't think you'll be able to, either. Storm called him yesterday and flat out begged. Then Memphis got on the phone and they tag teamed him. They were hoping to make him cave, but it didn't work. Phoenix doesn't want anything to do with Sharp Objects or music anymore."

"Give me a second."

Placing the phone down, I rub my temples. I could march up there and demand he pull his head out of his ass, but he'll merely refuse.

Phoenix gave it all up for me. And not while he was still chasing his dreams...while he was *living* them.

And now we're both grieving.

Only he doesn't have to because he can still live his dream.

He just doesn't want to.

A stab of grief arrows through me. I wish my dad was here so I could get his advice.

However, I know what he would tell me. He'd tell me to tell Vic to go fuck himself because he doesn't get to make even more money off *my* song.

I snatch my phone. "Skylar? Are you still there?"

"Yeah. I'm here."

It's a long shot, but here goes nothing. "Does Vic know we're married?"

I can practically see her smile right before she says, "No. Chandler wanted to tell him—and the world—but I made him promise me he wouldn't."

I'm sure he did. However, Chandler's need to keep Vic happy seems more important than his promises.

"Are you sure he wasn't just appeasing you?"

"I'm positive. Otherwise, it would have hit the news." There's an impish tone to her voice. "I also might have used my feminine powers of persuasion to ensure he'd keep his word. Well, that and contrary to what everyone thinks Chandler really does care about the band. He agreed to pretend he was in the dark about it all until I decided to announce it."

"Why haven't you?"

Although something tells me I already know the answer...and it means she's not just a good friend. She's the *best* kind of friend.

I'm getting ready to tell her that, but the phone disconnects.

A moment later, it rings. Only this time it's a video call.

Her gorgeous face lights up the screen after I pick up.

"Because I was waiting until you were ready to have this conversation." She chews the corner of her lip. "He stole your song, Lennon. And while I truly believe Phoenix loves you more than anything in the world and he's sorry, I wanted to give you time to make sure that marrying him is what you really want, because once it's out there...that's it."

I know.

"People aren't going to sympathize with him stealing your song and you'll have no grounds for legal recourse since you married the guy who did it," she continues. "It's why I didn't talk you out of wanting to file an annulment and hinted that you'd either be able to claim you were of unsound mind or coercion on Phoenix's part, given the circumstances. I talked to a lawyer, by the way, and I have his contact information if you want it."

I do, but not for the reason she thinks.

"Thank you, Skylar. Truly."

She gives me a sad smile. "You don't have to thank me. I just want you to know that even though I'm a publicist, I'm your friend first."

If I ever had any doubt about that, I don't anymore.

"I know." I swallow down the emotions rising up my throat because I can't be sad Lennon right now. I have to be *fuck with my husband and I'll make you wish you were never born* Lennon. "But I'm gonna need you to switch back to publicist mode, because I know what I want to do about Phoenix."

Or rather, Vic.

Her brows knit. "Okay, publicist mode activated. How can I be of service?"

"Is there any way you can set up a meeting with Vic Dougherty?"

"I have one scheduled later this week actually. Chandler's been talking me up to him and I think I passed my *trial period* and Vic wants to formally hire me to work for the label." She makes a face. "That's not gonna happen now, is it?"

"Not only will it happen, he'll probably want to give you a raise."

Because I just figured out how I'm gonna fix this shitstorm.

She blinks. "Why?"

"I'll get to that in a second. First, I have a very important message I need you to give him from me."

"Hold on." She places her phone in the mount. Then she fishes around her giant purse and pulls out a notebook and pen. "I'm ready when you are."

"Vic's not going to sue Phoenix."

Skylar looks up. "But—"

"I mean, he can try but he won't win. However, he *will* look really fucking stupid when we both walk into a courtroom and his wife swears under oath that Phoenix didn't steal my song…since I gave it to him." I tap my chin, pretending to think. "Actually, I can't believe I forgot. We cowrote it because he came up with some of the lyrics, too."

Skylar grins wickedly. "Talk about a boss bitch move. It's a shame you're already married because I totally just fell in love with you."

That gets a laugh out of me. "Then get ready to wine and dine me because you're really gonna like this part."

Her face lights up. "I'm all ears."

Phoenix loves me, but it doesn't mean he has to give up other things he loves.

However, I'm glad Skylar released a statement proclaiming he was taking some time off for his mental health.

Because even the sun can burn out.

Phoenix needs to recharge and fall in love with music again.

And when he comes back—because I'll make sure he does—his career will no longer be tainted with guilt because he'll know everything he has going forward is solely because of *him*.

He'll have a fresh start.

"First, I have a few questions."

She pulls a water bottle out of her bag and takes a sip. "Shoot."

"How long does it take to record an album?"

I remember reading that the new album was scheduled to come out at the end of January. It's the middle of September now so her answer will tell me just how long he'll have.

"It depends. Once the music is written and the songs are chosen, it mostly comes down to studio time." She chews the end of her pen. "The first album took the longest because they were new. It was a little over a month. The second album only took them two weeks to record."

"So, for this next album, they wouldn't have to start recording until…"

"The day after new year's," she supplies. "That *should* be enough time."

New year, clean slate. Sounds perfect to me.

"In that case, tell Vic to book studio time for the beginning of January. Phoenix will fulfill his contractual obligation, record the album, and do all the press that goes along with it. But *until* then, he's on vacation."

Something he desperately needs.

She winces. "I'll tell him, but he might decide to cut his losses and replace him. Phoenix is amazing, but this new guy doesn't have the bad press."

This is the part that's going to require me to be sneaky, because Phoenix won't like this one bit…given it will undo everything he did.

But I love him. Way more than the song.

"I'll be doing an interview a week before the album drops." This way it will get a buzz generating. "I'll tell everyone we're married, and that Phoenix didn't steal my song…he cowrote it. Only he didn't tell anyone because I specifically asked him not to. I didn't…"

A wave of grief catches me by the throat.

Sorry, Dad. I'm gonna need you for this.

Along with the nerve to disclose my own truth.

"I was afraid of being compared to my dad and not measuring up."

Skylar stops writing. "Lennon—"

My eyes burn, but I keep going. "Phoenix was only doing what I asked, but the guilt he felt for not giving me any recognition kept gnawing at him, so he decided to come clean."

"You know Phoenix isn't gonna go for that."

"That's why we're not going to tell him until after."

Then he won't be able to do anything about it because how could he? His wife, whom he claimed he stole a song from, is publicly telling everyone he didn't.

His status will be restored, and the world will go back to thinking he's a god again.

Because he was born for this.

"That should take care of his reputation."

"Oh, it definitely will." She makes a face. "But if for some crazy reason Vic doesn't go for it…what then?"

Then I do exactly what my dad would want me to do.

"Tell him this *small-town pussy from back home* will be the one suing him and him alone. For every penny he made off my fucking song." I sharpen my gaze. "In other words, he has two choices. He can either play nice and we'll all have a spot on the chessboard...or I'll light the fucking thing up and watch him burn."

Vic might be power hungry, but he's not stupid.

She throws her notebook. "That's it. I wanna be *you* when I grow up."

There was a time in my life when I wanted to be someone else, too.

I find myself smiling. *Now I'm married to him.*

"Are you sure you're gonna be okay dealing with the Memphis and Gwen baby extravaganza until January?"

It's a lot to ask and if she tells me it's too hard, I'll understand.

I just need a little time.

"I'll be okay," she assures me, although I catch the brief flash of pain in her eyes.

I'm about to probe but there's a tap on her window and Chandler comes into view...holding what appears to be a pair of panties in his hand.

What. The. Hell?

"Gotta go," Skylar squeaks before she disappears from my screen.

Dammit. I call her back, but she must have shut her phone off because it goes straight to voice mail.

Shaking my head, I get off the couch and go back upstairs.

Phoenix is still sound asleep when I come back so I crawl into bed beside him.

Placing my head on his chest, I trace the music notes over his heart.

But they're no longer mine. Or his. They're *ours.*

Because half my heart and soul belong to him.

The other halves are broken beyond repair.

But I don't want to think about that right now.

I just want to listen to my husband's heartbeat, feel his skin against mine, and inhale his scent into my system.

I thought letting him in again after he destroyed me meant I was weak, but perhaps it's valor.

Because I have what it takes to rise from the ashes after I've been burned.

I shouldn't wake him; he's been running himself ragged taking care of me and I know he needs his rest, but I miss him.

And there's no one on the planet who can make me forget about my pain like he can.

Hoping to rouse him, I slide my hand down his torso until I reach the waistband of his boxers.

When that doesn't work, I slip my fingers beneath the elastic and pull him out.

He twitches, growing hard in my hand, but Phoenix doesn't wake.

I scoot down until I'm hovering above his thickening cock. Opening my mouth, I lick around his head.

A low hungry groan leaves him, and his dick swells to its massive size, but his eyes don't open.

How the hell is he sleeping through *this*? Have I lost my touch?

Nope. Screw that. Phoenix said it himself, I give great head.

Probably because I genuinely enjoy satisfying my partner.

Although my partner doesn't seem very satisfied right now on account of being passed out cold.

Impatience billows through me and I wrap my hand around his base and suck him deeper, stroking him and my bruised ego in tandem.

I blatantly gag on him, giving it my all…and nada. Even though his body's responding because I can taste the precum leaking from his tip and feel him jerking in my mouth. He's *trembling,* for fuck's sake.

Growing more frustrated, I increase my suction and quicken my pace. If he doesn't wake up after this, I'm going to call 911.

"*Fuck*," he groans, his hands gripping the sheets and his hips jerking upward. "I can't take it anymore. This is goddamn torture. Please stop."

Wow. Embarrassment courses through me as I unhinge my jaw and release him.

I didn't think he'd mind waking up to a blow job, but boy was I wrong.

"I'm sorry. I didn't mean..." I feel like a total creeper. "I'm so sorry."

He peers down at me. "Lennon?"

Was he expecting someone else?

Narrowing my eyes, I sit up. "Yes?"

Confusion spreads across his face as he takes me in. "You're not drunk."

"I'm not drunk," I confirm, and now it makes a whole lot more sense.

But also...*seriously?* I've been drunk a handful of times in my whole entire life.

He scrubs a hand down his face. "Fuck. I thought..."

"That I was trying to give you drunk head again?"

He shrugs. "Yeah, but I figured if I didn't wake up, I wouldn't have to feel guilty for not stopping you and I could get off."

A paragon of nobility my husband is not.

"That's..." I scowl. "You made me feel like I lost my mojo. And then I felt like a creeper."

"You didn't lose your mojo, Groupie. Trust me." Smirking, he gestures to his cock. "By all means, creep away."

I will, but not without getting a little payback first.

Walking my fingers along his chest, I straddle him. "I'll happily suck you off, but only if I hear you beg again."

His mouth opens and closes in disbelief. "I did not *beg.*"

Oh, he most definitely did.

"I can't take it anymore," I repeat with a mock deep voice. "This is goddamn torture. Please stop." Crinkling my nose, I flash him some teeth. "Sure sounds like begging to me, Mr. Walker."

"Nah. You want to hear begging?" His hands grip my ass and in one fell swoop I'm pinned to the mattress and he's on top of me.

"You're about to hear a whole lot of it, Groupie…but it won't be from me."

I open my mouth with a retort, but his fingers thread my hair, and he claims it.

Desire surges through my bloodstream as his tongue slicks over mine and his hand moves between my thighs, rubbing me through the thin material of my sleep shorts, working me into a frenzy.

But I won't beg, I won't…

Oh god.

I cry out when he slips two fingers beneath my shorts and pushes them inside me in one long, deep, and gratifying stroke.

Then it's gone.

There's a cocky gleam in his eye as he glides his wet fingers along my swollen lips and the length of my slit, spreading my arousal around…making me feel the evidence of my want for him.

Squirming, I shift my hips, attempting to put them back inside me.

The gleam in his eye intensifies, and he drags his tongue over his lip ring. "Give me what *I* want, and I'll give you what you want."

A jolt of heat goes through me when the rough pad of his fingertip skates over my clit.

"We're getting closer." Taking mercy, he slides one long finger into me. I clench around the invasion, desperate to keep him there. "Stubborn girl."

I nearly whimper when he pulls out…only to push back in a moment later.

I stretch and grasp, needing more. Needing *him*.

"Please."

Triumph flashes in his gaze, but it's not enough. He's gonna make me work for it. And God help me I will, because it's always worth it.

"Take off your shirt," he rasps as he tugs my shorts and thong off.

When I do, his hungry stare rakes over my naked form. He

doesn't have to tell me I'm beautiful because he's looking at me like I'm the most perfect thing he's ever seen.

His teeth graze the column of my neck, sucking my skin, before he goes lower, drawing my nipple into his mouth.

A moan passes my lips. "Phoenix."

"I love it when you say my name." The gravel in his voice, along with his teasing, sends a hot shiver up my spine. "But I think we can do a lot better." He pinches my other nipple. "Spread your legs, Mrs. Walker."

Hearing him call me that shouldn't turn me on so much, but god, it *does*.

I eagerly follow his instructions and he stares at my open pussy like a man starved.

The look alone is enough to make me melt, but when he holds my gaze and slithers down, wedging his shoulders between my thighs, I'm completely done for.

The fucker knows it too, because he gives me the most arrogant grin right before his tongue comes out for a taste.

"More." When he shoots me a look, I add, "Please."

His chuckle is a half groan as he kisses me the same way he kisses my mouth. Passionate. *Needy.*

Tension in my core tightens and I unabashedly beg.

For him. For the way he's lighting my body on fire. For the way he's able to make me forget.

Phoenix settles into a rhythm, interchanging flicks of my clit with long greedy swipes, building me up. *Devouring* me.

My hand cups the back of his head, keeping him there. "Don't stop."

He doesn't, not until I'm shuddering, smashing my pussy into his face as I scream his name and drench the sheets.

He licks me through the comedown, causing little aftershocks that have me hissing, "Fuck."

"Trust me. I'm going to," he rasps against my slick skin. "First, I want another taste."

He laps at my orgasm, driving me out of my mind as he builds me up again, priming me for what's to come.

Crawling up my body, his mouth finds mine. When I part my lips, he feeds me his tongue, making me taste myself.

"Now, Phoenix. *Please.*"

I'm a desperate, aching mess.

Taking hold of my hips, he shoves inside me in a single thrust that's as harsh as it is pleasurable.

Our gazes clash, and I know that he's not only missed this, but he needs this as much as I do. This primitive connection. The intensity. The desire to consume each other insatiably.

He drops a kiss to my forehead, and we share a brief tender moment.

And then…

His composure snaps and he starts fucking me so hard—so deep—I forget everything.

Except him.

The hands on my hips tighten hard enough I know I'll have marks, but I want them.

I want him to brand me and mark me. *Burn me.*

I tremble as pleasure knots inside me again. "Oh. God."

Gripping the headboard, he picks up his pace, our skin slapping together in a wild, carnal cadence that's visceral.

And his kiss is just as brutal. All tongue and sharp teeth as he ruts into me. Taking and using, but also giving and providing.

"Fuck."

His hips strike mine ruthlessly, his thrusts a punishment and a reward.

A hoarse groan rips from his lips. "I feel you drip down my balls every time you take this fucking cock."

I claw at his ass, moving with him, meeting his savage thrusts. "Good."

He drags his lips along my throat, his hot breath gusting along my pulse point. I cry out when he nips my flesh. "If you want to come, you better beg for it."

His hand slides between us, finding my clit. A shudder moves through me and I bite my lip, biting back a moan. "Make me."

He withdraws almost completely before driving inside me again and again, the force of his thrusts pinning me to the mattress as those fingers strum me into oblivion.

I'm close. *So* close. He knows it too because there's a smug smirk on his lips as he looks on with hooded eyes.

Surging into me, his mouth settles over my ear. "Beg to cream this cock."

My body is strung tight, my lungs wrung out…but I beg so hard I'm sure poor Mrs. Palma next door can hear me.

Tension grows stronger, bigger, tighter until I have no choice but to let go.

I milk him, squeezing for dear life and digging my nails into his back so hard he grunts a string of curses.

I open my eyes in time to watch pleasure move across his face. His groan is guttural and his lips crash against mine as hot liquid floods me.

We kiss until our lips are swollen. Until we run out of air.

Phoenix was right. There was a whole lot of begging, but none of it was from him.

Because somehow, he knew exactly what I needed tonight, and he gave it to me.

"I love you," he whispers against my lips.

My heart flutters like the wings of a hummingbird and I smile, a rush of emotion jamming my chest. "I love you, too."

So much.

But the moment he slips out of me, the empty void—the grief ensnaring me—is back.

After Phoenix is fast asleep, I curl up into a ball and let the tears fall.

Because I know it will never go away.

CHAPTER 81

PHOENIX

Yesterday was rough.

Lennon stayed in bed and spent most of the day crying in my arms.

She's scared the pain will never go away, and I gave her the cold, hard truth.

It won't. Because she's always going to miss her dad.

But it won't always feel so raw like it does now. She just needs to give herself permission to start the healing process.

Fortunately, I think I figured out something that might help with that.

I'm pondering whether I should bring it up today when I look over on her side of the bed…and notice she's not in it.

"Lennon?"

I don't get a response.

Fearing the worst, I search through all the rooms before heading downstairs.

The muscles in my chest draw tight with relief—and surprise—when I find her in the kitchen, sipping coffee while pouring some cereal into a bowl.

I kiss the top of her head on my way to the fridge. "Hey."

She gives me a small smile. "Hey."

She ambles toward the kitchen table, but then she turns around, heading for the living room instead.

I want to get rid of that fucking table because I know every time Lennon sees it, she can't help but think about her father.

However, she hasn't reached that stage yet.

But she has an appetite again, and she's eating, so it's progress.

After fixing my own bowl of cereal, I join her on the couch in the living room.

I can tell she's lost in her thoughts because her brows are pulled together and there's a frown marring her face.

"What's going on in that head of yours?"

She chews and swallows carefully before she speaks. "What if I forget his voice?"

"You won't." When she starts to protest, I say, "We live in the digital age. There are voice mails and videos. All that can be preserved, and you'll be able to listen to it whenever you want."

She visibly relaxes…and then she pales. "What if I get dementia like my dad and I forget him?"

After placing my bowl on the coffee table, I brush my thumb over her heart. "He'll always be in there."

She takes another bite of her cereal. "I hate not having him around."

"I know."

But it will get easier.

Pulling her into my arms, I kiss her temple. "Do you trust me?"

Confusion clouds her eyes as she tilts her head to look at me. "Yes." She gives me a look. "Why?"

Because I know what's gonna get her through this.

Rising to my feet, I take her hand. "Come with me."

Despite the dubious expression on her face, she follows me up the stairs.

However, when we reach the door to her dad's bedroom, she shakes her head and plants her feet. "I can't go in there."

Lennon hates when I push her, and I get it. I feel the same way when she pushes me. It pisses me the fuck off and my first instinct is to shut down.

But we push each other because we get each other...more than anyone else ever could.

Music is therapy for Lennon, but she shoved it in a box and won't let herself open it.

She doesn't let herself create...but it's who *she* is.

It's what makes her whole.

I took it from her, but I'll do anything to give it back.

Including giving up music myself. Because I can't be whole until Lennon is again.

When she breaks...I break.

Even when I'm the one responsible for it.

Twisting the knob, I open the door. "Trust me."

People don't love her song because I sang it. They love it because they *feel* it.

Because they identify with her pain.

Because she poured every single ounce of it into her art.

Because her words—her music—her *creation* saved them.

It's time for it to save her again.

Her eyes flick to the piano, and those baby browns widen when she spots it.

While Lennon was sleeping yesterday, I went through her closet and found her old journal discarded in some box all the way in the back.

"I didn't read it."

I was fucking dying to, though. But I didn't. Not because I can't, but because it's hers. She gets to decide who she shares her art with. Not me.

Turning, I cup her cheek. "I know you got your stubbornness from your dad, but you also got your strength from him."

She visibly swallows. "I don't feel all that strong lately."

She is, though. She's the strongest person I know.

"I bet your dad didn't feel strong after your mom died, either." I gesture to the piano. "But he still created."

I can tell she wants to protest, but I'm not finished yet. "I know it's easier to walk out that door. I know it's easier to push me and everyone else away because it fucking hurts. I know it's easier to give in to the grief and let it take over."

Just like I did with my guilt.

I draw in a slow breath and let it out. "But someone way smarter than I am once told me that my mistakes didn't define who I was… it's what I do after that did." I tip her chin. "Don't let your grief define you, Lennon. Don't let his death be the end of him, because the greatest thing he ever did is still here. And he wouldn't want her spending the rest of her life mourning him. He'd want her to live."

A tear falls down her cheek and her gaze drifts to the piano again.

I see the longing in her eyes. Only unlike me, it's not so she can become a vessel for the magic.

It's so she can make it.

"It's been years since I've done any of that. I don't think I can anymore."

She's wrong.

She doesn't know it, but I listened to her and her dad talk that day…for a little while.

It wasn't my intention to eavesdrop, but when he made her sing her song, I found myself rushing back up the stairs and pressing my ear to the door so I could listen.

However, there was something he said shortly after that I'll never forget. Something Lennon needed to hear.

"Don't let your insecurities overpower that which makes your soul come alive. Otherwise, you'll walk this earth never feeling whole…and that's no way to live."

She goes still, pain and adoration battling on her face.

I walk over to the piano. "Spend time with your dad and get whatever's inside of you out. Because *that's* how you'll get through this."

She stares at the piano so long I think she's plotting her escape.

But eventually, she takes a few steps and then a couple more until she's sitting on the bench.

"Fine." A faint smile curves her lips. "But I know you only want me to write again because we don't have a prenup. Which means you're entitled to half our marital assets."

There she is.

Grinning, I drop a kiss to her forehead. "I fucking love you."

Giving her space, I stride out the door, closing it behind me.

I hold my breath until I have no choice but to take one.

Then it happens.

The corner of my mouth lifts as a dark, melodic sound fills my ears.

Because I know she'll be okay.

EPILOGUE

Three months later...

rritation rises within me when I check my watch. I'm forty-five motherfucking minutes late.

Fucking Memphis. Or rather, *Gwyneth*.

The reason *I'm* late right now is because *he* was late coming to the studio today.

I thought I was done with music for good, but a couple months ago, Vic called me up out of the blue. Did he apologize for trying to go behind my back and replace me? Of course not.

However, the prick did tell me that "Existentialism" could be the first single on the album and going forward, the band could have more input on the music we wanted to make.

I was shocked as shit because not only am I public enemy number one these days, Vic was dead set on getting rid of my ass… with good reason.

I'm not sure what prompted his change of heart, but according to Chandler, that's the closest thing to an apology the man has ever uttered.

Not wanting to give in so easily, I made Vic sweat it out and let him know I'd think about coming back. He moaned and groaned for a bit before letting *me* know he booked studio time for the day after new year's and he expected me to be there.

I never confirmed whether or not I would.

Until a certain person convinced me to go this morning.

I haven't sung in months and I was sure I'd be rusty as fuck, but Storm and Memphis were there—albeit one of them was *late*—and we decided to lay down "Existentialism" old-school style.

Meaning we recorded our parts at the same time instead of individually. It was fucking sick.

I'm wondering if I can convince Vic to let us do the rest of the songs on the album that way because there's an authenticity that bleeds into the music.

My phone vibrates and Chandler's name flashes across the screen. Pressing the ignore button, I open the door.

The dimly lit bar is small and there aren't many people here.

It's fucking bullshit. This place should be packed.

Not because of the cheap liquor and stale pretzels, but because of the entertainment.

A hoarse, sultry tone fills my ears as I make my way over to the bar.

Some redhead on the other side of it gives me a smile. "What can I get you, handsome?"

"Coke. Hold the Jack."

"Okay." Her nose crinkles as she fills up a glass with soda and slides it across the bar. "Here."

After placing some cash down, I turn my stool around.

Lennon and I made a deal a couple of weeks ago.

If she pursued her dreams…then I had to pursue mine.

My heart races as she reaches the climax of the song, her smoky voice a slow tug on my cock. Along with the little black dress she's wearing. I can't wait to slip my hand underneath it later and find out if she's wearing any panties.

However, the most beautiful thing about my wife right now is the happiness radiating off her. She's finally in her element and doing what she loves. What she was *meant* to.

The song ends and I rise from my seat, cheering her on. I know she hears me because there's a big smile on her face as she starts the intro to a new song.

One I've never heard before.

It's good. Really fucking good.

I sit back down, focusing on the dark and rough melody…and then Lennon starts to sing and I'm a goner. There's so much emotion in her voice, so much passion and depth. She blows me away every fucking time.

"She's amazing," some guy on the other side of me says.

I stare at the tattooed black band on my left ring finger with a music note. One that matches Lennon's.

"Yeah, she is."

And I'm the lucky bastard who gets to spend the rest of his life with her.

"Holy shit," the guy suddenly exclaims, his mouth dropping open. "*You're* Phoenix Walker."

Picking up my glass, I raise it in greeting. "In the flesh."

He takes a long sip of his. "I'm a big fan. Or should I say, used to be."

That's when I hear it.

'I stole your words, but you stole my heart.'

My chest recoils, and every muscle in me tightens because I *know* those words.

I fucking wrote them.

Our gazes clash from across the bar. Beaming, Lennon gives me a coy little smirk as her fingers flutter across the ivory keys.

Well played, Groupie. Well fucking played.

"Man, you were a legend." His sigh is expansive. "You had it all…and then you lost it."

The organ belonging to her contracts as I stare at my wife.

No, I didn't.

The End

Turn the page for a special treat.

SNEAK PEEK

Hey guys.

Wondering if there will be a book for the side characters? (*cough cough* Skylar and Memphis.) Well, I've been working on a little 'something-something.' Here's a sneak peek for the prologue.

I'd love to know if you're excited about their book. Let me know by grabbing it below. <3

Grab it here: https://dl.bookfunnel.com/vogmpigzdg

Join my newsletter and sign up for the latest news and updates on my books and releases: http://signup.ashleyjadeauthor.com/

Connect with me on Facebook: https://www.facebook.com/Ashley-Jade-Author-788137781302982/

Join my exclusive group for readers: https://www.facebook.com/groups/685774991573128/

ABOUT THE AUTHOR

**Want to be notified about my upcoming releases?https://
goo.gl/n5Azwv**

Ashley Jade craves tackling different genres and tropes within romance. Her first loves are New Adult Romance and Romantic Suspense, but she also writes everything in between including: contemporary romance, erotica, and dark romance.

Her characters are flawed and complex, and chances are you will hate them before you fall head over heels in love with them.

She's a die-hard lover of oxford commas, em dashes, music, coffee, and anything thought provoking...except for math.

Books make her heart beat faster and writing makes her soul come alive. She's always read books growing up and scribbled stories in her journal, and after having a strange dream one night; she decided to just go for it and publish her first series.

It was the best decision she ever made.

If she's not paying off student loan debt, working, or writing a novel—you can usually find her listening to music, hanging out with her readers online, and pondering the meaning of life.

Check out her social media pages for future novels.

She recently became hip and joined Twitter, so you can find her there, too.

She loves connecting with her readers—they make her world go round'.

~Happy Reading~

Feel free to email her with any questions / comments: ashleyjadeauthor@gmail.com

For more news about what I'm working on next: Follow me on my Facebook page: https://www.facebook.com/pages/Ashley-Jade/788137781302982

Thanks for Reading!
Please follow me online for more.
<3 Ashley Jade

ALSO BY ASHLEY JADE

Royal Hearts Academy Series (Books 1-4)

Cruel Prince (Jace's Book)

Ruthless Knight (Cole's Book)

Wicked Princess (Bianca's Book)

Broken Kingdom

Hate Me - Standalone

The Devil's Playground Duet (Books 1 & 2)

Complicated Parts - Series (Books 1 - 3 Out Now)

Complicated Hearts - Duet (Books 1 & 2)

Blame It on the Shame - Trilogy (Parts 1-3)

Blame It on the Pain - Standalone